Bolt

Bonnie Brunish

An Infernal Museum Book

To Uncle Glenn
who took me to the races

Mana was filling the mangers in the stalls when the horses began to shift and stamp. Virtuous Quota flung up her head, eyes rolling and nostrils quivering. Pious Remembrance, in the stall beside her, trembled as she stared into nothing. A chill crept down Mana's neck. She dropped the scoop in the wheelbarrow and hurried along the circular aisle toward the two pale gold mares. In all her years managing the stable, she'd never seen them behave this way.

"Easy girls," she soothed.

The mares didn't seem to see or hear her. Virtuous pinned back her ears and swung her head from side to side, tusks bared. Pious snorted and reared, her pale underbelly flashing.

"Easy!" Mana cried.

Then Pious screamed with such heart-wrenching anguish that Mana cried out in sympathy. The mare twisted and plunged in a motion that spun Mana's senses.

She was gone.

Mana screamed and ran over to peer past the chest-high door. The stall was empty.

Virtuous snorted. She too twisted and seemed to fly off in a hundred directions at once. A rush of grunts and hoofbeats went around the stable as panic spread, horses on either side plunging into the Deep. Within seconds Mana stood alone in the vast empty shell of a building that had held a hundred horses.

She ran outside and scanned the field. Grass flowed toward the horizon all around her, fresh and green. Wind moved through it with silvery ripples. Nothing else stirred; not a horse was in sight. Mana stood shocked and helpless, her heart pounding.

Had the horses been attacked by some monster from their own realm? But a deep-level creature would've taken the building apart like a child's sandcastle, and the building seemed untouched. She tried to calm herself enough to think clearly. It hadn't been anything she'd done, but something had scared them, something their deep-level senses had picked up, for there was nothing threatening in the here and now. Mana scanned the field again. It remained peaceful.

Perhaps the scare had come through their telepathic links with their riders. Since Pious and Virtuous had been most affected, they may have been the only ones to sense the threat, the others responding to their fear. Pious was the empress's horse.

Her throat tight, Mana scanned the pale blue sky. It remained clear, the few wispy, drifting clouds unruffled. But the capital lay on the other side of the planet.

Softly, the wind sighed through the grass, increasing Mana's sense of isolation. Because the horses' deep-level stirrings disrupted glowworm technology, Mana had no internal link, and the nearest System node was far removed. She considered walking to the tram that would take her there and checking the news.

No, she decided. Her duty was with the horses. Even if something terrible was happening in the capital, there was nothing Mana could do about it. The best thing she could do was to keep the horses content, and right now she was failing that.

She scanned the horizon again. Still nothing. She swallowed. If the horses decided not to return, imperial society would receive a jolt. But surely their fright would pass. They would be back to enjoy their feed. Imperial scientists made sure that they got tasty and nutritious fare with just the right combination of novelty and familiarity. And the horses enjoyed the attention and the grooming as well. And they enjoyed the races—why else would they choose to link themselves with humans? They felt their riders' urge to win as they pounded toward the finish line, and the the excitement of spectators rooting for their riders, and the thrill of bettors about to receive a flood of credits. They would be back.

But waiting, alone and in suspense and trepidation, was hard. Mana squared her shoulders and walked out a little farther into the grass. Surely her own horse would respond first to her voice. Taking a deep breath, she called.

"Ting! Ting! Come, Ting! There's nothing to be afraid of."

When a brown head popped up from beyond a grassy slope, followed by a glossy body sprinkled with small white spots, Mana sighed with relief. "That's right, Ting. Everything is fine here. Nothing to be afraid of. Come!"

The mare flicked her ears this way and that as she thought it over. Her official name was "Transporting," but since Genetic Algorithms had assigned an older horse the same name, Mana called her "Ting."

Her mind made up, Ting trotted over to Mana and put her head down for a hug. Mana let the love and trust enfold her. She hadn't felt so glad to hold her horse since the first time Ting had come to her on the Plains of Possibility.

"Oh, Ting, if I ever lost you, I don't know what I'd do!"

The mare gave an answering grunt, then pulled back slightly, as if suddenly recalling that she hadn't had her feed. Mana took a handful of the dark mane and vaulted onto her back. In a flowing canter, Ting carried her to the stable and around the aisle to her stall. Mana slid off and opened the door, and the mare went in and thrust her muzzle into the manger.

Moments later, as if they sensed what she was doing, the other horses began to trickle in. Mana hurried about opening stall doors and checking for signs of damage. The horses' downleveling directly out of the stalls had probably rearranged the molecular structure of the building, but she didn't see much: some splashes of color or swaths of odd texture on some of the walls, and a mysterious, gelatinous ring on the floor of Superhuman Prog's stall.

Usually she only filled the mangers once the horses had entered the stalls, and the horses soon caught on that most of the mangers were already filled. Virtuous decided to go into Growing's stall, snapping at the other mare when she tried to protest. But when the white stallion came toward her with pinned-back ears, Virtuous changed her mind and meekly moved on to her own stall.

Mana walked around the long aisle that curved inside the row of stalls, greeting each horse, checking the feed again, and closing the stall doors. They had all returned, except for Pious. Once they had settled in, Mana went to Trat's stall. She gave the stallion a little extra feed, and stroked his silken neck. "What would we do without you, Trat? Your grandchildren come and go, but you've been with us since the beginning. I'll bet you've known every single emperor and empress. Sometimes I don't think we appreciate you enough."

Eternal Trat nosed his feed and took a few bites, then lifted his head and contemplated something far away, his large, dark eyes softly shimmering. Mana bit her lip. He probably knew what was going on in the capital, but he couldn't tell her.

Mana left him and went to Ting's stall. When the mare had finished her feed, Mana groomed her and waited anxiously for someone to come.

Most of the riders liked to groom and exercise their horses every day. If they were too busy, they sent someone, usually a family member their horse knew, because neglected horses tended to choose new riders. But on this day, no one came.

Mana went to Trat's stall and brushed his coat, growing more nervous by the minute. The horses too grew restless, some circling their stalls, others pawing at the bedding, still others peering out the windows or over the doors.

Virtuous snorted, and instantly a dozen others were lunging about their stalls with upflung heads and flaring nostrils. Afraid that they might downlevel again and cause more damage, Mana hurried to open stall doors. Virtuous raced from the building with a loud whinny, and the others crowded out behind her.

As Mana watched them go, something nudged her shoulder. She turned to find Ting.

"Oh, of course. You expect your ride, and you're right."

Mana mounted and they trotted across the field toward the distant oval of the track. It wouldn't be much fun exercising all by themselves, but....

Hoofbeats swelled behind them. Mana looked back and found Virtuous coming at a gallop, carrying Katora. An imperious voice reached her ears. "Mana! What do you think you're doing! Why have you released all the horses?"

Mana tuned back and faced her grandmother as Virtuous skidded to a stop, throwing dirt over Ting's hooves and making Mana's mare dance away.

"The horses were nervous. They—"

"You're supposed to keep them calm! Is the job too much for you? Maybe you'd like to go back to Ulona."

Mana took a deep breath and concentrated on the feel of Ting's mane between her fingers. Katora's eyes were very bright, and her hair disheveled. Her face looked taut and tired and a paler shade of green than usual. Her peach-colored riding skin foamed at collar and cuffs. Whatever had happened had deeply shaken her.

"The horses downleveled from their stalls," Mana said.

Katora's mouth snapped shut, and her eyes widened. After a moment she said, "Don't tell anyone else about it. Thermeon has gone for the champions of Wamatu and Ulona. I tried to convince them that we could dispense with that in this emergency, but I'm afraid that my father and Galan didn't agree, so we'll have the Emperor Race when they get back."

"What happened?" Mana asked.

Katora eyed her as if she'd suddenly sprouted three heads and pedipalps. "The empress is dead!" she screamed. "I know you have no mindpowers, but I didn't think you were stupid as well!"

Mana tightened her grip on Ting's mane. She forced her breaths to flow deep and even, and reminded herself that Empress Pia had been Katora's beloved granddaughter, an awakened mindsea, a shining symbol of an enlightened future, and everything else that Katora could have hoped for in an empress. Mana was a granddaughter too, but she'd made an unfortunate choice in her mother, and her mindpowers didn't approach even mind-river level, so she didn't count.

"We'll need to rehearse for the race," Katora went on. "So get the horses back into the stable."

"No," Mana said. "Their routine has already been interrupted, and they're nervous. Better to let them forget about the excitement and have a fresh start tomorrow."

If you hadn't summoned Virtuous with your mind, Mana

thought, *rather than walking from the tram station like a mere mortal, they still would have been in their stalls.*

Katora gave her a furious glare. "Nathimeon and Karali are on their way."

"Good. I think they'll be able to call their horses the way you did."

"I find your attitude disturbing, Mana. The empire is in a state of crisis, and you want to create an impediment to a smooth succession. I think it's time you were replaced here."

Her words sent a shiver of fear through Mana. They almost wore down her efforts to remain calm and understanding. She stroked Ting's neck for comfort and reminded herself that whatever Katora might do, she could not take Ting away. At least, not legally. And thankfully, there were still people like Head of the Circle Raolin and Imperial Major Galan who insisted on upholding the law even when it was inconvenient for Katora.

Before Katora could say anything more, the sound of hoofbeats drew their attention. Two riders appeared on the horizon. Katora's smile quickly faded. They weren't her favorite son and daughter, but two of the late empress's daughters, Beteli and Polia. The two were Luminaries, the glowing white hair inherited from their great-grandfather Thermeon billowing like clouds about their heads. Mana had the same glowing white hair, but she wasn't important enough to be known as a Luminary.

"We're ready for the rehearsal," Beteli called out in a loud voice as she skidded to a stop on a pale stallion with a red mane and tail. Beteli's complexion was brown, but she had Katora's hard blue-gray eyes.

"We are waiting for Nathimeon and Karali," Katora told her.

Beteli exchanged a look with her sister, who had trotted up behind her.

"It was our mother's wish that Polia and I follow her," Beteli said.

Katora snorted, reminding Mana of her mare. "She may have told you that to soothe your egos, but she told me that she wanted Nathimeon and Karali to follow her."

"Don't make me laugh," said Beteli, steel in her voice. "That's what you want. Our mother never cared for your spoiled darlings."

Katora's eyes flared. "You're letting your primitive emotions rule you, Beteli. That is pathetic for someone who's studied at the mindsea academy. At a time like this, we need to put our egos on hold and focus on what is best for the empire. We need the strongest leaders."

Beteli smiled. "Then maybe we should let the races determine our champions, the way tradition dictates."

"Of course," Katora said. "That's exactly what I had in mind."

"Then we might as well start. But we'll need fourteen for the first champion's race."

Katora turned to Mana and roared, "Get the horses in their stalls!"

"Right away," Mana said. She urged Ting back up the slope toward the distant tiny shape of the stable. She would try calling the horses. Maybe they would come. They must know something was going on, and perhaps they'd be curious. She'd call the white stallion first.

As Ting lengthened her stride and the wind pulled at her hair, Mana smiled. If the twelve champions of Lal were chosen by racing, everyone, even Mana, would get a fair chance to be included in the final race for the throne. It would be a refreshing change after having the Emperor Race a mere formality with Katora deciding beforehand who would win. It would be done in the ancient, traditional way—a way that hadn't been practiced within human memory. History would be made.

Mana was worn out with frustration when she saw the two old men riding from the tram station. They were right on schedule.

Katora's father, Head of the Circle Raolin, and Member of the Circle Ietipa Huberimton Siger, known by everyone as Hube, rode every day despite their busy schedules. They always came after everyone else had left, in order not to be importuned about the issues on their desks, Mana supposed. Their horses knew the routine and always waited for them at the tram station. Raolin rode Mixing, a magnificent amber stallion with a chocolate mane and tail and a star on his forehead. Hube's mare, Baquer, was a glossy platinum color. She looked like dozens of the other mares, but she had carried her rider for thousands of years longer than any of them. The men themselves were almost mirror images—Raolin with his white skin and flowing black hair, black-skinned Hube with hair the color of Baquer's mane. Both had the blue eyes of the ancient aristocracy.

Like Mana, Ting had been getting bored and frustrated with the useless calling for the herd, but her ears pricked at the sight of the riders, and she rushed Mana over to greet them.

"We're setting up the perimeter," Raolin said.

Mana gasped. "Perimeter? What's happening? I haven't heard the news!"

He looked past her and gave a jerk of his chin. "Is she here?"

"Yes, but she didn't tell me anything."

"What is she up to?"

"She wants Nathimeon and Karali to take over the Palace Branch. But Beteli objected, so then she said that we would hold races to choose Lal's champions. I guess you'll need to participate too."

The two men responded as one to pat their horses, assuring them, no doubt, that they should not exert themselves too much.

"When is she going to retire and let the younger generation manage the empire?" Raolin muttered.

Mana didn't dare say anything, but Hube chuckled and said in his butter-soft voice, "I'm sure that people wonder the same about you."

"I need to protect the empire from *her*," Raolin said.

"But the perimeter," Mana prompted. "What's happening out there? Please tell me!"

Both men's eyes grew hard and sharp.

"There's a glowworm plague," Raolin said. "The city has ceased to function. Nothing animated is safe. The populace has been advised—"

"By word of mouth," Hube interrupted.

"—to flee into the Valley and try to live like peasants."

"The peasants who have kept to their ancient ways are all right, of course," said Hube. "Dro-carts are now the speediest form of transport in the capital."

"People will have a hard time getting through for her races," Raolin said.

"Oh! How horrible!" Mana cried. "How did you get here?"

They both looked at her for a moment, then Hube said, "Mixing and Baquer came to us in the city." He gave his mare another pat.

"Then you didn't come from the tram station."

"No."

"She should forget about the succession for now," Raolin said. "Things are far too serious for ceremonial nonsense. Galan can manage the Palace Branch."

"On the other hand," said Hube. "It will keep her occupied."

The two exchanged a look.

"You may be right," Raolin admitted.

"What concerns me more," Hube drawled, "is what he's going to do when he gets back."

Raolin groaned. Mana gathered they were talking about Thermeon.

"How bad is it out there?" she whispered. "What happened to the empress? Pious screamed—it sounded horrible!"

The two old men shook their heads, their faces etched with solemnity.

"The infection began in the shuttle lot," Raolin said. "Probably the mutation was caused by some fool pilot downleveling too near the space station. It had spread to air lifters before anyone noticed the pattern to the malfunctions, and by then, it was all through the city."

"People were falling from the sky," Hube said. "What an awful rain!"

Mana clutched her cheeks as she pictured passengers screaming and plummeting as their serene airborne rides went mad

"We grounded the air lifters and destroyed them," Raolin said. "For a while it seemed to be contained. But probably some fool held onto his air lifter, and it got into the System."

"Chaos ensued," said Hube.

"Bureau Headquarters and the Palace seemed immune, at first, with their independent systems," Raolin said. "But the plague-ridden glowworms found crossover points somewhere."

"Buildings and furniture went down next," said Hube. "Doors would not open, or they whirled people around or snapped them in half. Furniture went toxic. Clothing burst into flame."

Mana moaned. "Oh, no! How can that be?"

"It has happened before," Hube said. "But not on Lal."

"Hair-styling glowworms burrowed through skulls and infected people's internals," Raolin said. "They told me that it was like having an angry insect buzzing around inside their brains."

"How many colleagues have told us that they don't ride often because they would have to give up their internals," Hube said sadly. "They felt bad for us because we missed so much."

"People with copy insurance went to wonderdomes requesting euthanasia," Raolin said. "And they infected the float pools."

Mana gripped her stomach as she pictured people who had

come to wonderdomes in need of healing instead floating into madness.

"We scheduled a joint Wall Speaking," Raolin said. "Before our systems when down. Pia and Galan and I were there. The minors, by then, had shed their infected armor and their modern weapons, and they were armed with the primitive swords and javelins they train with."

"The Bureau's bioid guards had been infected," said Hube. "So whoever had questioned why the Palace still retains human guards has their answer."

"We tried to assure everyone that we had a plan," Raolin said. "They were to get into the Valley, without any glowworm-animated possessions, and await word. But people panicked. I think they were trying to reach the Wall, rather than any of us standing before it. The barrier, being glowworm-generated, was gone, and the guards had only those primitive weapons. They were overwhelmed. Galan and I managed to flee. I didn't know what had become of Pia until afterwards." He swallowed, his eyes bright.

"It's too awful," said Mana. "But what's going to happen now? Are we safe here?"

"Minors in space-planes are going to establish perimeters around a few places where people can take refuge—here, Seagamo, Vuduna Resort, the Valley. Anything glowworm-sized that tries to cross the perimeters will be vaporized. Once the city is evacuated it will be sterilized. After the plague-ridden glowworms have been eliminated, we can begin work on their replacement."

He glanced at Hube; then, without any visible signal to their horses, the two moved on in the direction of the track. Mana and Ting trailed after them.

The women's voices could be heard even before they came into view over the hump of the horizon. They sounded like crows squabbling over a baby bird. They fell silent when they noticed Raolin and Hube.

"Father!" cried Katora. "What are you doing here?"

"Don't I come here every evening?"

"I mean—"

"We are establishing the perimeter around the field. Bureau and Palace will make their temporary headquarters here for the duration of the crisis."

"How can you speak for the Palace?"

"Galan made the decision. I'm just passing it along to you."

Katora scowled. Virtuous stamped and flattened her ears at Mixing. The stallion ignored her.

"Galan can't speak for the Palace without an emperor."

"Yes she can. The major has always had that emergency power."

"Galan is your grandchild. I think that compromises the separation of the branches."

Beteli growled. "Our mother had every confidence in Galan. It's a slur against her memory to question her choice!"

"Katora," Raolin said in a patient tone, "Pia was my grandchild. Any descendant of yours will also be my grandchild. You can't invoke the separation of branches argument only when you aren't in the line of descent."

Katora looked frazzled, her hair in dark tangles around her drawn face, her eyes sunken. "Well, the specifics don't matter. I was speaking of the spirit of things. We need an emperor! We need someone to give the people hope!"

"They can take hope from human ingenuity and resourcefulness. They don't need an emperor to play god."

"You're giving people credit for attributes they don't have."

"Maybe if there were fewer emperors about playing god, they could find their inner strengths."

"So you're going to take another stab at ruling the empire without an emperor?"

Raolin fell silent. Virtuous squealed and struck out at Mixing with a front hoof, making him joggle back.

"Our mother was not playing god!" Beteli snarled. Her stallion had flattened his ears. He gave his head a nervous toss.

"I know, I know," Raolin said, patting his horse. "Katora, let's not dredge up the distant past. We all make mistakes. It's not learning from them that constitutes a character fault."

"I've learned from my mistakes."

Raolin looked at Beteli. "I know that your mother fulfilled her duties well, and she was not playing god. But others were at work trying to make her into a god figure."

"Father, I think you're confused. Pia and I worked together to try to bring about an Age of Illumination. Humanity is on the verge of the next step in evolution. Our work must be completed!"

"No!" Raolin shouted. "You worship mindpowers, that's all you do. And when have mindpowers made a better, kinder humanity?"

"We can't go back just because we're afraid that there may be a potential for evil. A human being is capable of greater evil than an ape, but we don't wish to have remained apes, do we? We must go forward to the next step!"

"That's not a valid analogy," Raolin said.

"Mindseas are the next step in evolution," Katora countered.

"I'll grant that humanity may someday develop greater minds than we possess at present. But we're nowhere near that point yet. Certainly not with your husband."

"Thermeon is the most powerful—"

"Powerful, yes. Human, no."

"You're wrong. His vision of the future is splendid and inspiring!"

"All he envisions is himself ruling the universe forever and you as some kind of star incarnate bathing him in the rays of perpetual adoration. He doesn't care a wit for anyone else."

"He loves all of his children!"

"He loves the reflection of himself in them. But if something set him off, he'd destroy all of us."

Katora forced a laugh. "You're raving."

"I am quite serious. You have not learned from your mistakes. First it was Quintillion, then Dino, now Thermeon."

She bared her teeth, her face momentarily twisting into an ugly mask. "I thought we weren't going to dredge up the distant past."

They both fell silent, and Mana could hear the wind stirring the grass and the soft thuds as the horses shifted their feet.

"We need to decide on the next emperor," Katora said.

"We can deal with that once the plague is under control."

"It needs to be now!"

"The Emperor Race can't be run now. The city's in chaos."

"That's why we need to dispense with formalities and simply have the new emperor take the oath."

"It can't be done. The Wall is unapproachable."

Once again father and daughter glared at one another. Katora's lips quirked. "If you're moving Bureau and Palace headquarters here, the Emperor Race can be run here as well."

"Yes."

Mana nodded and took in a deep breath of wind. Katora's pretend races had been staged in the city, but the real, traditional races had always been run on the track.

Katora lifted her chin. "Then let us prepare."

"First we have to run the races to determine the twelve champions of Lal," Beteli reminded her.

Katora heaved a sigh.

"An excellent idea," said Raolin. "I'll leave you to it."

He and Hube turned their horses toward the stable and rode off.

The stable was huge and round, punctuated by the hundred oval windows of the hundred stalls inside. Along its outer circular aisle, across from the stall doors, were corridors leading deeper inside. Two concentric rings of two-person dormitories, forty units per ring, opened onto the corridors from orange and purple doors. Thirty-two larger units in the two inner concentric rings had doors of blue and green. They nestled between two inner circular corridors. Other corridors like spokes joined the two circular corridors, and some of the rooms could only be reached by these. Four long straight corridors led from the outer circular aisle into the very heart of the building, which they divided into four pie wedges, two of them storerooms, and the other two the cafeteria and the gathering room. Mana didn't much care for these windowless, musty, shadowy places. At night, when the skylights went black, they had to be illuminated by chemical lamps, as there were no glowworms.

Raolin and Hube left their horses and entered the building. Mana hurried after them. She still had questions and concerns. As you entered the building and turned left, you passed the stalls of Eternal Trat and Serious Quiav, a mare whose rider had had her out for as long as Mana had worked at the stable. Then came Baquer's and Mixing's stalls. Raolin and Hube stopped between the two pairs of stalls, across from a corridor.

"We'll take the fist orange unit on the right," Raolin told her. "Put our names on the door."

"How long do you think the crisis will last?" she asked quickly, before they could slip away. "I usually get supplies every tenthyear, and we're midway through a cycle."

"The space-planes will supply us."

"How will we communicate with them?"

He smiled. "Without glowworms, and without mindseas. All we'll need are some chemical light sticks."

She nodded. "There's a bin of them in supply room A."

After the two had vanished into their room, Mana walked around to the first long corridor and down to the supply rooms. She checked the gauge on the primitive mechanical pump that supplied horses and humans with water. It indicated that the tank on the roof was filled. She took a supply bag and filled it with light sticks and chalk. She left the light sticks on the central table in the gathering room, then walked back to the door of the room Raolin had indicated.

She hesitated. Should she write "Head of the Circle," or "Bureau Headquarters," or "Raolin Hibary Violole"? Finally, with a shrug, she wrote "Raolin & Hube."

She walked back inwards to the cafeteria and began to ponder what she was going to do about preparing meals for all of the people who might arrive. The facilities were primitive, of course, and she usually settled for nutricubes of various flavors or an occasional soup or stew that came as a powder. All you needed to do was add water and heat it on one of the chem-powered hotplates.

She was measuring out soup powder when a flurry of footsteps came through the door and a voice shrieked, "Too late! The plague's here!"

Mana screamed and spilled powder all over the floor.

The room filled with laughter, and she met a pair of demonic red eyes beneath hedgehog cut of glowing white hair. It was Dino —Thermeon's son, Katora's ex-husband, and Mana's uncle on her mother's side and grandfather on her father's side.

"It's not funny!" she hissed. "People are dying! How did you get here, anyhow?"

"I shuttled over from Vuduna. Prog tells me you haven't been feeding her."

"Your horse is a liar." Mana stared at the mess of powder around her feet. "Dino, we have no glowworms here to clean up after us. Why don't you help me with this, since you made me do it. I think we need to get down on our hands and knees and scrub the floor."

He laughed again. Then, with a shrug, he went to the supply room for a broom and dustpan and started to sweep up. Mana moistened a sponge and scrubbed. She screamed when he tipped the contents of the dustpan into the pot of water she had set on the hotplate.

"What's the matter?" he asked, his eyes going big and innocent. "Do you think there are certain people here who shouldn't eat off of the floor?"

"We'll be eating off the floor too."

"It won't be the first time."

Laughing and weeping at the same time, Mana gave up her sponge and threw her arms around her uncle-grandfather.

No one else had arrived by the time she was ready to serve supper. By then, the late afternoon sun was drenching the field with golden light, and groups of horses could be seen grazing far out. The riders, including Mana, had changed from their skins into the plain, non-animated black robes from closets in the stable dormitories. Raolin and Hube got in line first and took their soup to one of the round white tables scattered through the room. Beteli and Polia followed and went to a different table. Katora came next. She stood for a second or two with her bowl in her hand, trying to decide where to seat herself. She joined her father and Hube.

Mana served Dino and then herself, and they joined Beteli and Polia.

"I can try to shuttle people from the city," Dino said.

"Don't," snapped Beteli. "The plague will find your shuttle faster than you can say 'oopsie,' and then you'll be stranded too."

There was not much conversation after that. In the stillness, all that could be heard was the clinking of spoons against bowls, and the crackle of Katora's voice from the other table, punctuated now and then by the lower voices of the old men. When she had finished, Katora walked by the women's table. "Beteli, we need to make plans."

The gold in the skylight had faded, so Mana turned on the lamps in the gathering room, and they all moved over there and seated themselves around the circular lounge in the center of the room. There was one unchanging gap in the lounge where you entered, and the caramel-colored cushions looked lumpy and worn. Raolin and Hube went to the right side, Beteli, Polia, and Katora to the left, and Dino went all the way around to seat himself across from the gap. Mana took her place beside Hube. The lounge could seat a dozen or more, so there was lots of empty space. In the center of the circle, directly beneath the skylight, stood a round wooden table.

Katora leaned forward. "I have been in touch with Galan and Nathimeon and Karali in mind-link. They are all safe, for the moment, on a dro ranch north of the city. But they have no means of reaching us." She clasped her hands, eyes brightening. "I propose a rescue mission! If we can load their horses onto the shuttle and fly out to them, they could ride back."

Everyone looked grave.

"It won't work," Raolin said.

"No," said Beteli. "The plague will hit the shuttle when you approach the the city, and everyone on board will die."

"We'll have our own horses with us too," Katora said. "If the horses sense danger, they'll downlevel. We'll be mounted, and we will safely downlevel with them."

Mana bit her lip and shook her head. "I'm afraid the horses will spook and downlevel the moment the shuttle starts to move, and the shuttle will be destroyed before it even takes off. They're not used to being on a craft like that."

Katora smiled at her. "You will come along to keep them calm."

Mana swallowed. She could understand Katora being anxious about her children, but her mission sounded like the height of folly. Then again, the terrible things that were happening seemed to call for drastic action. Her heart started to pound crazily as she pictured herself on board the shuttle trying to calm a bunch of edgy horses. The trouble was, if she was scared, they'd pick that up. But knowing that all she needed to do was project an air of confidence didn't in itself provide confidence.

"Oh, it'll be a cinch," Dino chortled. "No problem at all!"

Mana smiled at him and wondered whether he was really feeling confident, or whether he was just acting as if because he knew it was the only way to succeed.

"I think it's a bad idea," Raolin stated.

"You rode from the city," Katora pointed out. "Why shouldn't they?"

"Riding from the city isn't the problem. It's flying out there on the shuttle."

Katora clasped her hands still tighter. "If only you hadn't sent Thermeon off on that senseless mission to Wamatu!"

"It's the law," Beteli said.

Katora made a dismissive sound.

"I hope you're not planning to ride for the Wall," Raolin said. "Supposing you do get Nathimeon onto his horse, that is."

"I don't think it would be wrong," Katora said.

Beteli and Polia exchanged a look.

"Maybe we should come with you," said Polia.

Katora snorted.

Beteli gripped her sister's shoulder. "I think we had better stay here. This so-called rescue mission will probably end in disaster, and some of us should stay safe for the sake of the empire." Her voice grew sharper as she turned to Katora. "You ask what's wrong with rushing Nathimeon to the Wall? Just about everything. What about the races for the champions that you agreed to? You have no respect at all for the law, do you?"

"You see that we can't run races since no one can get here," Katora said. "Any more delay is senseless. While we sit quibbling about legalities people are dying for lack of leadership!"

Beteli half-rose as she yelled at her grandmother, veins standing out in her neck. "By leadership you mean yourself! You think someone gave you the right to run the empire forever and to decide who will sit on the throne and what their policies will be! And no one else's opinion means anything!"

Katora made a disgusted sound.

"Our mother did everything she could to please you for her whole life! She put aside her own interests—"

"If you mean her playing with snakes," Katora interrupted, "I'm sure that was for the best."

Now fully erect, Beteli shrieked, "I hate you! You take and take, and you never give anything in return!"

Katora stared at her in feigned amazement.

Polia rose and took her sister's arm. "There's no use talking to her. Come on, Beteli. It's been a terrible day. Let's mourn for our mother in private. We know her memory deserves to be honored, even if some people don't."

They threaded their way out from the lounge and left.

Katora forced a laugh. "You can see why I don't want *her* on the throne."

No one answered her. Mana's throat felt clogged with unshed tears. The big room was full of shadows around them, only a few pools of light radiating weakly from lamps. Dino's hair glowed. Raolin leaned forward to take a light stick from the box on the table in the center of the lounge. Idly he tossed it from hand to hand.

Katora swung toward Mana with a smirk. "At least you know your place. Maybe you should get some sleep, dear. Tomorrow will be a busy day."

Mana couldn't help but recoil against the cushion behind her as those blue-gray eyes played over her, the incalculable force of Katora's mindpower behind them, ready to manipulate reality itself to enforce her will. It was difficult even for Mana to swallow. Her instincts told her to flee, but she would need all her wits about her tomorrow, and there were questions she wanted answered. Her fear grew suffocating as those hard eyes told her that her grandmother would not care one way or the other if Mana died tomorrow. If her death was part of the series of events leading to Nathimeon mounting the throne, then, as far as Katora was concerned, Mana must die. Katora had probably been in one of her mindsea trances, peering into different possible futures and deciding which series of events would lead to the desired goal.

A still more horrible thought constricted Mana's throat. Had Pia's death been part of Katora's foreseen future? She hadn't wasted a moment in mourning before starting to push Nathimeon's succession. Mana moaned softly.

"What's wrong, dear?" Katora's solicitude was so false it burned.

With a huge effort, Mana tore her eyes from the gray wall of will and sought Hube's blue eyes. "W-what was it like, riding from the city? You must have gone through the Deep."

"Yes," he replied. "We rode across the Plains of Possibility. Very much like the obstacles on the racetrack—only there's no track. Quite a few riders across the millennia have ridden out onto the Plains of Possibility and never returned."

"Oh." That was hardly reassuring. Maybe he didn't intend it to be.

"Don't go," Raolin told her.

"Stay out of this!" Katora snapped. "It's Palace business!"

"Katora, you have not learned from your mistakes. Why are you trying to do the same thing with Nathimeon that you did with Habel when that turned out so unhappily for everyone?"

Mana stiffened. Habel was her father.

Katora laughed. "They're two entirely different people. Habel had *him* for a father." She glowered at Dino. "And he had to contend with her mother as well." Her eyes raked Mana. "But Nathimeon—his possibilities are limitless!" A smile transformed her face, and her voice went soft and dreamy. "Her mother once taunted me, saying that Thermeon and I could never have a mindsea son. But she was wrong! She didn't look far enough into the future! Thermeon and I have had to wait a long time, but at last we have a son who combines all of our best qualities, who can lead humanity onward into the future! Nathimeon is perfectly at home in the Deep, and yet he possesses a brilliant human intellect that can transmit understanding of that realm to ordinary citizens. During his administration the empire can advance on the technological level and the social level as well. As more intersection points are built, and customs built around them, everyone will be able to experience the Deep and make it part of their lives. Only when we complete the transition to become a deep-level species will we truly have immortality!"

"You mean," said Dino, "we'll finally be as good as our horses?"

"I wouldn't expect you to understand," Katora sniffed.

Mana sighed, remembering when Katora had spoken of her

father in those glowing tones, when she had declared her love for Dino to be true and everlasting, when she had scorned Thermeon as violent and brutal. No doubt Raolin remembered that too, and that was why his expression remained distant and somewhat weary. He must also remember when Katora had called Quintillion the greatest mindsea and the hope of the future, long before Mana was born.

"Nathimeon has loved riding through the Deep since he was a little boy. He's crossed the Plains of Possibility many times. Some peasants who've heard his horse go by believe he's the thunder god." Katora gave a fond chuckle.

She went on telling anecdotes about her son.

Suddenly glowing words appeared in the skylight. "COMMENCE COMMUNICATIONS"

"It's the space-plane," Raolin said. "Mana, could you turn off the lights so that they can read my answer." He ignited the light stick.

Katora laughed. "You're going to spell out words for them? Why don't you allow me or some other mindsea to mind-link for you."

"This will do very well. It will transmit nothing more and nothing less than what we intend."

"I see. But surely you don't think that you can command the minors!"

"They will allow me to confer with Galan."

"I can confer with her in mind-link!"

He said nothing more. Mana had turned off the lights. The glow stick traced words through the darkness.

Dino jumped up, clutching his glowing hair. "I had better leave before I'm misinterpreted!" Laughing, he scrambled away.

Katora snorted. She rose and moved off toward the faint glow of a doorway. Mana and Hube followed. When they stepped out into the corridor, Katora was gone.

Hube towered over Mana. As they walked, his soft voice wafted down on her. "Have you been in touch with your mother?"

"No," she said, surprised. "I haven't heard from her in years."

"Her knowledge of glowworms would be useful in this situation. If you hear from her, urge her to join us."

"Of course." Mana grimaced as she pictured her mother and Katora in the same room.

They walked outward through the long, straight corridor. When Mana stopped in front of the blue door of the large unit where she resided, Hube whispered, "Trust your horse, and you will be all right."

Mana hardly slept that night. Towards morning, she fell into a fitful sort of half-dream, where she was riding Ting along a path through a forest. For some reason, she dismounted and poked through the leaf litter on the side of the trail. There seemed to be a pile of toy horses lying there. They were wiggling around, which perplexed her, because all the glowworms were dead. Then she realized that they were actually the other horses and riders from the stable.

Mana awoke and tried to banish the unpleasant sensation of the dream as she stood naked in front of the mirror wall in her dorm bathroom brushing her long, straight white hair. The ends had grown uneven and needed to be trimmed by hand. As she had many times, Mana wished that she had a companion to help her with little things like that, and to help around the stable as well. The horses were wonderful, but it wasn't the same as human companionship. Maybe if she if she asked Katora, when they returned from the rescue mission.

No. She tightened her lips. Katora would delight in keeping things as difficult as possible for her. Why did she have to be that way? Mana's eyes burned with tears. All her talk about illumination and immortality was small comfort when what she delivered was meanness, pure meanness.

Mana stroked her hair harder. She would ask someone privately to assist her. Maybe Dino. But no, he'd probably ride back to Vuduna. Maybe Polia.

Life would be very unpleasant as long as Katora remained at the stable. Mana stroked hard to stem the threatening tide of self-pity. It was ridiculous to feel sorry for herself when people in the city were dying.

Still, she wondered why Katora had to hate everyone. Except for Thermeon and Nathimeon, whom she treated like gods. And Karali, who got some scraps of her attention.

Karali was mean too.

Mana hardly knew Nathimeon. Whenever he came to ride, Katora was there too, fluttering around him, cooing and laughing. Had she been like that around Mana's father when he'd been young? By the time Mana had come along, he'd been a bitter, cynical man, and Katora had always sounded exasperated by his failure to warm to his role as principal god of the theocracy the empire had become.

A sudden pounding on her door nearly made her drop the brush.

"Time to go!" Katora yelled from the corridor.

Mana walked out to the front of the long, nearly empty bedroom. "Wouldn't it be better—"

Katora stormed in. "We must go at once! The minors stopped responding. We must take things in hand!"

Mana gasped.

"Why aren't you dressed?" Katora screamed at her. Mana ran to the bathroom for her riding skin. As she pulled it on, Katora stood with arms akimbo examining her living space.

"You're taking up the room for ten people! You'll need to put the missing beds back in this room and move into one of the outer units."

Not answering, Mana finished dressing. "I'm ready."

"Come." Katora led the way at a run.

When they burst out from the building, Virtuous met them, dancing and tossing her head. Katora flung herself onto the mare's back, then yelled at Mana. "Get your horse and Galan's. I'll summon Thun and Will!"

Dino lounged on the back of his white mare, Superhuman Prog, and smirked at them.

Mana strode a few paces beyond them and called. Ting came to her, and Terraforming Thunder and Work-centered Will came to Katora. The two stallions looked about for their riders, then eyed each other and postured a bit like the long-standing rivals they were. Mana could almost see Katora's mindpower roll over them in a chilling wave, making their heads droop.

Galan's horse, Leader, didn't appear.

After a few minutes, Katora said, "We don't have time. Let's go."

Mana wondered if she had ever intended to rescue Galan.

The three of them rode out across the field, the two loose horses running alongside, switching their tails and kicking up their heels. The stable had fallen out of sight behind them, and the distant golden-browns of the desert came into view, the scent of warm sand mingling with that of grass. The shuttle, a shiny white ellipsoid, was parked on the verge of the sand.

A black hole appeared in the side and a ramp protruded. Dino rode Prog up the ramp and into the ship, and the others followed. The cargo hold had been fashioned to resemble two rows of stalls —the shuttle's glowworms still functioned, of course. Mana wondered why Dino hadn't volunteered to help communicate with the space-planes, but she didn't want to ask in front of Katora.

They dismounted and led their horses into stalls, then stayed beside them. Dino went up front. A faint rumble came from somewhere, and the craft began to vibrate. Ting tossed her head, but the other horses were quiet. Mana supposed Katora was using her mind to steady them. Dino returned.

"I've programmed our course for the ranch. Hopefully we'll get there."

The engine throb deepened and the shaking increased; the ship shuttle lifted from the ground. Ting snorted, and Mana soothed her. None of the other horses reacted to the motion. Mana wondered why she had come along. She wasn't helping with the other horses. If Leader had been there, she would've had an assignment, but Leader wasn't there. She sighed. It was too late to pull out now.

In the stall across from her, Dino smirked. He leaned against Prog's side and shut his eyes. The mare shifted, pushing back against him. A few shifts later, she had him pinned between her shoulder and the side of the stall. He slid down and emerged on her other side.

He leaned against her.

She leaned back.

It seemed to Mana that they played this game for hours before finally falling asleep leaning against each other. She had fallen asleep herself when a glowworm voice announced, "Impediments on landing site. Decision required."

Dino went forward, and a few minutes later the shuttle settled and grew still.

Dino came back for Prog, and everyone spilled down the ramp. Hot air filled with strange odors hit Mana's face. Virtuous snorted. Thun and Will whinnied. Their riders came running toward them across a stretch of sand littered with strange, twisted boulders. Katora cried out with delight. She threw her arms around her son and her daughter.

Mana's eyes slid away from their joyous reunion to puzzle over the boulders behind them. She gave a start when she realized that they were dead dros. Something had killed the ranchers' stock, and one of the odors mingling with the smoke was the stench of death. The sky was so dark with smoke that you could hardly see the afternoon sun.

Nathimeon and Karali both began to talk at once. He was very tall, with a mane of white hair like his father's—he was a Luminary, of course. But while Thermeon had a silvery complexion, his was golden. "You shouldn't have come here," he said in a low voice.

Karali tossed her own Luminary mane and yelped, "Speak for yourself, brother!" She turned and shook her fist at some vague smoky smudges on the horizon. "I can't get away from this hell hole soon enough!" Amber eyes flashed from her bronze face as she whirled back toward her mother. "We've been under siege! People from the city, who have no idea how to do anything for themselves, have been roaming about in mobs, naked like animals, trying to take everything from the peasants! We've been fighting them off with sticks and stones! Luckily they have no idea how to fight, either. But I sure wish we'd had those deep-level swords Father used to have. What happened to them, anyhow? Heads would have rolled!" She grinned.

Katora blinked in amazement. She pulled back the cowl of her riding skin and shook out her hair. Before she could say anything, shouts came from across the sand.

Galan came running, dodging around the dro carcasses. "Where's Leader?" she panted. Then she hung her head. "It's only to be expected. The minors told me I wasn't major any more."

"What?" Katora cried.

"Someone's touched the Wall and made themselves emperor."

"One of those animals!" Karali spat.

Katora's expression grew thunderous. "You and your stupid harping about the law," she growled at Galan. "I should have ignored you and gone straight to the Wall yesterday. Well, I'm sure we can straighten things out." She looked at her children. "Come."

"Mother," Nathimeon protested.

"Whoever it is will step down when they see us. Come."

The three of them mounted up. "Shake out your hair, Nath," Katora said as they trotted off, nearly trampling a group of peasants coming toward the shuttle. "Look like an emperor. Ride proud."

Galan started after them, then stopped. She opened and closed her mouth, but no words came.

The peasants, short men and women with green eyes and braided black hair who wore home-sewn garments of dro-hide, surrounded Dino in a grumbling mass.

"They've wrecked our homes and stolen our belongings!"

"They killed our animals and drove off the ones they couldn't catch!"

"They didn't even eat them!"

"Our livelihood has been destroyed!"

"What can we do?"

Dino waved his arms to quiet them. "My shuttle still works. I'll fly you to Vuduna."

They responded with a chorus of negatives.

"We can't make a living on your resort!"

"Yes, you can," he said. "You can offer classes in glowworm-free survival. They will be a big success!"

They all shook their heads.

"Take us to Galena Flats, we have relatives there."

"But stop at the Yakei Ranch first. They may need to flee too."

"And the Bemisat place!"

"And the Quegleog's."

"All right, all right," Dino said, flapping his hands at them. "Do you have everything you need to take with you?"

"We don't own anything any more."

"Then get on board." He looked at Mana. "Hm."

"I'll just be in the way, won't I?" she said.

"Why don't I take you to the Plains of Possibility, so you can ride back to the stable."

The peasants, who had started up the shuttle ramp, turned back with cries of dismay. "What if a mob comes when you're gone? They'll destroy this shuttle!"

"Look. It's on standby. Just tell it 'Go Home,' and it will take you to Vuduna."

"If you go to the city, you won't get back. The mobs will kill you."

"We're not going all the way into the city, and I'll ride Prog back to the shuttle. If it gets too crowded for her on board I'll just push her off."

The peasants scowled at him. Mana gasped.

He gave them all an innocent look. "She'll downlevel if she's falling. It's a fear response. But if we left our horses out here on the desert, they could starve to death, because they can't sift sand like dros."

"Wouldn't they downlevel to search for food?" Mana asked.

He shook his head. "It's a fear response. Like your hair standing on end. Could you make it stand on end if you were starving? But if you were falling from a shuttle, you could."

"We will not let you push your horse off the shuttle," said a peasant woman. "It's cruel."

"But Prog would forgive me. She'd know it was all in fun. Of course, she'd kick *me* off if I ever took her up in a shuttle again."

Prog stood at his shoulder, ears pricked with interest, black eyes bright.

Dino looked at Mana. "Would Ting forgive you?"

"I could never treat her that way," Mana said.

"You don't play enough games with her. Well, let's go. The nearest intersection with the Plains is through the museum back entrance."

They mounted and trotted south, side by side. Everywhere the peasants' rock walls had been breached and their animals slain. Prog and Ting rolled their eyes and flattened their ears at the smells of blood and sun-baked viscera. When Mana realized that some of the corpses were human, she clutched Ting's mane, bile rising to her throat.

"I-I don't think—"

"Don't look," Dino snapped.

Prog broke into a canter, and Ting sped to keep up.

Tears ran down Mana's face, blurring the world. Imperial citizens shouldn't die like animals. It was unthinkable in this day and age. But the most horrible thing was that they had not been killed by malfunctioning glowworms, but by their own fear. How could it be, that despite millennia of imperial civilization, something so primitive still resided in the human heart?

It made her wonder whether Katora's Age of Illumination had accomplished anything. Katora said said she was acquainting everyone with deep-level wonders, but what was she really doing? She had taught at a mindsea academy, but the students were few and nearly all from good families. She had popularized deep-level horse racing, supporting the movement to make high government officials on all the planets race for their appointments. She gave all imperial citizens the chance to bond with a horse. Every child visited a Plains of Possibility intersection. But unless you had wealthy parents you were trotted out in one great mass that was not likely to draw any horses. So with few exceptions, only members of established families had a horse.

"If I were emperor," Mana told herself. "I'd see that every citizen had a horse. If they could ride, they really would become acquainted with the Deep."

"Do you know how many citizens there are?" Dino asked. "That's a heap of horses!"

Mana hadn't realized she'd spoken aloud. But she forged onward. "There must be an infinite number of horses since they come from every possible universe."

"They wouldn't all fit in the stable."

"Each group of a hundred could have their own day."

"Their day would only come around one in a decade, and they'd forget their rider in the meantime."

"Well, we'd build more stables and more racetracks."

"Lal is a desert planet. It's not easy to find anywhere you can pump water without glowworms to maintain a field attractive for horses. They're not dros!"

"It can be done. You have that big lake at Vuduna. You could build a racetrack there."

"Huh."

"And not only on Lal. On all the planets. Then people would get out to the tracks, and they wouldn't sit around all the time letting glowworms feed and clothe and entertain them. They wouldn't panic if something like this happened." Mana was shouting out her thoughts. She fell silent when something moved on her left.

It was a mass of naked people moving many-limbed like a centipede. Shouts reached her ears, and a dust-cloud billowed up around the writhing human mass. A bolt of fear went through her. But the horses stretched out a little, and the mob fell behind.

Looking ahead, Mana saw the towers and bridges of the city rising against the dark, smoky sky. They looked almost normal, except that the air lifter riders who had always buzzed about them like the gnats that swarmed over the field on humid days were gone.

"We're nearly there," Dino said.

"I've heard that your sister makes her students at the Mindsea Academy of Eltien do everything without glowworms. Why didn't Katora ever try to make people less dependent?"

"She never expected anything like this to happen."

Mana fell silent for a while. There had always been glowworm plagues. She'd heard about them countless times on the news—always on some distant, unimportant planet. She had never stopped to think how terrible they must be.

"If I was emperor, I'd have some committee, or something, at least, looking into the problem. What has Katora been doing all these years?"

"Trying to produce Nathimeon."

"Oh. Of course."

Their horses sped down a long, grassy slope toward the museum's archway.

"Did she ever act the way she acts about Nathimeon with my father?"

Dino looked at her, different emotions going through his face. For a moment his eyes went glassy. Then he turned from her with a shout. "Katora's in trouble!"

Prog surged away at breakneck speed.

Mana had never ridden so fast, not even in a race. The wind whipped her hair and made her eyes tear. She was certain that Ting was running her fastest, and still Prog drew away, her legs threshing into blurs.

Why was Dino so desperate to save someone who treated him like dirt? Was he still in love with Katora?

Silent towers slid past as the horses clattered down the winding lanes between them, leaping over the ruins of bioids and other detritus Mana dared not examine too closely.

Katora had encouraged people to see her as a god who would bring them immortality, and she must surely have looked divine riding up to the Wall with her son and daughter, all of them on their beautiful horses, dressed in their pastel-hued riding skins while everyone else was naked. But something must have gone wrong. Despite Katora's focusing all of her tremendous mindpowers on guiding the future in the direction she wanted, it seemed that she could still miscalculate.

Mana wondered about that as she chased Prog though the long gloomy channels between towers, her hands gripping tightly to Ting's long mane. She caught her breath when a mob waving shards of wreckage churned out from shadows and blocked the white mare's passage. But Dino didn't even seem to notice. Prog hurtled toward the mob with no slackening of her pace, and at the last moment they fell aside. Moments later, when Ting raced past, they remained slumped and dispirited-looking by the wall of a tower.

It was impossible to gauge how far Dino and she still had to go; Mana had never crossed through the city except on an air lifter, high above the towers and bridges. Would they arrive in time to save Katora from whatever was happening? Was the mob about to trample or tear her apart, do whatever they'd done to the empress? Mana grimaced.

Katora had ridden off without the slightest suspicion that something bad might happen. She had thought herself immortal. But she wasn't immortal. The notion of a universe without Katora felt so much like dawn breaking after an interminable night that Mana guiltily shoved it away.

Ting carried her though one serpentine curve after another, her gallop never slowing as she strained to keep up with Prog. Mana felt the rushing of wind, the rhythmical surge of each stride, the occasional jar of Ting hurdling an object, as she flew along. The organic material of her riding skin clung to the mare's sweaty back, and she didn't slide about, not even when Ting followed one of the few sharper turns.

Thoughts kept bubbling out. Katora wasn't immortal, and she couldn't control the future. "Hah!" Mana cried as the towers fell behind and Ting chased Prog through the ruins of the retail sector near the city center. Anyone, without the least exertion of mindpowers, could have told Katora that if you treated people with callousness and contempt all the time, they weren't going to like you.

The ruined shops and restaurants fell behind. Prog was a small white dot far ahead when Ting joined her on the great, broad Way that was the backbone of the city, running as it did from Bureau Headquarters to the imperial palace. The two horses rushed toward the palace, which loomed immense in the distance, its golden skin tarnished by soot, its towers shrouded by low hanging tendrils of smoke.

Clusters of naked people moved along the Way, some wielding crude weapons. They all paused to watch Prog streak by. Some shouted and waved their arms or their sticks, and when she had passed, they quickened their steps toward the palace.

Something flashed in the sky behind Mana. As she twisted her head around, she saw a jagged violet river of light connecting a blinding white starburst high overhead with the ground. It looked something like a lightning bolt, only too wide, and it just hung there. Ting had seen it too, and her stride broke. She jolted to a stop and reared with a whinny of fear.

"Steady! Steady!" Mana shouted, clutching her mane.

A tattoo of hoofbeats, and Dino was pounding back, calling Mana's name.

"What is it?" she screamed.

"It's my father. It's ... his fear response." His voice grew sharper, more commanding than she'd ever heard it. "Put your arms around Ting's neck! Hold on tight!"

She obeyed. Something like a wave swept up the Way, soundless, invisible, and yet present in a form so solid it swept everything before it. The wave engulfed Mana and reality exploded.

It was the Deep. Suddenly she and Ting were at the intersection of innumerable universes. Racetracks had intersection points too, but Mana knew this one was deeper, had drawn more possibilities together than she'd ever experienced in a race. Wondrous vistas flickered before her. Worlds, events, cities, people and animals— they all flashed into magnificent reality, and then submerged once again into the churning alternatives, their brief, impossible beauty leaving her mind wrenched and aching.

Beneath her, Ting too had changed. She was a denizen of this immensity, and now Mana perceived her other selves, all dancing and leaping about the central core of her, her eyes whirling like kaleidoscopes, her million hooves tapping out a symphony of rhythm, manes like fire and frost and shadow glimmering and chittering and weaving about. Mana's riding skin, once part of a whale-like deep-level species from the planet Medne, glistened like an ocean with the reflections of clouds and great airships.

Mana wept and laughed and sang, hugging her multitudinous horse, many-armed.

Thousands at a time, the universes burst like soap bubbles, and were gone. Mana strove to engrave the last marvelous glimpses on her mind, knowing they would slip from her grasp like dreams. It was like living a million sped-up lives at once.

Then the wave had passed, and Mana found herself back in a single world once again.

It was not the world she had left. The city was gone. Mana understood—from her Patternistics lessons at the boarding school where her father had sent her—that everything in the city, just like herself and Ting, had been mixed up with all of those universes. When the fusion of universes had ended, and each universe resumed its separate existence, things that had no deep-level identity were torn apart, scattered across all of the possibilities. So whatever remained of the towers in this one universe was infinitesimal.

The smoke had been cleared, the starburst and violet light were gone as well, and the sun shone brightly down on the bare sands of Lal. A gleaming white monolith known as the Sword of Aturon, which had been encircled by the torus of Bureau Headquarters so that only Members of the Circle could see it, now rose naked at one end of the Way. Where the palace had stood, the sacred Judgment Wall also stood alone, no longer encumbered by its golden housing. The Way seemed to have reverted to some primitive version of itself. Broad and straight as ever, it was now surfaced in soft dirt that must feel sweet beneath the horses' hooves. The air, the sands, now flowing to the edges of the Way, seemed as they ever had been. Patternists—the men and women who studied the Deep without necessarily having mindpowers— still argued about whether planets had some sort of deep-level awareness, or whether it took more power to disrupt them simply because there were almost infinitely more possible threads of history where a planet existed than where a particular city or particular building did.

The people that had been roaming the way were gone, scattered across as many universes as the buildings. Mana gulped and patted Ting's mane. Without the mare's mind to enfold her tender being and guide her back, she too would have been scattered among the possibilities.

"All right?" Dino asked. He and Prog were beside her. His hair now fell to his shoulders in the typical "Luminary" style.

"I-I think so."

Dino stared off toward the distant spot where the violet bolt had touched the ground. Mana looked too, and soon she saw something like a white butterfly flitting across the sand. The object approached and resolved into a white-clad rider on a white horse. The hoofbeats grew in volume as the rider turned onto the Way and galloped toward them.

It was Thermeon, and he was riding Eternal Trat. His white hair swirled, his violet eyes shone, and his long fangs were bared in a triumphant grin. No simple riding skin for him—he had woven himself an elegant costume from the possibilities of the Deep, shining white and flowing, trimmed with intricate, scintillating golden patterns. Coming up between Ting and Prog, he leaned one way to embrace his son, and then the other to embrace Mana. His leonine tail switched. Dino's tail twitched in response. Mana didn't have a tail, but she had inherited the daintier, female version of the fangs, and she couldn't stop herself from grinning back at her grandfather; he was so overflowing with joy and pride in his accomplishment.

Didn't he realize that he'd just killed hundreds, if not thousands of people—just wiped them into non-existence? Hadn't he seen the people on the Way, from wherever he'd been? But he must have known, at least, that he'd killed everyone who'd been threatening Katora, for he was clearly no longer worried about her, or he wouldn't have stopped to greet Mana and Dino.

A faint cheering came from her left. People, most of them still wearing clothes, had emerged from the archway that marked the museum's front entrance. They must have taken shelter in the museum, both from the glowworm plague and the deep-level blast. Like the Wall, the museum had been designed for the Deep by the empire's founder. More and more people poured out and cheered Thermeon, while he acknowledged them with an upraised arm. They probably didn't realize either that there had been people on the Way.

A golden lion with a black mane strode out among the people and roared.

It was a bioid. Mana realized then that the plague was ended. Thermeon had wiped out the infected glowworms.

With another lofty salute to the crowd, he rode off toward the Wall. Prog and Ting cantered along on either side of the white stallion. When they neared the Wall, Mana made out some tiny figures standing before it. Only two of them were horses. The dark gray stallion, Thun, was missing.

Thermeon sped ahead, and by the time Mana arrived, he had leaped from the white stallion to sweep Katora into his arms. She clung to him, sobbing and floppy, giving him a full measure of feminine weakness that she never showed anyone else. Mana looked to see how Dino was taking it. His expression was serious, but impassive.

Karali stood staring at her parents with a grimace, until she felt Mana's eyes; then she smoothed her features. Behind her, standing with his back to the Wall, arms folded across his chest, was a man Mana had never seen before. He was very tall, yellow-complexioned, with short-clipped, dark blue hair. He wore an unadorned black tunic. After a moment, she realized that he was a minor. She had never seen one without their golden armor. But there must have been many of them before the Wall. Why had this man alone survived the deep-level wave?

She didn't dare address the man. His features were very severe, and he obviously felt himself still on duty. He must have just seen the emperor he had been sworn to protect disintegrated, along with his comrades, yet he had to maintain his composure and continue to carry out his duties as a member of the imperial armed forces.

Still shaking with sobs, Katora looked up at Thermeon. "They tried to hurt Nathimeon!" she wailed. "They wouldn't listen! They were hurting him!"

Thermeon said nothing, but his tail thumped against the sand.

Mana moved a little closer, trying to get a look at Nathimeon, who was sprawled on his back behind his parents. Then Katora and Thermeon turned and lifted him into a sitting position, and she clapped her hands over her mouth.

Nathimeon reeled between his parents. His riding suit, which had been a pale apricot color, was blotched as if with mold and mildew. His complexion was no longer golden, but silvery with splotches of green and brown. One eye was blue-gray like his mother's, the other violet like his father's. His white hair was interspersed with locks of crimson.

Katora stroked his cheek. "Nathimeon! Our enemies are gone! It's time to get up and put your hand on the Wall and swear the imperial oath."

"My name is Valen," he said.

"Nathimeon! You've had a shock, but everything is all right now! Please get up!"

When he spoke again, his voice was deeper. "My name is Halika."

Katora looked at Thermeon. "Help me get him up!"

Thermeon released his son's arm and rose, shaking his head. "He can't do it."

"Please!" she wailed.

Again he shook his head.

"Mother!" Karali growled. "Can't you see that Nath's out of the running? But I'm fine! I'll be emperor!"

"No, you will be major. Your brother is fine. He just needs to collect himself. Nath!"

Nathimeon flopped back. He began to twist and thrash, as if his body was fighting itself. Katora screamed and bent over him, trying to hold him still. He kept thrashing. The horses stamped and moved away.

"He's finished," Thermeon said.

"No!" Katora screamed. She tossed back her head, wild-eyed. "How can you say that? He'll be fine! Just help me!"

Nathimeon continued to thrash. Karali watched with a grimace of disgust. Mana clung to Dino. She turned her face away, but she could still hear the groans and the thumping. After a while the sounds grew fainter and Katora's sobs grew louder. She howled and wailed with abandon as the hopes and dreams she'd worked so hard for crumbled.

It was much later when Karali's voice cut through the sobs. "Mother! People are coming!"

They all turned to see. The people from the museum, a great crowd of them, approached the Wall.

Katora fell silent. "I think the worst is over. Thermeon, help me get him up."

Mana looked. Nathimeon lay pale and still, foam on his lips.

The only sign of life was a slight trembling of the fingers and toes.

"He's dying," Thermeon said.

"No!"

"It's your doing," he growled, tears spilling down his cheeks. "You should have left him alone to be what he was! You insisted on changing everything about him! You changed his name and his hair. You did not even let him keep the horse that first came to him!"

"It was a mare! You don't ride a mare!"

"Natural is better! You thwarted his spirit! It was worse than what happened to Habel!"

She rose to face him. "How dare you say that! I devoted myself to Nathimeon! He begged me to do everything I did for him!"

With a growl, Thermeon crouched and lifted his son's body. Nathimeon shuddered and hiccuped, then subsided, his head lolling. The crimson streaks in his hair looked like blood.

Thermeon walked off carrying him. After he had passed the five horses, who had wandered off a ways to stand in a disconsolate huddle, head to tail, he clucked to them, and they followed as he disappeared down a hole in the sand Mana hadn't noticed. She recalled that there had been a ramp in the lower palace that led to an intersection with the Plains of Possibility. It must still be intact, for she heard hooves scraping against stone.

Dino broke the silence. "Katora, my dear. You wanted a son who would be greater than his father. Don't you realize that Thermeon also chooses the future, and he would never permit such a possibility to come to pass."

Katora gaped at him, her face twitching.

"What about a daughter?" Karali asked. "Would he permit a daughter to be greater than he is?"

"Oh, certainly. All of his most talented children are female."

Karali grinned and switched her tail. "I will be emperor."

Katora whirled to stare at her, but said nothing. Dino walked up to his ex-wife, and with a hand on her shoulder gently positioned her to face the approaching crowd. He motioned to Mana to join them.

"If Karali becomes emperor," Katora whispered. "Who will be major?"

"Um," said Karali, eyeing the three of them. "I think it will have to be Mana."

Katora scowled. "I could summon Galan."

"No. It would make us seem unprepared. Mana looks the part."

"She has no idea what to do."

"I'll dismiss her and appoint someone else after a suitable interval. It's not like we're going to be enacting major policy decisions over the next few days."

Mana could hardly believe what she was hearing. She would be major! The position had once been the most powerful in the empire. Katora had worked tirelessly to strengthen the emperor in relation to the major, but Raolin had not permitted her to deprive majors of their power of command over the minors. Emperors had always had the ability to appoint and dismiss their majors—when they stood before the Wall. In the times when majors had been preeminent, they had prevented their dismissal by the simple expedient of denying emperors access to the Wall.

The crowd approached and spread out into a long line, faces craning to take in the magnificence of Attequol's Wall, which was now open to them in a way it had not been for millennia, if ever. Karali stepped up to the Wall, laid her hand against its grayness, and trumpeted, "I swear to serve the Common Mind!"

She was emperor. Her figure seemed to swell as she turned from the Wall to face the crowd. Her amber eyes blazed with triumph and self-satisfaction. She wasn't quite as tall as Mana or Katora, but she had a sturdier and more athletic build than either of them, and in the thrill of the moment her movements vibrated with barely-contained ferocity.

Now dedicated to her service, the minor turned toward her. "What is your insignia?"

"My insignia is the face of a leopard, roaring, against a field of gray."

If times had been normal, all the minors would have instantly displayed that insignia on the surcoats over their armor. But without glowworms to effect the transformation, the lone minor merely inclined his head.

Karali looked at Mana. Her features had something of the feral cast of Thermeon's, though she had not inherited the fangs, and she bunched them into a fierce scowl, as if she thought Mana might be too stupid to remember her role. "As imperial major, I appoint Mana Sinarl Boom."

Mana walked toward her, head adance with crazy thoughts. Had this day been a dream, a nightmare, a fantasy? She laid her palm against Karali's outstretched palm. "I swear to serve the emperor and the Common Mind," she said, her voice cracking a bit.

Mana was imperial major.

"I appoint Galan Potusen Pirunc as mind-river of Lal," said Karali. The mind-river had no oath to swear, so she did not need to be present.

The crowd cheered.

Side by side, the new emperor and her major stood before the Wall and faced their people. It was customary for the new administration to give a speech. In olden times, the major or mind-river had spoken, supposedly being in mind-link with a mindsea-emperor. Now it was more customary for the emperors to speak for themselves.

"These past few days have been a time of trial for the empire," Karali began. "But the crisis is over, the mutant glowworms have been purged, and reconstruction can begin. Even worse than the mutant glowworms was the rash of criminal misbehavior on the part of citizens who were assumed to have human brains. I myself have witnessed heinous acts of destruction carried out by these criminals—attacks against peasants, destruction of their property, and the slaughter of their animals. I promise you that the criminals will be rounded up and severely dealt with. Civilization must and will prevail, even—no, especially—in times of crisis!"

Karali fell silent. It was clear to Mana that she had not prepared a speech. Everyone had expected Nathimeon to be emperor. Mana cleared her throat. If she was only to be major for a few days, she might as well make the most of it, and express the ideas that had come to her during the ride to the city.

"The city will be rebuilt with new glowworms," she said. Karali and Katora started at the sound of her voice, but they couldn't very well make a scene. Anyhow, they didn't have the right to silence her. She was major—the emperor's equal.

"Experts from off-planet—" that would be her mother—"and

from Lal—" that would be Dino—"are already working with Members of the Circle to develop replacement breeds that will not have the uniformity that made the plague spread so widely. In addition, from now on, all citizens will find courses in glowworm-free survival included in their educational programs. As further protection against similar disasters, and to further the Age of Illumination by acquainting citizens with deep-level phenomena, new measures will be taken to insure that every citizen can bond with a deep-level horse. Additional stable-racetrack complexes will be built on all the planets and paid for by additional wagering on races for office."

With a slight inclination of her head, she indicated that she had finished, and the crowd applauded. The rushing sensation in her ears made her feel like she was still flying through the city on a galloping horse.

Once they had left the Wall and started down the ramp toward the Plains of Possibility, Katora and Karali began to berate Mana.

"You had no right to say what you did!" Karali growled. "Now everyone will expect me to carry out those ridiculous plans!"

"You think it's ridiculous to want safer glowworms?"

"Oh, who cares about the glowworms! I mean self-sufficiency courses. Educating a citizen already takes a hundred years. Do you want to make it two hundred?"

"I think teaching people how to live without glowworms would prevent the criminal behavior you saw."

"Bah! A thousand years of courses couldn't civilize the animals that attacked me! They need to be exterminated and their genes proscribed!" Her screech reverberated along the curving stone walls around them.

The ramp wound around and around. It had no lighting, and as they left the sunlit sky farther and farther behind, the darkness deepened, only the glow from Dino's, Karali's and Mana's hair showing the way.

"Mana," Katora lectured. "It was very wrong of you to promise every citizen a horse. The horses simply won't come to most citizens. You have just set the stage for a great deal of heartache."

Mana shook her head. "When I and my sisters and brothers and cousins went to the Plains, we were allowed to walk alone to the border so that the horses could take a good look at us. Most children are taken in a great herd by an indifferent museum bioid, who hardly lets them get a look at the Plains. Even if a horse was attracted to one of these children, they could hardly pick them out from the crowd."

"It's done that way because it would be a waste of time to take them one by one," Katora told her. "The horses find people with mindpowers most attractive, and mindpowers tend to run in families. Families with mindpowers have risen to the top of imperial society because they are the only ones who can maintain the deep-level services the empire requires. The mass of citizens have no interests and no abilities beyond sucking in the benefits of patternists' labors. They have no interest in horses beyond the hope of winning credits at the races." She sighed. "We can do it your way for a while, and then when people get tired of wasting their time, we'll go back to the old way. It's been tried before."

"Oh?" Mana had been frowning and thinking as her grandmother spoke. "But I think it's debatable whether horses are attracted to mindpowers."

"You choose to think that because you have none. But you're really very lucky that you've kept your horse for so long. It's probably only because you work so hard at it. Most of your Deep-blind relations get only a few years of riding, or they never bond with a horse at all."

Lengthening her stride, Katora moved ahead of the rest of them, but not so far as to lose the faint light cast by their hair. Dino squeezed Mana's arm. "I think it was a fine speech! Good thing you practiced with me, eh?"

Katora whirled back on them. "You foresaw what would happen?"

"No, of course not!" Mana cried. "He's just kidding." She gave Dino a kick.

"Hey!" he yelped, moving away from her.

"I think," Mana said, "that if even one child bonded with a horse they would not have gotten in the old way, it would be worth it."

Katora snorted, and Karali muttered, "Ridiculous."

A faint light came from below, and Katora quickened her steps. A few more turns and the light became almost blinding. It was as if they descended into an ocean of it. Then the ramp ended and they stood on a stone floor that bordered the Plains of Possibility. You couldn't focus on the Plains from the border; you saw only hazy reflections of the floor and ceiling of the spacious underground palace chamber, but light from countless suns that were always shining in universes somewhere filtered through.

Nathimeon lay on the floor, his father standing over him. Eternal Trat stood nearby, his head down, one hoof cocked and resting. The other horses were gone.

Katora rushed to her son. "How is he?"

"Quieter now," Thermeon said.

Katora knelt and stroked the crimson-streaked hair, her face quivering. "We'll take him to the wonderdome in Vuduna. Is your space-plane nearby?"

"It's gone. When I felt your call, I jumped overboard."

She looked at him, then quietly reached out, and he knelt to take her hand. They both stayed that way for some time, hands clasped above Nathimeon's chest. Finally Katora spoke. "The minors must have gotten the all clear by now. When they return to the city, they can take him to Vuduna. All right?" She looked at Karali, who would have to give the order to the minors.

The empress shrugged.

Dino spoke up. "I can take him my shuttle."

"Not fast enough."

Thermeon released Katora's hand and stood. "Floating will not help him. He suffers from a shattered spirit. He does not know who he is. I will put him on Trat, and he can journey across the Plains."

Katora jumped up, her face paling. "No! He'd be lost!"

"He is already lost."

She clutched his arm. "No, Thermeon! Don't give up on him! We can bring him back!"

"Floating will not help. His spirit is like a common rosebush that had another kind of bush grafted on to make prettier flowers. In hard times, the pretty, weak bush dies off, and only the hardier, common root remains. You must let our son return to his root."

"I don't know what you mean."

"Yes you do."

Perhaps he conveyed something in mind-link, because Katora gave a little start and scowled at him. "He did want to be emperor!

Maybe it's you who didn't want it. Maybe it's true that you don't want a son to become greater than yourself."

Thermeon studied her, his nostrils pulsing. He tossed his head and puffed out his chest, the golden patterns on his deep-level outfit twinkling. "I will always think myself greater than my sons! That is because I am living my life, and not theirs. It is for them to make themselves great, not for me, and not for you. You can't be greatness for anyone but yourself."

"You meant to thwart him," Katora accused.

"Why would I do that? I am not afraid of my children."

"Then why won't you help Nathimeon!"

His gaze dropped to the supine body. "I've told you want he needs. But you will insist on doing it your way and killing him."

"If I let you send him onto the Plains, we'd never see him again!"

"Maybe we would, and maybe we wouldn't. But his spirit would be whole."

"I couldn't bear never to see him again!"

He studied her. "I think you care too much about what happens in this mortal empire. As for myself, I feel that the Deep is my true home."

"I am trying to make this empire a gateway to the Deep. It was always meant to be one, since the foundation. We are an empire that looks toward the Deep, and we need only a little additional push to get there. Nathimeon could still be the man who awakens the people's minds and leads the transition."

"You think that people will awaken and become deep-level beings?"

"Yes."

He grinned at her. "I think that will happen too. But I think it has nothing to do with thrones."

"Who but the emperor can focus the people's attention? Do you think you have more power to awaken them with your lecture tours and your monster fighting?"

He made his hair puff out and switched his tail. "Yes. Fighting monsters is a good thing. And Puflet is out there fighting slavers. That's a good thing too!"

Hearing her mother praised made Mana smile. Katora, of

course, scowled ferociously and said, "Oh, I don't doubt that it's good, but that kind of spectacle doesn't make people pause and take thought."

"Grafting a throne onto a spirit that doesn't want it is not the way to make people take thought, either, except to wonder why you are going it."

"I've never forced anything onto him! He was always an eager student!"

"He wanted to please you. He let you mold him in ways he isn't meant for. He's weak."

"You're wrong, Thermeon. He was always so brilliant. He mastered the Tenets of Patternistics faster than any other student I've ever had, even Habel!"

"Yet he cannot heal himself. I think he worked very hard to present the illusion of mindpowers to you, because he knew it was important to you and he loved you."

"You think Nath's not a mindsea? We'll show you when he gets better!" She jutted her chin. "But why am I letting you waste precious minutes with your sophistry?" She whirled on Karali. "Go up there and tell the minors to transport your brother to Vuduna, at once!"

Karali switched her tail. "Mother, I am the emperor. I do not take orders from you."

The shock on Katora's face was almost comical. Then the scowl returned, and the blue-gray eyes fixed on Mana. "You do it!"

Mana's first impulse was to obediently run off. She reminded herself that she was the imperial major. She looked at Nathimeon, who lay so still it was hard to tell whether he was still alive. Then she looked at Thermeon, who stood glaring at Katora, arms folded across his chest.

"What are you waiting for?" Katora snapped.

Mana met her eyes. "I think Thermeon's right. I don't think floating would help. You can see that he's gotten different universes mixed together. It's a deep-level problem."

"You understand nothing about deep-level problems! Do as I say, or I will make you very sorry when your brief appointment is over."

"No."

Katora gasped.

"Karali and Mana are strong," Thermeon observed. "But you don't like it. Maybe you're the one who's afraid of our children. Maybe you want to keep them weak."

"I think you've all lost your minds!" Katora shouted. "I'm just trying to help Nath!"

"I'll go for the shuttle," Dino offered.

"All right," Katora agreed.

He whistled, and Prog stepped out from the haze of the Plains. She paused to touch noses with the stallion, then sauntered over to Dino. He mounted and clattered off up the ramp. Thermeon glowered at his departing back.

"I begin to wonder whether you truly are my goddess-star," Thermeon growled.

"What?" cried Katora.

"If you were truly my goddess, why would you worry so much about our children and think that you need to fix them? Wouldn't a goddess feel confident that they would grow as they should and let them be?"

"I'm also a mother!"

"But a goddess-mother would think of their spirits and not only their bodies. Perhaps my goddess still awaits me, somewhere out there." He stared into the haze.

"There's no one else for you, Thermeon! I'm the most powerful female mindsea in the galaxy."

"But maybe my goddess-star awaits me in Andromeda." He looked at Mana. "Isn't there a rider who rides her horse among the galaxies?"

"Oh, yes. Her name is Eria something. I've never seen her horse."

Thermeon smiled. "I think I will go find her."

Katora shrieked. "You can't be serious! Eria's an ancient hag!"

"A goddess is eternal. And I am certain she is beautiful."

"But she's Quintillion's sister!"

Ignoring her, he leaped onto the white stallion, and they plunged into the haze. A moment later, Virtuous appeared, and Katora mounted and charged after him.

"Woah!" Karali cried. She looked at Mana and laughed. "That

was quite a little tiff, wasn't it!"

"Historical, I'm sure. And poor Nathimeon's been completely forgotten by both of them."

Karali looked at her brother and shrugged. "Good old Dino will take him on his shuttle. Why don't you and I go up and issue some orders to the minors?" She smirked. "Of course, the first thing on my agenda will be finding a replacement for you."

"Then I might as well enjoy it while I can."

Side by side, they started up the ramp.

When Mana and Karali reached the top of the ramp, they found minors in armor guarding the Wall, holding the seething, babbling crowd at a respectful distance. Their surcoats were gray, and Karali's leopard roared silently on their chests. Mana thought the leopard-spotted plumes on their helmets a nice touch. Karali too smiled her approval.

Craning her neck to peer past the crowd, Mana made out a row of space-planes parked on the Way. People were swarming there too, like ants, approaching the space-planes unburdened and coming away accompanied by floating objects. Those were aid stations, Mana guessed, and emergency supplies were being passed out so that people could return to the city—such as it was. The floating objects—Mana couldn't quite identify them—were glowworm-powered. The minors must be satisfied that the plague was dead. The problem was that in their rush to get everything back to normal, the same old glowworm stock would be proliferated, and the city would remain vulnerable to another plague.

She turned to Karali. "We must make an emergency Wall-speaking."

Karali quirked her lips. "You have your agenda planned?"

"Yes. There are things that must be done at once."

"Like what?"

"Taking steps to make sure that this doesn't happen again."

"None of your horse nonsense?"

"Nothing I didn't mention before."

Another shrug. "It's not like I can stop you. But you'll be wasting your time and mine if we have to countermand your Proposals."

Mana smiled into her amber eyes. "I may be a temporary major, but don't forget that in Katora's eyes, you're a temporary emperor."

Karali's face fell, then bunched into a snarl. "We'll see about that! It's not like she'll challenge me openly."

"No, but she'll ask you to step down once she has Nathimeon mended, and if you don't; well, I'm sure she'll think of something."

Karali squeezed her eyes. "Even if she makes me race, she can't force me to lose. She was always talking to Nathimeon about how he might one day race for the throne if Pia was challenged, or if ... something happened to her."

An icy thrill went through Mana. Surely Katora hadn't *wished* the horrible events that had ended Pia's reign.

"But she always assumed he would win," Karali went on. "She really believes he is the best. But I know I could beat him!" Her lips set in a smile.

"Could you beat Katora as well? A lot of winners have named their children for the throne."

Karali swallowed, a little trickle of sweat running down from her bushy white forelocks as the desert sun beat down on them. "I'd be more worried about beating my father. Hopefully he's gone after that Andromeda woman and won't come back."

"And your mother will marry someone else?"

They eyed each other. Katora despised the children of her ex-husbands.

"She can't," Karali breathed. "After all she's invested in breeding with the most powerful mindsea in the galaxy? There's no one more powerful than him."

"Thank the stars!" said Mana, remembering that violet bolt of light. She turned to the nearest minor. "Announce an emergency Wall Speaking to take place an hour from now."

The man inclined his head, and word, presumably, went out through his internal.

The sun blazed overhead. Mana and Karali spotted an

opalescent dome-like pavilion where the Chamber of Planets once had been, and walked along the Wall until they reached it. Inside they found coolness and civilization: animated nooks, a System node, a serving bioid shaped like a blue-wooled sheep, who brought them drinks and fruit cups.

"I'm going to change out of this!" Karali plucked at the gelatinous pink collar of her riding skin. The pavilion wall extruded a shower booth toward her, and she stepped inside with a happy sigh.

Mana sat down at the node and began to issue orders to the minors—everything she could think of that didn't need to be proposed before the Wall and approved by the Bureau before taking effect.

She directed emergency services to the outlying ranches and requested a rundown of damages. She asked that her mother be summoned to the capital to work on the new glowworms. She appointed two of the younger, more enthusiastic riders as new caretakers at the stable. She ordered all of the supplies that she had ever wished were on hand. After a bit of further thought, she requested a patternist to come out to examine the stable for signs of unfusing damage and to determine whether it needed to be replaced.

Karali stepped out from the shower booth in a trailing pink gown with a leopard-spotted collar and a billowing silver-gray cape. "What are you doing?"

"Oh, just ordering a few supplies."

"Well, I need to order some things too. Move over."

Mana rose and went to shower. She hung her skin on a hook beside Karali's and relaxed for a few minutes while the water pounded over her. But thoughts continued to seethe inside her skull. It was all so unreal. She was major! She wished she could absorb something of the comportment of the great historical majors before she went on.

When she had been dried by the booth's warm air jets, she bade it weave her a tunic-style suit in olive green—emperors might cavort like racers, but the major was supposed to be the Palace workhorse—and stepped out.

Karali rose from the node and started to pace around swishing her cape. "Did you notice that the throne was gone? I'll have to order a new one. Should I duplicate the old one, or try something new?"

"Something new," Mana said.

"You have opinions about everything, don't you? You never spoke up much at the stable."

"Circumstances have changed."

Karali gave the dry rasp of a laugh. "That's the understatement of the day! Galan won't arrive in time to announce us, so one of the minors will do it instead. Are you nervous?"

"Yes."

Another laugh. "I would have ruled anyway. Nathimeon would have been my puppet!"

Mana let her thoughts return to the Proposals she planned to make, and didn't respond.

A few minutes later, a minor opened a door in the pavilion and said that it was time. When she heard him announce the Speaking, Mana walked out and took the major's position beside the silvery seat that was serving as interim throne. Karali strode out, magnificent and haughty, and swept herself into the throne. Mana cleared her throat and launched into her talk.

"As we begin our recovery from the double shock of glowworm plague and deep-level cleansing, we must keep in mind that the greatness of the empire lies not only in the glitter of its technology but in the hearts and minds of its people. Today I am laying before the Common Mind Proposals for nourishing our hearts and strengthening our minds. We must learn from this terrible experience, learn and grow, so that it is never repeated."

She went on to enumerate the ideas she had mentioned in her inaugural address, discussing them with greater detail and exactness, and presenting them as Proposals to be made part of imperial law: Every settlement in the empire should have a distinct non-interbreeding glowworm strain that could be deployed in emergencies. Education in glowworm-free handicrafts should be part of the mandatory educational curriculum. Every citizen should be offered at least three separate opportunities to familiarize themselves with the Deep by bonding with a deep-level horse.

As she finished expressing her thoughts on the bonding, another

idea popped into Mana's head, and even though she'd told Karali
that she wouldn't say anything new, she couldn't help but voice it.

"When a Challenge to the throne is to be decided by racing, the
final series of races should include eight champions from Lal, and
eight champions from beyond Lal, one for each sector of the
empire."

She was done. Her throat felt very dry. Turning slightly toward
the throne, she gave a little bow to indicate to the Emperor that she
had finished. Karali acknowledged her with an imperious nod, her
face set and angry.

"This Speaking is ended!" boomed the minor who was standing
in for the mind-river of Lal.

As she walked back to the pavilion, followed by Karali, Mana
wondered if he was the same one who had survived Thermeon's
purge. Had he been saved by mindpowers, or had he been in
contact with the Wall?

Once they were sealed away from the public's eyes and ears,
Karali began to growl about her Proposals, but Mana ignored her,
and said, "I'm worried about Nathimeon. Did you see Dino go by
during the Speaking?"

"No. But you're right. He should be checked on."

"I don't want to walk out in front of the Wall again. It would be
anti-climactic. But maybe we could walk around behind the Wall
to get to the ramp. No one's ever seen the back of the Wall, have
they? I wonder what it's like."

"Exactly like the front, I would guess."

"Let's go see."

When they stepped out from the pavilion and crunched over the
sand toward the back of the Wall, a couple of the minors followed
a few paces behind. The Wall was much thicker than Mana had
imagined.

"It's actually shaped more like a pillar than a wall, isn't it?"

"So what?" said Karali.

The sun had been directly overhead during the Speaking. Now it
began to sink, so that the deep shadow that must have lain behind
the Wall all morning had vanished, but Mana thought the sand just
behind it was a little cooler. The back of the Wall was marked by
parallel series of hexagonal grooves deep enough for a person to

step into and far taller than they were wide. The divisions between the grooves in each series were at different levels, but all extended as high as she could see. She studied them as they walked along.

"Well, of course it isn't really a wall, is it? It was part of Attequol's energy temple—or factory, or whatever—until Rathax wrecked it. And now it doesn't do anything any more."

"But by doing nothing, it makes people believe that it approves of the emperor standing in front of it." Karali chuckled and kicked happily at the sand with her leopard-spotted slippers.

Mana squinted up at the grooved surface. "Do you think maybe this side is really the outside, and the side we stand in front of the inside? That side is so smooth, it's hard to imagine that a block fell out of it."

"I don't believe a block ever fell out of it."

"So you don't think the Wall 'judged' Rathax?"

Karali snorted. "Remember your Patternistics lessons! There are many possible pasts leading to the present moment, more the further back you go. The possibility of a past where Rathax was actually killed by the Wall must be tiny. What most likely happened is that his enemies killed him and blamed the Wall."

"Well," said Mana. "There goes one of the empire's favorite stories!"

"Oh, the story is good," said Karali. "It helps us emperors maintain our position. As long as the Wall doesn't drop a block on us, it's showing approval." She chortled.

They reached the pit where the Challenger's Waiting Room had been—actually some levels below its vanished floor—and started down. "It's amazing, isn't it," said Mana. "The palace must have stood here, with the Wall at its core, ever since the successor of Rathax, whoever that was." She looked at Karali, and Karali smiled and shrugged. Without internals, neither of them could remember the successor's name. "I suppose a lot of emperors remodeled, but it was still an ugly heap. Now you have the opportunity to redo the whole thing!"

"You think I should change it?"

"Of course! You could build something beautiful!"

Karali shook her head. "It doesn't matter what the palace looks like. What matters is what it symbolizes to the people. So I'm going to have it rebuilt exactly the same way, because that's how people expect the center of imperial power to look."

"Oh. And I suppose you'll have the new throne look exactly like the old one."

"Of course."

"But you could start a new tradition. I think a truly great emperor would."

Karali's pale eyebrows drew fiercely together. "And what exactly do you know about greatness?"

"I think—"

"I don't care what you think! Greatness is something in the common mind of the masses, and they usually never realize how great you were until after you're dead, and future greatness is no good at all to you in the moments of your life."

"Well, I wasn't talking about greatness in the sense of public fame. I meant—"

"I don't care what you meant! By this evening, Taana will be here, and she and I will go over all the options for major. Your appointment will end very soon!"

Taana was one of Karali's and Nathimeon's older sisters. Mana thought she was very nice, but she hadn't inherited the glowing white hair, and that had made her a disappointment to Katora from the day the incubator had birthed her. "Taana's a wonderful architect! You should ask her for advice about reconstructing the palace. Maybe—"

"Then I don't need your advice, do I?"

Mana wondered why Karali was suddenly so angry. Perhaps she was worried about her brother. They descended turn after turn of the ramp in silence, the sun's heat and brilliance fading away until it was only a memory. Their steps echoed in the stillness, while stone floor, walls, and ceiling glimmered faintly in the light of their hair. At last light welled up from below, and they hurried down the last few turns until they rushed together to the hazy border of the Plains of Possibility.

The stone floor verging into the haze was empty. They both looked one way, and then the other, but all they could see was the more of the empty floor meeting the haze in a line that stretched to infinity.

Nathimeon was gone.

8

"Have I ever told you how beautiful you are?" Mana asked Ting as she groomed the mare. "Your coat is so shiny, and your little white spots are like snowflakes, and your mane and tail are rich and wonderful as chocolate fudge!"

Ting basked in the praise, her eyes half closed.

"And your eyes—they are such an exotic hazel color. You're the most beautiful horse in the stable!" Mana gushed as she brushed the long mane.

Ting was one of the most recent horses to appear from the Plains. Dino claimed that one of his sons—one he'd had before Katora—had been the first to bond with her some four thousand years before.

Mana paused her paean when she heard footsteps. Somewhere beyond the curve of the white wall across the aisle from the stalls, a person was approaching. It was probably Kusomba or Pasola.

Kusomba and Pasola were the young riders she'd appointed to manage the stable when she'd been major. Kusomba was a cousin, one of Dino's granddaughters. Pasola was an adherent of the ancient Code religion. Citizens made fun of them, but they believed in work and had maintained their traditional glowworm-free technology. Even though Mana's successor had rescinded their appointments and sent Mana back to her old job, the two still often came early and helped out.

It seemed to Mana, now, that her day as imperial major, along with the terrible destruction of the city, had been part of some unreal fantasy. It made it easier to go on with her life when she let herself picture the lofty and teeming metropolis as it always had been. Whenever she left the stable to take in the news, however, the shock of the devastation returned. Temporary habs like a field of bright flowers flowed out from the Way. The city's population had been reduced by two thirds, and yet Emperor Karali and her major talked as if the purging had been part of the plan, as if all the valuable citizens had evacuated as they had been told to, and only deranged killers had perished. It made Mana sick every time she heard one of their speeches, so she didn't go out to the Nexus very often.

The steps grew louder. Mana started when Karali came around the bend, clad in her pink riding skin and unaccompanied by guards.

"Mana!" she cried, her smile all-engulfing, as if they were best friends. "I bet you've been enjoying the quiet out here."

"What do you want?" Mana said.

Karali's amber eyes sparked. "Have you been following the news?"

For a moment Mana lost control. She gave Ting's mane a fierce pull, and the mare flung up her head. Apologizing, Mana patted her. Then she stepped out from the stall and faced Karali. "I've heard you proposing to end races for reproductive rights because the horses give people without mindpowers an even chance against mindseas. According to you, only people without mindpowers panic during crises, so they're a danger and should be bred out of existence. I agreed wholeheartedly when Raolin called your Proposal the worst idea since Quintillion put Nanders in charge of the trans-gates!" She began a laugh that ended in a sob. Her hands trembled, and the grooming brush slipped from her fingers and clattered on the floor.

"I suppose you feel threatened," Karali mused. "Like the apes must have felt when the first humans arrived on the scene. But no need to worry, Mana, I'm not proposing to euthanize anyone. You'll get to live out your life, meager as it is. I'll protect you from other mindseas."

"I don't want your protection!"

"Look, I know you'd like your two assistants back. I'll reappoint them. All you have to do is one little favor for me."

"No."

"You don't even know what it is."

"No! Just go away and leave me to my 'meager' life."

"Look, it's clear you haven't heard the latest news. I don't think you'd approve of the lies and calumnies they're spreading about me. All I want is for the truth to come out, and you can help."

Mana had no idea what she was talking about. She didn't think she wanted to know. It was strange, but as horrible and oppressive as Katora had been, Mana found herself wishing that she would come back and take her daughter in hand.

"They're saying I murdered Nathimeon," Karali told her.

"Did you?"

Karali blinked. "Of course not. Dino's been lying. He never took Nathimeon to Vuduna. They finally gave in to the alarmists and sent a firefly to snoop, and it reported that in no discernible past has Nathimeon been on the premises. He must've crawled onto the Plains, or else Thermeon came and took him."

"Oh. Well, if I'm summoned to testify, I'll share what I know. There's nothing more I can do."

Mana turned back toward Ting's stall, but Karali jumped in front of her. "Yes there is! You haven't heard the tenth of it! They're saying I murdered my parents too!"

Mana gaped at her.

"They're saying I'm not a legitimate emperor because I've never ridden the white stallion! Highlal's is coming soon, and if I don't ride Trat for the Showing, a Challenge will be around the corner."

It would serve her right, Mana thought. Trying to legislate Deep-blind people out of existence!

Karali grabbed her shoulders and shook her. "I'm not just worried about myself! There won't be an empire if the white stallion doesn't come back! You're in charge of the horses, Mana! It's your job to get him back!"

Mana shoved away the clutching arms. "I've called him every day, but he doesn't come. Thermeon's taken him to Andromeda. What am I supposed to do?"

"Ride after them! My father's just lost track of time, like you always do in the Deep. Remind him that Trat isn't his—he belongs to the empire!"

The last words Thermeon had exchanged with Katora had given Mana the impression that he didn't much care about the empire. She shook her head. "Riding onto the Plains is dangerous, especially for someone who's not a mindsea. If I fell off Ting, I'd lose the deep-level form she gives me. I'd go flat and inanimate, and no one would ever be able to find me again, even if they searched. Why don't you send one of your mindsea friends on this mission?"

The look on Karali's face told Mana that the emperor had already looked in vain for such a person.

"You're in charge of the horses," Karali argued. "Look—" A crafty gleam came into her eyes—"if you can do this, then you'll have proved to me that a Deep-blind person on a horse is as good as a mindsea. I'll give up my plans for granting repro rights according to mindsize, and instead I'll back your idea for giving more people horses. I swear it! What do you say?"

She was lying, Mana thought. If Mana returned from the Deep with Trat, she'd find some way to wriggle out of it, probably by claiming she'd never made any agreement.

Just then, Kusomba and Pasola came around the curve of the wall. Mana smiled. "All right, Karali. Swear before them that you'll change your policies if I bring Trat back."

Karali whirled. She hadn't heard the approaching steps. But her smile quickly reasserted itself. "Of course. I swear that if Mana can bring Eternal Trat back from the Plains of Possibility for my Showing, I will publicly acknowledge that a Deep-blind person on a deep-level horse is as capable as a mindsea, and I will advocate more people bonding with horses rather than trying to breed more mindseas. How is that?"

She'd still wriggle out of it, Mana thought. Even if she swore with her hand on the Wall, she'd still try to wriggle out. But Mana nodded and said, "All right, then."

Karali, Kusomba, and Pasola rode out with her across the field. It would feel like an intersection point on the racetrack, Mana told herself. Actually, it would feel more like Thermeon's bolt striking the city, because there would be no track. But it wouldn't sweep past her and let her return to her everyday world. She'd be immersed in it until she found her way to one of the edges. And she'd heard that it could be impossible to find your way out, even if you were a mindsea. You had to trust your horse to know the way.

From what she recalled of the Bolt, Mana knew why she would find the Plains disorienting. There would be an infinitude of vistas, some of the breathtakingly beautiful. She would need to keep in mind the deep-level time-contraction—minutes spent in the Deep could equal hours or days back home, depending on how deep you went. She couldn't pause to gawk at the wonders. She would be totally dependent on Ting to guide her to Trat, and then they could ride out together.

She patted the mare's neck, the mane flying around her hand. Ting knew something was up; she was already surging into a gallop, her ears pricked. If Mana fell off in the Deep, everything would end for her. It was only through her bond with the mare that she could experience its vistas, for she didn't possess her own deep-level organs of perception.

They approached the border. Mirror-like, the haze of the Plains reflected the field, making it look infinite, but Mana sensed the change in the wind, and then a shivery sensation went down her neck, telling her the Deep was near.

"Catch Trat!" she urged Ting, as she would during a race when there was a rider ahead she hoped to overtake. She didn't know for sure that Ting recognized the names of all the other horses, but she must know the white stallion's name. "Catch Trat!"

Ting lunged forward, leaving the other horses and their riders behind. The Deep enveloped her and Mana.

Once again reality burgeoned into vista after glorious vista. There were worlds that they might explore on every side, and many, many more sides than existed on home-level. Directions for which there were no words nor ways to describe now beckoned wondrously. Many-handed Mana gripped Ting's many manes and let the mare run. She couldn't even find her voice to urge her on. She felt outside of herself, free, exuberant, eternal.

At the same time she was utterly lost and more helpless than a newborn babe.

Something green and sparkling came at them from one of those deep-level sides. Some sort of marvelous gateway, it seemed at first, shooting out coruscating beams as new facets came into view one after the other. The overall shape was so dazzling and cleverly interwoven with itself, it made Mana laugh and hoot. Ting seemed to love it as well. Her joyous whinny echoed everywhere as she sped toward the gateway.

In the last instant, Mana realized that there was no passage through, that they were about to crash into a solid wall of crystal light. It felt like living liquid when Mana struck; the impact released a thousand voices that sang an incredible anthem of the Deep in perfect harmony, and light like a million green suns swam into her. She flew on a wind so wonderfully fresh that her mind exploded into cosmos after cosmos of tiny spiraling galaxies of sensation until she floated down, light and empty as a thistle seed.

With a start, Mana sat up at looked around. She gasped when she saw Ting a short distance away, cropping an emerald plain beside a red stallion with brown stripes on his legs.

A voice came from somewhere. "Don't be afraid. The splinter has a fusion field. You're safe."

Leaping up, Mana found herself looking into a pair of the most gorgeous violet-blue eyes she could imagine. Waves of bright, golden-red hair spilled around the face that contained those eyes, and a graceful feminine figure swathed in rippling blues completed the assemblage. The woman smiled.

"I'm Morning Glory."

"Oh!" Mana cried. "You're Thermeon's sister! Is it true that you've been lost here for thousands of years? I mean, well, but you wouldn't know how much time has passed out there, would you? Oh! Does it mean we're both lost now?"

"I'm sure your mare will take you back when she's ready. No, I'm not exactly lost. This is my home now."

"But where exactly are we? Did I leave the Plains of Possibility?"

"We still intersect the Plains, though I have a soul-gem splinter that maintains its own little bubble universe."

Mana looked about. "It's gorgeous! Heavenly! You're living the deep-level life. Isn't this what Thermeon wants for all of us?"

Morning Glory smiled. "Not really. It's too peaceful, too unchanging here for him. He was here a moment ago, and—"

Mana gave a wild leap. "I have to catch up with him! Which way did he go?"

The other woman held out a restraining hand. "Calm yourself! There are too many ways in the Deep. You'll never catch him by chasing after him. He is like a fly."

"But—"

"Have you ever tried to catch a fly that was buzzing around your house?"

Mana stared at her, tears of frustration brimming into her eyes. "I need to make him return the white stallion."

"No, of course you have never chased flies," Morning Glory said, as if to herself. "But in our homes in the Valley, we had swarms of them. They are very fast, and you could waste half a day chasing them about, but if you simply threw open your door flap, they would all go to the light and leave you alone. My brother is like that. Don't chase him. Create a light, and he will come to you."

"What sort of light?"

"The light of deep-level conflict. From wherever he is, he will home in on it. Especially if it involves people he knows."

"Oh." Mana frowned. "What exactly do I have to do? I'm in a hurry."

"You cannot rush, child."

It was a long while since anyone had called Mana "child." "Oh! I'm sorry, I haven't introduced myself. I'm Mana Sinarl Boom. Thermeon's my grandfather, so I guess that makes me your grand-niece. But I really am in a hurry. People are depending on me!"

Morning Glory's beautiful eyes shone on her. "Who is depending on you?"

Mana pictured Karali pacing, angry. Then she thought of children in their educational crèches, ready for their field trips to the edge of the Plains. "I want to help ordinary children get a better chance at bonding with deep-level horses, and the emperor said she'd support me if I brought Trat back in time for her Showing."

Morning glory beamed at her. "You want to make the empire a more equitable place."

"Yes!"

"I had such aspirations too, once. Let me tell you what happened, and why the empire is in crisis now. But first, I must be the good hostess and get you to relax. Because you really cannot rush when you are trying to direct the future."

"But—"

"If we were on home-level, I would offer you food and drink. But we don't need food or drink here."

"The horses are grazing," Mana pointed out.

"That's because they are horses, and they can't imagine anything finer than sweet grass. But you are human, so I will give you some interesting things to look at for a while. Afterward we will talk."

"But time is contracted here compared to home-level. Hours, days must be streaming by!"

"Yes. I'm afraid you are already too late for the Showing. So relax, and look at these things."

Four objects tumbled across the grass toward Mana. She picked up the first and examined it. It was a yellow ball with some sort of design on, or in it. The design seemed to represent some sort of scaly creature, but she couldn't quite make it out.

The second object was a macabre little statuette of a human skeleton clad in dragon armor with the wing folded over its chest.

The third object was a small rug with a flowered pattern. As Mana looked it over, a blossom fell from somewhere and became one of the patterns.

The fourth object was a small, flat, square piece of metal embossed with the picture of a mountain overlooking a lake and the words "Roldo Resort." Mana put it down and looked up into Morning Glory's celestial eyes.

"When you were thinking of the future," Morning Glory said, "you probably only considered two possibilities: the bad things that would happen if you did not bring Trat back in time for the Showing, and the good things that would happen if you did. Isn't that right?"

"Yes," Mana agreed.

Morning Glory nodded. "Most of us think that way. But the future really is full of so very many more possibilities—all sorts of things we can't even begin to imagine."

Mana wondered if that was why Katora had problems molding the future she wanted. Hearing herself voice this thought aloud, she clapped her hands to her mouth.

Morning Glory's laughter bubbled around her like a small stream. "Thoughts speak in the Deep, you know. But don't feel alarmed. I'm in no position to judge you, or even Katora, for I've done more than anyone, I think, to shape the disaster the empire faces. Though I did not intend to, of course."

Mana just shook her head. She couldn't begin to imagine what this glowing-eyed woman could have done. Certainly nothing Mana had learned about in her history lessons.

"Did Thermeon tell you about the glowworm plague on Lal?" Mana asked. "And about how he purged the capital? Are you telling me that you think you're the cause of all of that? I don't see how that's possible, if you've been here all along."

"Oh, but those disasters are only the beginning," Morning Glory said. "Worse is still to come. And yes, I set it all in motion."

A shadow fell over the glorious landscape around them. Mana gazed into a direction that had no name and saw a black cloud shaped like a dragon. A cold wind swept in from it, sighing through the emerald grass. The horses lifted their heads and switched their tails.

"What is going to happen?" Mana whispered. "Isn't there anything that can be done to prevent it?"

"I've been trying to think of something," Morning Glory said. "But I still don't know. But let me tell you the story from the beginning."

Mana settled down in the grass, hands around her knees, and waited. Sitting down across from her, Morning Glory began.

"When Attequol built his energy temples to hold the empire together, they were powered by a soul-gem that he imprinted with his mind. The secrets of soul-gem technology have been repeatedly lost and rediscovered throughout the empire's history. They say that Quokisa restored Attequol's soul-gem, but then, of course, Rathax destroyed it so that he could dominate multiple timelines. Before my brother took the throne, the empire enjoyed a resurgence of deep-level technology."

Mana nodded. That was when Imperial Major Horl had

dominated a succession of weak emperors.

"In order to defeat Horl," said Morning Glory, "my brother needed to destroy Horl's soul-gem and replace it with one of his own. I helped him. Do you understand how soul-gems work?"

"I just know they're a sort of deep-level beacon that helps galactic communications and ships converge on one timeline, so that the empire will have a unified history."

"Yes, and the way the soul-gem is imprinted determines its orientation. I wanted a future of happiness and fulfillment, but I was very young. I couldn't look that far ahead, and I didn't realize how many possibilities there were. Our soul-gem had a flaw."

Morning Glory's eyes shimmered with sorrow as the dragon cloud cast its shadow over her. She sighed deeply.

"I think you're taking too much blame on yourself!" Mana cried. "If there are really so, so many possibilities, then no one could forge a perfect soul-gem! Besides, the empire doesn't have a soul-gem any more. Wasn't Thermeon's destroyed at the end of the Great War?"

"Yes. But the direction of history had been set, and nothing has changed it since then. It's like you shatter a meteoroid, but all the pieces keep traveling with the same velocity."

"Oh."

"When a soul-gem is shattered, the splinters can turn up anywhere and anywhen. I found this splinter, and I've been using it to create my little hideaway. I suspect that Quintillion had another splinter, because his personality changed so much after the war. I don't know where it went after he died, but I suspect one of his descendants must have it."

"Is that why Katora advocated eradicating his genes?" Mana asked without really wanting to.

Morning Glory reflected for a moment. "Maybe she senses the splinter. That one had a darkness in it, though it could be washed away if all the splinters were reunited and forged into a new soul-gem."

Mana sat up straighter. "That sounds like a wonderful plan! You would know how to forge a new one."

"I know how, but it's very difficult. We would need four splinters, and I don't know where the others are. To overcome the momentum of the old soul-gem, we need to forge its replacement on Deep Six, but our ships don't fly that deep. When Thermeon's was forged, you see, we used the fusion field of the old soul-gem. There's a mountain that rises from the Plains, and it leads to the Stairway of Ice—the center of time and space. You can climb it as deep as you like, but you can't get back."

"Could your horse find its way back?" Mana asked.

"Perhaps. They say that Kokkiro rode up the Stairway of Ice when he led humans from Earth and first colonized the galaxy, but that was so long, long ago, that the stories aren't very probable."

Mana sighed.

"But still, I think it's time to try something. When my brother passed through, he was very agitated, and his wife was too when she came chasing after him. She refused to listen to me when I told her about flies."

"Katora is unbendable," said Mana.

"What they told me made me very uneasy." Morning Glory stared at the menacing dragon cloud. The wind was growing colder still, whipping back her red hair and Mana's hair and the horses' manes and tails. "Both of them are so fixed on building the future on just one thing, focusing on one dimension out of all the breadth of possibilities, it's a deadly thing. You see, when you care about one thing only, and nothing else, you're bound to destroy everything else in the quest for that one thing, because somehow, it seems you never can get it."

It was clear enough to Mana what Thermeon and Katora wanted: Thermeon must have his goddess-star, and Katora her perfect son.

"She was angry that her daughter had taken the throne," Morning Glory said. "She didn't seem to realize that this was as close as she would come to having what she thinks she wants. She told me that she expected her son to be well when she returned with Thermeon, and then she would arrange for him to challenge for the throne."

Mana bit her lip, but she couldn't stop the thought. "Nathimeon's vanished, and she doesn't even know. But there will be a Challenge with or without him, if Karali doesn't have the white stallion for the Showing."

Morning Glory nodded. "I'm afraid that the destruction of the capital is just the beginning of the troubles that will come if my brother and his wife decide they have to exert more power to get what they want. But maybe we can use the Challenge for our own purpose. I could bring my splinter to the races and talk about forging a new soul-gem. Everyone with ambitions for the throne would be drawn in, and I suspect that among them would be the holders of the other splinters."

"Do you think they would give them to you?"

"Of course not. Each of them will want all of the splinters so that they can imprint the new soul-gem for the history of their choice. So, it will have to be that the winner of the final race will get not only the throne, but the four splinters. And perhaps, if the racing is intense enough, the racetrack will intersect with Deep Six, and the soul-gem can be forged as the final race is won. But there must be one, single, incontestable victor to do the imprinting— having multiple minds in the soul-gem is disastrous."

Mana tried to picture a race culminating in a Deep Six intersection. It was true that the intersections reflected the focus of the minds of horses and riders, so she supposed it was possible. "But supposing Thermeon or Katora wins? Wouldn't that make things even worse?"

Morning Glory's eyes glowed in the fading light. "We must make sure that they don't win."

They stood.

"I am going to collapse the fusion field," Morning Glory said. "Get on your horse."

Mana started toward Ting, but suddenly both horses were prancing about, whinnying.

"Someone's coming," Morning Glory said.

The splinter sang out in its myriad voices as a horseman plunged from nowhere onto the emerald plain. Rings of light rippling outward from around him pierced the dragon cloud and transformed it into countless lesser dragons that fled in every direction.

"Mana!" cried the rider. "How did you get here?"

She recognized neither him nor his horse, and her confused thoughts bubbled out in an embarrassing cacophony.

The man dismounted and came toward her in long strides. His silvery face was rugged and attractive, his eyes a brilliant blue. Long dark hair streamed in the wind. His laugh boomed around her. "You know me as Nathimeon!"

"Nath? Have you really changed so much that I didn't recognize you? Or is it just some illusion of the Deep?"

"I have changed! Or perhaps it would be truer to say that I have returned to my best self. You see, my mother scoured what might have been thousands of timelines to find the person she wanted me to be. She took aspects of those me's from various timelines and combined them—somehow she was able to bring me back to home-level still having aspects that had fused in the Deep. She did this because I wasn't exactly the way she wanted on any of the timelines, and she thought she could combine all those elements and have a whole person.

"But I was confused inside, even though I tried not to show it, and even more confused whenever she pushed me into contact with the Deep. Until finally, when Father downleveled the city, I saw very clearly what had happened to me."

"It must have felt horrible," Mana said.

"I felt that I really wasn't a person at all. I thought I would dissolve, fly apart. But she saved me." He smiled at the mocha-colored mare he'd ridden in on. "She came for me as I lay on the border of the Plains."

"She's beautiful!" Mana cried. "She has the same hazel eyes as Ting. I've never seen her before. Is she from one of your other timelines?"

"Yes. Her name is Transcendent Point. The life where I bonded with her is the most satisfying of all the lives my mother tampered with. But of course you can see my mother wasn't satisfied with that me. For one thing, I don't have the Luminary hair." He laughed.

"It can be a nuisance sometimes," Mana said, running fingers through her wind-tangled hair. "Especially if you want to enjoy the darkness."

"And I'm not interested in sitting on a throne. I study oceans!"

Mana nodded and smiled into the oceans of his eyes.

"I'm going to go back there, so I suppose this is the last time I'll see you—someone else manages the stable in that universe."

"Oh." She sighed.

"But first I wanted to catch up with my parents and tell them to stop fighting about me. Transcendent brought me here when I told her to find Trat."

Morning Glory stepped forward and introduced herself. "My brother and his wife have already swept on. It will be useless for you to chase them. They're like flies."

"Flies?" He pushed the hair from his eyes.

Morning Glory explained about the flies in the Valley mud hut where she and Thermeon had grown up.

Nathimeon smiled and said, "I don't suppose many people understand my father the way you do."

"Don't return to your own timeline yet." Morning Glory said, and Mana's heart surged.

Morning Glory explained their plan to forge a new soul-gem. "You must join us, Nathimeon. Your parents will be drawn like flies to the power that the Challenge races will tap, and I think that your strength could help us to undermine their belief in their obsessions. Besides, the disaster looming over the empire affects your universe as well as Mana's, for its origins are far older than either of you."

Nathimeon's thoughts spoke aloud. "Of course I'll help!"

The three of them mounted.

"Let's go home," Mana told Ting. "To the stable! Time for your feed!"

The mare's ears pricked.

Then Morning Glory plucked the soul-gem splinter from the air above the center of the emerald plain, and the fusion field collapsed, removing the homey, interpretable sensations that Mana had experienced within it. The wild confusion of many universes rushed back in on her. But Ting was surging along in nameless directions, seeming to know the way, Transcendent and the red stallion following her.

It seemed only moments later when the flashing, exultant, teeming universes fell away, and the three horses trotted over the field toward the stable. Mana knew that it was indeed feeding time when horses poked their heads from stall windows and whinnied as they approached.

Pasola and Kusomba were waiting at the entrance. "Mana! We thought you were lost!"

"How long has it been?" she asked.

The two looked at each other. "Karali's been emperor for thirty-five years."

Mana's heart sank. "We had better exchange news, then."

They settled their horses, Ting in her old stall, which had something of a musty and unused smell, Transcendent in the stall that had been Thun's, and the red stallion, Stretching Meith, in Serious Quiav's stall.

"I'm sure Eria won't mind," Morning Glory said. "She's one of my grandmothers."

As they walked through the corridors to the gathering room, shadows cast by the skylights that marked each intersection dancing behind, then ahead of them, Mana said, "Eria must be one of Thermeon's grandmothers too. So why is he chasing after her? I'm sure I learned somewhere that Valley people frown on mating with their grandparents."

Morning Glory's soft laugh rippled along the corridor walls. "He has even fewer inhibitions about mating with close relatives than most imperial citizens. But only so long as they're female, of course."

The old circle lounge looked even more battered than before, but when Pasola brought them refreshments, the cubes were tastier than Mana remembered, and the fruit juice was tangy and flavorful.

"Karali has been out of control," Kusomba reported. "She couldn't get her plans for restricting repro rights for the Deep-blind approved by the Circle—no surprise there—so she's resorted to underhanded means. There's no doubt that she's been funding the Holy Crusade of Oceanic Love. These crusaders have been on a rampage of slaughter throughout the empire. They target people they call 'anachronisms' or 'obstacles in the path to the pure ultra-life.' They use deep-level attacks that can't be traced."

"They claim they have mindpowers," Pasola said. "They leave anonymous messages sounding very mysterious and scary, as if they were Thermeon himself. But Inspector Sunfox—he's the detective investigating the attacks—says they probably just use stuff that has been downleveled on ships to unfuse their victims."

Mana gripped her cheeks, unable to keep from thinking that she might have done something to prevent this nightmare had she not been gone for the past thirty-five years.

Morning Glory merely nodded, her expression somber.

Nathimeon sighed aloud and stared at the table top. "What were my parents thinking to have let her touched the Wall!" He looked at Mana. "You should have been emperor!"

She felt herself blushing. "Haven't there been challenges?" she asked.

"There was one early on," said Kusomba. "But Karali won easily, even with the eight Sector champions."

"Eight?" Mana murmured. Then she recalled that Raolin had stood before the Wall only hours after her Speaking and approved her Proposal about the races and the one about emergency glowworm strains before Karali could rescind them. She smiled grimly.

"Since then," said Pasola, "Whenever a movement to challenge gains momentum, its leaders have fallen victim to crusaders."

"We will organize a new Challenge," Morning Glory said. "I will stand before the Wall as its spokeswoman, and the galaxy will know that I have a soul-gem splinter." Like Thermeon, she had emerged from the Deep beautifully clad. Her azure gown flowed gracefully about her, and the splinter appeared as a sparkling green pendant secured by a delicate golden chain.

"The Crusade will target you," Kusomba warned. "They'll try to assassinate you and take the splinter."

Morning Glory smiled. "Let them try. They will learn how powerful a splinter is."

They all stared at the pendant. It blazed in the sunlight pouring down through the skylight, but it seemed to have an inner fire as well, a deeper, liquid green. It almost seemed to vibrate and dance.

The spell was broken by a whinny. Pasola jumped up. "We'd better go out and greet the riders as usual. A lot of them are Karali's lackeys."

Kusomba rose as well. "Most of them are," she growled. "They treat us like slaves, and we only have each other because we both refused to work unless there were two of us."

"Good for you," Mana said. "Do Raolin and Hube still come every day?"

"Yes, but always at different times, so the lackeys won't be able to corner them."

Kusomba and Pasola left the room.

"There is much work to be done," Morning Glory told Mana and Nathimeon. "First of all, the three of us need to reestablish our identities with Genetic Algorithms. I doubt that I have changed much, but I have been gone for a long time. You two have not been gone for so long, but from the story you've told us—" she was looking at Nathimeon—"you have changed a great deal."

He nodded.

"We should talk to Raolin, and see if he can minimize the red tape involved." She went on in a musing tone. "On most of the timelines I have seen, Raolin remains a pillar of the empire. Often Hube stands alongside him. There are a few universes where one or the other is gone by this year. Sometimes Hube is replaced by his daughter Cetila."

Raolin and Hube did not arrive until very late that night. After riding, they joined Morning Glory, Mana, Nathimeon, Kusomba, and Pasola in the gathering room. Morning Glory expanded on her plans for a Challenge.

"We can take no part in Palace affairs," Raolin said. "However, Genetic Algorithms is my purview, and I will see that your cases receive prompt attention, since I can personally vouch for your identities."

Morning Glory thanked him with a gracious smile.

Days later, she and Mana and Nathimeon walked across the field to the tram station and began their journey into the city, Morning Glory in her beautiful blue gown, Mana and Nathimeon in the simple black robes from the stable. The tram brought them to the Nexus, where they caught an underground bubble into the capital. In the short distance between their exit and the Genetic Algorithms office, Mana had time to marvel at the restored city. Tall towers buzzing with air lifter riders seemed no different than they had been before the disaster. She hoped that a separate glowworm strain had indeed been created and put in a secure reservoir as her Proposal had mandated.

The office was spacious and quiet, with a polite bioid lobster behind the counter, soft nooks in the waiting area, and shadowy corridors leading off toward the testing areas. A hovering globe offered to tell the story of Genetic Algorithms, and when Mana took it up on the offer, it showed her apes evolving into humans, accompanied by a solemn and worshipful narration worthy of a child of the Code—until it launched into the improvements on nature that imperial scientists had wrought.

"All the genes once responsible for human weakness, ugliness, and disease have long since been edited out!" the voice boasted. "The mating of the closest relatives no longer poses a problem, although, like parthenogenesis, it is considered rude and solipsistic. In addition, the human genome has been augmented to give imperial citizens a beautiful array of skin, eye, and hair colors, each as a separate allele, to prevent mixing and dilution. The addition of features such as enlarged heads, wings, or photosynthetic or chemosynthetic skin is practiced by some communities."

Mana turned off the globe when a gray-robed woman approached with whispering steps from the corridor on the left and called Morning Glory by her official imperial name, Eoflaxe Taleerous Ausen.

Moments later, a gray-robed man approached from the corridor on the right and called Nathimeon. For a few minutes Mana sat alone in the stillness, then the woman returned and called her.

The corridor led to a small room marked "Testing." "Step into the booth, please," the gray woman bade as she took her seat in an elevated nook in the center of the room. Mana did as she was told. On the wall in front of her, beneath the label "New Data," her genetic material and brain geography were displayed as intricate colored designs. On the other side of the room, the label "Old Data," floated in the darkness. The word "Confirmed" flashed between the two labels.

"You may go," said the gray woman.

Mana stepped out of the booth. "That's all? I've been identified? I didn't see any old data."

"Oh, it was all destroyed in the plague. The readings I just took will be on record for next time."

"How interesting. Well, thank you."

Mana followed the exit sign and joined Morning Glory and Nathimeon in the discharge room. "They had no old data for me," she told them. "Did they have any for you?"

They shook their heads.

"We could have said we were anyone! We could have said we were...." She gave Nathimeon a speculative look, and he laughed.

"Now that we have been identified," said Morning Glory, "presumably we have credits. Why don't we celebrate with lunch in one of the new restaurants?"

Three abreast, they strode out to explore the city.

With her identity confirmed, the next item on Morning Glory's list of steps to the Challenge was to register a Public Group, and to enlist a following numerous enough to give them a date before the Wall.

"In my speech," she told Mana, Nathimeon, Kusomba, and Pasola as they sat around the table one late night, "I will emphasize that I am not seeking the throne for myself, but for the person who can reforge the soul-gem and save the empire from the disaster it's heading toward."

"With the result that everyone will claim to be that person," Kusomba observed.

"Yes, but the proof will be in the races, and in the ability to handle the splinters. The counterfeits will quickly be weeded out."

"People of the Code will support your group," Pasola said. "That is, as long as we will have an equal chance to prove that one of our persuasion is the Chosen One."

"You will," said Morning Glory.

"I am a Blue Coder, of course." Seeing Morning Glory's raised eyebrow, she explained, "We hold that Maxuas, the son of Thermeon and our empress, showed us the true path. I am his descendant." She stroked her luminescent hair. "The Red Coders may disagree about the path, but they will make common cause with us."

"You will have your chance to forge the new soul-gem, along with everyone else who rides," Morning Glory promised.

"You Coders are numerous," Kusomba said, "but I believe my ancestry will prove more useful in getting our Speaking scheduled quickly."

"How so?" Morning Glory asked.

"My connection to Thermeon through Dino is not important." She thumped her tail against the cushion. "But my mother was a unique and special person. She was the daughter of Quintillion and a minor who loved him. Such love was forbidden, because, back in those days, they still had Contamination laws. My mother was conceived secretly and illegally, and after her birth, she had to contend with Katora's campaign to purge Quintillion's genes. But she prevailed, and I came to be. The minors still honor my grandmother for her selfless devotion to her illegal love, and for her sacrifice—she was killed in the Fissure."

Mana recalled that bit of history with a jolt. The recent purge was not the first time Thermeon had ravaged Lal with his mindpowers.

"My relatives in service at the palace will see that our Speaking moves up on the calendar," Kusomba concluded with a Dino-like smirk.

"Thank you," said Morning Glory.

The next morning she left the stable to establish her party headquarters in the city. Nathimeon went to his parents' mansion in Seagamo to work for the cause from there. Mana remained at the stable, since she had no important contacts, and her last job assignment had never been rescinded. She had found her old dorm just as she had left it, and moved back in.

Kusomba was good as her word. A tenthyear had passed like lightning when Mana, Pasola, and she took the tram to the Nexus to view Morning Glory's Speaking.

The sister of Thermeon looked regal as ever as she stood before the Wall's blank gray face, minors in Karali's colors bunched on either side, the throne sitting vacant behind them, citizens gathered in a great hall with a protective barrier between them and the dais and Wall. To Mana, it all looked exactly the same as it had before the plague and purge.

"My fellow citizens," Morning Glory began in a clear, ringing voice. "Today I come before you to lay a Challenge before the emperor. I come not on behalf of myself, but on behalf of an unknown champion who can repair the fault in our timeline."

This brought a murmuring from the crowd.

"I know there is a fault, because I myself am responsible. It was I who forged Thermeon's soul-gem, along with him and two others. As the gem coalesced in the heat and fury of Deep Six, I felt the wrongness of it: I saw a future leading not to the joy and spiritual expansion that I wished, but to terror and catastrophe."

Again the crowd murmured, an uneasy sound.

"I know that many of your emperors, especially Katora, have striven to bring an Age of Illumination, but they have been doomed to failure—doomed by the fault that lies at the foundation of our age."

There were more outcries, probably from Katora's faithful.

"The fault that marred Thermeon's soul-gem has brought us the Code War, the Great War, the Nander bloodletting, the Fissure, and most recently the Bolt that laid waste to this city. But this is not the end of it. Recently I met with my brother, Thermeon, and his wife, Katora."

Questioning sounds came from the crowd, but Morning Glory did not pause to elucidate.

"Their mind-states greatly disturbed me. I sensed that the doom foretold in the forging of the soul-gem approaches, and that if I did not act swiftly, the empire might come to an end."

Outcries of alarm from the crowd.

"Citizens, we must act. I reach out to all of you—put your minds and hearts into the mission that must be accomplished. Empress Karali is not strong enough, or wise enough, to save you. The Challenge will, through the time-honored means of a series of deep-level horse races, determine the champion who can save you. I possess one splinter of the soul-gem, that, though shattered, still controls your destinies." She laid a hand over the gem that blazed on her chest. Sounds of awe and amazement rippled through the great hall. "I ask that the holders of the other splinters bring them to Lal. When the races have determined the final four who will challenge the emperor in the race for the throne, let each of the four hold one of the splinters. Then, if the spirits of the Deep are with us, the magic of the final race will throw open the gateway to Deep Six, and a new soul-gem will be forged by the winner, by the champion who will became our next emperor and lead us into a true Age of Illumination."

There were some cheers, mingled with sounds of confusion.

"The winner must take all the splinters from defeated rivals in the final intersection," Morning Glory said.

Sounds of confusion intensified. Mana found herself nodding agreement. How could the riders know who the winner would be when they were in the final intersection? The race would not end until they returned to home-level and crossed the finish line.

Morning Glory lifted a hand to sweep back her blazing red hair, and smiled loftily out at the crowd. "The winner will be foreseen in the final intersection, if it goes deep enough. In Deep Six, the future can be seen. That is how I knew that our soul-gem was marred. As the gem fused, I beheld the fusion of the four people who had forged it. I saw our future, our descendants. The daughter of my daughter Fuerida mated with Quintillion to produce Salamano-Reborn, who mated with Puflet to produce the one who truly forged that marred soul-gem, though none of us realized it then."

Mana gasped when Morning Glory mentioned her mother. Kusomba growled, "Why is she saying that?"

"Why is she saying that this is the Chosen One?" Pasola complained. "She promised that everyone would have an equal chance!"

"I don't think she means the person she described is the Chosen One," Mana said. "I think she means just the opposite."

"Then why is she talking about this person?" Kusomba shouted. She whirled on Mana. "Is she talking about you?"

"Me? No, of course not! Puflet is my mother, but my father isn't related to Quintillion or Fuerida."

"Do you have sisters or brothers?"

"No. At least, I don't think so. My mother had three suitors, but when she set out to hunt down the slavers, she said that she didn't want children, because they'd make her vulnerable to hostage-takers. I guess she didn't count me because she didn't raise me."

Kusomba's nostrils flared. Pasola's brows remained creased.

Mana noticed that the Speaking had ended. "Let's go home," she said.

She couldn't sleep that night. Morning Glory hadn't returned from the city, but her words about the daughter of Puflet kept going around and around in Mana's head. What had she meant? Was this sister, or half-sister of hers from some other timeline?

She was still fretting, tossing herself to one side, then the other, when an unexpected sound made her freeze. There it came again—was it a footfall, a breath? She lifted her head, and saw by the light of her hair that three black-robed figures had entered her room.

A cold wave of terror went through Mana. She leaped from her bed and retreated into the bathroom as the figures advanced menacingly.

There was no escape. The three entered the bathroom and stopped just past the doorway while she cowered naked at the far end of the room.

"Get her!" growled one of the intruders.

Mana saw a pale tube in one of the men's hands. It must contain deep-level stuff that would escape if the tube ruptured. They were going to unfuse her.

With a gasping shriek, Mana tore her riding skin from its hook on the wall and charged the three, waving the skin wildly, hoping that its deep-level properties would shield her. The intruders seemed caught by surprise, and fell back with inarticulate yells. She got through them.

Depending on her intimate knowledge of the stable's layout to aid her escape, Mana ran a weaving path through the corridors, emerging in the outer circular aisle with the entrance on her right. A straighter path would have brought her out with the entrance to her left. She crouched at the end of the corridor, peering around the shadowed curve of the wall and listening. Shouts and thumps came from somewhere deep within the building, but she saw no one coming along the aisle, so she ran for the doorway, and out into the night.

The breeze felt cool on her skin, and the grass tickled her feet as she ran, gasping and straining, toward the Plains of Possibility. Horses grazing on the field appeared as darker or paler dots in the distance. When her lungs felt on fire and her legs felt heavy and weak, she stopped and looked back, leaning over and panting. There was no sign of pursuit.

Quickly, she pulled on her skin and slipped the hood up to cover her glowing hair. She crouched down in the grass and watched the building. A dreadful thought struck her. What if the intruders were killing Kusomba and Pasola while she sat out here thinking only of her own safety?

Swallowing hard, she rose. "Ting! Ting, come here!" Her voice was weak and crackly, but the mare felt her thoughts. Moments later, her hoofbeats came across the grass, and the warm and comforting bulk of her bore down upon Mana. Mana hugged her hard, then mounted, and urged her back toward the building.

As they pounded toward the doorway, a slight figure with glowing hair and a glowing tail tuft burst out, followed by two figures in black.

"Get them!" Mana screamed.

She had never asked something like that of Ting before, but her anger and terror must have transmitted the image of dangerous predators threatening the herd, for the mare flew into action. In two bounds she reached the black robes and bowled them over with her chest. She spun and stomped on them. She seized them in her teeth and gave them vicious shakes before tossing them high. When they fell back, she kicked them. She was still dancing on the floppy rags of the bodies when Kusomba returned on her silvery mare, Warlike Slime.

"Get to the Nexus and call the planetary police!" Kusomba shouted. "I'll keep watch here."

"Pasola?"

Kusomba shook her head.

Mana moaned. "Oh, if only I had—"

"Not your fault," Kusomba snapped. "It's Karali's fault."

Mana swallowed her tears and rode for the tram station.

By the next morning, the stable was in Challenge mode, the tram station guarded by units of planetary police, minors, and the Bureau's bioid guards, now powered by their own unique glowworm strain.

Investigation of the attack was being headed by Inspector Sunfox, a grandson of Thermeon with glowing orange hair. His team cordoned off Mana's unit and the corridor where Pasola had been killed and set up headquarters on the field in a golden tent displaying the red, blue, and yellow pennant of the Galactic Investigative Force. Though they had already related everything to the planetary police, Sunfox interviewed Kusomba and Mana again in the tent.

When it was Mana's turn to go inside, she found that the light collectors in the top of the tent combined with its mirror-like skin to keep its whole interior ablaze. Two lumpy chairs looked like they had been taken from the stable gathering room. Before he let her sit, Sunfox examined her riding skin, which she hadn't had the chance to change out of, from top to bottom. After that, he questioned her in great detail about the device that had been in her assailant's hand.

"Why is this important?" she asked him finally.

"We have not yet positively identified the weapons used by the Crusade, but evidence points to the pale cylinder you saw being an inter-level container that was destroyed in the unfusing caused by its rupture. A valid shipping container would not fail so easily, so it must have been made flawed or purposely weakened before the attack."

"They were crusaders, then."

He nodded.

"When will I be able to have my living quarters back?"

"After the body's removed."

Mana started. "There's a body in my dorm?"

The inspector pointed to a splash of violet-blue twisting around one arm of her riding skin."It seems that a lucky blow—for you, not for him—flung the device back against his chest with enough force to split it open. The edge of the resulting disruption splashed against your garment, but only discolored its deep-level material."

Mana crouched on the chair. She had killed someone! Not that she hadn't seen what Ting had done to his companions. But still, it made her feel sordid.

She felt even worse, later, after comparing experiences with Kusomba. Her friends would have been safe had they not rushed out to see why Mana was screaming. They hadn't paused to pull on their riding skins, so Pasola had had no protection from the crusaders' second device.

By early afternoon, the bodies had been taken off in wheelbarrows and the messes cleaned. The horses came in for their feeding. Riders who hadn't been seen in years appeared, along with friends or relatives to help them out with feeding, grooming, and exercising. They fought over the best rooms. When Mana tried to help out, they started jabbering about the attack. Everyone opined that the Crusade was after her because she was the Chosen One.

Nathimeon and Morning Glory returned. After the midday riding session they all met in the gathering room. Their eyes kept returning to the place in the circle where Pasola would have been sitting.

"The attackers have been identified as men with ties to the empress," Nathimeon told. "Citizens will stop believing her denials."

"I've already heard some of her former stooges singing a new tune," said Kusomba. "That sort of person senses a change in the political climate real quick."

Morning Glory sighed. "I should not have left you unprotected. I thought they would attack me, but it seems that our foe was too wise for that. Well, from now on, we will all stick together."

"I should have stayed too," Nathimeon said. "I didn't accomplish anything of note in Seagamo. I agree that we need to stick together."

"Why don't you all move into my room," Mana said. "There's plenty of space." *Space enough for ten people,* Katora's voice said in the back of her mind. She sighed. She'd never thought she would miss her grandmother, but as oppressive as she was, Katora was at least predictable. And she didn't *kill* people.

Well, not since she'd tried to purge Quintillion's genes. And when the Circle hadn't confirmed her Proposal, she had given up. She was courageous enough to openly state her agenda. She didn't use lies and assassins.

"There are four of us," Morning Glory said. "Every contender is allowed three live-in assistants, so let's agree that we'll all stay on to assist whoever is last to be eliminated from the races."

They agreed. Mana was certain that Morning Glory would be the last contender among them. She wondered whether Thermeon's sister wanted to become emperor, or only to reforge the soul-gem. If she won the Emperor Race, she could always abdicate in favor of her daughter Fuerida.

After their meeting, Mana wandered out across the field, which was starting to look like a fairground, brightly colored tents and pavilions—non-animated—popping up everywhere, pennants flapping in the breeze. She walked along a grassy aisle between the structures, taking in the scents of hot, spicy food, and inspecting the wares. Most of the vendors were hawking food and drinks kept cold in insulated boxes, without glowworms. A few displayed velvet-draped trays containing minerals and gems. One vendor motioned to her and excitedly whispered, "I have a genuine soul-gem splinter, especially for the Chosen One!"

She shook her and and walked on.

At the far end of the aisles stood a larger, cream-colored pavilion marked "LZ Node." A woman standing in the shadow beyond the rolled-up entrance flaps called out, "Communicate with anyone in the empire! Guaranteed clear and reliable message transmission!"

Mana smiled and shook her head. If they didn't garble things into imbecility, LZ nodes were guaranteed to bring you messages from some alternate timeline. She wondered if they'd work better in the light of a new soul-gem.

She moved to another aisle and wandered back toward the stable. The sun beat down, magnifying all the smells and burning in her hair. She passed Inspector Sunfox's golden tent. He wasn't to be seen, but an assistant with a red, blue, and yellow badge stood between the open door-flaps, trying to tell two bickering vendors that problems such as theirs would be dealt with by the planetary police. A bit farther on, Mana stopped to get a glass of cold ruberry juice, paying by impressing her thumb in a gelatinous slate beside the etched number of credits owed.

Someone called her name. She looked up to see Karali's sister Taana gliding toward her in a long, shimmering blue dress not meant for riding, her bronze hair ablaze in the sun. Taana had lost her horse years before Mana had ridden onto the Plains.

"For you," Taana said, thrusting a gel-pad toward Mana.

It was a message from Karali, telling her that she was fired, and ordering her to report to the palace for a new assignment. Mana laughed and handed the pad back to Taana. "I'm a contender, so it's my right to stay at the stable. If I'm eliminated, I have contender friends who've asked me to assist them. So no, I'm not leaving here. I'll be here for the next year. And after that, I presume that Karali will no longer be emperor, and she will have no further use for me."

Taana had dropped her eyes to the ground. "Look, I'm sorry, about everything."

"Can't you do something to hold her back? What she's doing is vile!"

"I know, and I've tried talking to her, but she laughs me off. She changed, Mana, after what happened to her on the dro farm. I think she still has nightmares about that mob."

Mana clenched her teeth. "Then she should go for a healing float, and leave the rest of us alone! And what about her major? Doesn't he have any humanity either?"

"Nobody knows anything about him, except that he comes from Elul. I don't think he was very prominent before Karali picked him out, so he's totally beholden to her."

Mana glared at her. "I thought she was going to take your advice about who to appoint."

"I'm afraid she didn't like my suggestions."

"Sometimes I think Morning Glory is right," Mana muttered. "I think the empire could be headed for even darker times. When people who have responsibilities can just turn their back on thousands of years of civilization! And that frightened mob doing it to her first does not excuse her behavior!"

Taana swallowed, her blue eyes bright with tears. "Do you think I don't worry about myself sometimes? I don't have any mindpowers. She thinks of me as a pet! I suppose our mother's to blame for that. I'll never forget the day I failed those tests at the mindsea academy. Something in my mother's eyes changed forever —as if any hope she'd had for me died, and the warm and loving person I'd thought she was went somewhere far away. I think my life has meaning, but no matter what I achieve, if it isn't deep-level, it means nothing to her."

"I think you're a fine architect," Mana said. "Did Karali let you help reconstruct the palace?"

"No. But I did design the new central wonderdome for the city." Taana's face brightened a little.

"I've seen the images," Mana said. "It's gorgeous! All shimmery and sparkling, like a giant blue teardrop. Oh, I don't know why I said that...."

Taana's eyes had clouded again. "Well, you're right. The city is in mourning still, though Karali doesn't see it that way. It's ironic. Grandpa Raolin's told me that when he was young, you tried to hide it if you had any mindpowers, because mindseas were thought to be stupid and brutish. And now it's just the opposite."

"Maybe it's just wrong to try to categorize people," Mana said.

Taana nodded. "Dino says that my mother was never so extreme about mindpowers being everything until she married Thermeon, and that he's been driving her, because he's that way."

Squeezing her eyes, Mana thought back to her own childhood. "Oh, I'm not so sure about that. She always gave me and my half-sisters and half-brothers attention exactly commensurate with our mindpowers. But I'm sure that Thermeon hasn't helped her any."

Taana sighed. "But it's not something he tries to do. He treats us all the same. I think it's because he believes in spirits. He thinks every living thing has a spirit, a deep-level mind, and if we don't seem to have mindpowers, it's just because we're not awakened. So to him, we all have potential. But our mother doesn't believe in spirits. She's a rationalist—she thinks she can understand everything. But her attempts to understand her husband, and to be the goddess-star he wants her to be, have made her a little crazy, I'm afraid."

"There is something unhealthy in the way those two bounce off each other," Mana agreed. "I was there when they had that argument before riding off."

"Karali told me about that." Taana bit her lip. "Even though we're grown, their behavior still impacts us. They're not only parents. They're so ancient and powerful—and historical figures as well—that they've always been gods to us. And when gods fight, it seems like the world could be falling apart."

Mana sighed. "It's true that they can do a lot of damage."

"Karali tries to act tough, but she was shaken by their fight, and their disappearance, and the father of the horses gone as well. And then, with this Challenge by the Chosen One, who she assumes is you—"

Mana yelped. "But I've told everyone—I can't be the Chosen One. I'm not descended from Quintillion or Fuerida. Besides, I don't really think Morning Glory meant that the person she described was the Chosen One."

"Then why describe her?"

"I think—" Mana began. She fell silent when she noticed two men in striped tunics coming toward them.

"Tell us about the Chosen One!" shouted the one in the red-and-black stripes. "I will convey your message to the galaxy! I have perfect recall!"

"My device inscribes sound waves in a crystal," cried the man in the green-and-gold stripes, thrusting a wand toward Mana's face. "The galaxy is waiting for news of the Chosen One!"

Mana clenched her fists. "I have already informed the galaxy that I am not the Chosen One. That there is no Chosen One!"

"You're wrong!" came a piping voice. A pale, golden-haired woman in a lilac riding skin came skipping up. "I am Cpice Maggariun Merl, and I am the Chosen One!"

Mana scowled. The two newsers turned toward Cpice. "Can you substantiate your claims?" asked Red-and-Black. Green-and-Gold thrust his wand at her.

"I am descended from Puflet!" Cpice grinned, showing small, sharp fangs. Anyone could grow themselves fangs, of course, but it would take lots of credits to grow them overnight.

"You're my sister?" Mana said, dubious. "My mother never mentioned having other children."

"Well, she didn't know," Cpice said. "Her mistress used her genes a few times when she was still a slave. One of the offspring was my grandmother. But she and my mother are both dead now, so their identity as the Chosen One has passed to me."

"Are you also descended from Quintillion and Fuerida?" Red-and-Black asked her.

"Well, of course! I'm riding Empty Alga. Watch for me!" Cpice flung up her chin and thrust out her chest.

A crowd was forming around them. When Cpice saw the newsers' attention drifting from herself, she scowled. The crowd jostled and parted. Morning Glory stood there in a pearlescent blouse and pantaloons, her hair a glorious coppery nimbus about her face, her eyes bluer than the cloudless sky above them. She looked Cpice up and down. "You are not related to Fuerida."

Cpice gnashed her fangs and stomped on a clump of grass.

"And probably not related to Quintillion, either."

"But I think I'm close enough," Cpice argued. "Besides, she doesn't want to be it!" A quick, narrow-eyed glance at Mana.

The newsers closed on Morning Glory. "Who is the Chosen One? The galaxy is anxious to know!"

A smile flitted over Morning Glory's face, and her wonderful eyes went distant. The crowd drew closer, silent and tense. She spoke, and the wind itself seemed to hold its breath.

"The Chosen One is a deep-level being. I beheld her in Deep Six. She encompassed many lives from many timelines. That is why there is probably no one person on any home-level timeline who is exactly like her." She smiled benignly upon Mana and upon Cpice. "She contains both of these young women. And she contains myself as well, for she folds past and future together. She contains Puflet, Thermeon, and Quintillion, and our ancestors, and descendants I could not quite make out."

She looked at the newsers. "That is the one who forged Thermeon's soul-gem. Unfortunately, she contained a flaw. Perhaps the flaw came from just one of her many selves. Perhaps from this one." She looked at Cpice. "Like the worm in an otherwise perfect apple."

"You're calling me a worm?" Cpice shrieked.

"Yes, I am," Morning Glory said sadly. She returned her attention to the newsers. "The Chosen One who will forge the new soul-gem is as yet undiscovered. His or her identity will only come to light as the races are run, as the Deep tests horses and riders."

A sighing went through the crowd, and Mana thought that, for a moment, she smelled the distant reaches of the Plains of Possibility.

Eight races would determine the eight champions of Lal. The first of the eight was scheduled to take place thirty days after the Challenge. The fourteen riders were chosen by lot from among the hundred who had horses at the stable by a primitive drawing of colored ribbons from a covered box.

Mana felt very downcast when she found that she was among those to ride in the first race. Her status as contestant would end, and she would have to become Morning Glory's assistant. It would be harder to resist Karali's machinations.

Also riding in the first race was the headmistress of the Mindsea Academy of Lal, Vedina Iynoolit Woat, a daughter of Thermeon born during his long-ago reign—one of his two well-known mindsea daughters. To make things even worse, Mana's half-sister Reselona was also slated for that race. Remembering their years growing up together in the unhappy household of their father, Emperor Habel, brought back mind-states Mana had hoped to have put behind her forever. Once again she felt the deficiencies that her step-mother and Grandmother Katora had heaped upon her, the longing for reassurances her father had been too tormented to give, and the dreams of fleeing to the real mother she knew was out there somewhere. Reselona had been held up to her as the good child, the child with mindpowers that Mana would never have. How Mana had resented her bright and cheery figure, even though Reselona had always been nice to her. After their father had sent

Mana off to school on Mosalno, she had returned home only when the emperor's schedule called for public appearances with family. After her father's reign had ended, she hadn't returned at all. She had lost touch with Reselona during the years she'd worked at the Ulona racetrack. After coming to Lal, she'd seen her half-sister when she came out to ride her mare, Avab, but they'd never exchanged more than a few words.

Now they would be measured against one another in a race to determine the empire's future. Mana had no idea whether Reselona still harbored ambitions. Once, she'd been the empire's shining star, their father's chosen successor. Then, in the moment when Katora had decided that her love for Dino wasn't so perfect, after all, Reselona's star had dimmed. Katora had turned her back on her and her siblings, switching her hopes for the future to her children with Thermeon and their descendants.

Mana wondered if it felt worse to be suddenly spurned by a grandmother who had always heaped you with praise than to never have been given any attention in the first place. Had Reselona suspected, before the change, that her grandmother didn't really love her? Katora could speak so passionately about love, about the strength and purity and wonder of the love she felt for her mate and their children and grandchildren. But the names she spoke weren't really the ones she loved, were they?

Katora loved a deep-level son, and she'd tried to make Nathimeon into him. But as Morning Glory had said about the Chosen One, no person on home-level could ever exactly duplicate a deep-level being.

As the days to the first race were counted down, Mana found herself still being dogged by newsers begging for the Chosen One's opinion about this and that.

"Do you have a message for your half-sister before the race?"

"Have you and Reselona made a pact to cooperate against the other riders?"

"Do you think Feber's grandmother had the right to participate in mating flights without a horse?"

Mana tried not to sputter at them. It seemed only yesterday— although it had been thirty-five years before—when Karali had been telling her that her opinions were not wanted.

"I wish my half-sister—and all of the other riders—good luck in the race," Mana said. "No, I have made no pacts. As a quadrupedal carnivore, Feber's grandmother would have found riding a horse unnatural, and the horse probably wouldn't have liked it either, so I don't think she had any choice."

Mana hoped that her words would not spark a surge of animal citizens using their own four feet in mating flights and making bipedal citizens who lost out to them blame her, but as a descendant of Thermeon, she could hardly condemn animal-human matings.

She looked forward to the newsers losing interest in her after the race. Perhaps then Cpice, who wasn't in the first race, would become the "Chosen One." Presently the newsers called Cpice "Worm" as they chased her around, seeming to enjoy her shrieks of protest.

On the night before the race, Mana could not sleep. Thrashing about on her bunk, she recalled her last sleepless night, when the crusaders had come. She had no fears for her safety now. The other bunks ranged around hers contained sleeping forms whose breathing assured her that she was in the midst of friends. Still, she couldn't relax, and finally, telling herself that her thumping about would wake her companions, she rose and tiptoed to the bathroom. She pulled on her riding skin, and then slipped out of the dorm.

A cool breeze met her as she stepped outside the building, and the stars blazed overhead in their myriad glory. The bright tents and pavilions all looked shades of gray beneath the stars. It was strange to see the aisles between them, now dirt tracks denuded of grass, empty of crowds.

Mana jumped when a black-clad figure emerged from a tent and hurtled toward her. A crusader! She shrank back toward the stable entrance, then decided that running for the Plains was probably the better option. She had taken only a couple of steps when the figure shouted, "Chosen One!"

Mana recognized Red-and-Black's voice. She stopped and spun around as he thumped up, his red stripes indistinguishable from the black ones by starlight.

"Why do you insist on calling me that?" she complained. "You heard Morning Glory's explanation. Didn't you believe her?"

He shrugged. "People don't want to hear patternistic obfuscation. They want something they can get their teeth into and shake around. Everyone loves the idea of a Chosen One who will save them from disasters of their own making."

"They'll be very disappointed when I lose, won't they? And it will all be your doing! What will you do then—call Cpice the Chosen One?"

His grin glinted beneath the stars. "See that you don't lose."

With a snort, Mana dove back into the building. She pulled off her skin, hung it back on its hook, and returned to her bunk. The next thing she knew, the skylight was filled with brightness, and everyone else in the dorm was already up.

Her knees watery, Mana prepared for the race. She showered, dried, and pulled on her skin. She went to breakfast. Food was now brought in every day, so there were cereals, fruits, and pastries to choose from, as well as assorted teas and real Triermian coffee. Morning Glory, Kusomba, and Nathimeon sat with her.

"You're going to do well," Nathimeon said, his blue eyes beaming at her.

"Just think about how angry Karali makes you," Kusomba advised.

"You could be the one to forge the new soul-gem," said Morning Glory.

Mana smiled gratefully at all of them, but tried not to take their words too seriously. She'd always finished in the middle of the pack in races, and those had only been training races. She'd never raced for office or taken part in a mating flight.

Toward noon, the horses came in for their feeding. Mana no longer filled the mangers. She'd been fired, after all. Kusomba had resigned after Pasola's death, so there was no official stable manager. Each rider had assistants to tend their horse, and a team of peasants had volunteered to muck out the stalls for everyone.

After feeding and grooming, riders mounted and went down to the track, its viewing stands now festooned with pennants displaying Lal's black-on-tan planetary logo. A banner of black-and-white checkers representing the primary otherness of Patternistics was stretched across the finish line.

After a brief warm-up, all the horses except for the fourteen in the race left the track. A race official with a black-on-tan badge on his chest blew a note on a carved and gilded dro-horn to summon the racers. The fourteen horses milled around behind a line of chalk sprinkled across the track. Mana's heart pounded, and Ting pranced, twitching her ears to try to take in everything that was going on. The other horses looked nervous as well. Working Nothing tried to tried to buck off his rider, one of the imperial major's sons. Only Vedina, wearing a green skin that matched her eyes, looked calm on her butter-colored mare, Godlike.

One of the peasant assistants dashed onto the track to offer a flower to Illuminated, the white-speckled black mare who was carrying Miesa Muatoni Sik-Basleop. The newsers called Miesa the "Peasant Champion." He was a grandson of Katora's long-ago peasant friend Galena, whose descendants had been active for centuries in their opposition to Katora's worship of mindsize.

"Off the track!" yelled the official, and the peasant scurried off.

The interruption had made the horses more restive than ever. Reselona's Avab reared. Feber's Mutant Time had backed toward the starting line and refused to turn around.

"We're not waiting for you," the official warned.

The stallion sighed and took his proper position, and the official waved his checkered flag.

"Go!" Mana urged Ting.

Maybe all the charging about they'd done recently had brought their minds into better harmony, for it seemed that Ting launched herself with greater alacrity than she ever had before in a race. Within moments she was pounding down the track with the rest of the field eating her dust. Mana smiled and sang out words of praise.

Then she concentrated on preparing for the first intersection point, halfway around the first turn.

They were in. The world expanded, though not so much as it had during the Bolt or on the Plains. The track curved across a vast mudflat bounded by an apricot-tinged horizon and smelling of the sea. On their right, the surf glistened and rolled, and pale crabs danced about where the foam had touched, lifting their claws aloft and crying, "Listen! Listen!"

They were only on Deep One or Deep Two, yet even here all

minds linked, allowing her to hear the thoughts—such as they were —of the crabs.

"Listen! Listen!" they cried, flipping their black stalked eyes and drumming the mud with their pincers.

Mana listened, and all at once she was aware of a voice so deep it shook the mud beneath Ting's hooves. "L ... I ... S ... T ... E ... N...."

Mana had to slow her own mind down to understand.

"Listen, a wave is passing," intoned the deep voice. "But who is there to heed? Everyone leads the life they love, and loves the life they lead."

The glow on the horizon faded to deep purple. The moon rose. The rolling surf flashed like the mane of a white horse. Was Trat out there? Before Mana could be sure, she and Ting were out of the intersection and racing toward the backstretch. None of the other horses were in sight. They must have whipped past while she'd been listening to the deep voice.

"It's all right." Mana patted Ting. "Just keep going. We'll get there when we get there."

The mare flew forward into the next intersection. They said that intersections reflected the minds of the riders who triggered them. Someone's mind must have been filled with sewage, because the murky gray wave that broke over Mana and Ting smelled vile and pelted them with all sorts of refuse, some bits sharp as glass splinters, others soft and disgustingly clingy. It reminded Mana of the home atmosphere she and Reselona and the other children of Emperor Habel had grown up with. She shut her mouth tightly and pressed her face into Ting's mane, willing the mare to hurry through this revolting place.

Ting responded.

Once again the track stretched ahead of them, and Lal's sun, low in the sky, poured its golden-orange rays down. The putrid droplets of Deep stuff flew off of Mana and Ting as they raced, fusing air molecules they touched. The downleveled home-level stuff could not maintain its cohesion for long, and unfused again with pops and chimes.

The next intersection point swept in with a cold, invigorating wind, and the track crossed a frozen sea.

"Careful!" Mana cried, as Ting's hooves skidded on the ice. "Don't try to go fast here. Just make sure you don't fall."

A crack appeared in the track ahead of them, and Ting leaped across to the next section of ice. Mana gasped, and Ting snorted and planted her hooves when the floe they had landed on lurched, then spun. The ice on the sea around them, the distant waves, and the pale gray clouds blurred into streaks as the ice floe revolved like a wheel.

"Steady, steady," Mana cried, clinging to Ting's neck. "We have to wait until it stops so we don't go flying off sideways, or something!"

She could not recall any previous race having such a difficult obstacle.

The spinning went on. Ting laid her ears back and put her head down. Mana's stomach verged on revolt. At one point she thought she glimpsed other riders already past the spinning floe, but it might only have been the shadows cast by ice formations.

At last the floe crashed into a larger floe and its motion stopped. Mana stroked her mare's steamy, trembling neck. "All right, we can go on now. Easy, but keep moving. Let's get out of here as fast as we possibly can."

Ting's head came up, her muscles tensed, and she leaped to the larger floe and careened across it far faster than Mana thought safe, but luckily she didn't fall, and moments later the intersection lay behind them.

Sighing with relief, Mana peered for the riders she thought she'd seen, but the track stretched empty ahead of her. Of course, things always looked closer in the Deep.

Ting flew into the final turn, and Mana braced herself for the next intersection. It came with a wash of indigo shadow. But she needn't have worried. A gorgeous landscape opened about them. The track had become a bridge spanning a breathtaking indigo canyon. As Ting clattered across, stars twinkled overhead from an indigo sky. They seemed to be humming a song that Mana couldn't quite grasp, though the melody was reassuring and invigorating and the rhythm matched Ting's hoofbeats. Only toward the end of the bridge did it occur to Mana that such a structure might be treacherous.

"Races don't kill people," she told herself.

Then she recalled that ancient races for the throne had often proved fatal, and the ice floe had already shown her that she should expect challenges here that weren't to be found in training races. By the time that thought flitted through her mind, the indigo intersection had faded, and Ting was hurtling toward the homestretch.

They plunged into the final intersection. The track became a pathway paved with white pebbles that wound through a vast and exotic garden. On every side rose fantastic trees and shrubs, some trained into marvelous shapes, others bearing enormous flowers. It should have been beautiful, yet a terrible air of sadness overhung everything, and gray skies silently wept. The branches of trees, blackened with wetness, bowed down, and all the flowers hung their heads. What were they mourning, Mana wondered. It was as if someone had laid out this garden with love and care, intending it to bring joy to everyone, but instead it had been forgotten.

The garden was the empire, she thought.

The melancholy garden vanished, and Ting galloped past a grandstand filled with cheering spectators and beneath the checkered banner that marked the finish line.

"Good girl, good girl!" Mana cried. "You can stop now!"

It seemed to take a moment for the idea to sink into Ting's mind, but she slowed then, and Mana urged her to circle back to meet the people who had run out onto the track toward them. As they turned, Mana saw the crimson sun touching the horizon. She had been so long on the course, all the other racers must have finished and gone home. But at least it was over. Her whole career as a contender in such high-powered, dangerous races was over. She patted Ting again, then slid to the ground.

Nathimeon, Kusomba, and Morning Glory rushed up to her. They gave her hugs, all babbling at once. The annoyingly familiar voice of Red-and-Black blared, "Chosen One, tell the galaxy how you achieved your stunning victory!"

She blinked at him, wondering why he was mocking her this way. Her friends didn't seem to notice. They all beamed at her. Green-and-Gold thrust out his wand. "Victory speech, Chosen One!"

She cleared her throat. "Where are the other riders?"

They all shook their heads.

"No one else has come out yet," said Kusomba.

It was as if the world were spinning again. Mana stumbled, and Nathimeon and Kusomba took her arms on either side. Regaining herself, she pushed past the newsers and stared back along the track. The setting sun deeply etched the hoof prints of a single horse.

Turning away, Mana lurched back toward Ting. Tears streamed down her face. "Apple," she whispered, and Kusomba handed her the apple Mana had bought from a vendor the day before as a post-race treat. Ting gave a happy little whicker and accepted her reward.

Mana faced the newsers. "Tell the galaxy that I owe everything to my horse. Ting is the best, the bravest, the most beautiful horse in the universe!"

The other thirteen riders all finished, in time. Reselona and Miesa were the next two to cross the finish line after Mana. Their names would go back into the covered box, and they would have another chance to win a place in the final races. The others were out of the running. The Headmistress of the Mindsea Academy of Lal, whom Mana had thought sure to win the race, came in sixth. Probably she had no interest in the throne.

But wasn't she at all concerned about forging a new soul-gem?

Riders who had been off-planet when the Challenge was announced continued to drift in to the stable. One of them was Morning Glory's daughter, Fuerida, a golden-haired woman with a very piercing voice who rode Shadow, a sleek black stallion with a silvery mane and tail. Accompanying her was a tall, solemn-faced man named Aspo, one of Katora's spurned children by Quintillion. He rode a white mare named Rational Shop.

Morning Glory invited the pair to move into their dorm without even consulting Mana, and suggested that they all sit down for a strategy meeting in the dorm.

"The gathering room is too busy these days," she said.

"And Karali's spies are everywhere," Kusomba added.

While she was major, Mana had provided her unit with a couple of couches. After additional bunks had been brought in and set up in two rows, the couches filled the rest of the space between them and the outer door. Everyone sat down, Mana, Kusomba, and Morning Glory on one couch facing Nathimeon, Fuerida, and Aspo.

"We need a strategy," Morning Glory began. "It's very important in working soul-gems, because the moments leading up to the forging will become part of the forging itself. I think, since Mana has already won a place in the finals, the rest of us should focus on supporting her."

Mana felt everyone's eyes on her, and she tried to look calm and composed, but not too self-important.

Fuerida's voice rang across the the room. "I think that's risky, Mother. What if Mana can't go all the way?"

"That's exactly what we must avoid thinking," Morning Glory replied. "We need to concentrate on making Mana win."

Kusomba tossed her head. "That's fine, but I think we also all need to try our best to win our races too. There are bound to be attempts to cheat, to win by murdering opponents, in the final races, when the most ambitious riders get the scent of victory in their nostrils, and Mana isn't really a fighter. We'll need to protect her."

"We will attempt to defuse those schemes from outside the races," Morning Glory said. "Besides, I will give Mana the splinter for protection."

Once again Fuerida's voice pealed out. "Isn't it a bit premature for that?"

"No. There's already been one attempt on her life. And I'm sure that I won't be carrying the splinter through to the end. I've already had my chance to forge a soul-gem and failed. It's time for someone new to try."

Hadn't Fuerida also been part of Morning Glory's attempt, Mana wondered. But if Mana was part of the "Chosen One," then perhaps she wasn't new herself. Her gaze passed over the others in the room. They were all related to either Morning Glory or to Quintillion or to Thermeon, so they wouldn't be new either. And yet, just picking a random person like Karali had picked her major wasn't necessarily a good idea.

"Have there been any signs of the other splinters turning up?" Fuerida asked.

Morning Glory shook her head. "I think we will need to wait to see who wins the other preliminaries." She fixed her gaze on Aspo. "I feel certain that your father had the black splinter. Have there been any rumors in the family about where it went after his death?"

Aspo sat flopped over the back of the couch. His chest rose and fell in a long sigh. "There isn't any family, just a few scattered remnants. The only one I've talked to in the past hundred years is my sister Shell. And we don't talk about things like that. So, no, I have heard nothing."

Nathimeon gave him a sideways glance. "Can't you be a little more negative?"

Aspo's lips quirked. "I am quite the optimist for a child of Quintillion."

Kusomba scowled at him.

"I don't think that your father was naturally depressed," Morning Glory said. "I think that the splinter did it to him."

"So we should look for someone very melancholy to find the black splinter?" Mana asked. "What characteristics do the other splinters instill?"

Fuerida's laughter rang out like a bell.

"It's just Morning Glory's hypothesis," Kusomba growled. "There's no evidence that Quintillion ever had it."

"I'm almost certain that he did," Morning Glory said. "And perhaps the red and violet splinters are also drawn to descendants of a certain bloodline. Quokisa was the first to gather them and forge them into a soul-gem. Besi, who claimed to be her descendant, used the splinters of Quokisa's soul-gem to forge hers. Katora claims to be descended from Besi. Maybe she or one of her family has those splinters now."

Mana and Nathimeon both shook their heads.

"I heard Katora talk about Besi," Mana said. "And how she was going to fulfill Besi's vision of a city of beauty, on Ulona. But she never expressed much interest in soul-gems."

"That's right," Nathimeon said. "Although, by the time I came along, she'd abandoned the Ulona idea too."

"Too bad," said Mana.

Morning Glory wrinkled her brow. "Well, perhaps those splinters didn't pass from Besi to Katora because Horl had taken them. Perhaps one of his descendants has them now."

They all looked at each other.

"Who do we know is a descendant of Horl?"

Mana spoke up. "Probably Cpice. When she appropriated my mother's genes, her mistress probably gave them to some of her relatives, and she was a daughter of Horl."

"Cpice?" Fuerida cried out. "The Worm?"

Morning Glory turned toward Mana. "She's been picked for the second race. Perhaps you could give her some tips."

Before Mana could respond, the door slammed open, and an orange-bearded figure almost as broad as he was tall invaded them with a collection of ill-matched blotches of color that made the skin Nathimeon had worn during his illness seem soothing by comparison. It was Orgmorgan, Head of the Pilots Guild, Fuerida's father. The whaleskin he wore wasn't actually a riding skin, but the flying suit of a deep-level pilot, for it bore golden rings at the shoulders and hips.

"You done solvin' the galaxial problems yet?" he roared. "C'mon, Glory, let's get out for an evening ramble."

"Excuse me." Morning Glory rose and went to him.

"Thought you was gettin' shed of that gewgaw," Orgmorgan said.

"Oh. Yes. I think Mana should have it."

"Our little Puffball's girl?" Orgmorgan took the gold chain in his stubby, hairy hands and lifted the green splinter from around Morning Glory's neck. Crossing the room, he lowered the chain over Mana's head and very gently placed the warm gem against her skin.

"Thank you," she said.

"Jus' don't come cryin' to me if you change your mind." He and Morning Glory left the room.

Mana stared at the jewel that seemed to capture and magnify every ray of sun coming through the skylight. When she tried to lift it in her hands, it felt strangely slippery, as if it were actually composed of liquid. Somehow it ran through her fingers, no matter how tightly she pressed them together..

Kusomba leaned down to look at it and poked at it with a finger, but her finger slipped off, and she jabbed Mana's breast.

"Ow!"

Fuerida's laugh chimed out with disconcerting brightness.

Mana looked up. "How do I use it for defense?"

"You probably can't do anything with it, seeing as you can't handle it. At least not on home-level. In the Deep your horse will help you make something of it. But splinters actually make wonderful weapons. Let me show you something."

Fuerida went over to the bunk she'd claimed and pulled out the carryall she'd stowed under it. Fishing inside it, she produced a long, thin cylinder wrapped in pink fabric. She stood, gave it a shake, and the fabric fluttered away, revealing a gleaming silver sword with an eyeball-sized violet jewel for its pommel.

"This is Starflash, the Sword of Foske. It used to be paired with Starbolt, the Sword of Brodan, but Starbolt, unfortunately, had to be destroyed to forge the soul-gem, because it was powered by the violet splinter. The gem on Starflash was created by Horl. It's a quasicrystal, but not nearly as powerful as a splinter. Thermeon gave Starflash to me when I fought the Ghost War." Her grin was bright as her voice. "Would you like to try holding it?" Approaching Mana, she held the sword out, hilt first. Mana put her hand around it, but when Fuerida let go, the sword pulled away with the force of a bolting horse.

Smiling, Fuerida picked the sword up from the floor and offered it to Kusomba. Kusomba gritted her jaw and grabbed with both hands, but the sword pulled away from her too.

Fuerida offered the sword to Nathimeon. He took it, one-handed. Rising, he tested the blade with a couple of cuts through the air. Its wake had the crackling sound of unfusing air molecules.

Nathimeon and Fuerida exchanged a smile. Mana saw something leap between the two of them. Her heart clenched. The tentative bond she had felt growing between herself and Nathimeon withered and died in that instant. It was the same old story. She was too ordinary, untalented, uninteresting.

At least Ting loves me, she told herself.

She looked at Kusomba, and at Aspo, and saw that they understood.

"Why don't we go outside, and I'll give you a few pointers," Fuerida chirped.

She and Nathimeon left.

Mana heaved a sigh. "Well, I suppose I ought to go out and look for Cpice and try to surreptitiously pump her for information about splinters while pretending to be helpful."

"I might as well come along," Kusomba said.

"I will too, if you don't mind," said Aspo.

The three of them wandered among the bright tents and babbling crowds, but Cpice was nowhere to be found, and for once, even the newsers seemed to have deserted Mana. Perhaps they'd caught a glimpse of the sword. As she walked, she ran a fingertip up and down the delicate chain supporting the splinter. It was a bit of a relief to know that probably no one except a mindsea would be able to snatch the jewel away from her, but it was also disconcerting to think that she probably would not be able to take it off.

None of Mana's friends had been picked for the second race. When the day came, they all sat in the grandstand together, sipping cold drinks that vendors brought to their seats. They watched the fourteen horses surge away and vanish into the haze of the first obstacle. Mana had wished Cpice luck, but the Worm had remained hostile and suspicious, and had revealed nothing about the possible whereabouts of splinters.

It was a long wait with nothing to see until the horses reappeared between intersections. When you were racing, it seemed as if the time you spent between intersections was about as long as time spent in them, but for spectators, the deep-level time was a hundred times as long.

Grandstands had been placed to allow viewing of the track between obstacles. Orgmorgan and Morning Glory sat together and quaffed beers and wines until they both began to giggle drunkenly. Nathimeon and Fuerida sat pressed together, whispering about the wonderful properties of splinters. Kusomba and Aspo were exchanging tales about Quintillion. Mana ran her finger up and down the chain around her neck, a new habit she couldn't seem to rid herself of.

Fuerida had been right, when mounted on Ting, Mana could feel the splinter and move it about. She didn't even need to be in an intersection. But when she had entered an intersection in a training race, she understood the splinter even better. Parts of it came from other places and times, and that was why it felt slippery, and it didn't react to home-level physical forces like an ordinary object either. Somehow people with mindpowers were able to get their hands around all the exotic facets of it when Mana couldn't. Maybe their hands had fingers from other places and times. But if Thermeon was right, and everyone had a deep-level spirit, Mana should be able to command the far-reaching fingers of her hands if she could just remember how she'd done it when she was riding.

Her finger moved up and down, up and down, but she couldn't get the feel of the other places and times, no matter how hard she tried.

A swelling of voices pulled her from her reverie. A horse had burst from the final intersection to come galloping along the last lengths of the homestretch to the finish line. He was dark brown, almost black, with a flaxen mane and tail. He wasn't Cpice's silvery stallion, or Miesa's speckled black mare—the only two Mana was rooting for.

As horse and rider swept past, an official with a bullhorn blared, "Baran Etro Geed is Lal's second champion!"

Reselona ran down from the grandstand to greet the rider, and Mana recalled that two of the contenders in this race were her grandsons. But when the man had dismounted and turned toward her, Reselona let out a scream.

"You're not Baran! I've never seen you before in my life!"

Mana heard the man chuckle and say something in a deep and mellow voice, but she couldn't make out the words. She stood and started moving toward the track, but everyone else was doing the same thing, blocking her view and drowning out the words that were being exchanged. Soon Red-and-Black and Green-and-Gold were adding their voices to the tumult, but Mana caught only a phrase here and there. Something about the Bolt that had destroyed the capital.

Finally most of the spectators settled back, and Reselona began to make her way up to her seat, her face still perplexed. Mana hurried over to intercept her.

"What did he tell you?"

Reselona paused and swiped back a strand of her glowing white hair. She turned and faced Mana with an air of annoyance. "Don't expect me to give you any tips to use against him in the finals."

"Oh! I wasn't even thinking about that. It was just that, when I had to reestablish my identity after riding the Plains of Possibility, I noticed that all the old data had been erased, so—"

"I see. Well, Baran is no imposter. He remembers all the details of his childhood. And the horse knew him. I shouldn't have made such a fuss. It's just that I hadn't seen him since he'd had himself tattooed."

Mana looked back at the track, where Baran was still expounding to the newsers. Blue spirals shimmered against his brown cheeks.

"Excuse me," Reselona said. She moved on.

Mana rejoined her friends as Baran was making his victory statement.

"I am honored to be here, on this wonderful planet, on this beautiful day, in this fantastic year of one hundred six thousand, five hundred and nine, in the presence of all of you great citizens of our gloried empire!"

Mana frowned. The way he stressed his words struck her as a bit odd. He sounded like Thermeon or Morning Glory, who were very old and had been raised in the Valley, rather than a young person.

Orgmorgan growled, "If he's Baran Etro Geed, I'll eat my whale!" Lurching to his feet, he windmilled his arms and bellowed, "Hey, Stripes! Whatcher doin' here?"

Baran looked up at him. "Michiy! How delighted I am to see you!"

"I'll Michiy him," Orgmorgan grumbled under his breath. Mana supposed that must be his birth name, and he didn't want anyone to know it. He bellowed, "Come up here and share a drink or six!"

Baran smiled and signaled a vendor. He purchased a foamy mug and saluted Orgmorgan with it. Orgmorgan lifted his own mug.

Baran's stallion, Virtue, came up behind him and nuzzled his shoulder. Turning, Baran offered him the mug, and the stallion guzzled its contents. Baran purchased another mug, and let the stallion drink that one too. Then Virtue reared and beat the air with his hooves in a playful way before spinning and trotting off the track and away over the field. Baran purchased a third mug and climbed the grandstand to join them.

"You had to give that nag two ales?" Orgmorgan greeted him.

"Power requires sacrifice." Baran laughed.

Mana had the feeling he was continuing some long-ago conversation.

"Think he'd run jush as fash for'napple," slurred Morning Glory. She flapped a hand toward Mana, who was seated to her left. "Jush ash her."

Baran smiled at Mana and extended his hand. "Baran Etro Geed."

Mana gave her full name and took his hand. His grip was warm and firm. Wavy, shimmering blue lines encircled his fingers, hands, and wrists, as well as his neck. His short, spiky hair was the same shade of blue as the tattoos.

Baran introduced himself to each of the friends seated to Mana's left.

Fuerida grinned at him and chirped, "Would you like to hold my sword?" She was wearing flame-colored pantaloons and a billowing iridescent blue surcoat secured by a diamond-studded white sword belt.

"No thank you," Baran told her. "I am afraid of swords."

Her laugh bubbled out. Nathimeon laid his arm around her shoulders and smiled, a triumphant gleam in his eyes.

Yells and hoots announced the approach of a second horse. Again the rider was someone Mana didn't know.

"That is Velan," Baran said.

"A son of the major?" Mana asked.

"Yes."

"That mage's got more spawn than a blessed sliverfish," said Orgmorgan. "An' they're all twenty years old!"

"And all fine citizens, I am sure," Baran said in his deep, regal tone.

Rather than sitting at either end of their group, he stood staring at the small space between Mana and Kusomba until they all slid along the bench to give him room. He sipped his ale and leaned forward attentively when Velan gushed a few words about the support of his family and how he'd do even better in his next race.

A third horse crossed the finish line, another stranger to Mana.

"That is Barento," said Baran.

Barento was Reselona's other grandson. She went down to congratulate him, but Baran remained where he was.

"I guess that Cpice and Miesa are out of the running," Mana said. "Did you see them during the race, Baran?"

"No."

With a drumming of hooves, Cpice charged from the last intersection on her silvery stallion. Some of the watchers cheered, but it was very subdued. Cpice raced up to the two horses standing beyond the finish line and commanded Empty Alga to halt in a loud, cheery tone, probably thinking that she was third.

In a moment she learned the truth. Mana saw her grin collapse. A sob carried up to the now hushed grandstand.

"What words does the Worm have for the galaxy?" Red-and-Black blared.

"That's cruel," Mana said.

"She was arrogant," Baran said. "She boasted about herself before the race. No one likes that."

"What are your plans, Baran?" Nathimeon asked. "If you win the whole thing, what philosophy will you use to forge the soul-gem?"

Baran scratched his spiky hair. "I have no plans. I am here just for the delight of taking part in this fabled event. If Virtue wishes to win, then I must step back and give my place to another. This is done, yes?"

"Usually people give their places to a son or daughter," Kusomba said. "Do you have children?"

He glanced up at the sky and laughed. "No."

Weary spectators were starting to filter down from the grandstand, leaving small clumps of people still waiting for their riders. Mana noticed a group of disconsolate peasants who had pinned their hopes on Miesa.

Fuerida jumped to her feet. "I think it's time for some more swordplay, Nath." She shot a glance at Baran. "You don't happen to know where I could find another sword, do you?"

"No."

"Then let's go."

She and Nathimeon marched down from the grandstand and crossed the track where Cpice was still sobbing.

"Do you know where the other splinters are?" Kusomba asked Baran.

"No."

As far as Mana could tell, he'd never even glanced at the jewel that still hung around her neck by its gold chain and blazed like a green sun above the bodice of the violet dress she'd bought for spectating. She ran her finger up and down the gold chain.

Baran smiled at her. "Will you walk among the tents with me and explain everything?"

"Why, of course," she said, wondering why he would need things explained.

They rose.

"Don' go!" Orgmorgan yelled. "Have s'more t'drink!"

Baran gave him a dismissive wave. Then he and Mana made their way over to a ramp and descended toward the track.

"Those two, they are in their own world," Baran said. "Inside a bubble of alcohol."

"I guess. But I never saw Morning Glory drink before he came."

"Perhaps he frees her from her self-restrictions."

Mana considered this, running her finger up and down the chain.

Baran paused to deposit his mug in the vendor's collection box. Then he and Mana walked across the track. Cpice pointed a finger at them and moaned, "I think I understand now. They were in league against me!"

The newsers closed on them. "Is the Worm's charge true?"

"Did you combine forces against her?"

"We never met before today," Mana said.

"But you will combine forces in future races?"

"All the challengers should combine against an emperor who has made problems," Baran said.

The thunder of approaching hooves saved them from further questions. As they crossed a long stretch of undisturbed grass toward the tent city, Baran said, "You should not feel sorry for Cpice. Things have gone as well as they could for her."

"Are you sure?" Mana asked.

"Yes. She would not have made a happy empress, so it was best that she lost this race. But years from now, she will boast about how she played an important role in this historic time as the Worm."

Mana shrugged, unconvinced. The movement made the golden chain bite into her skin. She ran her finger up and down along it. "Nathimeon changed himself on the Plains of Possibility. His mother probably won't recognize him, and he might have had trouble proving his identity if the old records hadn't been erased. Did something like that happen to you? I heard you say something about Thermeon's Bolt."

He was silent for a while before speaking. "Yes, I said that. But I lied. I am not Baran Etro Geed. I am a time tourist. I claimed his identity because it was convenient, and because he looked like me."

"What happened to the real Baran?"

"I believe that he died in the Bolt. I found his name on a list of the missing."

"But you made Reselona believe that you were him! I think that's cruel!"

"She allowed me to convince her. But she truly knows that I am not him."

"If she realizes you lied, she'll bring charges against you."

"She cannot prove that I am not Baran. But I hope that there will be no trouble before the culmination of the Challenge. After that I will be gone."

"You're here just to see the Challenge!"

"Yes."

She lowered her voice. "What's going to happen?"

He smiled. "I do not know. My being here will change events, even though I intend only to observe."

"How can you know something important is happening, without knowing what it is?"

"Sometimes events create a disturbance, a wave that travels through the ocean of possibilities. Then time tourists are drawn like sharks to thrashing prey."

Mana tried to digest this as their steps swished through the grass. Once again she heard that deep voice from the intersection intone, "Listen, a wave is passing." She ran her finger up and down the gold chain.

"Does that thing bother you?" Baran asked.

She stopped. When he stopped and turned back toward her, she said, "The splinter?"

"Yes. You do not seem at ease with it."

Mana frowned. Suddenly she recognized feelings that she had been suppressing since Morning Glory had given her the jewel. "I hate not being able to take hold of it. I feel like its alternate-time facets are worming their way through my body. Every now and then I move the wrong way, or something, and I feel it tugging against me."

"You are fighting it. So you should not carry it. Give it to someone else."

Mana nodded, swallowing her angry tears. She ran her finger up and down the chain, then flung her hand down in exasperation. "How can I hope to forge a whole soul-gem if I can't even carry this splinter?"

"I cannot say. But carrying it now will only fatigue you."

She nodded. "But who should I give it to?"

"Fuerida would like to have it. She longs to make a sword of it."

"But the sword would have to be destroyed when the four splinters are united. Maybe I could give it to Nathimeon."

"I think that you would cause conflict between the couple if you gave it to him."

"They're hardly a couple! They just met!"

He chuckled, his black eyes crinkling. "You would like to see them fight?"

"So tell me why giving him the gem would make them fight."

"He loves her, and he thinks that she loves him. But she loves her sword. She carries it about like her man-part, and she needs him only to applaud her. But if he had the gem, her desire to take it from him and make a sword of it would spoil the illusion for him."

Mana fingered her lip. "How do you know this from just sitting near them for a few moments?"

"Their faces were most eloquent."

She ran her finger up and down the chain. "But I have to give it to Nath. There's no one else. Where do you think they are?"

He pointed. "I saw them go that way."

They walked in the direction he had pointed out, and soon, coming over a slight rise, they saw the distant figures of a man and a woman. Nathimeon swept the sword this way and that while Fuerida, standing well back, gestured and posed. It was not long before the ringing tones of her voice reached Mana's ears, though it took much longer before she could make out the words.

"When you're fighting a large animal, like the crokso, you want to hold it thus!" Fuerida took a stance, one arm thrust upward, and Nathimeon mimicked her. "Then, when the beast bears down on you with its long neck, you do thus." She leaped, spun, thrust. Nathimeon leaped, spun, thrust with the sword.

Mana had seen had seen most of the battle with the monster reenacted by the time she and Baran were close enough to attract the participants' notice.

Fuerida grinned at Baran. "Changed your mind about engaging in some swordplay?"

"No." He planted his feet and gripped his hands behind his back.

Mana walked up to Nathimeon. "Nath, will you please take the splinter? Carrying it around tires me out."

"Sure." He extended the sword to Fuerida as she came to his side and reached for the gold chain.

"Give it to me!" Fuerida chimed. "I'll fashion a sword for it!"

The splinter dangling from his fist, Nathimeon turned to her. "But we'll need it to forge the soul-gem."

"It can power a sword until then. Give it here."

Laughing, he held the jewel high, out of her reach. "How are you going to make a sword?"

"I'll fashion it in the Deep. Give it here, and I'll ride out onto the Plains. It won't take long." She jumped at the splinter, but he swept it away.

"That's what you'll think. But you're forgetting the time distortion. You'll miss your race. We can worry about another sword after the soul-gem has been created. Until then, just wear this and look glorious!" He set the chain around her neck.

Her high-pitched giggle made Mana wince.

Mana and Baran walked on toward the tent city that glowed like a flowered meadow in the distance.

"He is more insightful than I gave him credit for," Baran said.

Mana sighed. "He told me that he found his true self on the Plains of Possibility."

When they reached the next rise, Baran stopped. They stood looking at each other. He wasn't as tall as Nathimeon, so they were nearly eye to eye.

"Your face, too, is eloquent," he said.

Mana's lips parted, but she could think of nothing to say.

"You have been waiting for someone to notice you. You are attracted to that young man, but he turns away. The other one, the dark one—"

"Aspo," she supplied.

"He too moons after the Lady of the Sword, though she has abandoned him. They do not understand your worth."

Mana tried to resist the rush of self-pity his words were unleashing. She did feel unappreciated. She had always felt that way, always felt relegated to the sidelines while some more vivacious, greater-mindsized person basked in attention from parents, teachers, lovers.

"They are wrong," Baran said. "The Lady of the Sword has her nose glued to the quintessential two-dimensional object, while you stand open, ready to experience new things, like a flower turned toward the sun!"

Mana had never been compared to a flower before. Not knowing what to make of it, she reached up to run her finger along the chain, only to find it gone.

"If you will allow," Baran said, "I will appreciate you."

With a hand on either side of her face, her pushed back her hair. Then he planted his lips on hers and kissed her.

His lips tingled. She felt a sudden longing that was painfully intense. She wanted to wrap her arms around him and kiss him back; she wanted to fall with him into the grass and.... Resisting those urges, she pushed him away. "You," she panted. "You're going to return to your own time!"

"Yes. When I am gone, you must find someone else. But let me be the first."

She forced a laugh. "I've had lovers before!" A man had come to the Ulona racetrack and courted her. It had been wonderful. Then Mana had discovered that he was one of her mother's old suitors and that Mana was his second choice.

"Let me be the first to appreciate you." Baran put his arms around her and kissed her again. The thrill went deeper. It threatened to split her in two. She found herself kissing him back, pressing herself against him and moaning, all before she knew what she was doing. That was what came from putting sex out of mind, never hugging anyone except a horse, never going to the Nexus for relief in the bioid brothel and even neglecting to take unsex pills. Yet she hadn't actually been aware of the need that now threatened to unseat rationality altogether. With a gasp, she again pushed him back.

"It's not right for you to make me get attached to you when you're going to go away!"

"There will be others after me. But first, you must recognize your worth. That is what I want to show you." He reached toward her.

She backed away. "If I do this, I'll feel abandoned when you leave!"

"You will always have the knowledge that I have loved you. I will never reject you or treat you with indifference. As long as our timelines intersect, I will appreciate you."

"But you can't stay here, in my time!"

"No."

"And you can't take me back to your time?"

"No. But surely you are not like the White Fire, who thinks that he can burn in his goddess-star forever?"

She frowned. Did he mean Thermeon?

"The joy of coupling is one of the marvelous gifts that existence grants to living creatures. It is an intoxication. Let it submerge us in its bubble and make us forget everything else for a while. But you know it is not good to remain intoxicated forever."

Mana wavered, her vision blurred by tears. The longing made her want to give in. Another voice in her mind told her that he was just wrapping very nice words around what amounted to casual sex.

He extended a hand toward her. "Please, Mana. Let us forget the tents and go straight to my room and indulge ourselves. Your need has made me very aroused." He placed the other hand over the bulge in his golden riding skin.

She was still arguing with herself when her hand, seemingly of its own volition, took his.

When Baran had Mana in his unit, one of the small outer ones, she suddenly realized that he had stripped her both of the protection of the splinter, and of her friends. If he had evil intentions, there would be nothing she could do.

Such thoughts—indeed, all thoughts—quickly vacated her mind, as he commenced to guide her along the path of raptures she had never imagined while in the arms of of a bioid. First they shed their clothes and showered together. He soaped her and admired her aloud. Tattoos covered his body from head to toe, and they shimmered like little rivers in the pelting water of the shower.

After they had dried, he threw all of the blankets and pillows from the two beds onto the floor between them. Then he lay down with Mana in the soft mess and commenced to explore her with fingers, lips, and tongue—her earlobes, eyelids, throat, breasts, thighs, clit. He made her feel like one, great, enormous, beautiful bud of sensations so extraordinary and intense she wondered why no one else had ever noticed them. Of course they must have, but she had never sampled any erotica. When at last he entered her, waves of ecstasy coursed up and down her body. She arched and moaned and knew in her heart that this was the reason for living, that nothing else mattered, not empires, nor soul-gems, nor even looming disasters. And then all the rivers of joy met in such a flood of revelation that screams of testimony burst from her lips.

It was only much later, after the wondrous wave had passed, that it occurred to her that the primitive walls of the stable dorms had no sound-proofing, and that everyone in the whole building must have heard her screams.

They lay side by side on their backs, holding hands. Mana's body still tingled as the tide of bliss slowly subsided. Her mind felt light and empty; it reminded her of when she and Ting had crashed into the splinter, and she wondered if you could go Deep on sex.

"You never told me your real name," she murmured.

"It's Sarl," he said.

"Sarl." She squeezed his hand, and he squeezed back.

Of course you could go Deep on sex, she told herself. She drifted into a dream where instead of racing they were forging the soul-gem sexually, while Sarl snored softly at her side.

A burst of light awoke her. A glowing figure stood in the doorway. When she recognized Thermeon, she scrambled up, discovering simultaneously that Sarl was gone from her side and that he had thrown a blanket over her. Clutching the blanket around herself, she tumbled up onto a bed.

"O cruel Sun!" Thermeon roared. "Release my granddaughter from your burning rays!"

Mana couldn't find Sarl among the shadows of the room. Hours must have passed since she had drifted off. Not a glimmer of sun remained in the skylight, which made her grandfather's ranting about the sun seem all the weirder. Then the chemical lamp in a wall sconce came on, and she saw Sarl standing at the foot of the bed wearing one of the generic black robes.

"I salute your concern, O Dragon," he said. "But there is no need to destroy anything here. Mana is safe and well."

"Grandfather, I'm fine!" Mana whispered. "Please don't make a scene and wake everyone in the building!"

Thermeon's mane bristled. "Go back to your friends, Mana. They're worried about you!"

Confused and angry, she sat up on the bed, still clutching the blanket around herself. "They have no right to try to manage my life. Sarl explained everything to me. I know that he'll have to return to his own time."

"Did he explain that he doesn't believe in love?"

She blinked. How did he know Sarl's views on love? Was he ripping his mind? She glanced at Sarl, but he looked as composed as anyone could be when facing Thermeon in one of his rages.

"Grandfather, I'm not sure that even I believe in love the way you do."

"So you allow this world-destroyer to seduce you? I had hoped you were raised better than that! He won't even give you a child, will he?"

Mana couldn't find words. Her mouth opened and closed.

"No," said Sarl.

"See?" Thermeon bared his fangs. His tail lashed.

"Grandfather, have you and Sarl met before?"

"He told me that I would never meet my goddess-star!" Thermeon's violet eyes blazed with furious indignation.

Mana heaved a sigh. It *would* have to be about the goddess-star.

"I was trying to help you," Sarl said.

Thermeon drew himself up and laid a hand over his heart. "You spoke out of bitterness and envy, because your own goddess had rejected you!"

"I do not pursue goddesses," Sarl said.

"What about Ul!" Thermeon cried, triumphant.

"Ul?" said Sarl. "Who is Ul?"

"The planet Ulona."

Sarl cast him a perplexed look. Thermeon shut the door behind him and began to pace about the small space between it and the beds.

"Grandfather," Mana said. "You're not making any sense."

"I am making perfect sense!" Thermeon whirled suddenly and grinned at the two of them. "I have found my goddess-star!"

Sarl regarded him with a stony expression.

"What about Katora?" Mana asked.

"She had me fooled."

Mana swallowed. Katora had rejected her previous husbands, but she had never been rejected herself. This could be quite a blow to her.

"Where is she?"

"I do not know, and I do not care. Because now I have found

my true goddess, the one whose shining rays have ever gently rested upon me, though I did not locate their true source until now." His face shone with joy and wonder, and his white mane bristled and quivered with a soft susurration that sounded almost like a cat's purring.

He went Deep on sex, Mana thought. That's why he thought the object of his desire must be a goddess, that the act of love was the ultimate goal of existence. She sat with the blanket tented around her, gripping her drawn-up knees beneath it, and shivering, just a bit.

Sarl sat down on the side of the other bed and contemplated her grandfather. "I had a dream about you, once. It was a long time ago, and I don't quite recall it any longer, but there was a curtain of white flame that obscured a land in the sky. The land symbolized the Deep, I would suppose. The white fire became a white dragon with violet eyes—yourself, of course. I could not help but feel that something wonderful and creative might be accomplished with those brilliant flames."

Thermeon regarded him with narrowed eyes, nostrils pulsing, the tip of his tail twitching.

Sarl touched a finger to his forehead. "If only you would occasionally take thought instead of always blindly following your instincts!"

Thermeon snarled. "You dare lecture me after what you've done to my granddaughter!"

Mana gasped and protested, "I'm perfectly fine, Grandfather!"

"I have done nothing but give her a little of the attention she deserves."

Thermeon directed his searing gaze at Mana. "In the future, if you are in need of attention, just tell me, and I will direct a suitable mate your way. There is no need to let yourself be used by cosmic bullies!"

Cosmic bullies? Mana's throat went tight as her suspicion that Thermeon knew something about Sarl that she didn't grew stronger. Did Sarl roam through time seducing girls at every stop? And what had Thermeon meant about the planet Ulona? Aware suddenly of the need to urinate, she scooted off of the bed and hurried to the bathroom, dragging her blanket behind her.

She lingered to shower and dress, and to think. Thermeon exaggerated, hyperbolized, but he didn't lie. Sarl must have done something to earn the epithet "cosmic bully." On the other hand, if he had been truly evil, Thermeon would have simply killed him rather than call him names. She pulled the violet dress on over her head, adjusted the filmy sleeves and smoothed the skirts, and checked herself in the mirror.

Thermeon's emotions were exaggerated compared to those of ordinary people. So he wasn't actually angry—just slightly annoyed. And Sarl probably hadn't seduced a string of girls across every era. Maybe just one, but someone Thermeon cared about. Perhaps a daughter, or some other granddaughter. But the planet Ulona? She frowned. Her grandfather did tend to conflate celestial objects with people. He must have been speaking of someone he regarded as personifying Ulona. Katora had done more than anyone to restore the planet that been lost for nearly a hundred thousand years after its reduction by Attequol. But Thermeon would not have called her Ul. Mana finger-combed her hair and squinted into the mirror. Was there some old Ulonan myth she didn't know about? There had been an undead mindsea of Ulona, but that had been a man.

She would ask Sarl about it, after Thermeon left. She didn't want to sound like she'd been kept in the dark and give her grandfather more fuel for deploring her lover. When she opened the bathroom door, she found Sarl still seated on the edge of the bed and Thermeon still pacing about at the end of the room.

"She exerted all of her mindpowers to keep me deceived," Thermeon grumbled.

Mana gathered that he was speaking of Katora.

Thermeon took two more turns between door and beds, then poised with one hand raised, as if about to continue his discourse. But instead of speaking, he just stood that way for several seconds, while Sarl and Mana watched him in silence. Slowly, Thermeon lowered his arm and turned toward the door. He threw back his head and sniffed the air.

Mana heard his voice in her head. *Someone is sneaking up. I do not like their smell. Hide yourself.*

She stepped back into the bathroom and pulled the door almost shut, leaving a crack so that she could peek out. Moments later, two women in black tunics and trousers slid into the room. One of them, wild-eyed, brandished a white cylinder.

"No one move or you will be unfused! The Holy Crusade will prevail!"

Mana's heart pounded. Even a mindsea could be killed by unfusing if he couldn't downlevel before he was struck. She wondered why Thermeon's fear reaction hadn't made him go Deep.

"Blindfold him!" commanded the woman with the bomb. She was looking at Sarl.

"What about Thermeon?" asked the other. "We didn't expect—"

"Ignore him!" snapped the first crusader. "Just take Baran!"

That explained Thermeon's lack of fear. He wasn't the target.

The second crusader produced a sopping strip of black cloth from a pouch on her belt and strode over to Sarl, who still sat on the bed. "Turn around," she commanded.

"Please don't," he said.

"It is necessary to remove the familiarity of your surroundings," said the woman. "Now turn around or you will be unfused!"

He twisted away from her, and she flung the wet cloth over his eyes and knotted it at the back of his head. "Now put your hands behind your back."

He did, and she produced a rope from another pouch and tied his wrists together. "Now stand up! Move!"

Behind the door, Mana was shaking with terror and outrage. There was nothing she could do, but why didn't Thermeon do something to stop this? Surely he didn't hate Sarl enough to wish him harm.

Sarl began to shuffle toward the outer door, the woman shoving him from behind. Thermeon stood between him and the door, looking slightly amused. When another shove would send Sarl careening into him, the crusader looked at her leader.

"We have to tie Thermeon too," said the woman with the bomb.

"Don't try," Thermeon said.

The second crusader produced another rope and started to move around Sarl. In a flash, Thermeon was on the first woman. He ripped the bomb from her hands, and the two fled, squawking and cursing.

Thermeon pushed past Sarl and set the cylinder down on a bed. "Don't disturb that. We will dispose of it later. First I will catch them."

Grinning, he bounded back to the door and was gone.

Mana rushed out of the bathroom and started struggling with the knots that bound Sarl's wrists. "It's horrible! I thought we would be safe from them with all the guards around!"

When his hands were free, Sarl pulled off the soggy blindfold and stood staring at it.

"Did it hurt you? What do you think they intended to do?' Mana found her hands reaching for the nonexistent chain, and clasped them together.

"I think that they wished to stop me from from riding in the finals. The second-place finisher would have my position."

"That would be the major's son. Probably a supporter of Karali. She never wanted children of her own. She had her sex turned off permanently, too."

Sarl raised his brows. "She must be a woman of few affections."

Mana fell back onto the bed behind her. "She didn't count on Thermeon returning, or she never would have tried this. He'll rip their minds. He's probably ripping them now, and he'll know exactly who gave the orders. Even if it wasn't Karali herself, he'll dig into the minds he sees in theirs, and find his way up the chain of command. Or he'll just look into her mind—Karali's. I'm sure he won't kill her, but he'll let her feel his disapproval." She grimaced.

Sarl draped the blindfold over the bedpost and sat down across from her, rubbing his wrists. "Are you all right, Mana?"

When she shook her head he rose and stepped over to her side. He stroked her hair and kissed her lips. She wanted to melt into him. "What if my grandfather comes back?"

"He is too busy now meting out justice. Come to the other bed. You are sitting too close to that bomb."

Mana jumped up with a gasp. Smiling, Sarl gathered pillows and blankets from the floor and threw them onto the other bed. He turned off the lamp. Mana undressed again, then joined him in bed. She felt safe and warm in his arms. Soon they began another journey into delight.

In the morning, Mana and Sarl joined Nathimeon, Fuerida, Kusomba, and Aspo in the cafeteria for breakfast.

"I hear that you had an exciting time last night," Kusomba said, smirking.

"It was terrible!" Mana replied.

For some reason, this evoked laughter and more smirks. Fuerida and Kusomba were stealing furtive sideways glances at Sarl. Suddenly Mana realized that they were pretending that she had been talking about the sex. She felt furious.

"Thermeon has gone to the capital," Fuerida piped. "Karali will be sorry she was ever born! Morning Glory and Orgmorgan spent the night at the Nexus, so they missed everything."

"Oh," said Mana. "Is Katora here?"

They all looked at each other, shrugged or shook their heads.

"I am saddened by what I hear of Katora," said Sarl. "I had hoped once that she would be a greater emperor than Thermeon or Quintillion."

For a moment no one spoke. Finally Kusomba said, "When did you hope *that*?"

He wrinkled his brow. "It seems like it was only a millennium ago."

Mana wanted to ask him how many visits he had made to their timeline. She had a great many questions to ask, but she didn't want to sound as if she didn't know things she ought to know. Her friends all seemed determined to mock her. Why were they being so unfair? No one was sneering at Nathimeon for his infatuation with Fuerida.

Fuerida smiled at her. "Since you don't need our protection any more, Nath and I are moving to our own room."

"Oh."

"It would be silly of us to stay in that big unit all by ourselves," Kusomba said. "So Aspo and I are moving out too."

"Oh." Mana felt sad and a bit shaken. Was their whole group breaking up because of Sarl? "Where will we meet for conferences?" she asked.

They shrugged or made indifferent sounds.

"I'm sure you won't need our help any more," Kusomba said, with a meaningful look at Sarl.

They all hated him, and Mana had no idea why. But clearly, they thought she must know and had chosen to side with him despite whatever it was. She wanted to yell out, "Tell me, already!" But of course she couldn't.

Sarl seemed unperturbed by their hostility.

Maybe they were just angry because they knew he was an imposter, and he hadn't explained himself to them. But Thermeon had known who he was, and had some sort of grudge. Was it only because Sarl had made a negative comment about his goddess-star? Well, that was probably enough.

"We'll move our things out after breakfast," Fuerida said.

Mana swallowed and nodded.

"I will take the bomb to Inspector Sunfox," Sarl said.

Fuerida squeaked. "You have the crusaders' deep-level bomb? Give it to me! I could—"

Nathimeon shook her arm. "It's evidence in a criminal investigation, Fue."

"But—"

Sarl looked at her. "If your intent is to do deep-level engineering, I am certain that you can find better sources of material."

"Do you know of any?"

"You have access to deep-level intersections from the racetrack.

Use one of them."

Fuerida fingered her lip. A smile curled her pert pink lips.

"But not during a real race, Fue," Nathimeon warned. "Or you'll fall behind the other riders."

"Pshaw!" She grinned at Sarl. "Baran ... um, do you want us to call you Baran, or...."

"Call me Baran. It is a good name."

"Have you detected who has the other splinters yet?"

"The only splinter I 'detect' is the one you have around your neck. But then, I have little interest in such things. If they interest you, put your mind to work and deduce who is most likely to arrive with one of them. Who—aside from yourself—loves them the most?"

Her face suddenly went solemn, and a little paler. "Horl did. But, you don't think ... I already had to fight him once when he tried to come back. You don't think...."

"Who can say?" Sarl rose from the table. "I will take the bomb away."

Mana got up too. "I guess I'd better get my things."

Smiling, Sarl laid his hands on her shoulders, drew her close, and kissed her lightly on the lips. She thought she heard an intake of breath from everyone at the table. She felt eyes drilling into her back.

Sarl took her hand and they walked from the room together. Every step of the way, Mana felt her back burning from the stares. The agony seemed to go on and on. People sitting at the other tables watched their passage too, but less intensely, perhaps only because Mana and Sarl were certain of places in the Final Sixteen Race.

The moment they reached the doorway and turned into the corridor, Mana let out her pent breath. "My friends all hate you!"

He chuckled. "They do not hate me. They are merely perturbed and perplexed by my presence here."

"Why?"

"They did not expect me to visit this era."

"Oh. They know something about you."

"I am certain that Orgmorgan told them at length."

"You met him before."

"Yes."

"Thermeon too."

"Yes."

"Thermeon hates you."

"He is angry with me because I told him that he would never meet his goddess-star. Before that, he was ready to kiss my toes."

Mana couldn't imagine Thermeon lowering himself before anyone. She squinted at Sarl. "Are you one of his ancestors, or something?"

His laugh boomed in the narrow corridor. "Heaven forfend!"

"Oh, right. You said you had no children."

"I said that, yes."

"But it's not true?"

"No."

"What are you hiding from me, Sarl?"

He took her hands and kissed her fingertips. "There is a wonderful magic in our relationship, Mana! I hate to ruin it!"

"You think my knowing the truth will ruin it?"

He looked her in the eye. "Yes."

"Then our relationship isn't real."

"I told you that it was destined to last only for a short while. It is a glorious soap bubble, all the more beautiful for its fragility and ephemerality."

"But—" She froze as a couple she didn't know entered the corridor. Sarl walked on, and she followed him to a circular corridor, and around it to the connecting corridor that led to his dorm.

When they stepped inside, memories of their exquisite lovemaking welled up in her. It was all based on lies, she told herself.

"You don't trust me," she murmured. "You don't trust me to still love you if I knew the truth."

He stood between the beds, contemplating the bomb. Then he looked back at her. "And you do not have trust enough to love me despite not knowing."

"I think you are more wrong than I am! You could be someone dangerous. I have no power to hurt you."

"You can hurt my feelings." He picked up the bomb, then

turned toward her. "Go ahead, ask your friends about me. Then, if you still care, you can join me here tonight. Otherwise...." He shrugged.

"You won't tell me yourself?"

"No." He walked up to her. "A last kiss!" Putting one arm around her, the other still holding the bomb, he kissed her lips. She didn't dare resist, because of the bomb, though the rush of sensations was exquisite agony.

Releasing her, he went on to the door.

"Is your name really Sarl?" she flung after him.

"Yes."

"But?"

"My name is Sarl in the same way that your name is Mana."

"It *is* Mana."

"But to the galaxy, you are the Chosen One." He went out, closing the door behind him.

Her mind jumped on the clue. He was known by some appellation. He had some connection to Ulona. Could he be the Undead Mindsea of Ulona? She shuddered.

She could not bring herself to ask her friends. It would be utterly humiliating. If she had to, she would go to her grandfather and confess her ignorance and her stupidity. But he was in the city, and not likely to be finished with Karali soon. She would ask Orgmorgan or Morning Glory if she could find them. Perhaps she should go to the Nexus and seek them out there.

Then another thought came. She would ask Dino. She knew that he was spending most of his time in Vuduna, but he must have come over for the race the day before; so, if she was lucky, he would still be around.

She went to the unit that had his name on the door and knocked. Then, thinking she heard a voice, she opened the door.

Dino sat on one of the beds, holding the sobbing Katora in his arms. He looked at Mana over the dark waves of Katora's hair and shook his head. Mana backed out and quietly closed the door behind her.

For a while she remained standing in front of the door, close to weeping herself. She wanted to go and curl up somewhere, but there was no place to go. Her friends were probably still in the big unit getting their stuff, and she was certainly not going back to Sarl's room.

Voices drifted along the outer circular aisle of the stable, and a group of the peasant caretakers came trundling a wheelbarrow full of manure and another full of fresh bedding and carrying pitchforks from one stall to the next. Mana walked over to them.

"Would it be all right if I helped out? I know it might seem odd, but I used to do all the work here myself, and sometimes I miss my old routine."

Four pairs of luminous green eyes stared at her. Finally, one of the women said, "We don't mind, if you don't. But, you know, you'll stand out something right huge amongst us. Why with your height, you make us all look like yearlings."

"I don't care." After being stared at for being the Chosen One, for kissing Sarl, what injury could she suffer from a little more staring? She went to the supply room for a pitchfork, and soon she was going from stall to stall with the two women and two men.

"I'm sorry Miesa lost," Mana said.

"At least no stuffed-noses have won yet," said the woman who had spoken to her first.

"What's a stuffed-nose?"

"When a dro gets hook flies in its nose sieve, it runs around with its head in the air and its eyes closed. That's how some folks act around us—like they's way up on some higher level, and can't even see us."

The woman's three companions nodded.

"That Cpice was like that," she went on. "We all laughed when Morning Glory called her the Worm."

"We like Morning Glory," added a man.

The woman nodded. "She grew up in the Valley—on the land, like us."

"Her brother too," said the man.

"And Dino helped us after the plague, so we know he's all right, even if he does strange things to his mare."

"I think he calls it playing games," said Mana.

"We think you're the right sort too," said the woman. "Wanting to help out like this."

They all nodded.

"And Baran is polite to us, so we're glad he won."

"But you know," said Mana, "he's not really Baran."

"We heard the woman screaming, but we thought it was set straight."

"He told me that he was a time tourist."

They all ooh'ed.

"Do you have any idea who he might be?" Mana asked.

The peasants looked at each other.

"Well, he has tattoos, so he's probably Attequol."

They all nodded.

"Attequol was a friend to our people, because he married Queen Lala."

"We weren't peasants back then, you know. We were the rulers of the land."

"Now that we know who he is, we'll need to show our respect."

"We could bring his meals to his door."

"Or get beer for his horse!"

Mana smiled and nodded at them, but inside she was groaning at their silliness. She'd forgotten that the peasants were exempt from most of a citizen's educations programs, and believed in a host of nonsensical myths—for instance, that Attequol lived inside the Wall and would appear whenever the empire was in danger.

The peasants made lunch for themselves before serving the rest of the building. Their meal consisted of dishes made from plants native to the sands of Lal, such as red carrots and dust-roses, as well as confections that had dro milk as a major ingredient. Mana ate with them, then went back to her big dorm. Everyone else's belongings had been cleared out. Feeling lonely and rejected, she lay down on her bed and fell asleep.

She was awakened by loud neighing. Stallion trumpeting was interspersed by the angry squeals of a mare. As she ran out to try to help, she realized the altercation came from the direction of Eternal Trat's stall. Her dread rose. She'd never seen him fight before. What could be happening?

Skidding out from a corridor into the broad aisle, Mana saw the tableau: Trat and Stretching Meith with arched necks, fanned-out tails and flaring nostrils in front of the stall beside Trat's, while a brown mare Mana had never seen before stamped as she eyed the open stall door behind them.

Two women came running up just ahead of Mana. The first was Morning Glory, the second a very small woman with buttermilk skin and bright red hair.

"Meith, no! Away from there!" Morning Glory came up alongside her stallion, grabbed fistfuls of his mane, and tried to push him away from the stall; but he planted his hooves, ground his tusks, and kept his eyes fixed on his larger rival.

The small woman leaped onto the mare's back. "Come, Serious." She rode toward the exit.

When the mare had passed him, Trat wheeled around and followed her out. Meith watched him go. His ears swiveled forward, and he tossed his head, snorting with satisfaction and triumph. Then he turned toward the stall.

"No, Meith!" Morning Glory cried. "I'm sorry, but we're going to have to find another place for you."

Morning Glory mounted, saw Mana, and greeted her. "Do you think you could try to calm Trat? He's very agitated this morning."

"I'll get a brush," Mana said, though she felt intimidated by the thought of facing a furious white stallion. "That was Serious Quiav? And Eria? They've come back from Andromeda?"

"Yes. She says that Thermeon was chasing her all over the multiverse. Unfortunately, Trat still seems to think he needs to chase Serious."

"I'll get a brush. And some treats." Mana ran back down the corridor.

The brush in one hand and a bag of apples in the other, she hurried back along the corridor that intersected the outer aisle just to the left of Serious Quiav's stall. She was several paces from the intersection when she saw Sarl walk past along the aisle. She cursed under her breath and slowed her pace. Flattening herself against the corridor wall, she peeked around the corner.

Sarl was standing a few steps away, back to her, studying the white stallion, who was staring over the closed door of Serious Quiav's stall. The mare stood in the back of the stall, as far from him as possible. Trat whinnied.

Sarl spoke to the stallion. His words were incomprehensible to Mana. Was he speaking the Ulonan language? Trat backed away from the door and looked at him.

Eria leaned out over the door. "Attequol! Is it really you?"

"Eria," he responded. "How great a pleasure to meet you once again!"

"You're not still twisted?"

"No, I am fine."

"And you have more tattoos now. But they're blue! And your hair!"

"I am in disguise. I am going by the name Baran Etro Geed."

Eria looked up and down the aisle to see if anyone had overheard her greeting, and Mana shrank back out of sight. She slid down the corridor wall and sat in a heap. One by one, tears rolled down her face.

Eria's voice flowed on as she complained about Thermeon's behavior, and Sarl responded with a few soothing and inconsequential words here and there. Finally, Eria cried, "What will I do?"

"He enjoys the chase," Sarl said. "So facing him is best."

"He doesn't seem to hear when you speak to him."

"Yes, I think he has grown too much to love his own myth, and finds no reason to stop. Even this horse now has the myth in his mind."

"Poor Trat," said Eria. "I know it's not his fault, but he's been terribly annoying to Serious, trying to herd her where Thermeon wants us to go. Can you calm him? Surely he knows you."

"He knows me. But that does not mean he prefers me to the White Dragon. Thermeon has let him indulge his power and wildness. Still, even a horse can realize that self-discipline has its merits."

"Do you think that a bit of riding around could make him understand that the chase is over, and we can all relax now? I don't know who at the stable is supposed to exercise him. Do you know?"

"No."

Mana could have told them that only the man or woman currently occupying the throne was supposed to ride Trat. When Pia had been that person, she'd stuck to Pious except for ceremonial occasions, and Trat hadn't gotten much attention. Of course, such rules meant nothing to Thermeon.

"Why don't you and I go for a short ride," Eria said. "Now, before anyone else comes around."

"Why not?"

There came the crunch of hooves over the stall bedding, then Trat's happy nicker as the mare emerged. Hooves clopped away along the aisle, growing fainter as they turned toward the exit. Then they were gone.

Mana picked herself up and fled to her room to cry.

Mana did not emerge until almost all of the riders had taken their horses out. Apologizing for her lateness, she gave Ting the apples she'd gotten for Trat, then brushed her with extra care. Finally, she rode her around the track all by herself. Usually one horse and rider didn't trigger intersection points, but Mana's mind-state was so agitated that the rule didn't hold.

All the deep-level sensations she experienced were depressing. She crossed an abyss on a bridge; it was not beautiful as the indigo chasm had been, but gray and unlovely, more like an abandoned open-pit mine than a wild place.

She rode through a dense, dark forest, full of vines that reached out to snag her and leafy barricades that stung her with their allergy-producing spines. She itched violently, and even after leaving the intersection her skin remained irritated.

Next, Ting clattered along a gloomy thoroughfare in an underground city full of strange chemical smells, where mushroom-like inhabitants followed their passage with bitter glares. This was a real place, Mana reminded herself; real, yet located in some place and time she would never find again, while her own appearance would be attributed to some inexplicable deep-level phenomenon.

She rode Ting through a relentless downpour across an island that seemed to be dissolving into the sea that surrounded it. Rivulets streaming down from the high place where the track was laid out carried away soil and vegetation, and the track itself seemed to melt into ever widening puddles that Ting splashed through.

The last intersection brought them to another underground land, where Ting galloped along a track of dark clay washed by the translucent briny ripples of a somber sea. A sea of tears, Mana thought as the last glimpse of it dissolved.

After releasing Ting, she sat down cross-legged on the field facing the Plains of Possibility and gave way to her fury and her desolation.

What she had wanted had been the love of a man, someone like Nathimeon, but she would have been better off sticking to loving her horse, because now she had neither friends nor lover.

At least she still had Ting.

If Ting ever left her, there would be nothing left for her at all. She bowed her head, buried her face in her hands, and wept. Poor, stupid, Mana! She'd hoped that someday she could outgrow that feeling of always being the unwanted child. She'd told herself that somewhere she would find a person who liked her—her, Mana, and not her mother, and not some squeaky-voiced bimbo who played with her sword. Attequol had seen her need. It must have blazed like a beacon to his god-vision. She ground her teeth as she thought about how blithely he'd passed his mindpowers off as ordinary, human perceptiveness. It was pretty obvious that everyone's thoughts shouted to him the way they did in the Deep. All her friends had caught on to what he was, but poor, stupid Mana had been so desperate for a companion that she'd refused to see. She had convinced herself that she had found love. Instead, she'd been the plaything of a god. She was an utter, hopeless fool. She would never be able to look any of her former friends in the face again.

She bawled like a baby.

Chosen One, indeed! That was another farce. She had nothing to offer the galaxy. She wished that she could just run away, far away, never to return, take the splinter and Ting and go live in a private bubble like Morning Glory had. No one would miss her. In fact, that was a good idea, if she could just get the splinter back.

But she couldn't. Fuerida would never give it up. Mana would have to crawl back to the stable and endure everyone's sneers. She wondered if her idiocy had ruined Morning Glory's plan for forging a new soul-gem. She'd certainly destroyed their bold little group. Did that mean disaster would crumble the empire? She remembered how she'd dismissed disaster as unimportant when she'd been in the throes of sexual ecstasy. She'd been mind-warped.

Something made her look up. Attequol was standing there, watching her.

She leaped to her feet with a shriek. "Go away! Leave me alone!"

He smiled. "Come back to the stable. It is time for dinner."

She whirled to flee, but he caught her arm and pulled her away from the haze of the Plains—she'd forgotten how close to the border she'd been sitting. This additional evidence of her stupidity, plus the aggravation of his touch, snapped the last thread of her self-control.

"I hate you!" she shrieked, pummeling him with her free fist.

He wrestled her backwards across the grass, while her shrieks and struggles grew more frenzied, until finally he fell over onto his back and lay laughing at the sky. It was a deep, robust laugh that brimmed with joy.

"How dare you laugh at my misery!" Mana wailed, kicking his ankle.

She started to run back toward the stable, but he scrambled to his feet and again caught her arm. "It is not because you are miserable that I laughed. It is because you are alive! And you are beautiful. You are so full of feelings and yearnings! That is such a wonderful thing, Mana. You do not realize it now, but you are anything but miserable!"

"Let go of my arm!" she screamed. "Go find some other mortal to amuse you!"

He released her, but continued to follow behind her. "I do care about you. Someday you will know that."

She whirled around. "I suppose you've seen the future. But it's very unfair for you to use your god-powers against me. Besides, how do I know you're not lying? You told me before that you didn't know what was going to happen in this Challenge."

He laughed. "Many things will happen in the Challenge. But

you can only reach one conclusion about me."

"You're hateful!" she growled.

As she stomped up over the next rise, she saw the colorful tent city outspread below. She paused, and Attequol came to her side.

Thinking about the Challenge brought back all the hopes Mana and her friends had entertained, hopes ruined now, unless her friends could go on without her to gather the splinters and somehow figure out how to.... Her thoughts skidded to an abrupt halt. She stared at Attequol. "Why, you know everything about soul-gems! You designed the first one, didn't you—the original that Morning Glory's splinter is a piece of?"

"Yes."

"Then why didn't you offer to explain to me how it's done?"

"You would not have found my explanation authoritative when you did not know who I was."

"I know now. So tell me."

He sat down cross-legged in the grass, and motioned her to do the same. When they sat facing each other, he said, "I find the plan that Morning Glory outlined, for attempting to forge the gem during a race, very strange indeed!"

"Well," said Mana, twisting a grass stem around her finger. "What would you suggest?"

"Why worry about finding all of the old splinters? Create a new soul-gem."

"That would require working on Deep Six, wouldn't it?"

"Yes. But you require that depth of focus to reforge the splinters, too."

"You think that we can create a whole new soul-gem during the Emperor Race?"

He shook his head. "I do not understand why you wish to attempt this during a race, which will be filled with chaos and extreme passions."

"It's the only way we know to reach Deep Six. The mind-states of the riders will help to form a deep intersection."

"That all seems strange to me. Perhaps this way of thinking began with Horl. He seemed to believe that deep-level engineering required intense emotions. Thermeon thinks that way as well. Does Katora?"

"No, but she doesn't actually do any deep-level engineering herself. She uses her mindpowers to try to shape a future in which she'll have a son who can do it."

"How curious. Why not approach the problem in a straightforward way and focus on the engineering rather than these strange manipulations?"

"No one knows how. The patternists who understand how things should be engineered don't have the mindpowers to actually do it. And mindseas like Thermeon who can affect deep-level stuff can't think through what they're going to do. He just explodes, like the horses when they bolt into the Deep."

Attequol smiled. "I know. But it is not necessary to behave in that manner. Deep Six is not inaccessible." He gestured broadly. "It is everywhere around us, not creating a dangerous fusion field as when an artificial intersection is created, but naturally intermingled with our home-level. To create an artifact with the requisite patternistic depth, it is necessary only to observe the patterns—to count the number of holes, and so on. Perception is necessary, but perception can be informed by knowledge. You understand?"

Mana sat up straighter, gripping her knees and frowning as she stared at him. She knew that he was offering vital information, but it threatened to slip through her mind. "I'm trying to! I don't think I'm the person who could see that deep-level shape. Why aren't you sharing this information with patternists?"

"You are open to ideas, Mana. You think that you cannot see what I am attempting to convey, but you will keep trying until at last it becomes clear. I have found that those who believe themselves to be experts do not wish to hear advice that contradicts their own cherished ideas. Horl was perhaps the greatest of deep-level engineers in your recent histories, but he was extremely unreceptive to my suggestions."

Mana plucked at the grass, frowning as she tried to picture Horl and Attequol meeting. "Will you help us forge a new soul-gem?"

He shook his head. "No. It must be forged for this time. If I interfered, my imprint would connect it with times long-ago. This is clear to you, yes?"

She wrinkled her brow. "Is that why you wouldn't touch

Morning Glory's splinter or Fuerida's sword?"

"One reason." Smiling, he rose, then extended a hand to help her to her feet.

Mana scooted away and jumped up by herself. "You're putting your imprint on me!"

He threw back his head and laughed. "You are perceptive! But let us walk down among the tents together."

She gazed at the swarm of colors between them and the stable, which sat on the field like a giant white mushroom cap. She didn't feel quite so devastated as she had a while before, but she didn't want to touch Attequol and let her emotions start to roller coaster again. Maybe, now that she had gotten some advice about the soul-gem, she could approach her friends and talk it over with them.

"Please don't follow me or touch me. I want companionship with my own kind."

"Can you not think of me as a man?"

"No. Will you keep your distance? I don't want to create a scene where people, and especially the newsers, might be watching."

"Go. I would like to spend more time with you, but I do not wish to hurt you."

"Thank you." She ran down the long slope toward the tent city, looking back over her shoulder a couple of times to make certain that he wasn't following. He remained standing on the top of the rise.

She hurried along the dirt path between lines of tents and booths, many of them closing up for the evening. The newsers had pitched their tent closest to the stable, but like other members of the public, they were not permitted inside the stable, and guards were now stationed outside the entrance to enforce the rule. Mana saw no sign of Red-and-Black or Green-and-Gold as she rushed by.

Arriving in the crowded cafeteria, she looked around for her friends. Kusomba, Aspo, Fuerida, and Nathimeon were seated together around a table near the far corner. She got a bowl of red carrot stew and a glass of rosehip juice from the peasant servers and joined them.

"I talked to him about soul-gems," she announced.

When everyone's eyes had fixed on her, Mana realized that she didn't actually have anything helpful to report. "He's not going to help us. He said that he doesn't think we should try to forge a soul-gem during a horse race, or even try to find the splinters. He thinks we should just be able to create a new soul-gem by picking deep-level stuff out of our surroundings, by counting holes, or something."

"Twistor him!" Kusomba muttered. "Why's he even here if he's not going to help? To mock us?"

"My father wrote an opera called 'Attequol and Rathax,'" said Aspo. "It was a tragedy. He felt that Rathax was right, and Attequol was wrong, that he was a destroyer, like Thermeon."

"You look ravaged yourself," Fuerida chirped. "Maybe you should stay away from him."

Mana nodded. "I think you're right."

Eria won the third position in the Final Sixteen Race, her red hair flying wild as she rode Serious Quiav over the finish line. Before the newsers could ask her for a victory statement, Thermeon rushed down onto the track, declaring that his heart was melting with love for her, and Eria made a rude gesture at him.

Moments later, Fuerida finished, blazing with her jewels, and cursing when she learned that she hadn't won.

Beteli came in fourth, but within minutes she'd convinced the unknown who had come in third to cede their chance in another race to her, and she spoke at length about how her mother, Empress Pia, would not be forgotten.

An elderly granddaughter of Thermeon came in fifth, and the major's son who had placed second in Baran's race came in sixth.

Morning Glory joined Mana, Kusomba, Aspo, Fuerida, and Nathimeon at dinner that evening.

"I talked to Eria about joining us," she reported. "But she is quite the loner, I'm afraid. She seems more concerned about Thermeon's antics than in the fate of the empire."

"I'd be concerned about him too," Mana said.

The looks everyone gave her made her uneasy. The rift that had opened when she'd walked off with Attequol had not yet healed.

No one had talked about returning to the big unit, so Mana spent another night alone there. Every sound she heard as she tried to sleep made her imagine that crusaders were about to crash in, or that Attequol was about to appear at her bedside and run his hands across her body. Then she would squirm about as tides of longing smashed against tides of anger and self-pity.

Perhaps she had been lonely and needy before he'd played with her, but she hadn't realized it, and she'd been content with her life. Now she knew what a pathetic loser she was, and the knowledge ate at her with a slow burn.

"Chosen One, indeed!" she grumbled at the silence of the night.

She hadn't even gotten any useful advice from Attequol. The more she thought about it, the angrier she grew. "Like hell you care about me!" she muttered at the figure she imagined standing over her. "Oh what wonderful wisdom you've passed on to me. I should count holes. Count holes!"

She plunged her face into her pillow and sobbed for a while before finally slipping into a restless sleep.

The next morning, names were drawn for the fourth preliminary race. Both Fuerida and Kusomba would ride. When Mana joined them for lunch that day, all attention naturally fixed on them. Once, Kusomba turned to Mana and asked if the obstacles in a real race really were more difficult and dangerous than those in practice sessions, and Mana said, "Yes." Other than that brief exchange, she felt as if she might have been invisible.

Her friends would face Katora in their race, as well as a daughter of Katora and Dino named Dilora. Katora was the big concern, of course.

"What is she thinking these days?" Fuerida wondered aloud.

"She has asked my sister Taana to room with her," Nathimeon said. "But she won't speak to me. When I went to the door, she called me an impostor and yelled at me to stay away. Dino tells me that she will come around, but you know how much that's worth."

"Doesn't she recognize you from having seen all those future timelines?" Mana asked.

"I don't know." He spoke as if his mind was elsewhere, not even looking at her, but exchanging glances with Fuerida.

"She has avoided the newsers," Kusomba noted. "That's not like her."

"Thermeon's desertion has really shaken her," Mana offered.

Again no one seemed to notice that she had spoken.

Fuerida laid her hand on Nathimeon's arm. "We should give her another try. It would be wonderful if we could bring her on board!"

"Katora won't want our future," Kusomba growled.

Mana sat in silence, but she wondered what Fuerida and Nathimeon could be thinking.

She did not accompany them to Katora's room, but Katora's shrieks carried all through the building. Most of it was unintelligible, though one phrase was repeated over and over.

"It's all your fault!"

When they gathered again for their evening meal, Morning Glory turned to Nathimeon and said, "I'm very sorry if my talking you into coming here has caused you pain."

Morning Glory had been joining them for meals and training races, though she spent nights at the Nexus with Orgmorgan.

Nathimeon shrugged his broad shoulders. "I know my mother. She's just lashing out because she's hurt and confused by my father's desertion."

Mana couldn't stop herself from saying, "But in your other timeline, Thermeon and Katora are still together, aren't they?"

Everyone gave her a look. Fuerida tittered.

"I don't know," Nathimeon said, and went back to his meal.

"When we determine the future in the Emperor Race," said Morning Glory, "we will bring all the timelines together."

Mana frowned. "But doesn't that mean that the winner must be an older rider, someone who exists in all the timelines to be gathered?"

"No," Morning Glory said, though her brow wrinkled, and she didn't seem entirely certain.

"Shouldn't we just worry about our own timeline?" Mana persisted. "Then a younger person could be emperor, and we wouldn't need to worry about going so Deep to gather all the timelines. It's moving all those histories that makes it so difficult, isn't it?"

Morning Glory shook her head. "Mana, a galactic empire always requires deep-level fusion. Otherwise interplanetary voyages and messages would disperse along countless random timelines."

"Oh. But you're talking about keeping a single timeline going into the future. Not about gathering timelines from the past."

"Yes. The past isn't important."

"Then a young person could be emperor."

Morning Glory looked mystified. "That's what I said."

Mana saw everyone's heads turn toward the doorway. Attequol and Eria had entered the cafeteria.

Kusomba's eyes slid toward Mana. "Better to leave the ancient ones to each other."

Mana said nothing, and tried to keep her face from revealing anything, but she couldn't help thinking that Attequol and Eria were not from the same era. Eria had been born in the Seventy-seventh Millennium, but with all her intergalactic travels in deep-level time-contraction, she probably wasn't nearly as old as her birthday suggested. As for Attequol, traveling about through time —why hadn't Mana thought to ask him how time tourism worked —could he really be said to have an age? Probably Hube and Raolin, who avoided deep-level travel of any kind, were the oldest humans.

While these thoughts tumbled by, Mana watched Attequol and Eria stand in line for their dinner, then wander back to seat themselves at a nearby table. He did not touch her the way he had touched Mana. She talked and gesticulated the whole time, probably about Thermeon. Attequol was sitting facing Mana. He smiled at her, and beckoned with a finger.

She fixed her eyes on the plate in front of her.

Moments later, a soft whooshing sound followed by an intake of breath from people on every side made her head jerk back up.

Thermeon stood framed in the doorway.

"My goddess-star!" he whispered.

"Stay away from me!" screeched Eria.

Wearing his usual gorgeous gold-trimmed white tunic, his mane fluffed out, his tail undulating behind him, Thermeon strode toward the table where Eria and Attequol sat. "Why do you test me, my love?"

"Stop calling me names! Go away!"

Thermeon looked at Attequol. "Why do you attempt to keep my goddess from me?"

Running a finger over one of the spiralling tattoos on his cheek,

Attequol studied him. "Why do you think that I am in any way concerned with you?"

"You think that you can keep my goddess for yourself, but you do not understand love! You understand only power and possession! What coercion have you used to make my goddess disavow our love?"

Attequol seemed at a loss for words.

Eria tossed her wild red hair. "I have never allowed any man to dominate me! Not him, and not you! Certainly not you!" She clenched her small fists.

Morning Glory rose and hurried over. She laid a hand on Thermeon's sleeve. "Brother, this is not the way to woo a woman. You must be gentle."

"I am gentle!" He grinned, fangs winking in the lamplight.

"You must be patient."

"I am very patient! I have waited for nearly seven thousand years for her to fulfill the promise she made to me."

"You must take thought before you allow your passion to do what cannot be undone. Before you unleash your dragon-spirit, you must carefully consider what has gone before. How many times have you been mistaken about the human form your goddess-star would take?"

"Well...." For a moment he lowered his eyelids with a sheepish expression. "But I am not mistaken now! I feel the glow of her deep-level starry spirit! She alone pursues glories of the unchanging world, feigning no interest in the affairs of mortal realms!"

"Yet, if she were truly your goddess-star, would she not welcome your love?"

Thermeon pointed a clawed finger at Attequol. "I fear this cruel sun has snared her with his burning rays. Perhaps he has threatened to immolate her children!"

Morning Glory tightened her grip on his sleeve. "I do not think so."

"He still festers from the rejection of Ul!" Thermeon gnashed his fangs. "The sight of lovers arouses his bitterness and envy!"

"No!" Morning Glory cried. "Come outside and let the coolness of the night and the glitter of the true stars calm your agitation. It would be wrong for you to give way to anger that could harm innocent people."

"Well...." He allowed her to pull him away. When they had vanished through the doorway, Mana heard sighs of relief.

Fuerida tittered. "I remember when he was pursuing the Code Empress with the same conviction. His misguided passion has started most of the major wars of the past several millennia."

Her piercing voice rang through the stillness of the room. Eria rose from her table and stomped over. "You wear a sword—why don't you cut off his head?"

Fuerida laughed again, with an almost hysterical note. "He's my uncle. Besides, he doesn't mean any harm."

Eria rolled her eyes. "You would dare say that to the victims of his wars?"

Nathimeon rose and laid a hand on Eria's arm. "It's a passing fancy. He'll get over it."

She shook him away. "I want it over now!"

When no one answered, she swung around to glare at Attequol, who had remained seated at their table. "Why don't you put an end to him?"

Fuerida squeaked in alarm, and Nathimeon let out an inchoate bellow. Mana jumped to her feet. "Please! You don't know what you're asking!"

Still seated, Kusomba pointed a finger at Eria. "Why don't you just get over yourself."

Growling, Eria flung herself away from them and stomped from the room.

Attequol didn't follow her. When he saw Mana looking his way, he again motioned to her, and she again dropped her eyes to her untouched plate.

She could guess how Eria must feel, being pursued by a relentless, godlike being. At least Attequol remained in control of himself. And while Thermeon might allow the explosion of his lust to downlevel and unfuse unfortunate lovers, Attequol had only acquainted her with delights that she probably would never know again.

Perhaps her lot was even harder than Eria's.

While the preliminary races were being run in Lal, other sectors of the empire were choosing their champions according to a schedule that would allow all the riders to travel to Lal in time for the finals. Sector Three, Niom Sector, lay on the far side of the galaxy. The name of their champion reached the capital before Fuerida and Kusomba's race was run, and the newsers asked Mana, Baran, and Eria for their reactions to the success of Saku Fanweroug Leopasi in securing a position in the Final Sixteen Race. Mana had never heard of the woman. Attequol and Eria said they hadn't either.

Life at the stable continued to seethe. Thermeon mooned after Eria. If Morning Glory wasn't around to drag him away, Dino or Nathimeon took on the task. Katora remained sequestered in her room, allowing only Taana and occasionally Dino access. Nathimeon kept trying to talk to her, but without success. Attequol continued to invite Mana's company, and she resolutely ignored him, although the fantasies she endured each night involving his creeping into her bed grew unnerving. A third newser, a woman wearing pink and purple stripes, joined Red-and-Black and Green-and-Gold. In the city, Karali had loudly proclaimed her intention to root out the Holy Crusade. No more attacks occurred at the stable.

Mana felt weary and drained from her nightly struggles when the day for the fourth preliminary race dawned at last. Kusomba looked as if she had hardly slept either, her luminescent hair bedraggled, even her tail hanging listlessly. Fuerida was her usual bouncy, shrill-voiced self. Nathimeon kissed her and patted her butt as she leaped onto Shadow's back. Katora sat pinch-faced astride Virtuous and met no one's eyes. When the newsers approached, Virtuous bared her tusks and snaked out her neck to drive them back.

The official started the race with a flourish of his checkered flag. Virtuous charged into the lead with Shadow on her heels, the remainder of the field in a bunch behind them. They vanished into the first obstacle, and the waiting began.

Mana walked slowly across the infield behind Nathimeon, Aspo, Morning Glory and Orgmorgan, and they took their seats on the grandstand that had been placed for viewing the stretch of the track between the first and second intersections. Voices swelled around them as more spectators and vendors arrived. Orgmorgan got ice-covered, vapor-billowing mugs for himself and Morning Glory.

Clouds gathered overhead, and the distant grumble of thunder could be heard. Mana sat on her hands, because they kept wanting to search for the golden chain she hadn't worn for two tenthyears. She wondered if the splinter would give Fuerida luck. She wondered if she should strike up a conversation with Nathimeon, who was seated beside her, ask him about his latest attempt at Katora's room. Or would that just annoy him? Before she could decide, he turned to Aspo, who was on his other side, and said, "I think my little Fue will be able to take my mother."

"She seemed confident," Aspo said.

"Too confident!" bellowed Orgmorgan, who sat on the other side of Morning Glory from Mana.

"It was still wrong of you to bet against her," Morning Glory said.

"I calls 'em like I sees 'em."

"But you know that you're affecting the Total Configuration when you wager, even when you think! You should be thinking positive thoughts for our daughter."

"Bah! She's a grown-ass woman, Glory. She don't need coddlin' from us." He lifted the mug to his lips. When he lowered it again, icicles encrusted his beard.

Morning Glory tasted her drink. "These Tyle Cold Eagles have a bite!"

"Thass the eagle's beak."

The two of them seemed to sink into their own frozen universe, smiling at each other through the swirling vapor.

On Mana's other side, Aspo was saying, "How I met her? You recall the shallow-level tower that Thermeon attached to the palace when he was emperor?"

"He's mentioned it," came the low murmur of Nathimeon's voice.

"Well, by the Hundred-fifth Millennium, the thing was broken."

Aspo went into a long tale about adventures with Fuerida in the broken shallow-level tower. A profound restlessness crept over Mana. She tried to fight it by sitting as still as she could. She could almost feel Attequol sneaking up on her. Her discontent probably zinged right to him, and he was drawn like a bee to nectar. She was not going to turn her head, because she would only see him smiling and beckoning her.

She was not going to turn her head.

She was not—

A chorus of whoops erupted from the crowd. Two horses burst together from the first obstacle—they were Virtuous and Shadow. The two raced neck-and-neck around the end of the first turn and onto the backstretch, where the second obstacle enveloped them.

Minutes later, a second pair of horses appeared. One of them was Kusomba's silvery mare, Warlike Slime, the other a golden stallion with a silver mane and tail and a blaze on his forehead. His rider had a green face and a Luminary's hair. It took Mana a moment to remember Dino and Katora's daughter Dilora. Both women yelled and urged their horses on. Warlike Slime put her nose in front moments before the second obstacle swallowed them.

Other horses emerged, raced past, and vanished again. Mana and her friends waited until all fourteen had gone by. This early in the race, the field was still fairly close together. Later on, the leaders might emerge from one obstacle before the last horses emerged from the previous one.

They walked down the ramp from the grandstand and moved

across the infield grass toward the next viewing spot. Mana trailed behind the others, feeling alone and neglected. Morning Glory and Orgmorgan were a couple, and Aspo and Nathimeon were more interested in talking about Fuerida than in acknowledging Mana's existence.

With a whisper of steps, Attequol came alongside her. "Why don't you sit with me?"

Before Mana could gather herself to respond—quietly but firmly, she hoped—Orgmorgan turned back and yelled, "Hey, Stripes, you gonna join us for a few? What's next on our list, Glory?"

"The clouds look threatening," Morning Glory said, "so I thought maybe Xuptam Warm Velvets would be nice."

Orgmorgan glared at Attequol. "I'll order three."

"I would be pleased to join you," Attequol said.

They mounted the grandstand, and he sat between Mana and Morning Glory. Orgmorgan waved his hands at the alcoholic beverage vendor, his fingers frenetic.

"He is indicating that he would like three drinks from planet nine-sixty," Attequol told Mana.

She felt like an ignoramus. Every child was supposed to learn the planetary order, but without an internal, her memory of it was very hazy. She realized with a start that Orgmorgan, as a pilot, no doubt knew not only the numbers of all three thousand plus imperial worlds, but also their locations in the galaxy.

Attequol probably knew them too.

The vendor gestured back at Orgmorgan. It seemed that he didn't have their beverage in his cart, and he had to send a note back to his main tent. The note traveled along a continuously moving wire that had been strung high above the track, and sometime later, a basket containing the three drinks returned via the same wire.

The Warm Velvets looked like black oil with a fuzz of mold, and Mana was glad she hadn't been asked to join the drinkers.

"Y'know," said Orgmorgan, raising his glass, "I find that most mindseas can't hold their liquor. You find that too, Stripes?"

Attequol shook his head. "I wouldn't know."

"You don't drink enough. Did I ever tell you 'bout the time I drank Fang-face under the table?"

"I have not heard that story," said Attequol.

Fang-face was Orgmorgan's name for Thermeon. He launched into the tale.

"And then he tried to tell me that his mind was perfectly clear," Orgmorgan concluded, "only the words got cut off when he fell down and rolled across the floor. Hah! So much for mindseas claimin' they never get drunk."

"I have also heard the claim that they are never unconscious," Attequol said. He proceeded to tell a tale about Horl.

On Mana's other side, Aspo was recounting a sequel to his shallow-tower story that involved murders on the planet Medne. He and Nathimeon drank dwi juices and crunched bamboo chips.

Clumps of people to their right and to their left, above them and below them on the grandstand were jabbering and munching as well, filling the air with sounds like a flock of twittering birds. Mana felt as if she sat in the silent center of the universe, with all of creation spinning about her, yet separated from her by some invisible wall.

Attequol tapped her arm and handed her a fruit mashup in a crystal goblet. "You need sustenance."

Her fingers closed around the goblet's cool stem, and she sat helplessly staring at the pink foam inside it. She needed to do something to get out of her rut. She had to find someone to love. Someone who was just an ordinary person like herself. She needed the sustenance of human companionship. For years she had told herself that she needed only Ting, but she had been lying. She craved the touch of her own kind.

Attequol was not her own kind, and he knew that as well as she did. From now on, she promised herself, she would meet every new person with special consideration, as if they might be the one. There were innumerable humans in the universe, especially if you considered all of the alternate timelines, so it was a certainty that one of them would fit with her.

Maybe one of the champions from the sectors.

Unfortunately, any ordinary person would be frightened off if Attequol was shadowing her. She had to firmly tell him, sometime when they were alone, to stop it. She risked a sideways glance.

Attequol met her eyes and smiled.

She tore her eyes away. "Did you lie about not knowing that woman who won Sector Three?"

"I have never heard her name before."

"But you think you know who she is?"

"It seems that no one in the empire knows her, which is strange. Perhaps she is a time tourist like myself."

"Oh! But who could she be?"

"Someone with an interest in soul-gems."

"But who? Before, you said Horl might attempt to return to our timeline."

"Yes. But I do not imagine he would appear as a woman. More likely this tourist was once a mindsea-empress who forged soul-gems."

"Empress Besi or Empress Quokisa?"

"I am not familiar with their histories."

"You aren't? My history classes made Besi seem very kind and gentle. Katora claimed that she patterned herself after Besi, even though her temperament is entirely different. Quokisa was a rapacious thief, so maybe the Sector Three champion is her."

"There, you have solved the mystery!" Mana heard the smile in his voice, though she kept herself from looking at him.

"Ain't never seen Quokisa," Orgmorgan said. "But I found notes from her at the Planet Hunters Club."

"What sort of notes?" Mana asked.

"Why, 'structions for mixin' her favorite drink, of course!"

Mana made a disgusted face, and he guffawed.

"There was a note from your son there too," Orgmorgan said.

Mana assumed he was talking about Aturon, but Attequol made no comment. History celebrated Attequol as the most successful conqueror in all of human history, but he'd had two notable failures. One of them was Ulona. The other was his son. Aturon had been trained to succeed his father as emperor, but instead he had run away, a hundred thousand years ago, and he was still running. He'd explored galaxies beyond Andromeda and beyond them. Perhaps one day he'd return to his starting point, having made a circuit of the entire universe.

At least, that was how Mana had always pictured him. But if

Orgmorgan had really found a note wherever this Planet Hunters Club was—she'd never heard of it—then perhaps he hadn't gone so far, after all.

"Aturon would not take part in a spectacle such as this," Attequol said.

Mana bent her head and nibbled at her fruit mash. The sweetness dissolved on her tongue. It reminded her of sex.

There came a crackling, a thunder of hooves, and yells from the crowd. Katora and Fuerida rode from the second obstacle, still neck-and-neck, their faces intent. Virtuous and Shadow were lathered in sweat. Only moments later, Kusomba and Warlike emerged to give them chase. Mana cheered until she was hoarse. Dilora and her golden stallion came out several minutes behind her.

This time Mana's group didn't wait for the rest of the field to appear, but moved on toward the grandstand between the third and fourth intersections. Nathimeon and Aspo surged ahead on their long legs. Morning Glory and Orgmorgan held hands and discussed their next drink selection. Mana fell behind and thought about telling Attequol to stop following her, but before she could frame the words, Dino edged up on her left.

"How's the Chosen One doing today?"

"Please stop it," she replied.

Dino darted around to her right, squeezing himself between her and Attequol. "My granddaughter and I need to have a private conversation, if you wouldn't mind."

Attequol nodded and walked on after Morning Glory and Orgmorgan. Mana and Dino stood watching him go. Finally Dino turned to her and said, "You're the Chosen One in more ways than one, eh?"

"Please!"

"They say he conquered two thousand, two hundred, fourteen worlds before he took time off to woo Queen Lala, and that was a hundred thousand years ago. You may be one of only two girlfriends!"

"I'm not his girlfriend! He's just playing with me."

His red eyes might have contained a gleam of sympathy for a moment, but it quickly passed. "I've been trying to bring Katora around. I told her not to marry my father, but she didn't listen. They were never meant to be together, but it's not sinking in very quickly. Anyhow, that's why I never got back to you after you came to my room the other day. What did you want to tell me?"

Mana seethed. That had been over a tenthyear ago! "I was just wondering how long you've known who he was." She nodded toward the receding Attequol.

"Oh, I didn't recognize him. I'd never seen him before. So I knew nothing until Orgmorgan called out his name."

"I wish I'd heard that," Mana muttered.

"You did. You were sitting right there. 'Stripes' means 'Attequol' in pilot lingo."

She sighed. "I thought it was just one of Orgmorgan's stupid nicknames."

"Let's go wait for the riders." He started toward the distant grandstand, and she followed along.

"I feel conflicted today," Dino said. "On the one hand, I want my love to win, but I'm also hoping that Dilora will! She's such a perfect combination of myself and Katora, right down to her name!"

"I think you should forget about Katora," Mana said. "Why don't you find someone who loves you back?"

He paused and struck a pose, hand over his heart. "I am too loyal for desertion!" With his hair long, and his dazzling, ruby-trimmed white tunic and white pantaloons, he looked a lot like Thermeon.

"Sometimes I think you are just trying to outdo your father."

Dino heaved a sigh. "I believe that I know how Aturon felt," he said, staring after Attequol. "The galaxy wasn't big enough for both of them, so he left. And I'm sure the sense of it never occurred to old Stripes there. There were times when I hated my father, especially after I first realized that he didn't love us. Sure, he'd attack our foes if we were threatened, but it was for the pure love of battle! We were never important to him. Only his goddess-star and his eternal starry dominion are important. But after years of struggling with my hatred, I realized that I was only damaging myself. What was I going to do, start a war like Max? I decided that I might as well accept the little bit of love that he could give."

"Yes, I think that was a good decision." Mana wondered why he was baring his soul to her. He'd never talked this way before. "But you could find a lover who gives you more than just a little bit."

He smiled at her. "You know all about love, Mana?"

"I know very little, but I also know that it's infinitely easier to solve someone else's problems than your own."

"Let's go watch the race."

When they had climbed the ramp, Mana took her seat on the very end of the grandstand bench. Dino sat beside her, effectively screening her from Attequol. They ordered from vendors and waited. A few bursts of rain dashed down onto the grandstand roof.

Three horses exploded into view at once as three riders—Katora, Fuerida, and Kusomba—battled for the lead. Mana and Dino waved their arms and whooped.

Then they went on to the next viewing station on the final turn.

Kusomba was the first to appear from the fourth obstacle, her silver mare dark with sweat. Mana and Dino cheered her on—she was his granddaughter, after all—and her face set into a grim, but confident smile. Katora and Fuerida, still neck and neck, appeared a few minutes later.

Mana and Dino went on to the grandstand overlooking the finish line. People who hadn't bothered to walk all around the infield were already seated there. More streamed across the track to join them. Mana watched Reselona and a couple of her grandsons climbing a ramp. They were following behind Reselona's mother, Eadin, the stepmother who had caused much of Mana's childhood misery. Taking their seats in a clump, they called and gestured to the vendors. The blare of Eadin's voice carried to where Mana and Dino sat. Old, bad memories stirred. Dino seemed to understand, and clapped a hand on Mana's shoulder.

"I think they hate your boyfriend even more than they hate us," he said.

It was true. Eadin and those around her were directing glares toward the spot where Attequol sat between Morning Glory and Nathimeon. Mana's ire surged, and she pictured Reselona suing him for identity theft and getting slapped down by his god-powers. (Exactly how was a bit hazy.)

She shook the fantasy off. Dino was right. Hatred was a self-destructive habit.

As the late afternoon sun broke through clouds, Mana savored her third fruit mashup, and reflected that using food as a sex substitute probably wasn't a very good habit either. She wished she could forget about her shortcomings and concentrate on directing strengthening thoughts toward Kusomba. Morning Glory was right about even thoughts being part of the total configuration of the universe and having some connection to everything else that happened. Though only mindseas seemed able to see the shapes of the connections and to manipulate things to get their way.

Crack! A single horse and rider burst into view and raced down the homestretch. People strained forward as one to identify them. Mana's heart sank as she realized that the rider wasn't Kusomba.

Her face was green.

But the horse had a blaze. It wasn't Virtuous. After seconds of mental flailing, Mana realized that Dilora was about to secure the fourth position in the Final Sixteen Race. Dino was on his feet, whooping for his daughter. Orgmorgan let forth a series of bellows. He must have wagered on her victory.

When the golden stallion realized that he'd won, he pranced about, tossing his head and swishing his tail. His nostrils were are red as his rider's eyes, and all the veins stood up on his steaming hide. Dilora pulled back her cowl and tossed her glowing white hair. Sliding to the ground, she faced the newsers with a triumphant grin.

"I want to dedicate this race to my parents!" she cried. "To my father, who always believed in me and stood by me!" She inclined her head toward Dino, who had run down from the grandstand to congratulate her. "And to my mother, who didn't." With a quarter turn, she faced the track she'd just raced across. "She tossed me aside so that she could devote all of her attention to my brother Habel, and when that didn't work out, to my half-brother Nathimeon. So here's to you, Mother!"

She stared toward the haze that cloaked the final obstacle, her lips twitching into a smile when Katora and Fuerida appeared, their horses still racing neck-and-neck.

"I beat you, Mother!" Dilora screamed.

The two riders seemed to realize in the same instant that they weren't battling for the lead any more, that they would come in second and third, and the order didn't matter, because both of their names would go back into the box. Their horses faltered, showing their weariness, and Mana realized that if Kusomba came through the haze at that moment, she might race past the two of them.

But the moment passed, and no other horse appeared. Fuerida crossed the finish line a little ahead of Katora. Dismounting, she patted Shadow and smiled at the newsers.

"Dilora rode a clever race," she said as she smoothed back her golden hair. "She let us tire ourselves battling for the lead, and sneaked past in the labyrinthine ruins of the final obstacle."

Katora rode from the track without a word to anyone. Dino started after her, mounting Prog, who had been waiting at the far side of the track. Taana had rushed from the grandstand toward her mother, but she didn't have a horse. She stopped in the middle of the track, looking forlorn in her pale blue gown. Nathimeon walked out and hugged her.

Orgmorgan swept down upon Dilora with a pair of foaming mugs, and they toasted her victory.

No other horses had appeared.

People began to leave the grandstand. Eadin and her followers marched off. Mana watched Beteli, Polia, and a few other members of the late empress's immediate family, whom she hadn't noticed before, walk away. She waited.

After a long time, the fourth horse appeared. The rider was someone Mana didn't know. A fifth rider came, another one unknown to her. Finally Kusomba and Warlike galloped down the homestretch, finishing sixth.

Mana went down to give Warlike the apples she'd purchased. The mare's head drooped. Kusomba sobbed into Aspo's arms. "We got turned around in those stupid ruins! Oh, I've ruined everything!"

"No, you haven't," he told her. "You're part of a team, and it's the team that counts."

Unneeded, Mana left them and went back to her big, lonely room.

The Sector One champion was a man named Calomil Fnused Wupern. He was a Blue Coder, descended from Maxuas, the son of Thermeon and the Code Empress. The followers of Maxuas had separated themselves from the Red Coders, who prided themselves on being free from the infusion of Thermeon's genes.

The Sector Five champion was Quox Selped Sea-Shey, a daughter of Katora and Quintillion who had been spurned by her mother long before Dilora had suffered similar treatment.

Morning Glory's name had been drawn for the fifth local race. Beteli and Polia would ride in that race as well. Unfortunately for all of them, Thermeon's name also had been drawn.

There were no surprises. Even though he rode his personal horse, a pale gold stallion named Military Call, rather than Trat, Thermeon coasted to an easy victory after leading out of every obstacle. Still mounted, he made a speech, magnifying his voice in Mana's mind, and probably doing the same for everyone else in the grandstand whom he knew.

"I dedicate this race to my beloved goddess-star, the ineffable Eria Megtu Luv-Pet, who has pierced the skies of my mind with her eternal light! I dedicate every race to her, hoping that I may please her and coax her out of the mysterious occultation that she tests me with. If I should win the Emperor Race itself, I will throw the fruits of victory at her feet, or bequeath them to our first-born daughter or son, who will grow up wild and free on the shores of the universe by the ocean of the Deep. O my beloved, think of that person who is yet to be! How beautiful their spirit will shine! Think of them, and tarry no longer, but come to me and enfold me in the glorious light of your love!"

Mana didn't see Eria in the grandstand, but no matter where on Lal she was, Thermeon could make certain that she heard his speech.

Morning Glory finished second, and Beteli was third. Mana didn't wait for the stragglers to drag in, but she learned the next morning that Polia had finished last.

Everyone was grim when they met for their strategy session later that day—they had resumed meeting in Mana's unit, although she still spent nights alone there.

"I swear, I don't know which of your parents is worse," Fuerida grumbled at Nathimeon. "They behave as if the empire is a bauble for the amusement of whoever their favorite kid is at the moment."

Nathimeon nodded. "I'm afraid you're right."

"We have a very big problem," Kusomba agreed. "Who can beat him?" She looked across the room at Mana. "Can you?"

Mana shook her head.

Kusomba looked at Morning Glory, who was sitting beside Mana. "You've already shown us that you can't. I certainly can't. I won't even have a chance to try. Fuerida—" She turned her head to study the woman beside her. "You couldn't beat Dilora. Will you beat Thermeon?"

Fuerida scowled. "Maybe racing isn't my strongest facet. But Nathimeon will beat him!" She smiled up at the man beside her.

"Do you think you can beat your father?" Kusomba asked.

"I'll try," Nathimeon said.

"That's not enough. You have to succeed."

Nathimeon gazed over his steepled fingers with calm blue eyes. "What you must understand, is that my father becomes extremely violent if he feels something he loves is being threatened. At the moment, he's in love with a child who hasn't even been conceived yet, who he feels is entitled to become the next emperor. Trying to push against his dream will only make him push back harder. I think you can imagine how hard he'll push back if he thinks he might lose."

Mana saw again the violet bolt falling on the city and nodded.

"The only way for me to win," said Nathimeon, "is to convince him that he doesn't want his dream-child burdened by the cares of the galaxy, that he'd rather have me on the throne instead."

"Of course," Morning Glory murmured.

Aspo chuckled. "Good luck."

Mana wrinkled her brows. Hadn't Nathimeon told her that he had no interest in occupying the throne? Had he changed? Or were circumstances simply different now that it wasn't his mother, but Fuerida, who was pushing him? Still, he seemed the most likely member of their group to succeed, so it was a good thing he was accepting the challenge.

"There's another factor to consider." Kusomba glared at Mana. "What about the so-called Baran? Could he beat Thermeon? What does he plan to do if he wins? Did he tell you, Mana?"

Heat flooded her face. She clasped her hands and tried to think clearly. "He's just amusing himself observing our foibles. I told you before what he thinks of our plan to try forging a soul-gem during a horse race. He said we should forget splinters and forge a whole new soul-gem and we could access Deep Six if we just counted holes."

Frowns surrounded her.

"What sort of holes?" Nathimeon asked. "Was he talking Topology?"

"I suppose so. But it felt like his aim was more to laugh at us than to actually help."

"Fuerida and I will talk to him," Nathimeon said.

Mana nodded. She would feel even stupider if they learned something useful that she'd been too obtuse to grasp.

The days flew by. Morning Glory and Aspo were chosen for the sixth race. They would ride in a field that included Raolin, Hube, Eadin, and Beteli. From across the galaxy came news that Rondo Faar Won-Yeosh, one of the Six Sages of Mosalno, was champion of Sector Two. Mana had been schooled by the Six Sages of Mosalno, but she didn't recognize the name. One of her old teachers must have been replaced by this Rondo.

The identity of the champion of Sector Seven stunned her still more—it was her mother.

Mana's mother had come to Lal to help clean up after the glowworm crisis, but Mana had missed her because she'd been on the Plains of Possibility searching for Trat. But now they would meet for the first time in many years. Hopefully Puflet wouldn't be dragging any suitors around. Whenever she had visited Mana on Ulona, there had been at least two of them. Mana would relish a good, though long-delayed, heart-to-heart mother-daughter conversation. Perhaps Puflet would share her big room.

Of course, she would have assistants, and they'd probably be those men.

In the meantime, her room was growing cluttered with stuff that Nathimeon had gathered for his deep-level engineering discussions with Attequol. They'd brought in a table and set it between the two couches at the front of the room. Then there were various snacks to serve as patternistic elements—donuts to represent the holes, gumdrops for vertices, cross-eyed pies for edges, diamond cakes for surfaces, and dwi fruit for solids. Mana watched along with Fuerida, Aspo, and Kusomba as Attequol took Nathimeon through various exercises for identifying deep-level intrusions into home-level spacetime.

Attequol would stand there and say things like, "And where are the other event-dimensions?" or "Show me the next possibility," or, "Now slide an object-space," and Nathimeon would move the food around.

Mana couldn't follow any of it, but one day she looked at the donuts and cakes and pies lined up on the table and exclaimed, "That pattern reminds me of something," and Attequol smiled at her and said, "Then you understand."

The sixth race was run on a stormy day. Winds howled about the grandstands and whipped the finish line banner into a gray blur. Rain pelted down until the surface of the track oozed, and the field squished beneath hooves and feet.

Imperial citizens accustomed to their weatherdomes had no rain gear, but the riders found that their whaleskins shielded them well, and those who had no horses wore the generic stable robes, which could be hung on hooks once they got beneath a grandstand roof, and allowed to shed some of their excess moisture. Attequol seemed to have become part of their group, and though Mana tried to keep Nathimeon between him and her, she somehow ended up sitting between them. Orgmorgan sat on Attequol's other side. With a chuckle, he nudged Attequol's ribs. "Now, since she's racing, Glory'll insist that I toast her and think 'bout her the whole time. So you gotta help me, Stripes. How many drinks made from morning glories do you know of in the galaxy?"

After a pause, Attequol said, "There is the Morning Glory Soother, from Kono."

"Right you are!" Orgmorgan signaled the vendor. Kono must have been far down on the planetary list, because the finger-flicking went on for a while.

The official waved his soggy flag, and the horses were off. Morning Glory and Beteli led the field going into the first obstacle, and Mana and her friends moved on to the grandstand at end of the first turn, where Attequol and Orgmorgan decided on sparkling morning glory wine from Lukopa. The waiting for the field to emerge, as rain continued to drum against the roof, seemed interminable to Mana. At last, horses and riders came splattering out from the haze, Beteli's pale, red-maned Running well in the lead, followed by Morning Glory's Meith, with Eadin, Raolin, and Aspo in a group farther back, and the rest of the field scattered behind them.

The rain slowed to a drizzle as Mana and her companions walked along the backstretch. Orgmorgan and Attequol moved on to Zigmu Morning Glory Comfort. Nathimeon and Fuerida decided to join them.

"Kusomba, Mana, let us order them for you as well," Nathimeon said.

It was pathetic how Mana's nerves buzzed at this tiny bit of attention, how she nodded like a one-bit bioid. Using alcohol as a sex substitute was no doubt even worse than using food. On the other hand, refusing to join in would just thicken the invisible wall around her.

"What comfort!" she whispered sarcastically, under her breath, as she sipped the stinging greenish-yellow drink.

Perhaps the alcohol slowed the racing of her thoughts a bit, for the next thing she knew, a rider was galloping along the track in front of them. Mana blinked in surprise, because the rider was Hube on Baquer. He also seemed surprised to find himself in the lead, and looked back over his shoulder, but there was no one there.

Mana gasped as blue flames erupted from Baquer's ears. For a heart-pounding moment she thought that the Deep had followed the mare and her rider from the intersection. Then she noticed that the tall poles suspending the vendors' wire also sported blue flames. Though strange and beautiful, it was only a home-level phenomenon.

Baquer vanished again. Morning Glory emerged, closely followed by Raolin and Eadin. Aspo and Beteli must have fallen far back. After waiting for a little while without seeing them, Mana and her companions walked ahead to the next station.

It was time to sample Morning Glory Warmth from Hedoc. The blood-red drinks came in tall, fluted glasses. They did provide a bit of a rush to combat the chill of the damp afternoon, making Mana find the waiting somewhat more companionable.

"I still find this an odd method for choosing the next emperor," Attequol said.

"We have become a meritocracy of sorts," Nathimeon told him. "The races are a test of a rider's ability to bond and cooperate with deep-level beings and navigate deep-level landscapes—both very necessary skills."

"I see." Attequol's tone didn't suggest that he necessarily agreed.

"I thought," said Mana, "that the races were an ancient tradition."

"It may be so," Attequol said. "But they do not go back to the earliest years. We did not have so many horses then."

"But you had Eternal Trat, didn't you?"

"Yes. We had the white stallion and the black mare."

"But the black mare was too wild to ride, and ran back to the Plains. At least that's what I remember learning."

Attequol smiled at her. "You know the story of the white stallion? Where he came from?"

"Well, I thought he was just always...." She trailed off, feeling foolish.

"He came from Mars, a small world in the same system as

Earth. It was there that Kokkiro built the first steps to the Stairway of Ice. He rode the white stallion up the Stairway to lead mankind to the stars."

"You know that legend?"

"Yes. It is far older than the empire."

"Oh. But there's not much chance that something so long ago can be knowable, is there?"

His smile broadened. "Some day I will visit that time period. I think it is most fascinating!"

"How do you travel through time?"

He laughed, deep and mellow. "The center of time and space is everywhere and everywhen."

On her other side, Nathimeon said, "The Tenets of Patternistics tell us that there is nowhere but here and no time but now. Of course, actually working the First and Second Tenets is far from...."

The spatter of mud beneath hooves interrupted him. They all swung around to see. Raolin and Morning Glory galloped past, closely followed by Hube and Beteli. They waited for a few minutes for Aspo, but he didn't appear. They were just filing down the ramp when his white mare streaked past. Aspo looked relaxed, his cowl pushed back and his dark hair swirling.

At the next stop they all quaffed purple Overheated Morning Glories from Airrie. Mana excused herself to use the latrine, and Kusomba went with her.

"I don't think it's fair for him to participate in these races," Kusomba whispered. "If he can travel wherever in space and time he feels like." Her tail lashed.

"I agree," said Mana. "And, of course, he knows everything we're thinking, too."

"That's shit," Kusomba muttered.

"Our lives are just a game to him. He'll go off to some other place and time, and we won't even exist to him any more." Mana burst into tears.

"Woah," said Kusomba. "I thought you liked being his little sidekick."

"Not at all!" Mana wailed. "He tricked me! I never would have let him touch me if I'd known what he was!"

168

"Now, now." Kusomba gave her a clumsy hug. "Why don't we sit by ourselves when we go back up? We're entitled to a little girl talk."

Mana nodded her head and wiped her tears with the back of her hand.

They found a spot on the highest bench by the back wall of the grandstand, equally removed from the men and from Reselona and grandkids, who must have come to cheer for Eadin. When the riders appeared, Raolin and Hube were in front, despite their best efforts it seemed, for they both checked their horses and looked back for signs of pursuit. Minutes later, Eadin, Aspo, and Beteli came along in a bunch with two others. Morning Glory was nowhere to be seen.

"The lead keeps changing so much," Mana said. "I have the feeling the obstacles are very difficult."

"You're right," Kusomba said as they headed back to the grandstand that overlooked the start and finish. "The obstacles in these races are mad. And I think it's only going to get worse. I'm almost glad that I don't need to worry about them any more."

Again they sat at the back by themselves. It was a very long wait, and dark and somber clouds had gathered about the setting sun when the sound of hoofbeats roused the weary spectators. Elongated shadows swept across the ground ahead of two horses, one dark, and one pale. The pale horse surged ahead to win at the last moment. It was Aspo on Rational Shop. The second rider was Raolin. Sometime later, Eadin finished on her brown mare, Living. The fourth finisher was a man with glowing orange hair. Mana was surprised to recognize Inspector Sunfox. She hadn't known his legal name, which was Faxoe something. She decided that she must have seen him ride now and then over the years, but she hadn't paid any particular attention to him, and she hadn't known that he was a detective. His horse was a honey-colored stallion with flaxen mane and tail named Glacial.

Morning Glory appeared next. Meith charged down the track. He was only a half-length behind Glacial and closing fast when they crossed the finish line.

Aspo was making his speech for the newsers. "The obstacles were scary! First there was this thick forest of stone trees, and then a cemetery on a world so hot the land was steaming! After that we had to ride by an electric sea. The foam shocked you if it landed on your skin! After that we crossed a field with some sort of alien grass that was exhaling acid. It burned your eyes and lungs! But the last obstacle was the worst of all! An ocean of chaotic dimensions threatening to plunge you into its maelstroms! I finally just closed my eyes and let Rational take me home!" He patted the mare.

Mana hurried down to give an apple to Rational and another to Meith. Orgmorgan threw one arm around Morning Glory and handed her a lopsided glass with the other.

"Here ya go! Issa Mornin' Glory Tilt from Aarpux! We been drinkin' you all day!"

"T-t-thank you," Morning Glory whimpered. She drained the glass.

Raolin faced the newsers and said, "I withdraw from the competition so that my adopted son, Faxoe Coacace Aater, can have another chance."

He and Inspector Sunfox bowed to each other.

Morning Glory gasped. She must have realized how close she'd come to getting another chance herself. But would Raolin have withdrawn for her?

Eadin bustled up to the newsers and trumpeted, "I have every faith that these intelligent horses will help me to restore the glory that the empire knew during the reign of my late wonderful husband, Emperor Habel!" Then, with her family closing around her, she swept away, and Living wandered off across the field.

"I will always ride for justice and fair play," Inspector Sunfox told the newsers.

Hube had just galloped up on Baquer. He, Raolin, and Sunfox rode off slowly together.

Morning Glory and Orgmorgan congratulated Aspo, then headed for the Nexus.

Fuerida, Nathimeon, and Kusomba gathered around Aspo as he walked Rational from the track, hurling more questions about the obstacles.

Mana had been deserted again. She looked around. The sun had set, and someone had lighted lamps that hung from the overhang of the grandstand roof. Polia sat alone up there, waiting for her sister to finish. Suddenly Mana realized that she had forgotten about Attequol. He was coming across the track toward her.

She fled.

The Sector Four champion was one of Mana's mother's old suitors, Kael Biari Moot. The Sector Eight champion was Quixa Pyen Soam, Thermeon's most famous mindsea daughter. She had been born in the Hundred-second Millennium, during his reign. Longtime headmistress of the Mindsea Academy of Eltien on the planet Meru-Iola, she was famed for subjecting her students to a glowworm-free existence.

On Lal, Nathimeon's name had been drawn for the seventh qualifying race. Also in the field were Sunfox, Reselona, and Karali's major, Aidon Eotro Bociety.

The race fell on a cool and windy day. To Mana, it looked much simpler than Aspo's race had been; Nathimeon led the whole way and came in an easy winner. Sunfox finished fifth, and the major and Reselona were farther back.

After dismounting to give Fuerida a big hug, Nathimeon credited the team for his victory.

"Let's go to the Nexus and celebrate!" Fuerida chirped.

Orgmorgan and Morning Glory whooped their agreement. Attequol said to count him out, so Mana gladly agreed to come along, and Aspo and Kusomba did as well.

But once in the Nexus, under the visored gaze of minors bearing Karali's leopard-spotted plumes, traversing tunnels lit by news broadcasts praising the empress's latest charitable activities, Mana felt much less confident. They entered a nightspot and gathered around a silken black table beneath a black dome illuminated by tiny flying bioids in jewel colors and pulsing to complex rhythms of the newest musical mania. Aspo and Nathimeon continued their comparison of the obstacles they had encountered during their races.

"The ground was shaking, and rocks were falling on every side," Nathimeon said, waving long arms.

"Not as bad as my oceanic chaos, which came at me from more sides than that!"

"But my next one outdid any of yours," said Nathimeon. "The track enters this big yellow building, and inside, I swear, there were people like us sitting at tables in niches eating and drinking as they watched us race by."

Orgmorgan lifted his mug. "If I get one of those in my race, Glory, I think I'll stop off for a few!"

"The last obstacle was a sheet of ice," Nathimeon told. "Sparks crackled under Transcendent's hooves, and the jolts went right through my body."

"My poor baby," Fuerida said, running her hands up his arms to his neck. "*I'd* like to send some jolts through your body!"

Oozing into one another, they moved out onto a dance floor that expanded to accommodate them, and began to gyrate to the music.

Orgmorgan regarded them with a twinkle in his eyes as he finished his drink. He extended a furry hand to Morning Glory. "Let's show the younguns how it's done."

They too rose and began to dance.

Aspo and Kusomba looked at each other. They each gave Mana a brief, apologetic glance before joining the others.

Mana rose and went home.

The last sector champion to be announced was the champion of Lal's sector, Sector Six. She was Lelin Sposhoob Weapoa, matriarch of the Red Coders. Soon afterward came the final qualifying race for Lal's champions. It was almost a repeat of the fourth race—Fuerida and Katora emerged neck-and-neck after every obstacle and finally battled it out down the final stretch. No Dilora had gotten past to spoil it for them, and the sight of the empty space beyond the finish line sent both women into paroxysms. Fuerida's piercing entreaties to Shadow to run faster and Katora's blaring commands to Fuerida to give way rose above the thunderous hoofbeats, until, with a final lunge, Shadow put his nose in front as they crossed the finish line.

Mana and her friends whooped and leaped up and down before charging down the ramp to congratulate the victor. Katora rode off in a huff.

Orgmorgan and Dino finished third and fourth, but only first counted in this last preliminary race—unless any of Lal's champions dropped out. Then the second and third finishers in the eighth race, who had been deprived of the second chance they would have had in earlier races, would be first in line as replacements.

When her friends decided on another celebration in the Nexus, Mana said she had a headache and went to her room. She showered and dried and combed her long, straight white hair in front of the mirror, picturing Katora trying to convince Dilora to give up her championship. The imagined scene made her dissolve in a fit of giggles.

A pounding on her door made her drop the comb.

"Mana? Are you in there?" It was Katora's voice. "I need to talk to you!"

Cursing, Mana pulled a black robe from its hook and threw it on. Before she could reach the outer door, Katora sailed in, almost crashing into the table covered with stale snacks. She wore a pale green scarf tunic and pantaloons.

"What is this mess? You live like a pig, Mana! And you're still taking up room for ten, aren't you? That will change when the sector champions arrive."

Mana walked up to the side of the table across from her. "What do you want?"

Katora took a deep breath. "You've always known your place, Mana. You know that the final races are not for you! The stakes are very high, and the danger will be very great, perhaps lethal."

Mana smirked at her. "You've had your chance to rule the galaxy, Grandmother. You ruled through my father. You ruled in your own name for fifteen hundred years. Then you ruled through Pia. And what's the final result of all your great leadership? Karali and the Holy Crusade!"

"I never meant for her to be emperor! You know that! Progress was made under Pia, but we have to complete the transition." She rubbed her long, slender green hands together in a nervous and distracted manner.

"Transition to what?"

"If you haven't understood yet, then there's no sense in trying to explain it to you. You need to drop out, Mana!"

"I'm sorry, but I'm part of a team. If you can convince my team that you should ride in the finals instead of me, then I will drop out. But not until then!"

Katora scowled. "What team."

"There's your son Nathimeon."

"He's not my son!"

"Your son Aspo."

A chin lift and nostril flare. "I have no son by that name."

"Why do you hate all your children?"

"I don't hate my children. I love my children! But what do you know? You've never had any, and most likely never will. I loved your father so much!" Her voice quivered.

"Then why did it all turn out so badly?"

"Your mother, Mana, was filled with hatred. She was a monster! She destroyed everything I had!" Katora's voice had become a wail.

Mana shook her head.

"Someday you will learn, to your sorrow, what your mother is." Katora heaved a deep, tremulous sigh, then seemed to gather herself. "Are there other members of your so-called team?"

"Fuerida, Morning Glory, and Kusomba."

"I'll talk to Morning Glory." Katora left, slamming the door behind her.

The following day, after the afternoon practice on the track and before dinner, Morning Glory came to Mana's room.

"Why did you tell Katora that you wanted my permission to drop out of the races?"

Mana hopped in annoyance. "I didn't say that! She demanded that I drop out, and I told her that I wouldn't unless the team agreed."

Morning Glory gave her a sad smile. "You should have just told her no. The team would never agree to your dropping out."

"Oh. But I won't be able to help in the final races. The competition is way beyond my level."

"Mana, can't you see that Katora is hurting the team by making you feel negatively about yourself?"

Mana blinked. "I thought she was being realistic."

Morning Glory's expression grew stern. "No. She was exerting her mindpowers to make you doubt yourself and thereby hurt our cause. Don't think she has lost her strength of will just because she can also play the poor, deserted wife. We need you on the team, Mana. You are essential! You were the first one to join with me in resolving to do something about the terrible danger that faces the empire!"

"And Nath," Mana sighed.

Morning Glory studied her, tilting her head a little. "I'm aware that you feel left out sometimes. But I thought the attention from Attequol would make it better."

"Why?" Mana heard the note of bitterness in her voice. "I want human companionship, and he's not human."

"It's wrong to talk about mindseas that way!"

"He's not just a mindsea. He's a god! You heard him say that he could just step through space and time. He shouldn't be here interfering in our human affairs."

"But he's a beneficent god, Mana," Morning Glory's voice was warm and soft. Her blue eyes glowed. "He saved my life when I was just a little girl. And I think there's some set of rules he's following, for how gods should interact with humans. I get the sense that he can only encourage and guide us, but that we must do the actual work ourselves. That's why he just gives hints about soul-gem engineering." She gestured at the chaos of the snack-laden table.

Mana shrugged.

"He knows you are essential to our hopes," Morning Glory went on. "You must resist Katora and other voices of pessimism. We have four riders with positions in the finals, and it takes four splinters to reforge the soul-gem. Each of you is an essential player. You must all employ all of your strength, ingenuity, and heart to make it to the Emperor Race. Katora was trying to injure your heart, Mana. Don't let her!"

Mana nodded. "I'll do my best. But—"

"No buts!"

Mana bit her lip and nodded again.

The arrival of the sector champions loomed. A beribboned archway had been erected near the tram station, festooned with planetary logos and crowned by golden letters spelling out "Welcome Sector Champions." The newsers had contacts in the Nexus, who were to launch colored flares when a champion was spotted.

Everyone watched the sky.

The first champion to arrive was the champion of Sector Six, the Red Coder champion, Lelin Sposhoob Weapoa. She stepped from the tram in flowing robes of crimson and gold, a golden crown sparkling on her black hair, with the deportment of an empress. Numerous attendants and functionaries, all clothed in red, surrounded her and escorted her to the blue unit they had prepared for her in the stable. The newsers tagged along shouting questions from the edges of this cloud of activity, only to be told that the champion would grant a news conference upon some later occasion.

When the horses came in for their feeding, Lelin called her white stallion, Oppressive Reif, and rode him to the stall that her assistants had prepared for him, the stall that had belonged to Pasola's horse.

In the afternoon, she exercised Oppressive Reif with a couple of local Coders who had horses.

In the midst of the training racing, another flare burst in the sky. It broke into filaments of gold and ultramarine, indicating Sector Seven. Mana's heart pounded. Her mother was coming. She left the track and rode Ting to the tram station to greet her.

Puflet Wuner Doom was a small, curvaceous woman, much shorter than Mana, with a silvery complexion inherited from her father, Thermeon. Her face was triangular and elfin, with an upturned nose and a pair of big blue eyes. She had a Luminary's hair, but whereas Mana's hair fell straight, hers fluffed out around her face in a downy mop. She had piloted her own ship to Lal, and emerged from the tram station in her powder blue flying suit, gold rings sparkling in the afternoon sun.

"Mother!" Mana cried, running to her.

"Mana!" she responded, giving her a hug.

"I was hoping you'd share my room," Mana said. "Do you have luggage? Assistants?"

"Pooh. I just brought myself. And this." She swung around a whaleskin carryall.

Thermeon and Dino galloped up and dismounted to hug Puflet.

"Would you like to go to our room now?" Mana asked.

"I've interrupted your practice." Puflet indicated Ting, Prog, and Military Call, who stood shoulder to shoulder eyeing them. "Why don't I call Les and join you for a little gallop? But first, could you take this to my room, Bro?" She tossed her carryall at Dino.

"Your wish is my command, Sis."

Green-and-Gold had been describing the scene into his instrument. Now he and the two local newsers, as well as newly arrived newsers from the sectors, crowded forward, babbling questions.

Puflet raised her own small hands to silence them. "I have one thing to say about the upcoming races. Someone from my family will win it all!"

"Who? Who?" cried the newsers, but she shook her head and walked off, flanked by Mana and Thermeon and their horses.

When the haze of the Plains lay before them, she called, and a mouse-gray mare with a chocolate mane and tail stepped out to join them. Her name was Mirrored Les.

"I've had to interrupt my hunt for slavers twice during the past half-century to solve your problems," she grumbled as they rode toward the track. "The first time, both of you were off in the Deep. I was rather surprised at you, Mana. You never seemed so adventurous before."

Feeling criticized, Mana smiled tightly.

"But if we can put someone on the throne who's really tough against slavery, I'd be satisfied. I think any member of the immediate family would do. Well almost. I can't believe Karali with her Holy Crusade against the Deep-blind." Puflet glared at Thermeon, as if it were his fault.

He threw up his hands. "I talked to her, and I believe she has seen the light. You know that souls are imprinted with the shape of their most focused moments, just as soul-gems. It seems that the rioting during the glowworm plague made a deep impression on her."

Puflet glared at Mana. "I can't believe that you called me in to deal with your problems. But no matter. I worked on independent glowworm strains for both the Bureau and the Palace, and I left some backdoors in place. In case you ever need to sneak into the palace for anything." She snickered.

Thermeon grinned as if he thought that an excellent idea.

The way they saw themselves as above the law wasn't much different from Katora's outlook. It made Mana think of the ancient saying about the rot of power.

Dino rejoined them as they reached the track. Their horses, familiar with the routine, broke into a gallop. Other groups of riders had gone ahead of them, but each group had its own aggregate mind-state that brought forth its own obstacles at the track's intersection points. Mana and her family had a pleasant ride that afternoon.

They passed through a quiet garden that brought to mind the garden Mana had seen on the day of her champion race. But this garden was vibrant, its flowers smiling in the sun.

They rode beside an ocean that cast great churning waves onto the sand. Voices seemed to grumble in the waves, and Mana thought of the voice she'd heard in the sea of the dancing crabs, but these were too low and indistinct to make out words.

They passed beside a glowing lake in a nighttime world. A great stillness surrounded the lake; only when they were nearly past did she realize that what had looked like an island actually was the carcass of a great beast. Then she identified the scent of asphalt and understood that danger lurked beneath the lake's placid surface.

They went on to visit a city of crystal in an underground world. Everything was beautiful, though muted by the dimness of the light.

Their final intersection took them past a gorgeous castle of amethyst that glowed and glittered as its crenelated towers played with the sun's rays.

After releasing their horses, they went into the stable cafeteria to dine together.

"I suppose you know that I have left Katora," Thermeon told Puflet over their meal.

"Not a moment too soon!" She stirred her carrot stew around with a fork and regarded it with less than enthusiasm.

"They don't have much meat here," Thermeon said. "I could ask the peasants to bring some dros, and we could roast them out on the field."

"That's all right," said Puflet. "It's better than slave gruel."

"I have left Katora," he resumed. "She had me fooled, for all those years, but when Nathimeon fell ill, and she went on about the throne and insisting that Nath should be made to fit it, my eyes were opened. Katora is not my goddess-star!"

"I could have told you that long ago."

His violet eyes slitted. "Then why didn't you?"

Puflet didn't give him the obvious answer—*when have you ever welcomed advice?*—but merely glared back at him.

His thoughts flowed on, and he smiled. "But at last I have found her—my true goddess!"

"Oh?"

"She is known to you as Eria Megtu Luv-Pet."

Puflet's pink lips formed a circle of surprise. "Quintillion's sister!"

"Yes, it is she!" His voice became dreamy. "How could I have overlooked her for all of these years? But in the Deep I saw her true fire! Her focused eyes were incandescent blue, and the long strands of her hair billowed like a starry corona! She flew before me with such wild grace and beauty, my heart was hammered into a state of pure and utter awe! Even here, in this home-level pile, her spirit outshines all others!"

Puflet exchanged looks with Mana and Dino.

"Yet she turns from me," Thermeon went on with a tone of incomprehension. "She tries to hide her light, though that is impossible. What have I done to merit such treatment? Does she wish to chastise me for all the years in which I neglected her? Is she angry at me because she blames me for her brother's demise?

She will not explain, and I suffer tortures of doubt and confusion!"

Puflet cleared her throat. "You're certain that this isn't another case of mistaken identity?"

"Impossible! She is the one! I recognize the spirit-voice I heard long ago in the Valley!"

"Before you told us that you recognized Katora's voice."

He made a dismissive gesture. "That's what she told me. But I should have known better, because she hadn't been born yet."

"Didn't she say that she cast her voice back through time?"

"Yes, but it is clear now that she lied! Eria is my goddess-star!"

"Still it seems strange that—"

Thermeon raised a hand to silence her. "Hark! She approaches!"

The Red Coder champion swept into the room with her large retinue. Among them, also wearing red, was Eria. Going into one of the corners of the quarter-disk-shaped room, they rearranged tables, then seated themselves. Lelin and Eria took the tip of the corner, with the others at tables ranged in a protective arc about them. Thermeon clenched his fists, digging his claws into the flesh of his palms. "See! She hides herself! She refuses to explain anything!" He whirled toward Puflet with his white mane frothing. "You have met her. Will you talk to her. Learn the reason for this cruel behavior, and tell me what I must do to make her relent?"

"I'll talk to her," Puflet said.

Thermeon smiled.

Mana watched Lelin and Eria in animated conversation. They must have a lot in common with reference to Thermeon. When Thermeon had pursued the Code empress, mother of Maxuas, she must have been a close relative of Lelin, if not Lelin herself. (The Coders had always been mysterious about the identity of their empresses, and now of course, they weren't permitted to call their matriarch "empress.")

Thermeon sniffed the air. "They have brought their own home-grown meat and vegetables."

When they had finished eating, Mana and Puflet excused themselves. Leaving Thermeon still slavering over his goddess-star, and Dino keeping an eye on him, they went to Mana's room.

"What's all this?" Puflet asked when the table covered with snacks confronted them.

"Attequol has been lecturing us about deep-level engineering."

Puflet gave her a sharp look. "Attequol. As in the guy who founded the empire? That Attequol?"

"Yes," Mana said wearily. "He took the identity of someone named Baran Etro Geed, but Orgmorgan recognized him. And Thermeon."

Puflet fingered her lip. "Baran Etro Geed is one of the champions. We'll be riding against him!"

"Yes."

"So it seems that Morning Glory's call to forge a new soul-gem has been answered. But I don't think this is right! He's already had his age! If he wins the Emperor Race we'll be going backwards in history!"

The spark of rage that animated her features alarmed Mana. She stretched out a calming hand. "He doesn't intend to win, I'm sure. Or to forge a new soul-gem himself. He wants to show us how to do it. That's the reason for this." She gestured at the table.

Puflet snorted.

"What bothers me more, is that he's been following me around, sort of like Thermeon with Eria."

Puflet's eyes opened wide. "Attequol is courting you? He must want to beget another Aturon."

Mana shook her head. "He said he doesn't want a child. He said he just wanted a casual affair."

"A casual affair?" Puflet's voice became a hysterical squeak. "No, no, no! Mana, my dear, my poor child, the founder of the empire would not travel to our era for a casual affair! He has something grand in mind, something dear to his heart, and the only thing I can imagine would be to restore the empire to what it was in the beginning. Look, look, he's a powerful and subtle man, and he must be manipulating the mind-states of everyone around him, including yours—or maybe especially yours. Don't they call you the Chosen One? You must be a key to whatever is about to happen in imperial history."

She picked up a donut. "This is you, Mana. And this is me." She touched a diamond cake. "And these others are everyone else here. Hasn't he been showing you how patterns taken by ordinary matter can point to the Deep? Well, he's creating such a pattern with your minds, a pattern that will lead to the desired conclusion. We can't let that happen!"

A tear trickled down Mana's cheek. She felt more used than ever.

"When my father pursues Eria," Puflet said, "that's exactly what he's doing. No other thought or idea intrudes. But when Attequol does it, you can be sure that there's some political motive. He conquered the planets with systematic single-mindedness until he reached Lal, and then he courted Queen Lala because it was expedient for his plan to make Lal the imperial capital. He's not capable of romance, dear. Political power is everything to him."

Mana broke down and sobbed in her mother's arms.

The next sector champion to arrive was Rondo, Sage of Mosalno. Mana joined the crowd that greeted him at the tram station two mornings after her mother's arrival. She was delighted when she recognized the man accompanying Rondo as one of the sages she had known when she had attended school on Mosalno: Vica Miname Vifurt. After the sages had made their announcement of intentions for the newsers—Rondo would ride to remind the galaxy of the important role education played in opening up possibilities for imperial citizens—they came to Mana.

"Greetings, Mana," said Vica in his soft, dry voice. He had a long, lugubrious face. Sprung from the old aristocracy, he was black-skinned and blue-eyed like Hube, and his wispy gray hair suited his very self-effacing personality.

"It's so good to see you again!" Mana gushed.

With a sad smile, he introduced Rondo. "Rondo joined us this millennium. Zerelia is no longer with us. Rondo was the protege of Ir and his contemporaries."

Mana had forgotten, if she ever knew, who Ir was. She smiled and shook hands with Rondo, a short man with a pointy nose. He was very pale, with dark hair and eyes, and the kind of pinched in expression she she associated with too much study.

"Delighted to meet you," he said in an absent-minded way with a bioid-like smile.

"I was hoping that you could help us find a room," Vica said. "And stalls for our horses. Galaxy—that's Rondo's stallion—is used to exercising with Sexy." He spoke his mare's name very softly, as if embarrassed.

"Of course," Mana assured him. "Riders who have been eliminated and aren't assisting one of the eight champions of Lal have left the area, and their horses have not been allowed into their old stalls, so there is plenty of room for the horses from the other sectors. Why don't we choose your room first, and then you can call your horses and find stalls for them."

The two sages nodded. Mana started off, and they followed, one tall, the other short, their long ultramarine sage robes sweeping the grass, bags in hand. They declared themselves satisfied with one of the small rooms in the outer ring.

"Let us adjust ourselves and we will be out to call our horses in, say, an hour's time," Vica told her.

Mana left them. When she searched for them later, she might not have recognized them in their riding skins, except for the disparity in their heights. She joined them near the border to the Plains. They called, and after a few minutes, a honey-colored mare and a sand-colored stallion came trotting out and happily greeted them. Ting had been grazing on the field, and came over without needing to be called. They rode to the stable together.

Mana found stalls near Ting's for Sexy and Galaxy, and wrote their names on the doors with a piece of chalk. She brought the three horses an early feeding. She and the sages were lingering, watching the horses and chatting about the school, when steps pounded down the aisle.

Attequol appeared. "It seems that we will be neighbors!" he boomed. "Baran Etro Geed. I am delighted to make your acquaintance!" He extended his hand first to Vica, then to Rondo, and they murmured their names and accepted his handclasp.

Then it seemed to Mana that he went still for a long time, staring at Rondo, while continuing to grip his hand. Rondo winced. Attequol released him. He laughed. "Shall we ride our horses together this afternoon?"

"No, no," Rondo murmured. "The Lalian gravity has fatigued us. Perhaps on another day."

"Another day, then!" Attequol bowed, and the two sages returned the gesture. Then he walked on the way he had come.

Vica and Rondo stood as if frozen in place, Vica looking baffled, and Rondo utterly blank. At last Rondo seemed to return from his trance. In a low voice, he said, "No doubt he means well."

"What ... did he...." Mana faltered.

"He mind-spoke me," Rondo said.

"He's a mindsea?" Vica murmured.

"He is Attequol," said Rondo.

Vica's jaw dropped. "That man? I never pictured Attequol with blue hair."

"He's in disguise," Mana explained. "Though it seems like a lot of people recognize him."

"I did not recognize him," said Rondo. "But I think he took me for my original."

"Original?" Mana's heart sped. Who was he a copy of? Horl?

Both sages wore embarrassed expressions. Finally Rondo said, "When the Six Sages were led by Ir Wirarn Oine, they embarked upon a project to create a copy of Kokkiro, and I am the result. But, you understand, there were no memory-dumps or temporal retrievals, only an old gene spec file passed down from some long-forgotten era. And so I am a very poor copy. I have no mindpowers and no memories of what Kokkiro did or might do. I fear that I was a great disappointment to my six parents."

"No, not at all!" Vica protested.

Mana stared down at the little sage. "Oh." She felt sorry for him. Having people expect you to be Kokkiro must feel very much like it did when they expected you to be the Chosen One. "Are you really too tired to ride today?"

The sages looked at each other.

"We are tired," Vica said. "But riding should prove invigorating."

"He was tiring," Rondo said. "Merely looking at him was tiring." He looked at Mana. "You are not tiring."

She laughed.

When the horses had finished eating, they rode around the track together.

Two days later, the champion from Sector Five arrived. Quixa

Pyen Soam, Headmistress of the Mindsea Academy of Eltien, was a striking woman with her black skin, luminescent white hair, and violet eyes. She wore a violet-trimmed pink suit with a black-and-white checkered vest and a checkered flower in her lapel. Her sister Vedina, Headmistress of the Mindsea Academy of Lal, had returned to the stable with her to act as her assistant. Mana stepped forward to greet her along with Puflet, Dino, and Thermeon.

The afternoon meetings in Mana's room grew unwieldy. Since Puflet had arrived, Thermeon insisted on joining them, and Dino came along with him. Mana had invited the two sages to come as well, and they did, even though Attequol would be there. When Quixa arrived, Thermeon invited her and Vedina. The deep-level lessons had ended, as there was no room for the table with so many people present. It had been removed, and two more couches that had sat along the walls of the gathering room carried in. The four couches were arranged in a rectangle with gaps at opposite corners so that people could squeeze through.

Conversation was awkward. Mana would exchange glances with Morning Glory and Kusomba, knowing that they wanted to talk about how to outrace Thermeon and Attequol. Instead, they could only speak in vague terms about how the team spirit would bolster all of them. The first eight finishers in the Final Sixteen Race would go on to the next race, but there were nine of the final sixteen among them, so this talk had a false note.

"I'm certain that I won't be among the first eight finishers," said Rondo. "I don't have the drive or the focus of the rest of you. But if my riding helps people to remember the Six Sages of Mosalno, who were led so ably and so long by Ir Wirarn Oine, I will be content."

He and Vica always grew moist-eyed when speaking of this mentor, but no one else reacted to the name.

"I do not know of him," Attequol stated.

"He was born more than a millennium before Hube," Vica told. "He kept the light of knowledge burning throughout the Decadent Epoch, when Horl attempted to possess all of the secrets of Patternistics for himself."

"There are no secrets," said Attequol. "The universe willingly displays its treasures to anyone who looks."

This brought a little snort from Puflet, who was watching him with narrowed eyes.

"Eria was born long before Ir!" cried Thermeon. He could not keep his mind from his favorite topic for long. "Have you spoken to her, Puf? What is her excuse?"

Puflet shrugged. "She disclaims any resemblance to your goddess-star."

"But her spirit, it burns so!" His hands wove a feminine shape in the air. "How can she pretend to be other than what she is?"

They all sat silent for a couple heartbeats. Then Quixa spoke, her voice dry and her tone caustic. "Father, you are chasing your own reflection! Haven't I been telling you since the eve of the Code War that this goddess-star is a figment of your imagination?"

"No!" He tensed, his mane abristle, violet eyes flaring. "She is the most real thing in the universe! I felt her mind reach down to me from the stars. When I was most alone and most lost, she reached out to me. She promised to meet me with glorious fulfillment one day!"

"It's a day that never will come," Quixa said.

Mana saw Attequol's lips quirk as Quixa voiced his own opinion about the goddess-star. Quixa noticed his reaction as well. She turned to him. "The ultimate truth of the universe is that we are all alone. We are all struggling with phantasms created by our own minds. Is that not so?"

Thermeon swung around to direct his fury at Attequol, and Mana felt a surge of annoyance at Quixa. The last thing any sane person would want was for these two behemoths to go for each other's throats, but Quixa looked as if she relished provoking them. Mana hadn't met Quixa before, but the rumors of her cruelty to her students had prepared her for something like this.

"Yours is the solipsistic view," Attequol responded. "I do not hold with it. The wonders of our age spring from the fact that we are not alone. We recognize and bond with one another, and cooperate to envision and achieve goals that no one could reach alone."

"I concur!" Rondo cried, his voice sounding high-pitched and weak after Attequol's boom. "The solitary existence of a creature battling its environment is characteristic of a wild carnivore.

Human civilization arose when we looked at each other and recognized minds similar to our own behind the eyes of others."

Attequol smiled at him, as if their agreement was important to him, as if he still saw Rondo as Kokkiro.

Quixa flashed her fangs in a grimace. "The Third Tenet of Patternistics states that there is no one but you." She directed a challenging glower at Attequol.

"That can be understood in many ways," he said. "Just as the First and Second Tenets can be understood in many ways. We can take 'There is no time but now,' to mean that we are trapped eternally in one instant, that no other times exist, or we can use it to travel gloriously to many other moments. In the same way, we can understand 'There is no one but you' as trapping us within the isolated ruins of our own mind, or we can use it to recognize that we are part of a profusion of minds, all as real as our own."

"And we can subsume them," said Quixa.

Attequol blinked at her. "Or allow them to subsume us. But if we understand the Fourth Tenet: 'There is no volition, only affirmation,' we see that there is no choice. All minds simply are, and the lines we draw to distinguish 'me' from 'thou' are as ripples in water."

Quixa sat back on the couch between Vedina and Vica, seemingly taken aback. Then the gleam returned to her eyes. "But, still, my father will never find his goddess-star, will he?"

Thermeon's lip curled. "She is real!"

Attequol regarded him thoughtfully, eyelids half-lowered. "She may exist. But you constantly change her parameters. That is why you cannot find her."

"I do not change parameters! I seek the owner of the voice that called and said, 'Come to me!'"

"A deep-level voice?"

Thermeon nodded.

"A mind cast a thought to you, whether from that time or another. But the divisions between minds are as ripples of water. You can truthfully say only that the universe called to you."

"She was a woman!"

"Do you think this mind that cast this thought would remember doing so?"

"Yes."

"You think this mind loves you?"

"Yes."

"Then I do not think this mind would deny that she had called. You should eliminate anyone who does so from your search."

Thermeon clenched his fists.

"Katora told you that she was the one who called," Attequol continued. "You once believed that she was your goddess-star. Why did you change your mind?"

"She harps on thrones and other stupid home-level matters!"

"You changed your parameters, then."

"No. I always expected her to be a goddess."

"Yet you expected her to take mortal form."

"Yes."

"And have no mortal failings?"

Thermeon sat silent, nostrils pulsating.

"Do you have no mortal failings of your own?"

Thermeon lifted his chin. "Mortal politics are inconsequential matters that have never interested me."

"And yet you sat on the throne yourself for, how long—" Attequol glanced around the room. "A thousand years? Two thousand? Why did not not abdicate at once?"

Thermeon said nothing. The rasp of his fangs filled the room.

"The lines drawn between minds are ripples of water," Attequol said. "So think less about adding more and more requirements for your goddess-star to meet, and think rather about the choice of goddess-star that will be good for the most people. It seems to me that if you recognized Katora as your goddess-star despite her flaws, and that if she recognized your son as a wonderful young man despite any minor disappointments, everyone around you would be much happier."

"That's an excellent idea!" cried Morning Glory.

Others murmured their agreement.

Thermeon's gaze traveled around the room, and finally rested on Nathimeon. "If Katora were my goddess-star, she would love our son in his natural state. I will never love a woman who does not love our son!" He sprang to his feet and stalked from the room with lashing tail.

"Now someone just needs to get through to Katora," Morning Glory said.

Seven days before the Final Sixteen Race, the champion from Sector Five, Quox Selped Sea-Shey, arrived. She was Aspo's sister.

"She will want to join our group," he told them as they prepared to leave Mana's room to go out and meet her. "She is a sweet and gentle person who wishes good for all living creatures. But she is very shy and retiring. I think it would be wrong to confront her all at once with so many people, especially people who can be intimidating." He looked pointedly at Thermeon and Attequol. "Also, she hates her name, and prefers to be called by her nickname, Shell."

So only the members of their original group went out to meet Shell. Like Puflet, she had piloted herself to Lal, and emerged from the tram station in her flying suit. Her complexion was blue, her eyes a paler blue, and waves of lilac hair cascaded about her face. She came tromping along with her carryall slung over her shoulder, her gaze searching the field's distant horizon, when she became aware of people surging toward her. She stopped, a look of alarm on her face.

When the newsers blared their questions, she fixed her eyes on the ground and whispered, "I can't understand you. One at a time, please!"

Aspo pushed his way through them. "She will give you her racing philosophy at a later time."

Shell said, "Oh, if that's what they want, I can tell them now." She squared her shoulders and faced the newsers. "When people are kinder and less aggressive, more of them can fit in the same environment without degrading it, like more molecules of most substances fit in the same area when they're cooled down. So I am riding for cool minds."

"Cool minds!" echoed a newser. "You're the Cool Minds Champion?"

Shell murmured, "Um...." and Aspo motioned her to follow as he dove toward the stable.

Mana and the rest of the team closed in a protective curtain around Shell. When they were safe from the newsers inside the building, Mana introduced herself and said, "Would you like to room with me, Shell? I have a big unit, and there's just me and my mother, Puflet."

"Puflet?" From the look on Shell's face, Mana might have invited her to sleep on a bed of carnivorous fungus.

"Perhaps you'd like to share a room with me and Kusomba," said Aspo.

Kusomba introduced herself. "I'm your niece—Tami's daughter."

"Yes," said Shell. "Can we go there now?"

She and Aspo and Kusomba moved off, without even bothering with introductions to Morning Glory, Fuerida, or Nathimeon.

"I don't think molecules of *her* would fit into anything smaller than a medium-sized world-dome," Fuerida pealed.

"Maybe, if we introduce her to one new person a day...." said Mana.

Three days before the Final Sixteen Race, the Sector Four champion arrived. Kael Biari Moot, Puflet's one-time suitor, was now a prince consort on the planet Gilkay. He arrived with his wife, Princess Aobida, and Puflet's other two longtime suitors, Oakiza, a Coder, and Serpenlino, a son of Quintillion and grandson of Quixa.

Puflet rushed up, laughing, to hug all three men. As soon as Kael had made the requisite speech to the newsers, saying that he rode for "Safer glowworms and the understanding that mindpowers are a continuum rather than an either/or proposition," she invited them all to move into Mana's big unit with her, making Mana let out a gasp of surprise and annoyance.

"Thanks, but we'll find our own rooms," Kael responded.

He was Mana's favorite among the three suitors. He had never pursued her after Puflet's rejection.

The following day saw the arrival of the Sector One champion, the Blue Coder, Calomil Fnused Wupern, a bronze-skinned man with glowing blue hair and red eyes. He wore a stately blue robe with silver trim and brought a panoply of blue-clad attendants. The red-clad attendants of the Red Coder champion spilled across the grass to greet them.

Watching the action from a distance, Fuerida chirped, "It looks as if they're pairing off, all right. Coders believe in arranged matings, you know. And they also birth their young straight out of their bodies."

"We do that at my academy as well—men and women." Quixa added in her acerbic way, "It can be a very instructional experience."

It was two days before the Final Sixteen Race. Morning Glory had kept everyone abreast of news from the Nexus: Katora had been in the capital, trying unsuccessfully to get Baran disqualified for falsifying his identity before the race so that she could fill his spot. Reselona had defended him, and the court had refused to act with the necessary speed to help Katora, ruling that the question of identity should be kept separate from the mechanics of the Challenge. Now she began to insist that the Sector Three champion was not going to arrive in time, and that she, Katora, should fill *her* spot.

On the day before the race, a blue flag marked by a yellow sun flew from the officials' black-and-white pavilion to indicate that an announcement would be made at noon.

When Katora, contenders, and assistants had filed into the sweltering pavilion, an official spoke.

"If the Sector Three champion fails to arrive in time, her spot belongs to the person who came in second in the final Sector Three race."

"They won't be here either!" Katora argued.

"Then fifteen will race. However, I do not think this will be the case. Some time ago, we received a communication from the Sector Three champion telling us to expect her arrival at the last moment."

Katora stormed out, muttering, "I do my best to keep this empire intact for thousands of years, and this is the thanks I get!"

After their daily exercise on the track, Mana's extended group met in her unit for the last time before the final series of races—The Final Sixteen Race, the Final Eight Race, and the Emperor Race. Kael had joined them as well as Shell, so they now comprised eleven riders out of the final sixteen. They filled the four couches to overflowing. Fuerida sat on Nathimeon's lap, and Puflet sat on Serpenlino's lap. Shell sat on a bed, back in the shadows. Rondo sat on the floor.

"We have spoken of various goals," Morning Glory began. "But we all want the same thing. Tomorrow eleven of us will ride for a better future, a future free from the ugly shadows of hatred, slavery, and injustice. It is my hope that by remaining focused on our collective vision of the future we can avert the accelerating catastrophes that bad government will inevitably inflict upon an empire.

"The red, violet, and black soul-gem splinters have not yet appeared, and that is a disappointment. But somehow I still feel that they will appear, perhaps with the mysterious Sector Three champion. When we ride tomorrow, let us keep our minds and hearts firmly fixed on our quest to forge a new soul-gem in the last race. Let us ride as a team, not in competition with one another, but all of us striving to help those who are best suited—not by our own measure, but by the measure of the universe—to go on to the next races, and ultimately, to forge the soul-gem!"

The gathering murmured their agreement.

"You speak very well," Attequol said. "I begin to understand how you are creating a pattern of deep-level action."

"You have voiced the hopes of the future," said Rondo. "I am honored to take part in this endeavor."

"When we race, our true spirits can no longer be hidden," said Thermeon. "My goddess-star will emerge from her eclipse!"

Colorful pennants representing the eight sectors and the planet Lal snapped in the wind. Members of the public crowded the grandstand, vendors swarming up and down the ramps to serve them. Fifteen horses fidgeted and stamped behind the starting line. Katora sat astride Virtuous by the outer edge of the track.

"She's not coming!" Katora shouted. "I will take part in this race!"

The race official perched on the black-and-white checkered podium waved her back.

A piercing whinny floated from afar. Katora and the fifteen riders and the spectators and vendors all strained to see. Two horses swept down from the direction of the Plains, one black, the other white. A group of peasant workers who had gathered along the rail to watch the start of the race babbled excitedly. Mana, as winner of the first qualifying race, was positioned nearest to the rail.

"It's a sign! A timeweaving!" she heard them say. "The white stallion and the black mare pointin' to big changes on the way!"

Only the black mare had a rider. The skinny, angular woman wore a bright orange whaleskin mottled with black, and a white fur around her neck. Her streaming dark hair had a greenish tint. As she approached, the horses on the track lifted their heads and whinnied. The black mare whinnied back at them, sharp and high.

The white stallion whinnied, thunderous and deep. His tail, held high, swirled like a mist plume behind him. Mana recognized Trat.

The black mare pushed past Virtuous, who meekly gave way.

"Who are you?" Katora demanded.

"The champion of Sector Three," the woman replied. Golden eyes shone from her square-jawed coppery face. She wore a sword on either hip. One had a blazing violet gem for its pommel, the other a deep crimson gem. Mana heard Fuerida's envious gasp.

"And these are 'Hush' and 'Rush,'" the woman said, touching the swords.

The black mare pranced and bared her tusks, and the other horses lowered their heads as if to pay her homage. Trat cavorted behind the mare. He seemed eager to take part in the race. As none but the empress was supposed to ride him, and the empress was not permitted at the track until the last race, there was no one to take him in hand. The golden-eyed woman guided the black mare toward her place in the lineup between Rondo and Kael, but Galaxy and Kael's chestnut stallion, Ghostly, shied away from her.

"Remove your fur!" the official blared from his podium.

As the woman unwound the fur from her neck, it wriggled and flung out a triangular head with two black eyes and a pointy black nose.

Laughing, Morning Glory ran out from the grandstand. "Let me take him!"

The woman leaned down to pass the white fox into her hands.

"Stealth Shadow!" Morning Glory called her. "I hoped it would be you!" She paused to stroke the black mare's nose, then hurried back across the track, the fox struggling free of her grasp and climbing up her arm.

When she reached the rail, Mana leaned down from Ting and whispered to her, "Is she Quokisa?"

Morning Glory allowed the white fox to drape itself around her neck. "Yes."

"And that black mare—she's Trat's first mate, the grandmother of our horses?"

"Yes. Her name is Ahaha. She comes back to us every now and then, though she prefers her freedom."

"Riders, take your positions!" shouted the official, and Morning

Glory ran back to her seat.

Mana straightened, patted Ting's neck, and looked down the row of riders. Attequol sat beside her on his dark brown, foamy-maned stallion. He smiled when her eyes met his, and she forced her gaze past to Eria and Serious Quiav, Dilora and her golden stallion, and Thermeon on his paler gold stallion. Beyond Thermeon was Aspo on his white mare, Nathimeon on his mocha-colored mare, and Fuerida on her silver-maned black stallion. Then came the sector champions: Calomil on a pale gold mare, Spacious Quoya, Rondo on Galaxy, Quokisa on Ahaha, Kael on Ghostly. Shell's horse was a honey-colored mare named Ruling Shore. Beside her, Lelin whispered Code mantras to her white stallion. Then came Puflet on her gray mare, and finally Quixa on Inspirer of Fusion, a black mare sprinkled with white spots that made her resemble a starry sky.

The official whirled his flag, and the horses surged forward in a wave. Trat galloped beside them for a short ways; then, as they went into the turn, he crossed the outside of the track, which had no rail, and they left him behind.

Rondo's Galaxy had grabbed the early lead, with Dilora and Shell chasing him, followed by Puflet, Quokisa, and Calomil. Ting kept her nose right behind Spacious Quoya's rippling tail, running easily.

The first intersection enfolded the horses. They galloped across a desolate landscape beneath a night sky. The stars shone brightly. Peering ahead, Mana made out two globs of luminescent hair, her mother and Dilora. She wondered where Thermeon was, and Quixa, but she didn't look back.

A star brightened suddenly, drawing her gaze. As she watched, it grew into a fireball that cast snaky shadows of the galloping horses and of the dwarf trees growing alongside the track. The shadows leaped as the fireball swelled and streaked toward collision with the land. A blinding flash blotted everything from view. Moments later a deafening boom blasted them, and the land rocked beneath Ting's hooves. A wave of heat turned the sky into an oven. The dwarf trees burned.

Gripping tight to Ting's mane, Mana cried, "Steady, girl! Steady, girl!" though she couldn't hear her own voice for the ringing in her ears.

Her wonderful mare galloped on, her shoulders and neck streaming with sweat. But Calomil's mare pulled away, and all at once another rider shot past both of them. Her hair flickered red-orange in the firelight. Mana recognized Eria. Serious Quiav left Mana and Calomil behind, then overtook the two patches of luminescent hair on the track ahead of them.

Mana was about to urge Ting to run faster when they surged past Shell, and she realized that Ting was working hard enough; there was no sense in exhausting her this early in the race. She tried to radiate encouragement to Shell as she went by; they were teammates, after all. Then she patted Ting's steamy neck and cried, "Good girl! That's the way!" wondering if the mare could hear her.

They left the intersection, and Lal's sun drenched them with its light, though Mana's ears continued to ring and afterimages of the fireball danced before her eyes. Disturbed by her inability to hear who might be about to overtake her, she risked a glance over her shoulder and saw that Fuerida and Attequol had passed Shell and were racing side by side a couple of lengths back. Attequol smiled at her. She faced forward again.

The grandstand with its silently screaming spectators swept past, and the horses plunged into the next intersection. The track ran through the center of a deep, rocky crevasse beneath a purple sky washing into turquoise where a sun lurked behind the horizon. Cold air soothed Mana's sweating face. Mist poured from the horses and gathered over the track in an ethereal white river that swirled and eddied around the churning hooves. Ting seemed to like her surroundings, and increased her pace. As the turquoise tint in the sky gradually paled to blue-green, then to apricot, Mana passed Rondo, Quokisa, and Calomil. She had just come alongside Dilora when the intersection ended.

Another grandstand hurled its cacophony over the track. Mana smiled because she could hear it. Lal's sun was lower in the sky.

Still neck-and-neck, Ting and Dilora's golden stallion carried their riders into the next intersection. Darkness and silence surrounded them.

"No you don't!" Dilora cried, her voice suddenly sounding lightyears away.

"Steady, girl," Mana soothed Ting.

She couldn't see the track, and Ting's hoofbeats sounded faint and distant, as if her body had been grotesquely elongated. The image disturbed Mana, but she could see nothing. Even when she held a hand up to her hair, which usually made it stand out in its luminescence, she caught only the ghost of a hand shape.

But there was no time to dwell on the eerie sensations. Dilora's far-off voice was urging her stallion to pull ahead. Mana concentrated on keeping Ting going straight and steady. A faint and tiny glow ahead became Puflet's downy mop of hair. Silently, their horses bore them past her. Then Dilora's stallion seemed to tire. Her voice and the faint glow of her hair fell behind. Mana sailed through utter darkness.

Home-level exploded over her with its noise and light. Ting seemed to be running all alone. Had other riders passed them in the void of the last obstacle? A rider without glowing hair would have been silent and invisible. Mana looked at the grandstand and thought how nice it would be if her teammates waved flags to tell her about the riders who had passed them before her. That wouldn't be illegal, would it? She should have studied the rules posted in the officials' pavilion more carefully. Maybe then she would also know why the officials said nothing to the riders who carried their swords onto the track, but had objected to Quokisa's fox.

The next intersection transformed the track into a switchback trail descending the steep and jumbled rocky side of an abyss beneath a dull gray sky that held no hint of day or night. The abyss itself blended into a deeper and deeper grayness before finally becoming utter blackness far below. On either side of the trail, smaller trails branched off, winding across smaller jumbles of stone, and even smaller trails branched off from them. Once, as Mana peered down at a small trail, she saw a small horse and rider racing along its zig-zags.

With a start, she realized that the rider was Eria, and the trail was the same trail she and Ting traversed, revealed as a branch of a larger trail by the distance. Mana shivered as the suggestion of an infinite regression brushed her mind. She dared not look up, for fear she would see a giant horse descending upon her.

Ting snorted once, to show her disapproval of this obstacle, and the echoes of her snort split into overtones and undertones that sounded in rich cascades all about them. But, despite her misgivings, the mare ran on as fast as the steep and bendy trail permitted, and no other horses caught her.

Once again they raced along the track beneath Lal's late afternoon sun, passed the screaming spectators and rounded the final turn, with no other horse in sight, either ahead or behind. They entered the final intersection.

Ting galloped along an immense rampart beneath a starless night sky, the myriad red-orange gleams of the enemy's campfires to the left, the shadowy bulk of the fortress on the right. Mana peered along the broad, straight top of the rampart. She thought she saw a shadowy horse and a rider with long hair that caught the firelight in its swirling strands.

Without warning, a section of the rampart just ahead exploded. Dirt and rocks dashed against them. Mana screamed and clutched Ting's neck as the mare reared with a squeal of pain. Hoofbeats came from behind, and Attequol was there. He laid a hand on Ting's neck, calming her.

"We're all right!" Mana cried. "Just frightened."

"We can still get through," he said, riding ahead. Virtue leaped down into the crater that had been formed by the explosion, then scrambled up the other side.

When another explosion sounded behind them, Ting snorted and followed the stallion across the crater.

"You're right," Mana told her. "Let's get out of this place as quickly as possible."

She no longer saw Eria ahead, but Virtue's pale tail rippled like a pennant in the darkness, and they followed until night became day and they were back on the track, racing toward the finish line. Spectators were shrieking and waving their arms. Virtue and Serious Quiav awaited at the end, but Mana saw no other finishers. She heard another horse gaining on Ting, but it didn't matter. They only needed to finish in the first eight. Looking over her shoulder, she saw Calomil on his pale gold mare. The pink nose drew even with Ting's flank as the finish line flashed toward them. Calomil grinned at Mana, and she felt his high spirits and his happiness just to be finishing, and she knew that he, like herself, didn't care which of them was in front. Spacious had been through the hot and cold and the explosions just like Ting, and her hide was flecked with dried sweat and dirt from the last obstacle, but she wasn't laboring.

Mana grinned back at Calomil. Then they had finished. Mana's team closed around her, leaping up and down. "You're third! You're third!"

Blue-clad Coders flocked to Calomil, telling him that he was fourth.

Mana slid down from her mare's sweaty back and took the apple she had asked Morning Glory to have ready. She gave the treat to Ting and hugged her. Through the babble of voices she heard Eria's angry rasp as she gave her victory speech.

"Freedom is my passion, and the empire would be a happier place if more people shared it. We all need to say 'No,' to tyrants, whether they try to cow us with threats or with blandishments, or with lies about how only they know what is best for us, or how they have found some secret truth that holds the keys to immortality and it only will be shared with us if we obey their every whim, or even when they claim they love us."

Galloping hooves could be heard. Mana looked back to see Puflet and Aspo racing toward the finish line, Thermeon right behind them. In quick succession, Nathimeon, Shell, Quokisa, and Dilora emerged from the haze of the final obstacle. With excited yells, the riders urged their horses to make one last great effort. Military Call pulled ahead of the others to finish fifth. Shell caught up with Aspo, and then brother and sister galloped side by side, clasping hands. They finish sixth and seventh. The black mare Ahaha whisked past Nathimeon and Puflet to secure the last position in the Final Eight Race for Quokisa.

Puflet gave a furious howl as she saw victory snatched away from her. She finished ninth, a length ahead of Nathimeon. Dilora's golden stallion, dark with sweat and wheezing loudly, struggled toward the finish line. Lelin's white stallion emerged from the haze, followed by Rondo and Kael together. Looking as if he had barely exerted himself, Galaxy breezed past Lelin and Dilora to finish eleventh. Rondo dismounted and congratulated the winners while the three behind him finished.

"You can hide no longer," Thermeon told Eria.

"Tyrant!" She remounted and fled, and he gave pursuit.

Orgmorgan trundled up to Quokisa and handed her a wicked looking chalice filled with something that effervesced. She threw back her head and bellowed out laughter.

"Where is Fuerida?" Nathimeon demanded. He stared toward the last intersection as if he thought he could ride back and search for her. That, of course, was impossible. The intersections never took you to the same place twice.

"She's been way behind since the third obstacle," Morning Glory told him.

Red-and-Black, Green-and-Gold, and Pink-and-Purple had converged on Mana. "Chosen One! Tell us about the race! What strategy did you use?"

"I trusted my wonderful horse to see me through," Mana said. "As well as the support of my teammates."

Leaving her as quickly as they had come, they joined some of the sector newsers around Aspo and Shell. "You are the children of Katora and Quintillion," one of the sector newsers announced importantly. "Does your victory over the son of Katora and Thermeon mean that Quintillion was a greater mindsea than Thermeon?"

The siblings looked bewildered. After a moment, Aspo said, "We were just lucky. Nathimeon is a superb rider. He probably would beat us nine times out of ten."

"Which of us wins has nothing to do with our fathers' mindpowers, anyway," murmured Shell. "It might show something about their relative ability to sire good riders, but there aren't enough data points in a single race. You would need to take all the children of Katora and Quintillion—"

"That's just us, I think," interjected Aspo.

"And race us against all of the children of Katora and Thermeon, many times, to...." Her voice trailed off, for the newsers had grown bored and gone on to confront Nathimeon with the same question.

"I don't care about the race," he said. "I'm concerned about Fuerida. I should have stayed beside her. Some of the obstacles were dangerous."

The newsers surged forward. "How dangerous?"

One eye on the track, he described the fireball and the void, the fractal trails into the abyss, and the rampart bombardment.

Kusomba handed Mana a brush, and she guided Ting to the side of the track and started to work some of the encrustations out of her hide, while the mare shut her eyes and rested one foot at a time. The murmur of voices continued behind them. When Lelin and Calomil had concluded their statements for the Coder newsers, they moved off, escorted by a single cloud of red and blue assistants. When they passed her, Calomil waved to Mana, and she waved back.

It was so rare for her to get any attention from a man that her pathetic heart flip-flopped, and her mind raced. It was stupid to imagine romance with a Coder, of course. Calomil probably had matings set up for him. Mana had been courted by a Coder before —her mother's former suitor, Oakiza—and he'd been free to choose his own partners, but Calomil was probably much more important and restricted. And then there was the Code religion. They seemed to feel there was something wrong with you—she supposed it was their upbringing—unless you believed what they believed. They'd nag you and nag you. Oakiza had done it in a nice way, but still....

It was very much like Thermeon and his goddess-star. He insisted that everyone believe that this voice he thought he'd heard one time when he was starving and light-headed from blood-loss signified that some woman was waiting to give him eternal love. If you doubted him, he took it as a personal attack.

Mana shook her head and continued to groom Ting as the twilight deepened around them. At least the Code religion supposedly benefited everyone. It told you that there was an awareness guiding human evolution, that messages had been inscribed inside your genes, and that if you took care to read the messages you would learn wonderful things and have the goddess's overmind embracing yours. No wonder Thermeon had thought, for a time, that the empress who personified this goddess was meant for him. He never realized how selfish his personal creed was. A goddess loving him wasn't exactly helpful to anyone else, was it?

She rather liked the idea Attequol had suggested, that he stop changing his mind about who the goddess was, and just pick one according to how much that choice would benefit others. She wondered if Nathimeon was having any luck in getting through to his mother, and whether he'd told her that accepting him as her son might get her back together with Thermeon.

She gave Ting a final pat and sent her off to graze on the field with her herd. Then she started across the track toward Nathimeon to ask him. He stood, back to her, staring intently down the home stretch. There came a sudden crackle, a flash of green, and Fuerida and Shadow appeared. Her face looked green in the splinter's glow. Nathimeon raised his arms and bellowed. "Fue! C'mon, girl!"

She grunted encouragement to Shadow, and they pounded the rest of the way home to Nathimeon. Fuerida dove from Shadow's back into his arms. They never noticed Mana walk by.

Everyone was gone now, even the newsers. Only the official remained on duty on his pedestal, and Vedina sat alone in the grandstand, waiting for her sister Quixa, the last of the sixteen to finish. It reminded Mana of the other night when Polia had waited for *her* sister.

"We Thermeon-spawn aren't completely selfish," Mana told herself. "We do have some sense of loyalty."

She walked up into the grandstand to wait with Vedina.

The next morning when Mana entered the cafeteria, she found the crowd considerably sparser than it had been the day before. Already some of the losing riders and their assistants had left for their homes, or at least the more civilized parts of Lal in the Nexus and beyond. Her mother and Quokisa had accompanied Morning Glory and Orgmorgan to their usual haunts the night before, and none of them had yet returned. Mana sat at a table with Nathimeon, Fuerida, and Kusomba. Aspo and Shell pulled up a second table so that they could sit close by without crowding. Everyone seemed subdued, hypnotized by the steam rising from their coffee cups.

"Well," Fuerida finally said. "I guess I will need to pass this on to someone." She fingered the golden chain that suspended the green splinter. Just watching her touch that chain made Mana's fingers itch. "So which of you three is going to take it?" Fuerida looked at Mana, Shell, and Aspo.

Mana shook her head.

Aspo and Shell remained silent. Finally, after several seconds, Shell spoke in a tiny voice. "If no one else wants it...."

Fuerida unclasped the chain from her neck. "Do you want me to help you get it on?"

"No, I think I can manage." Shell stretched out her hand, and Fuerida leaned across the table to place the gem in her palm. Mana expected it to slide through her fingers, but it didn't.

Shell gazed into the splinter as her nimble blue fingers turned it this way and that. "So many facets! This is really a wonderful artifact!"

"Yes," Fuerida choked. Tears ran down her face.

"I still love you, Fue!" Nathimeon put his arms around her. She turned toward him, and they kissed.

Mana clasped her hands together and imagined herself kissing Calomil.

A moment later, the Blue Coder champion walked into the cafeteria with a couple of his blue-tunicked assistants, and Mana hastily dropped her eyes to her coffee cup.

After breakfast, she roamed around the outer aisle of the building with a sponge, intending to clean off the names of horses who were no longer there. She wasn't sure which riders were gone for good, so, seeing some peasants cleaning a stall, she asked them if they knew.

"Stuffed-nose is gone," a woman told her.

Mana nodded. That would be Dilora.

"And the two magpies."

That would be Quixa and Vedina.

"And the three moons."

That would be Kael, Oakiza, and Serpenlino.

"The red empress and the two sages ain't gone."

"I see."

"Be quiet around Serious Quiav's stall. She be sleepin' there with her rider."

"They's hidin' from Silverlance," a second woman added.

"Silverlance?" Mana said. "That's Thermeon?"

The peasant woman pressed a finger to her lips. "Don't speak it! That's his bad name."

"His good name is Silverlance," said the first woman.

"Does he know that?"

All the peasants nodded.

"Do you know about his goddess-star?" Mana asked.

Again they nodded. "Galena is his goddess-star."

"Oh! Galena, who was Katora's friend before she became empress? The grandmother of your champion Miesa?"

"She's the only true spouse of Silverlance."

"Miesa be their grandson—his'n and hers."

"When he remembers what's his true name, he'll hear Galena callin' him from the spirit world."

"But his bad self don't want to die, so he don't hear her."

Mana soaked all this in, fingering her lip. When steps approached, she and the peasants looked up. Morning Glory and Quokisa came around the bend. They both wore flowing surcoats and pantaloons, Morning Glory's blue and Quokisa's orange. Quokisa wore her sword belts, and her fox as well.

"Good morning, everyone," Morning Glory called. "Have all of you met Stealth Shadow?"

The peasants all dipped their heads to Quokisa, and their spokeswoman mumbled, "'Tis an honor to meet the granddaughter of Queen Lala."

"Your grandpa is here," a second woman said.

"I know." Quokisa winked at Mana.

"The others are meeting us in your room," Morning Glory told Mana.

"Oh! Now?"

Morning Glory nodded. "I wanted to meet early before any of the later hangers-on drop by."

Mana guessed that she was referring to Attequol and Thermeon.

They bade farewell to the peasants, and turned down one of the corridors that led deeper into the building.

When they walked into her room, Mana found Nathimeon, Fuerida, Kusomba, Aspo, and Shell awaiting them.

When they were all seated, morning Glory said, "I wanted to bring Quokisa into our group, since she has found us two more of the splinters."

Quokisa grinned, indicating the gems on her swords. "Hush bears the violent splinter, and Rush bears the red. The last splinter is here too. The black one."

"Where?" everyone cried.

"I scented it during the race. One of the riders carried it, but hidden."

They all looked at each other.

"Could you tell who it was?" Morning Glory asked.

"It passed through each obstacle ahead of me. It left its scent-trail, but its rays were cloaked. I will sniff it out the next race."

"You're sure the one who has it will be in the next race?"

"Yes."

"That's one of eight people," Morning Glory said, her eyes passing over everyone in the room. They rested on Quokisa. "One of seven."

"And three of them are in this room!" Mana gasped. "But I don't have it."

Aspo and Shell shook their heads. "We don't have it!"

"That leaves Attequol, Eria, Thermeon, or ... Calomil," Mana choked.

"Attequol is not the carrier," Quokisa said. "He and I fell in together for a spell during the second obstacle, and exchanged some barbs." She smirked. "It was our first encounter."

"I know Eria doesn't have it," Morning Glory said. "Their father's spirit directed it to Quintillion and not to her. And my brother doesn't have it, because Quintillion was his contemporary. It must be with whomever Quintillion passed it on to." She looked at Aspo and Shell. "I think it could have been passed on without the recipient realizing it."

The siblings both started.

"That is so," Quokisa mused. The way her golden eyes played over the two offspring of Quintillion would have made Mana nervous. The siblings drew together protectively.

Mana addressed Morning Glory. "Didn't you tell us that the black splinter changed the person who carried it? Made them depressed and hopeless?"

"Yes."

Everyone was still looking at Aspo and Shell.

Shell swallowed. "Can you detect that splinter now?"

"The black splinter casts off swirls of memory," Quokisa said. "The scent of pines of an ancient forest, the cool refreshment of water from a fishing stream, the blood of the kill. These are its tracks. The memories pool in the downdraft of the Deep, but home-level noise dissipates them and renders them too faint to follow."

"But ... if we rode a training race together. That's still the Deep, isn't it? Could you tell then if we had this thing?"

"Yes."

Morning Glory clapped her hands. "Then we will all exercise our horses together this afternoon, and that will settle things."

Everyone nodded.

"After the fourth splinter has been tracked down, the Chosen One must be prepared to gather and meld them." The golden eyes fixed on Mana.

"Oh, but I'm not—"

"My instincts tell me that you are. You must carry at least one splinter in the Final Eight Race." Rising, Quokisa unbuckled one of her sword belts.

Mana recoiled into the couch back, a hand extended to ward her off. "I can't touch deep-level artifacts! I think maybe Shell is the Chosen One!"

"There's no evidence for that!" gasped Shell.

Quokisa laughed at them both. She held the sheathed sword out to Mana. "Belt and sheath are special weavings that embed the Deep intersection in home-level. They will comfortably hold the sword for you. When you venture into the Deep, you will gain power to wield the sword. If the carrier of the black splinter resists the disgorging of it, you must cleave it free."

"Cleave? Wouldn't that injure them?"

Silence surrounded Mana. Quokisa continued to stand before her, holding out the sword, her lips curled with amusement.

"Mana." Morning Glory's voice came softly, but firmly. "Remember the stakes we are riding for. It is almost guaranteed that not every rider in the last race will return. At this moment Karali is without doubt perfecting the deep-level weapon she will carry."

"Weapons are permissible?"

"It's our tradition," said Morning Glory.

"We are a mindsea empire," said Quokisa. "And a mindsea needs but a thought to arm in the Deep."

"So you see," said Morning Glory, "long ago challengers who were not mindseas argued that they must be allowed weapons to defend themselves if they rode against mindseas. So weapons have been allowed for many millennia. I don't know exactly how long."

"Since my time." Quokisa laid the sword across Mana's knees. Then she unbuckled her second sword belt and handed that sword to Aspo. "And Shell has the third splinter, and knows what to make of it, I believe, so you will all three be prepared for the next race. I myself will watch over you, also. But I do not think it would be fitting for me to take part in your Emperor Race. Then you must fend for yourselves."

The sword felt as heavy to Mana as a battleship. "If this is our tradition, why did the official disallow an innocent little fox?"

The fox lay draped around Quokisa's neck, beneath her hair, head and front paws dangling over one shoulder, tail and hind paws over the other. Hearing himself mentioned, he opened his black eyes and looked at Mana for a moment. Then he shut his eyes and went limp again.

"He made some of the horses nervous," Morning Glory said.

Mana stared at the gem on her sword. She had been given the crimson one. The intense, spidery rays emanating from it looked cruel. "I've never held a sword in my life. How can I fight with this thing?"

"You should have practiced swordplay with me and Nath," Fuerida said.

"But I can't even hold any of these deep-level weapons!"

"Better if you acquaint yourself with the sword's feel when we ride this afternoon," Quokisa said. "Your mind and your arm and hand will be different in the Deep."

"When you race," said Morning Glory, "focus on what you're riding for. Remember the team. Remember that we're trying to heal the empire, trying to end the corruption and injustice."

"Think of Pasola," Kusomba said. "And the thousands of others Karali has murdered. If that doesn't make you mad enough to kill, nothing will."

"Mad enough to kill," Mana murmured, half to herself. When Thermeon grew mad enough to kill, he unleashed destruction with a thoughtless spasm of mindpowers. She would need the same unthinking mind-state, because if she thought about hurting someone, even Karali, she'd never be able to do it.

"I know how you feel," Aspo said. "I've never struck a blow in anger either."

Quokisa snorted, as if she could hardly imagine how two such innocents could exist.

The group broke up. Mana sat for a long time staring at the crimson rays of the splinter. Finally she rose and went out to help the peasants feed the horses. All too soon it was time for their exercise. Mana went back to her room to don her riding skin, and reluctantly buckled the sword belt over it. She felt oafish, grotesque, with the sheathed sword banging against her ankle as she walked. Would she even be able to mount Ting?

Somehow, with her friends all waiting on their horses in the broad, curving aisle alongside the stalls, she managed, and they rode out to the track together. When they galloped into the first intersection they found themselves on a broad thoroughfare traversing green hills dotted by close-spaced rows of stone monoliths, all elaborately carved with interwoven designs that seemed to express personalities, though no element resembled anything human.

"Mana! Aspo!" Fuerida cried. "Unsheathe your swords and copy me!" She flew along the verge of the road, slicing off bits of the carvings.

"But aren't these some life-form's memorials for their dead?" Mana protested.

"Please do it," Morning Glory said.

Mana grabbed the sword's hilt and pulled. It slid free from the sheath as easily as water, and felt light in her hand as a shadow. She swung at the monoliths as she rode along, and chips of stone flew. It was like slicing jello. Aspo did the same, then shook his head with a bemused look.

"Be sure to sheathe your swords before you leave the intersection," Fuerida warned. "Or you'll drop them."

They obeyed.

In the next intersection, they were engulfed by choking clouds, and had nothing to fight, so they urged their horses on. The third intersection landed them on a path amongst sparkling sapphire ice formations. Mana didn't feel too bad about slicing them, and concentrated on aiming her swings to take off exactly the pieces she decided on beforehand. She almost forgot to sheathe her sword before the ice world dissolved. The last two intersections took them across flat landscapes, so again, there was nothing to practice on.

After releasing their horses, they walked back toward the stable, following a long, circuitous route to avoid the bustle of the tent city.

"I did not scent the black splinter," Quokisa said. "No one here carries it."

Mana tripped over the sword and almost fell. "Then, that means Calomil must have it!"

"Indeed."

"But why? How?"

"Well," said Morning Glory. "He comes from Wamatu, and that was Quintillion's homeworld."

"Oh."

"But it does seem odd," she went on. "Because he's too young to ever have met Quintillion."

"Perhaps he chanced upon the splinter and swallowed it," Quokisa suggested.

"Swallowed?" Mana cried. "You mean, like, for instance, it was inside a fish, and he ate the fish?"

Fuerida laughed.

"Perhaps," said Quokisa, narrowing her golden eyes.

"He won't cooperate with us," Morning Glory said. "As a Coder, his mission is to convert the galaxy to his religion. At least his only possible ally, the Red Coder, was eliminated. Three of you will be able to take him on."

Mana clutched her throat. "We'll have to ... kill him?"

"No one dies in the Deep," said Quokisa.

"You'll just change him so much he won't be able to return to home-level," Nathimeon explained.

"Like slicing him in half," Fuerida supplied.

Mana walked the rest of the way to her room in a daze. She unbuckled and tossed the hateful sword onto a couch, peeled off her riding skin and rinsed off in the shower, then pulled on a generic black robe and threw herself face-down on the bed to weep.

Morning Glory had never warned her that she needed to become a murderer to forge the soul-gem. She wasn't going to do it. She would drop out. She should have listened to Katora, as hateful as her grandmother was. She had no stomach for the role of Chosen One.

If she dropped out, Aspo and Shell would still attack Calomil. She jerked up her head. Should she warn him? But that would be betraying her friends. Her head dropped back.

Maybe Aspo and Shell wouldn't be able to do it either. They seemed like gentle people. Though they hadn't protested the idea. Or had they? Mana realized that she hadn't heard a word her companions had spoken after Fuerida had mentioned slicing Calomil in half.

The effort of trying to retrieve the moments hidden in that haze sent a knife thrust of pain through her skull. She clutched her forehead and moaned. What was the use of trying to make the empire a better place if you had to become evil in order to have the power to do anything?

"The rot of power," she moaned, rolling from side to side. "The rot of power."

How had she gotten herself into this situation? How could she get herself out? The crimson rays from the splinter pierced through the intervening furniture and her eyelids with their promise of mayhem. She saw Calomil riding up alongside her, his smile open and friendly, suspecting nothing; and the sword, seemingly of its own will, dragging her hand along as it swung to cut through his body.

Her tears became a torrent until at last she slipped into an exhausted sleep.

Mana dreamed that Calomil was riding alongside her. Grinning, he reached out to take her in his arms.

She woke with a start. "They're wrong!" she gasped. "He's too happy!"

"Who's wrong?" came a voice.

Mana sat up and saw her mother sitting on the bed across from hers, wearing the same generic black robe. "Oh. Morning Glory was trying to convince us that Calomil has the black splinter. But they're wrong. He's too happy. And that's that!"

Standing up, she pulled strands of hair back from her face.

"You look a mess," Puflet observed. "Your eyes are all puffy! Too much victory celebration? I had a few too many fire-dragons trying to drown my disappointment last night, but I reckon I look a big bit better than you."

"No celebration," Mana said. "I've been wrestling with moral dilemmas."

"That's not a recognized sport. That I know of." Puflet laughed.

Mana laughed too. She was just so happy to have solved the Calomil problem. She had to tell the team. What time was it? She glanced up at the skylight. "Have you seen the others? We're still having our afternoon meeting, aren't we?"

"I don't think so. I passed a bunch of them at the tram station. They were taking Thermeon into the city to try to reconcile him with Katora."

"Oh. Who was taking him?"

Puflet shrugged. "Morning Glory, Dino, Nath, Fue." Her brows drew down. "I can't believe they're stupid enough to actually fall for our glorious founder's suggestion that Thermeon should just arbitrarily decide that Katora's his goddess-star. I've heard him talk about his vision, and Katora has no resemblance to it! He was talking about a real goddess, someone with knowledge and power of deeper realities. Even if they do get back together, Katora will do something crass again, in a few years, and the crisis will repeat itself."

"I suppose," Mana murmured. "She isn't capable of loving an actual person. But—"

"Eria isn't his goddess-star either! But she could get the whole ordeal over with a lot faster if she just let him beget a few kids on her until he figured it out for himself."

"I don't think she's a mindsea," Mana said. "He could unfuse her."

"Oh, there's that." Puflet wrinkled her nose. "But he still has the right to pursue his dream, no matter how inconvenient it is for other people! I mean, as long as he doesn't actually restrict their freedom."

"Chasing Eria around comes pretty close to that."

"You'd think the stupid woman could find a way of setting him straight." Gripping hands behind her back, Puflet paced up and down along the aisle between the two rows of bunks. Reaching the bathroom door for the second time, she whirled around and stopped. "Oh, maybe I should try to talk some sense into him!"

"That's a good idea. Maybe you can get through."

Puflet resumed pacing. "I still say he has the right to pursue his goddess, whether or not it pleases Katora and their children. Everyone is responsible for their own happiness! You can't try to please the world!" She stopped in front of Mana's bed and looked at her. "So what dilemma have you been wrestling?"

"Morning Glory and Quokisa were trying to convince me that I would have to use that deep-level sword to kill Calomil during the next race. They have this idea that he must have the black soul-gem splinter—inside him, or something. But I realized that they're mistaken. I need to tell them."

Puflet snorted. "Good luck convincing them of anything. But cheers to you for seeing through whatever net of falsehood they wove. I want to puke every time one of these fusled celebrities from the past pokes their twistored nose into our history and starts telling us what to do! They've all had their chance! Morning Glory, Thermeon, Quokisa! And Attequol! What are we? A comedy act for their entertainment?"

Mana merely sighed. "Well, Morning Glory promised that her speech and her splinter would draw other splinters and people who had them or coveted them."

Puflet resumed her pacing, reminding Mana of Thermeon. "Hah! I could've laughed myself sick when Katora got shut out of the Final Sixteen Race! The twistored old witch thought she needed her hand in as well! That's the problem with this empire! Old mindseas never die, and young people never get a chance! Everything is old, old, old!"

"Quokisa said she wouldn't ride in the Emperor Race," Mana said.

Puflet whirled and glared toward the outer door. "She shouldn't be riding in any of our races!" A sudden smile spread over her face. "But the way she shut Katora out was mega-sweet!" She looked at Mana. "Did your lover Attequol tell you he was going to drop out at some point?"

"No. And I never wanted him for my lover! I told you he tricked me! I want the love of a man, not a god!"

Puflet came over and sat down by her side, stroking her sweaty hair. "Try not to feel bad about it, sweet! He would've fooled anyone. At least you fought back once you understood what he'd done. I just wish there was some way we could get rid of him!" Her eyes searched the room.

Mana clung to her mother, wondering whether she should broach her budding feelings for Calomil. It was too premature, she decided. She had probably misunderstood his smile.

A knock sounded on the door.

"Who is it?" Puflet yelled.

The reply was too muffled to make out, but Mana said, "Come in," anyway.

Vica and Rondo entered. The two sages stopped in the small space between the door and the back of a couch. The two of them clasped their hands and regarded her with embarrassed faces. In their sage robes, they looked like a pair of pious statues in assorted sizes. Mana rose and walked over, squeezing into the center of the couches. "I'm sorry you were eliminated yesterday, Rondo. Will you be staying much longer?"

"That is what we wanted to check with you," he said.

"With your permission," Vica said, "we would like to stay on as your assistants. The voyage here was long, and we so seldom get away from the school, that it seems a shame to hurry back."

"The accommodations here are simple," said Rondo, "but we don't mind. We would feel honored if you would allow us to exercise our horses with Ting."

Warm feelings flooded Mana. "Oh, yes, of course!" she babbled.

"Then we will see you tomorrow afternoon," Vica said.

The two bowed and went out.

"They're very nice!" Mana exclaimed.

"Two old fogeys," said Puflet. "But harmless." She joined Mana between the couches.

"Do you think Calomil is dangerous?" Mana asked.

Puflet laughed. "Not very! Coders are like bees, Mana. The hive is everything to them. They don't believe in individuals pursuing their dreams. They have one collective dream. And they like to breed people so they pretty much all think the same way. So, whereas we have hordes of imbeciles, sluggards, and crooks, and a few absolutely extraordinary minds, they have hard-working, competent, good, and intelligent people, but no brilliant, innovative thinkers, and no mindseas."

"Oh."

"Calomil is racing because his people want him to, but I doubt whether he has any personal ambitions."

"Oh."

"I don't think the Coders really expect to put their champion on the throne, anyhow. Our empire is too—"

She was interrupted by a firm knock on the door.

"Come in!" Puflet yelled.

Attequol entered and squeezed into the center of the couches. He too wore one of the generic black robes. Puflet rose to face him. "I have a few things to say to you!"

He said nothing, merely stood and waited.

"First of all, keep your filthy hands off my daughter!" The sword lay on the couch beside Puflet. With a snarl, she unsheathed it. The air crackled as molecules touched by the gleaming blade unfused.

"Mother!" screamed Mana.

The blade flashed, and Attequol's right arm and the right sleeve of his robe fell to the floor. Blood spurted from the wound.

Mana shrieked and tried to tackle her mother from behind, but Puflet kicked back and sent her reeling into the gap between two couches. While Mana struggled to regain her feet, she sliced off Attequol's other arm. He fell back onto a couch.

"Secondly, I don't want you riding in any more of our races!" Two more flashes of the blade, and Attequol's legs lay writhing on the floor.

Mana scrambled up only to slip on the cascade of blood and crash down on her tailbone. She clutched her mouth, her stomach heaving. She had been certain, in the instant when her mother had attacked, that Attequol would unleash his god-power and disintegrate her. Or else vanish into the center of space and time. Or something. This didn't make any sense!

"I can't die," he said.

"We'll see about that," Puflet growled. "I'll keep these for a trophy." She sliced off his genitals and stuffed them into a pocket of her robe. "The rest of you, I'm going to eat!"

"I will still come back, once my molecules leave your body."

"Then I'll think of you every time I poop!" She struck off his head, and it rolled along the back of the couch and dropped off the corner onto the floor. Blood geysered from the tattooed neck.

Black clouds were closing in on Mana, and a buzzing filled her ears. The last thing she saw before the blackness enveloped her was Attequol's heart still beating as Puflet sliced open his chest.

W hen Mana awoke, blackness filled the skylight.

"I've been lying asleep since I drifted off after the exercise," she told herself. "I dreamed that my mother sliced Attequol up with that sword."

The room had a funny smell.

She did not want to get up to investigate. She wanted to lie in bed forever. She lay for a while, listening to the thump of her own heart. But it was no use. She had to get up. She walked to the bathroom and switched on the chemical lamp in the sconce by the door. She looked down at herself. Her hands and robe were covered with blood.

She tossed the horrible, soggy garment onto the floor, showered, and pulled on her whaleskin. Arming herself with all the towels and extra robes hanging in the bathroom, she ventured out again. She didn't light another lamp; the glow of her hair showed enough. The entire end of the room where the four couches were arranged was black with blood. She made a path for herself by throwing the towels and robes across the floor and walking on them until she reached the door. She slipped out the door, shut it behind her. She spat on her hand and tried to rub her name from the door. It had been there for a long time, and wouldn't come off.

Giving up, she went to the supply room for some chalk. She returned to the unit and crossed out her name. Then she went up along one of the radiating corridors and put her name on the door of a free two-person orange unit.

"There you go, Grandmother! I'm not taking up space for ten any more."

She went in, lit a chemical lamp, and made certain that the room was clean. Then she showered in her whaleskin, hung it on a hook, and showered again. Finally, she crawled into one of the two beds and fell asleep.

When she woke, Mana couldn't understand for a moment why she was in a strange room. Then the horrible images leapt back at her.

"Attequol won't bother me again," was her first thought. Her second thought was, "There is something very wrong with my mother."

She dressed in a generic black robe and went to the cafeteria. To her vast relief, she saw Aspo, Shell, and Kusomba seated at one of the tables. She got herself a cup of coffee and went to join them. "I've changed my room."

They looked at her.

"Is something wrong?" Kusomba asked.

Mana clutched her coffee cup with shaking hands. She nodded. "M-m-my m-m-mother sliced up Attequol with that sword."

No one said anything for a while. Finally Kusomba said, "I think you must have had a nightmare, Mana."

She shook her head. "Y-y-you'll see! B-b-baran won't be there for the race."

"All right," Kusomba said, disbelief plain in her voice.

"Another thing," said Mana. "Calomil doesn't have the black splinter."

"How do you know?"

"He's too happy!"

"Do you know him?" Kusomba asked.

Mana shook her head. "But I'm not using that sword."

"I agree with you on that," said Aspo. "This soul-gem stuff is all too hypothetical to start killing people over."

"Attequol said we didn't need to find the splinters," Mana said. "And I'd rather count holes than cut people up with swords."

"I think the pressure is getting to you," Kusomba said.

Mana fell silent and huddled over her coffee, too nauseated by the images that kept flashing back into her mind to want to ingest anything.

Morning Glory, Fuerida, Nathimeon, and Thermeon came in and pulled a table over next to theirs.

"Calomil doesn't have the black splinter," Mana told them. "And I'm not using the sword."

They all looked at her.

"What happened?" Morning Glory asked.

"My mother cut Attequol into pieces with that sword!"

Fuerida smirked. "Did she really? I think he had it coming. If I were Eria's mother, I'd cut Thermeon into little pieces too."

Thermeon's mane bristled. "I'm not as bad as him!"

"Mana had a nightmare or some kind of hallucination," Kusomba suggested.

Mana glowered at her. "I wish." She looked at Morning Glory. "I changed rooms. We can't have meetings in my old unit any more. It's filled with blood!"

Once again everyone stared at her. Thermeon rose. "Let's have a look."

They followed him from the cafeteria and through the corridors until they reached the door that bore Puflet's name beneath the scratched out "Mana." Thermeon opened the door and they filed inside. The four couches were gone. The floor looked clean, except where it met the wall in a dark line. There was a slight discoloration on the wall above where the back of the couch had been. Thermeon sniffed.

"I can smell the blood."

Part of Mana that had been paralyzed suddenly snapped awake. "I'm going to tell Inspector Sunfox."

She marched out from the building and through the tent city until she reached the golden tent displaying the red, blue, and yellow pennant of the Galactic Investigative Force. Her companions followed her, and when the newsers saw them go past, they tagged along as well.

"I want to report a murder," Mana said.

Sunfox rose from the armchair where he'd been enjoying his morning coffee. "Where is the body?"

"I don't know. She told me she was going to eat him."

This drew a laugh from the crowd. Sunfox raised his eyebrows and scratched his bushy orange hair. Then he started to ask Mana questions. When she had told him everything she had seen, he stepped out from the tent and started toward the stable. After a few steps, he stopped and stared up into the sky. He looked over his shoulder at the people following him.

"Does anyone smell something cooking?"

Thermeon pointed, and Sunfox turned to follow the new direction. As they moved away from the tents, a pillar of smoke could be seen rising from beyond the next ridge. They headed for it. At its base was a large bonfire, above which an enormous pot was suspended from an iron crook. Puflet was tending the fire, feeding it couch legs and gobs of stuffing from the cushions.

"I'm not sharing!" she yelled at them.

Sunfox walked up to her. "You are under arrest for the murder of Baran Etro Geed."

"Oh, please," she said in a sarcastic tone.

As she was marched away, she called over her shoulder, "Save my stew until I get back!"

Mana did not go to the Nexus to watch the proceedings, but her friends kept her apprised. When Puflet claimed that her victim had not been Baran Etro Geed, but Attequol, tests were made. The victim's genetic material showed that he'd had not even a very distant kinship with members of Baran's family. Orgmorgan and Thermeon testified that they had recognized Attequol.

As there were no laws forbidding the killing of a god, Puflet was set free.

Katora renewed her petition to replace Baran in the races, pointing out that gods were not permitted to participate. The race officials ruled in her favor, but as she had not participated in the Final Sixteen Race, they would not give her Baran's position from that race. The eight first finishers, aside from Baran, from the Final Sixteen Race would still advance to the Final Eight Race. Katora would be added to make an unprecedented field of nine.

But to Mana, the strangest news item to come from the capital was Karali's reaction to Puflet's murder and cannibalism.

"Her effort to intimidate me with her ferocity has failed," the empress said.

Once again the pennants flapped, the crowd overflowed the grandstand, the vendors swarmed. Nine horses pranced and tossed their heads as they awaited the official's signal to run. Once again Mana had the position on the rail, but this time it was Katora beside her on Virtuous rather than Attequol. The green face glanced over at her with a smug smile. On the other side of Katora, Eria stroked Serious Quiav's neck and kept her face turned away from Thermeon, who was next in the lineup. Past him sat Aspo on his white mare and Calomil on his pale gold mare. Aspo was not wearing the sword. "Someone might just take it from me," he had argued.

The black mare Ahaha stotted and growled on the other side of Calomil. Swordless astride her sat Quokisa, her hair flapping like great green wings with each bounce. Presumably she would sniff Calomil when they entered the first intersection.

Shell and Puflet completed the field.

The checkered flag descended, and the historic nine-horse Final Eight Race began. Ting felt eager, and flew down the track. Aspo's white mare drew ahead as they entered the first turn, and Ahaha crept up alongside, but the rest of the field had fallen behind. Why wasn't Quokisa holding back to sniff Calomil, Mana wondered.

They plunged into the first intersection, and suddenly Mana was gripped by a cold so terrible she could barely breathe. Her eyeballs felt on fire. Numbed, her hands lost their grip on Ting's mane. *If the cold penetrates my legs, I'll fall,* she thought. She heard the scrape of Ting's hooves over blocks of ice that covered the track and felt her slide. Terrified, she tried to stay upright on Ting's back. If she fell here, would she become part of this frozen world forever? She did not want to find out.

Through the crystals forming on her eyelashes, she saw the white blur that was Rational Shop receding, but she dared not urge Ting to increase her efforts, even if she could have. Quokisa seemed to have fallen back. But then new scraping sounds came from behind, and Calomil edged up beside her on Spacious. Was he trying to smile? It was too cold for smiles. Still, she felt a tiny bit warmer.

A series of swift crunches sounded, and Mirrored Les bounded past both of them. Bathed in the ruby glow from the jewel on the sword she wore at her hip, Puflet was grinning.

The scene dissolved, and the blessed rays of the sun poured down on humans and horses alike, returning sensation and flexibility. But all too soon the next obstacle was upon them.

Once again biting cold enclosed Mana and Ting as they labored along a strange liquid track at the bottom of an abyss so deep that the sky was only a narrow ribbon of grayness far above them. Why were these obstacles so cold? They seemed to radiate a hatred that Mana hadn't been aware of on home-level. Whose mind was triggering such sensations? Was Mana experiencing what it felt like to be Katora?

She hadn't seen Katora since the start of the race. But she wasn't cut off from all the other riders. Calomil's pale gold mare kept pace alongside Ting, and his presence, despite the impossibility of smiles, kept her hands warm enough to grip Ting's mane. The horses' hooves sent intricate patterns of ripples through the surface of the track. Ahead of them, the jewel on Puflet's sword burned like an angry red sun.

Aspo's white mare came from behind, and as the obstacle dissipated, the three horses galloped down the track together. Mana was unfrozen enough to notice a pink flag waving in the grandstand. It was a signal from her friends, letting her know that Puflet had emerged before her. She waved to them as she swept past.

The third obstacle unfolded another desolate setting, windswept and chill, though not so inhumanly cold as the first two. The track led among the ruins of a once-magnificent complex. Fallen pillars and shattered fountains of red stone made Mana picture elegant temples and luxurious palaces where the aristocracy of a vanished civilization had prayed and laughed. What cataclysm or series of disasters had ended their existence?

An ominous crunching and scraping rose above the moan of the wind. Another great pillar was tilting, about to topple across the track ahead of them. With a cry, Mana urged Ting to race past before it fell. Puflet had checked Mirrored Les, and Mana flew past her, Calomil and Aspo following close behind. With a tremendous C-C-CRACK the giant pillar broke free from its base. The mass of stone came hurtling downward. Mana had miscalculated; she and her friends would be crushed. She raised a protective arm and screamed as the falling giant blotted out the sky above her.

The impact came light as a breath of air. Mana and Ting were safe back on home-level. Anxiously she looked back and saw Calomil, Aspo, Puflet, and Eria galloping along the track behind her. Her hammering heart slowed. She noticed a white flag in the grandstand, indicating that she led the field. She waved to her spectating friends and then faced forward to meet the next obstacle.

The track led over the drawbridge and beneath the portcullis of a tremendous, five-towered castle of dark gray stone. Once inside, Ting charged down a long, winding stone hallway lit by flickering torches set in iron sconces high on the walls. The stones oozed with moisture and smelled of mildew. Multiple shadow horses leaped ahead of her. The clatter of Ting's hooves within the narrow space between walls was magnified by echoes and echoes of echoes, and it sounded as if a thousand horses were following close behind.

The hallway branched, and Ting veered to the right. The new hallway sloped downward, curving sharply. Ting skidded to a halt as the hallway ended in a small windowless chamber where an iron-bound wooden chest mouldered.

"We've gone the wrong way!" Mana cried. "Back!"

Ting snorted and wheeled and they raced back up the curving

hallway. As the intersection came into view, Calomil, Eria, and Puflet shot through it. A moment before Ting reached the place where she had taken the wrong turn, the black mare Ahaha reached the intersection and turned right, blocking their passage.

"This is the wrong way!" Mana shouted.

Quokisa's golden eyes glowed in the torchlight. "I know. But I have tidings for you. I have sniffed out the carrier of the black splinter."

Mana gasped. "Who?"

"It is Puflet."

"My mother!"

"It is an ill thing that you allowed her to take Rush. I will wrest it back from her in the next intersection."

"Oh!"

The black mare spun away, and resumed her race through the long, winding hall. Ting followed.

But Mana felt as if her heart had dropped out. What did this mean—that they would have to slice her mother to get the black splinter? Maybe Puflet didn't know that she had it. And what was her connection with Quintillion? Perhaps Quokisa was mistaken, as she had been mistaken about Calomil.

But the memories of Puflet wielding the sword were too real and too terrible to leave any doubt. There must be a magnification of the malevolence when the red and black splinters came into proximity. Mana had been entrusted with a powerful and dangerous artifact, and she had foolishly left it lying unguarded. She recalled the connection between Puflet and Quintillion, too. They had both been held by the same slavers.

The castle was gone. Ting rounded the final turn past the grandstand where red, blue, and pink flags appeared, indicating the three riders who had taken the lead inside the castle.

The final obstacle blasted Mana with searing heat. If the earlier obstacles had indicated hatred, this one was fury. The horses galloped along a levee alongside a steaming river. Timbers supporting the levee were burning, sending up walls of flame on either side, leaving only a narrow passage of safety. Acrid smoke boiled up, blotting stars from the night sky.

Somewhere ahead of her rose a tumult of screams and curses.

Two horses reared and spun and bucked, silhouetted against the flames. Mana thought she recognized her mother's voice. Quokisa must be trying to take the sword. While she gaped, Thermeon and Military Call galloped past.

"I will sort this out!" he shouted.

Then Aspo swept by, and Shell came alongside on Ruling Shore. Mana realized that she wouldn't make the cut for the Emperor Race if she didn't hurry.

"Come on, Ting!"

Her mare surged forward.

But the burning levee had vanished, and the finish line loomed at the end of a short stretch of track. Again Mana whispered to Ting, and the mare responded. Wind stung Mana's eyes as they pounded past Shell and Aspo, past Puflet, who rode swordless on a faltering Mirrored Les. They were gaining on Eria when the checkered banner flashed overhead, and it was over. They had come in fifth.

Mana patted her mare and fed her the apple that Morning Glory had handed her. Kusomba handed her a brush. Aspo and Shell were galloping in hand in hand, as they had in the Final Sixteen Race. The official with his bullhorn announced that their horses had finished in a dead heat.

Calomil, who had come in first, was making his victory speech.

"I give thanks to all the people of the Code who raised me, taught me how to live, and sustained me through my lows and highs, and to the Goddess who is life itself."

Puflet reached the finish line, cursing darkly.

"I withdraw my name from consideration for the last race," announced Quokisa, the second-place finisher. She inclined her head toward Mana.

Her withdrawal meant that Mana would ride in the Emperor Race. Mana was surprised by the number of people in the grandstand who responded to the announcement by shouting, "Chosen One!" and cheering.

Thermeon and Military Call, who had finished third, were circling around Eria and Serious Quiav. "My love, destiny has called us to the final race for the future. Let us ride with one mind and one heart!"

"You're like some infernal mind-tick!" she growled.

He laid a hand over his heart. "Without you I am lost and empty, and as useless as the tiniest bug. If only you would open the floodgates of your love to revive me before I crumble away in the desert of your disapproval."

"Crumble away!"

Katora and Virtuous passed under the finish line and stopped. The mare, knowing she had done poorly, hung her head. Katora glared warningly at the newsers who started to approach.

Eria raised an arm and pointed toward the last-place finisher. "There is the woman who wants you. Go back to her!"

Thermeon gave Katora the barest glance. "Her time is past!"

Katora sat up straighter and sent him a withering look. "It's you who have cut yourself off from the future! You'll never have love again! I promise you that!"

The newsers quivered as they took this in with their perfect memories or recording devices.

Aspo and Shell had left the track. Mana rode after them. When the voices from the finish line had faded into the distance, she became aware of the black mare shadowing her.

"You must wield Rush in the final race, Mana."

Mana folded her arms. "I refuse! You can't make me kill."

"You must embrace the road you have embarked upon. Will you be the Chosen One, or not?"

Mana's thoughts whirled. If she withdrew, Aspo or Shell would take her place, or both of them, depending on the rules about ties. Then they'd be faced with the same terrible dilemma. "All right, then. But I'll only use it to defend myself, if I'm attacked."

"Take care that your mother does not wield it." Quokisa made to unbuckle her belt as they rode side by side.

Quickly, Mana said, "Can't you wait to give it to me until right before the race? Since my mother can draw it on home-level, and I can't, I can't very well stop her from taking it if she wants to."

With a smile, Quokisa handed her the sword. "That is your test."

"Thanks." Mana buckled on the clumsy weapon, Ting pinning her ears in annoyance when it thumped against her ribs.

Mana stopped on a gentle rise that overlooked the stable, that giant mushroom aglow in the twilight. She brushed Ting, then left her grazing, and walked to her room.

Morning Glory, Kusomba, Aspo, and Shell awaited her there, sitting on the beds.

"Good, you have the red splinter," Morning Glory said.

Aspo rose. "Let me give you the violet one too."

"And the green one," said Shell.

Mana felt as if she were about to be buried beneath a mountain of neutron star stuff. "Wait! Shouldn't we think this through for a moment?" She looked at Shell. "Since you can handle the pendant, you could wield the swords too. Home-level I mean. Maybe it would make more sense for you to ride in the final race. I can withdraw."

Shell's blue face paled. "No! Mana, I do not have a feel for politics!"

"She's right," said Aspo.

"Like I have a feel for politics?" Mana said.

They all nodded.

"You accomplished a great deal in a single day as major," said Morning Glory. "More than Karali's man has done in thirty-five years."

"The imperial palace must feel like home to you," Aspo said. "The only time I ever visited, I got lost in a shallow-level tower and almost didn't survive."

"I have never been there," Shell said. "I don't want to be there. Even when a newser asks me something, I don't know how to respond so they will understand. I could never speak before the Wall, as you did."

"Well, I guess I understand." Mana sighed. "But how can I keep these imperial treasures safe until the day of the race?"

"Hide them," Morning Glory suggested.

Mana unbuckled the sword and let it fall to the floor. Then she bent down and shoved it under one of the beds. She motioned to Aspo, and he slid the other sword in beside it, and Shell rolled the pendant after them.

"Maybe I'll think of a better place in the morning," Mana said. She seated herself beside Kusomba.

"Now," said Morning Glory. "There's the question of the black splinter. Did Quokisa say anything to you?"

Mana froze. No one else knew. If she didn't tell them, they wouldn't expect her to do something drastic to her mother. But if she didn't tell them, she wouldn't be able to talk it over with them and get their advice. She drew in a deep breath. "She told me that my mother has the black splinter."

They all looked astounded.

"How could Puflet possibly have gotten hold of it?" Morning Glory wondered.

It seemed they didn't know about the slaver connection.

"But that would explain a certain viciousness in her," said Kusomba. "Sorry, Mana."

Mana shrugged.

"She's not riding in the final race," Morning Glory said. "So you must get the splinter from her before then."

Mana fidgeted. "But if it's in her body, as Quokisa seems to suggest, I'm not sure if she could remove it even if she wanted to. It's a deep-level artifact, so glowworm surgery wouldn't work, would it?"

"No," said Morning Glory. "But if you ride training races with her, it could be removed when you're in an intersection."

"Maybe she could just spit it out," Kusomba said.

"I'll see if I can convince her to try," said Mana.

Morning Glory smiled. "Good. Now that we have a plan, I insist that all of us go to the Nexus to celebrate tonight."

Mana shook her head. So did Aspo and Shell.

"It won't be safe for us out there," Mana said. "I'll be riding against the empress, and Shell and Aspo are next in line, if anything happens to me."

"Orgmorgan will be there," said Morgan Glory.

Mana shook her head again.

"I could get Thermeon to come along with us."

"I think I'd feel safe then," Mana said. "But, you know, it still isn't much fun celebrating without a partner."

"Thermeon makes me uneasy," Shell said.

"Besides," said Mana. "Isn't he the one we really need to worry about stealing the victory from us?"

"That's why it would be good to talk things over with him in a relaxed setting."

"But he never relaxes from his fix on his goddess-star, does he?" Mana said. "Nathimeon might have had a tiny chance of convincing him to let us win, but he'll hardly do it for me. He might try to stop Karali from attacking me or the other riders—if he could take his mind off of his supposed goddess for even the tiniest fraction of a second—but he won't slow down for us. I don't suppose he cares about the splinters, though, so he won't try to take them from us. But we—" She gave Shell and Aspo a guilty look —"I won't be able to forge the soul-gem."

"A little celebration will take your mind from these negative thoughts." Morning Glory smiled. "In primitive times, troops often would carouse together on the eve of a great battle."

Shell shuddered, as if at some dark memory.

"When Karali is gone we should celebrate," Mana said. "Until then, it would be premature."

"You girls are difficult to please."

Firmly, Mana asked that everyone leave her room.

After showering and changing into a black robe, Mana went to the cafeteria to see about dinner. She found the big room empty. It seemed that just about everyone was either celebrating victory or defeated and gone. She walked up the axial corridor to her old unit and knocked on the door.

"What do you want?" came her mother's voice.

"I need to talk to you," Mana said. She went in.

Puflet was wearing a black dress with frills that brightened slowly through brown and maroon to reach a vivid crimson on their edges. It made her look a bit like a cooling lava splatter. She was stuffing things into her carryall.

"Well, make it quick, dear. I'm ready to see the last of this place."

Mana paused where the couches had been. Her eyes traveled to a faint stain on the wall.

Puflet smirked. "You have to admit it was the best solution. People don't seem to realize that talking and analyzing and whining about problems don't get you anywhere. Problems require decisive action. It infuriates me when I think of all the slavers and pirates who go free because they can talk their way out of the jaws of legal punishment."

"Attequol wasn't a slaver or a pirate."

"No, but he still had no right to be here interfering with our lives. There should be a name for what he was—time-pirate maybe."

"He *let* you slice him up."

Puflet paused in her packing and gave her a long look. She snorted. "Well, he's still gone. He's not bothering you any more, is he?"

"No." In retrospect, Mana wondered whether her crying about him hadn't been a bit babyish. He hadn't intended to stay for very long. She wondered suddenly if he'd known from the very beginning exactly how he would be leaving. The way he'd just stood there and let Puflet go at him with the sword; and long before that, when he'd told them that swords scared him, had he known?

She wrenched her mind back into the present. "Mother, you have the black splinter."

"I see. Is this Morning Glory's latest idea? You told me the other day that she said Calomil had it."

"Quokisa smelled it on you. In you. During the race today."

Puflet flopped back onto her bed. "She's playing with all of you, Mana. She's a time-pirate too."

"She said you might not know you had it."

"Do you have any idea how ridiculous you sound? Do you want to search my carryall? Or what? What I think you need is a new set of friends."

"Think, Mother. When you were in Ix's camp, on Puztak, did Quintillion give you something?"

A look of utter astoundment wiped the sneer from Puflet's face. She stared at Mana, not really seeing her. Her jaw hung open. After a few moments, she blinked and shook herself. In a low voice, she said, "Well, so. He gave me something. Not a splinter. He gave me my mindpowers. But deep-level artifacts can have many aspects." She laughed.

"Mother, we need—"

Puflet sprang to her feet, her pale face suffused by rage. "No! It's mine! Quintillion gave it to me, and it's mine! It's part of me. I need it to fight slavers. Morning Glory has some ridiculous idea that she can create Queen Lala's Rainbow Land if she gets all of these artifacts together. Well, she tried it once, and failed, and I see no point in wasting all of our energies a second time. She can no more make the future perfect than Katora could make the Age of Illumination or Thermeon can embrace his goddess-star! All of these grandiose, all-encompassing schemes are doomed to failure! But I can use my splinter—if you want to call it that—to root out some of the vile criminals who infest the galaxy, and that's what I'll continue to do."

She pulled a pair of crimson-soled, crimson-lined black slippers from under the bed and dug her feet into them. "I'm out of here, Mana. You're welcome to look me up someday, if you ever get free from this place." Hefting her carryall, she started for the door, then paused and looked back over her shoulder at Mana, who was still standing in the aisle between bunks. "If you ever become emperor, please don't let people like Morning Glory tell you what to do. The world would be a much better place if more people thought for themselves instead of believing in convenient nonsense."

She strode to the door and went out, slamming it behind her.

Mana just stood where she was, taking deep breaths, until the shock began to subside. Then she went back to the cafeteria. She found Aspo and Shell there. After reconstituting a bowl of stew by adding water from the pot that was boiling on a hot plate—the good food was all gone—she joined them.

"My mother admitted that she has the black splinter. But she's not going to give it up to forge the soul-gem. So Morning Glory's plan has failed." She heaved a deep sigh and stared uninspiredly into her bowl of stew.

"That's too bad," said Aspo. "You'll still need to carry a sword in the Emperor Race to defend yourself. But there's no need for taking three splinters."

"That's a relief. I think I'll take the violet sword. I hate the red sword!"

For a while they ate their stew in silence. Then Mana said, "Attequol said we didn't need the splinters to forge a new soul-gem. I wish I could've followed whatever he was trying to show us with those patterns on the table."

"Deep-level stuff is ordinary matter," Shell said. "Just arranged differently. What he was showing were things that the builders of deep-level ships need to know. The soul-gem is deeper than any of our ships, so the pattern is more difficult to see."

"How do you know what he was showing us?" Mana asked. "You weren't there."

She shrugged. "No, but Aspo told me about it. It's just standard deep-level engineering."

"It must be extremely difficult, or the empire would have a new soul-gem already," Mana said. "Has anyone aside from Attequol ever made one from scratch? Or has the empire been just repeatedly piecing his old one back together?"

"I think so," said Aspo.

"Then we're twistored." Mana sighed.

They finished eating and went to their separate rooms. Mana dreamed that she was riding with Quokisa.

"Sometimes my splinter shatters," Quokisa told her. "And then my travels become dangerous."

When Mana woke, she wondered where Quokisa was. She hadn't put her name on a room, nor did Ahaha ever walk into a stall. She asked Aspo and Shell at breakfast if they knew, but they had no idea.

After breakfast, Mana joined one of the peasant crews going from stall to stall. She asked them if they knew where Quokisa and Ahaha were.

"We call her Stealth Shadow," said a peasant woman. "No one can find her 'less she wants bein' found."

Mana roamed the field far and wide, but Ahaha was not among the horses grazing around the stable.

Morning Glory and Kusomba were back in time for lunch. Mana told them about Puflet and the black splinter.

"I'll ask Thermeon to talk to her," Morning Glory said. "Hopefully he can convince her to come back and help us."

"Why should he care if our plan succeeds?" Mana asked. "Doesn't he intend to win the race for some child he wants to have with Eria?"

"Yes, But—"

"Would it be possible to make a new splinter to replace the black one? Or find another one? Or were there only ever four splinters in the galaxy?"

"Oh, Horl had his own soul-gem," Morning Glory said. "When it was broken, its splinters surfaced somewhere in time and space."

Mana sighed. "Nine days until the Emperor Race! We don't have much time to find one of them."

"No." Morning Glory frowned. "I felt certain that my Wall Speaking would attract all the splinters we needed. We will simply have to convince your mother to help!"

That afternoon, Mana exercised Ting with Galaxy and Sexy. She thought about bringing the violet sword, and decided against it.

"Do you think that it would be right for me to use the sword against Karali?" she asked the sages as they headed for the track.

"I know how you feel," Rondo answered. "Because my parents —the Six Sages under Ir—intended for me to become emperor. They reasoned that my genetic heritage made me fit for the position. But they were scholars who had long avoided the empire's centers of political power, and they did not take into account the cauldron of ugly human emotions that surrounds such centers."

"So you never became emperor," Mana said.

"No. I had to ask myself the same questions you are asking. If you ride in the Emperor Race, it is almost certain that you will be forced to use the sword to defend your life. I have no doubt that you want to make the galaxy a better place. You must ask yourself if this is the best way to achieve your goal. Is your participation in the race necessary to defeat Karali? Will the position of emperor make the best use of your energies and talents? And above all, do you want to become a person who can kill? If the answer to any of these questions is no, then you must withdraw from the race."

Mana swallowed. "Yes, I see." It was obvious, of course. How could she have imagined that she could win the most contested position in the galaxy without being prepared to kill? And if they didn't get the fourth splinter, and there was no chance of forging the soul-gem during the race, why should she ride?

She had nine days to think it over.

It seemed as if she spent all of her days and nights, except when she was actually talking to people or riding training races, thinking or dreaming about the Emperor Race. She dwelt upon the ramifications of every possible outcome.

If Calomil won and became the next emperor, the Code religion would be preeminent in the galaxy. Calomil was civilized and not a fanatic. But he'd be under pressure from people like Lelin to accelerate the conversion of the empire. Movements like the Holy Crusade would arise, and how could Calomil stand firm against people with whom he ultimately sympathized?

If Eria won, the galactic situation could deteriorate far more precipitously. She'd call on the minors to keep Thermeon away from her, and he'd explode into one of his deep-level manifestations.

If he won—the most probable outcome—he'd continue his pursuit of her, ignoring the galactic situation, until the empire devolved into chaos.

Mana didn't waste much time imagining herself winning, since it was so unlikely. But there was one other possibility that made her blood go icy.

Karali might win. She'd use her deep-level weapon to eliminate the competition. She wouldn't try to kill her father, of course, but she'd do something to slow him down, and since he had some kind of inhibition about striking out at his children, she'd get away with it. Mana would be forced to taken action to stop her.

When she pictured this, the scenario always reached the same conclusion. She was slicing up Karali the way her mother had sliced Attequol. Blood was spurting, enough blood to drown in, and Karali, unlike Attequol, screamed louder after every cut.

In the dreams, she wouldn't die, no matter how many times Mana sliced her. She just kept screaming, bleeding, and arguing.

"How can you do this to me, Mana? I've done nothing wrong! All I was trying to do was protect people from the feral creatures that attacked me at the dro ranch!"

Each morning Mana awoke in a sheen of sweat, her hair matted, a sour taste in her mouth. Over breakfast, Morning Glory would try to soothe her.

"I have the feeling that we'll still be able to forge the soul-gem! Thermeon has been in mind-link with your mother. She's on her ship, but she hasn't downleveled yet, so she's still thinking it over.

He'll get through to her, you'll see."

"But he's not planning to drop out or let us win, is he? So how can I forge the gem, even if I have the splinters?"

"There will be a way. You are thinking again that the future must be this or that—but there are other possibilities you cannot imagine."

Each day, Mana thought about taking the sword to a training race, and each day she decided not to. Rondo and Vica always joined her for training. Sometimes Morning Glory or other members of the team came as well. The track was closed to all riders except those involved in the Emperor Race, so the only other riders they encountered coming or going from the track were the Coders.

It was the afternoon of the fifth day. Mana and Ting emerged from the final obstacle of a training race after a pleasant enough course consisting of various lush and steamy wilderness settings. None of her training partners had reached the finish line, but she saw Calomil, Lelin, and a couple other Coders there, presumably waiting for their own friends. Calomil acknowledged her with a smile and a wave.

Mana waved back. She rode up to him. "Could we talk?" Her heart pounded. Despite her fantasies, she'd never really spoken to him before.

"Let's sit in the grandstand," he said. "I'll ask Gaadan to bring us some cool drinks. What would you like?"

"Um. Dwi juice?"

"Good. I will have ruberry. No native Wamatuan likes to drink dwi juice away from home. The dwi is our planet's tree. You probably know some flavor native to Lal that isn't nearly as good anywhere else."

Mana shrugged. "Red carrot stew, maybe? Or fern juice for an Ulonan. I've spent more of my life on Ulona than Lal."

"Regretfully, I have never visited Ulona."

Gaadan rode off to fetch their drinks, and they climbed into the grandstand.

Aspo came past the finish line on Rational Shop. Mana waved to him. She turned to Calomil. "I wanted you to know that I will probably carry a sword for the Emperor Race. If I do, it will only be to defend myself if Karali attacks me. It will not be a threat to you, or to any of the other riders."

"I understand," he said. "I will not be armed."

"Oh. I've been informed that Karali is preparing a deep-level weapon for the race. Perhaps you should reconsider."

He smiled at her. "Your concern shows that you have a good heart. But I must rely on the defenses my genes and my upbringing have provided me."

"Your reliance on nature and your people is commendable," Mana began. She was going to mention that she had an extra sword, but a commotion on the track tore away her attention.

Eria had ridden up on Serious Quiav, followed by Thermeon on Military Call. Mana hadn't seen either of them come out to train since the Challenge had begun.

"The Deep can't hide your light from me!" he called out. "It only shines with trebled brightness as you achieve your full splendor!"

"They are not serious about this race," Calomil observed. "You and I, Mana, are the only two taking part in the Challenge whose aim is to replace Karali's corruption with a better government."

"True," said Mana.

On the track below them, Thermeon was shouting. "I will prove to you that we are meant to be together! Ride into an intersection! I will follow later, and yet I will find myself in the same deep-level place as you."

Without answering, Eria rode off down the track. He waited, grinning. He exchanged a few words with Morning Glory, who had just finished the training circuit, then looked up into the grandstand and waved to Mana. She waved back.

"His behavior is disgraceful," Calomil said.

"Yes." Trying to ignore Thermeon, Mana looked at the man beside her. "I gather that all of your people are united in supporting you for the throne."

He nodded. "We have been preparing since the petitions for the Challenge first circulated in the planets. My sister Pasola was one of the first organizers."

Mana gasped. "Your sister? Oh, I should have realized! You look so much alike! She was a wonderful person, and I miss her so much! Then ... you have a personal reason for wanting Karali gone."

"I have many reasons for wanting Karali gone—one for each innocent her crusade murdered. It would be wrong to give more weight to a single death because she was dear to me. But of course, I have fallible human emotions."

A tattoo of hoofbeats sounded as Thermeon took off after Eria.

"Of course," Mana said.

"Pasola is with the Goddess," Calomil murmured. "She has been fulfilled."

Mana bowed her head for a moment to show her respect for the departed.

Gaadan climbed up the ramp and handed them their drinks, then descended again. The rest of Mana's team had finished their training and lingered below, talking with the Coders.

"We have studied the Proposals you made when you were major," Calomil said. "And we approve. The changes you sought in education would have brought the imperial norm more into line with how children of the Code are raised."

"Without the religious aspect, of course," Mana said. "I very much admire your self-sufficiency, your willingness to learn ancient technologies, which, although not so convenient, prove to be of inestimable value during crisis situations. But the empire comprises a large and varied population that embraces many belief systems. It would not be right to try to impose any one belief system on all people."

"I understand that," he said. "But the Code is also science. You may be more familiar with the older school—" She gathered he meant the Red Coders—"but modern people of the Code have embraced all of humanity's most advanced scientific findings, and our beliefs have been reinterpreted in light of that knowledge. The teachings of the Code are no more religious than teaching that men and women should be courteous and kind to one another. They should be part of every young citizen's curriculum."

"I would never say no to teaching courtesy and kindness," Mana said.

"But are these vital concepts stressed in today's crèches? How can young people learn what is right without science, as discovered by the Code, showing them the way?"

"I am of the belief that all healthy human societies find kindness and courtesy adaptive. People of the Code are not the only group who teach their members good behavior. The Lalian peasant also has a strong ethical system. There are too many others to name."

"These belief systems are based on tradition, not on science. They can erode as times change."

"The interpretation of the universe by the Code is one way of looking at reality. But science isn't just one theory, one interpretation of the facts. It comprises every interpretation that fits the data. And it collects new data constantly, and constantly evolves."

"Code science evolves."

They continued to discuss education, ethics, science, and the belief systems of various groups while their friends waited below. It was a good way of feeling one another out. But, alas, Mana realized that their relationship must be political rather than personal. If she became emperor, she would need to work with the Coders, who, though not perhaps the most numerous religious group in the galaxy, were the most organized and active, and he was their spokesman. She felt certain that he was a good man, though imbued with the same unwavering, obstinate faith of all Coders.

She heard a horse galloping toward them. It was Serious Quiav. From the speed of her return, Mana guessed that Eria had encountered only relatively shallow obstacles in the track's intersections, Deep One, or at most Deep Two.

One of the peasant workers held out a tall glass as she crossed the finish line. Eria slid to the ground and accepted the glass. The black-clad woman who had handed it to her screamed, "The Holy Crusade will prevail!" and dashed something into Eria's unprotected face.

Some of the deep-level stuff the fake peasant had discharged at Eria must have struck Serious Quiav, who was standing behind her. Screaming with rage and pain, the mare reared and unfolded hooves and tusks and maddened eyes too numerous to count. The crusader had started to flee, but the mare seized her without taking a step, crushed the body in her jaws, and flung it aside. Then she turned toward her fallen rider.

Mana and Calomil rushed down from the grandstand to join the crowd around Eria. Mana staggered when she saw the devastation the bomb had caused—nothing remained of Eria's head except for the long red hair. Calomil caught her before she could fall.

"It's all Thermeon's fault," Mana sobbed. "He hounded her, he wouldn't let her be, he disrupted her peaceful, happy life out among the galaxies!"

"Alas," Calomil said, his arms comforting around her.

Looking like a normal, home-level horse once more, Serious Quiav hovered over the body, her breath stirring the outflung hair. After a moment she moved away, scanning the horizon with desperate eyes, as if she hadn't recognized the dead thing on the ground, and expected to find Eria somewhere else. She whinnied.

"Poor thing," Mana whispered. "They were together for so long."

The mare called again, and again, each whinny reaching a

higher pitch of anguish. Suddenly her ears pricked at some distant sound Mana couldn't hear, and she raced away, still calling.

Another set of hoofbeats approached. Thermeon had finished his circuit. "What happened?" he called.

Mana opened her mouth to scream at him, but Morning Glory cried, "Don't!" and she fell mute.

He dismounted, and the crowd parted to let him see. Thermeon stared. He knelt and touched the hair. A strange, wild cry worked its way from his throat. Then he bared his fangs, and a savage gleam came to his eyes. But after a moment the fury gave way to confusion. He crouched, shaking his head, his hair trailing through the dirt of the track. "Karali didn't order this," he moaned.

"Or maybe she gave someone the authority to plan attacks without letting her know," Mana said. "So you couldn't see them in her mind."

Thermeon didn't seem to hear. He howled his anguish, sounding strangely like the mare. "No, no, no! This cannot be! My goddess, how can you leave me this way?" All at once he surged to his feet, looking wildly about. "You must still exist somewhere! In the Deep! On another timeline! I will find you!"

He ran to Military Call and leaped onto the stallion's back. They hurtled away in the same direction that Serious Quiav had taken.

Someone must have run to the golden tent, for Inspector Sunfox came sprinting up, followed by a horde of newsers. Sunfox briefly examined both corpses, then addressed the crowd. "I will need to take statements from everyone. A list of those present will be drawn up, and then I will call you to my tent one by one for questioning."

"I want you to hold me," Mana whispered to Calomil when they walked to the tent to give their testimony. "I don't want to be alone for one more night."

"There is a Code sanctuary in the Nexus," he whispered back.

Mana knew that the sanctuary would contain a Pool of Revelation where men and women of the Code formalized their bonding. "Is it all right for you to take me there, even though I don't belong to your people? You don't have commitments?"

"I find you beautiful, Mana, in your body, mind, and soul. My people have put narrow views of genetic suitability behind them."

After each of them had related what they had seen to the inspector and exchanged their riding skins for street clothes, Mana and Calomil walked to the tram station beneath twilight skies and twinkling stars. The stars were fully out when they reached the sanctuary, a small complex of native sandstone buildings set apart from the noise and motion and glowworm glitter of the rest of the Nexus. After a light dinner of decapod salad washed down with blue wine, Calomil lit a torch from a ceremonial fire that was kept burning at all times, and conducted Mana to the pool.

The Pool of Revelation lay in an underground grotto that had been carved from Lal's sandstone. Round and shallow, it breathed out a hot, salty atmosphere. Although it looked primitive in the torchlight, Mana suspected that it was artificially heated and circulated. Parting in front of the pool, they went to separate booths where they undressed and rinsed. They returned to the pool to openly study one another's naked bodies.

Genetic Algorithms made certain, of course, that all citizens were physically attractive, with only moderate variations. Mana was not as buxom as her mother, but she was tall, slender, and well-proportioned. Calomil was a little taller, lithe and well-muscled, broader at the shoulders than the hips. She saw no trace of Thermeon's animal features nor any strangeness due to different beauty standards held by the ancient Code people.

"Accept me as your mate," Calomil said. "And I will focus my male instincts and energies in the celebration of your femininity for as long as you wish."

"I accept you as my mate," Mana said.

His smile glittering in the torchlight, Calomil took her hand and led her into the pool. She wondered how he had known that she would understand the ritual. Had he and Oakiza talked about her while Oakiza had been at the stable assisting Kael?

The water caressed them with the warmth of a womb. They floated side by side, gently stroking one another and kissing. The delicious sensations Mana had feared she never would know again began to race up and down her body. When Calomil's eyes were dark with desire, and they both gasped for breath, he guided her from the pool through a drying tunnel—the air jets were modern, but the rough sandstone walls gave it a primal appeal—and into an egg chamber.

The gently yielding bed, fluffy pillows, and silky sheets were far more comfortable than the hard beds at the stable. Mana let everything else slide from her mind as she plunged into reacquaintance with her body's special delights. She had feared that an ordinary man wouldn't have the skill (or the ability to magnify his skill with mindpowers), but Calomil knew what to do. He knew where to touch her, how to slowly increase the intimacy and the rhythm of his touch until she clutched him and kissed him with wild delight and urged him on with her hands and tongue. When he entered her, she felt all golden inside. He held her there, waiting until the tide of ecstasy began to subside, and then moved slowly, tantalizingly, to bring it back. Arching, groaning, she gave herself over to the ride into the depths of erotic wonder. Like a conductor of the orchestra that was her body, Calomil evoked one wave of excitement after another, leading her higher and higher into an amazing awareness. She was Woman—all women. She was Female—every female who had ever mated since the beginning of time. It seemed an unassailable truth that some eternal goddess had programmed humans to know her truths by weaving this marvelous mating urge into their genes. But then, hadn't Attequol said something of the sort too, calling it Existence?

At last it was too much; the golden tide burst its barriers and Mana screamed unabashedly as the delicious pulsations swept through her, while Calomil burst deep inside her and shuddered in her arms.

As she drifted along in the aftermath, still entwined with her lover, feeling like a boneless puddle of dazzlement, it occurred to Mana that she had been a goddess in that instant, when the highest peak had been crested. And wasn't that what the Coders believed; that the goddess had gifted all humans with the ability to be united with her in their moment of supreme passion?

So why did Thermeon insist that his goddess take on a permanent human form? Why didn't he—but her mind was too full of buzzing, flitting stars to frame any more thoughts. She drifted into sleep.

In the morning, Mana and Calomil shared a breakfast of fruit and cream in a little stone gazebo overlooking a garden with trickling fountains before joining others in a larger room where they gathered in twos and threes with coffee cups in comfortable nooks and watched the news from the capital.

Reports from the murder investigation came like a dash of cold water to subdue Mana's glorious mood.

"I am entirely innocent!" Karali's face proclaimed. "This is the work of a copycat killer!"

Inspector Sunfox reported on his investigation. "The killer entered the stable area with the crowds on the day of the Final Eight Race, then bided her time, protecting herself from prying eyes by blending in with the peasant workers, although never mingling close enough with them to arouse their suspicions. Scanners at the tram station should have detected the inter-level material of her bomb, and reports from the planetary police scanner indicate that it did register an alert on the bomb, but that it was overruled by the Bureau and Palace scanners, which both deemed the item safe."

A race official appeared to report on the adjusted lineup for the Emperor Race.

"Since Aspo Irsifitial Miad and Quox Selped Sea-Shey were tied for fifth place in the Final Eight Race after the withdrawal of Saku Fanweroug Leopasi, they both will take the place of Eria Megtu Luv-Pet. If Thermeon Pestire Toom does not return in time for the race, his place will be taken by Puflet Wuner Doom. If she does not return in time for the race, her place will be taken by Katora Srenlendens Miosony."

Katora's face appeared. "Like you, I am shocked and dismayed by the series of horrible events that has led to the unraveling of our imperial system culminating in this highly disordered Challenge. I apologize for any part I had in bringing about these disasters, and I pledge to apply all of my energies to their speedy and complete rectification.

"As you know, my husband of many years was Thermeon, an extremely powerful mindsea whose wild energies I had hoped to channel into expressions beneficial to mankind. I realize now that I failed in my mission. He remains a wild animal; and, unfortunately, our children are tainted by the feral streak that they inherited from him.

"Therefore, I pledge to do my utmost to uphold the tradition of the Challenge on Horseback and to remove the flawed emperor Karali Iamorri Doom from the throne."

Hearing her words, Mana realized that all of Katora's most recent offspring, including Nathimeon—whether or not he had changed—and even inoffensive people like Taana, were now no longer to be recognized by Katora as her children. She sighed, and Calomil squeezed her shoulder.

At about noon, they left the sanctuary and traveled to the stable with the rest of the Red and Blue Coders, bringing their own luncheon supplies to serve in the cafeteria, and then going to the track to exercise their horses. Mana made a quick circuit of the building between lunch and riding to check with her friends.

"I'll be training with Calomil so that we can cooperate against Karali in the last race," she told Morning Glory. "Aspo and Shell should join us too."

Morning Glory seemed very subdued, not saying much. Mana thought that she was probably still in shock about Eria.

"You'll need to carry the pendant and one of the swords," Mana told Aspo and Shell. "And come out to train with me and Calomil."

Sister and brother nodded, but they both wore long faces, and they didn't ride with Mana and Calomil that afternoon.

Fuerida and Nathimeon weren't around. They hadn't said anything to Mana about quitting the team, but since Fuerida had given up the green splinter, Mana had seen less and less of them.

After their training race, Mana and Calomil returned to the Code sanctuary for dinner, and after dinner delights in the egg chamber.

The morning news involved accusations and counter-accusations about the algorithms of the checkpoint scanners, and speculations and various opinions about the whereabouts of Thermeon and Puflet.

Katora opined that Puflet had left Lal and would not be back.

Orgmorgan, as Head of the Pilots Guild, reported that Puflet's ship was orbiting Lal in home-level space, which gave her the option to return.

Puflet herself made no statement, neither withdrawing from the race nor promising to be there. Mana recalled how greatly she had enjoyed Quokisa's last-minute appearance. Was she aiming to provide similar dramatics?

Days and nights slipped past in the same pattern. Mana's happiness would have been perfect if it hadn't been for the Emperor Race looming closer and closer.

One morning she awoke to realize that the day of destiny had arrived, and for a long moment she clung to Calomil with shaking arms and wished with all her might that she would never have to get out of bed.

But, of course, there was no escape.

The pennants and crowds were back. Now too a contingent of imperial minors in leopard plumes and special non-animated armor appeared to safeguard the empress, each man and woman equipped with a deep-level weapon, a long pole tipped with a blade shaped like a crescent moon. The blades crackled and shimmered with rainbow lights as the minors escorted Karali, mounted on Eternal Trat, onto the track and took positions along the rail. Mana and Ting had to cede their position on the inside to the empress. Karali looked at Mana with a sneer.

"Your day before the Wall bit you with the addiction to power, did it? Well, I have the cure." She shook her spear.

Mana swallowed and shifted her weight, making Ting crowd closer to Virtuous.

"You are a disgrace to the throne!" Katora spat at her estranged daughter.

"Take your positions!" roared the official from his podium.

On Katora's far side, Aspo, Calomil, and Shell tried to align their nervous mounts.

At that moment, as Mana had suspected she might, Puflet galloped up on Mirrored Les, a huge grin on her face. "Get out of the lineup, Katora!"

"You're too late!" Katora yelled.

"The race has not yet started," shouted the official. "Katora, you must give way."

"She's too late, and she's purposely delaying us!" Katora argued.

A peasant woman stepped onto the track, walked up to Les, and offered the mare a red carrot. Mana smiled, recalling how they'd offered Miesa's mare a flower before her race. Although it seemed an odd treat, since red carrots were extremely spicy.

The mare crunched the carrot. Puflet didn't notice as she continued to smirk at Katora.

"Off the track!" The official pointed his furled flag at the peasant woman.

She scampered to the outer edge of the track where she blended into large group of her compatriots.

With a squeal of outrage, Les started to buck and spin. Puflet went flying into the dirt.

"Revenge for Attequol!" chorused the peasants.

Puflet picked herself up. "This is unfair! Cheating! They've poisoned my horse!"

"You are too late, and you're delaying the race!" blared the official. "Clear the track immediately!"

"No!" screamed Puflet.

"Get your horse off the track!"

Les continued her demented gyrations back and forth across the track, wheezing and farting. Finally she spun across the outer edge and continued to move away.

The official raised his flag. Trumpeters on hand for this special occasion began to blow a fanfare. Puflet looked wildly about.

Like a shadow, Quokisa and the black mare slipped around the crowd of peasants and trotted up to her. Quokisa dismounted and Puflet sprang onto the shiny black back. As she turned to join the lineup, Quokisa looked straight at Mana, pointed at Puflet, and slid a finger across her throat. Then she whirled and bounded away.

The fanfare ended. The flag dropped. Seven horses charged down the track.

Ting felt eager beneath Mana, galloping as fast as she had in the previous two races, but the white stallion blew away from her, with Virtuous in determined pursuit, and the black mare right behind them. The three horses vanished into the first intersection.

A moment later, Mana joined them. She found herself riding

along a narrow, winding trail through a forest of trees that stretched up on every side with their crowns lost in the clouds. Everything was gray. Whorls of mist spun across the trail and vanished among the great gray boles. A whispering filled the air. At first Mana thought it must be the leaves up above the clouds that she heard, chattering in the rain. But the voices were human. Everything that had been said to her since the death of Empress Pia was being spoken again.

"My father's fear response," said Dino, while Attequol boomed, "You'll know that I care for you," and Katora sneered, "At least you know your place," and Rondo asked, "Are you a person who can kill?"

All the while vast, unseen crowds chanted, "Chosen One! Chosen One!"

Mana urged Ting to increase her speed, and the mare stretched out. She veered from the trail for a moment to pass Virtuous. Then Mana saw the black mare racing just ahead, her long tail whirling from side to side. She seemed fractious, pausing for a moment to buck, making Puflet clutch her mane and yelp. Ting shot past them.

The red jewel burned like fire against Mana's side. The forest whispered with Quokisa's voice, "You'll have to slice the black splinter out of her."

Mana shook her head and rode on. If she hadn't caught the flash of white from the corner of her eye, she would have been caught completely off guard when Karali charged out from among the trees with the moon-spear leveled at her heart. She checked Ting. The mare reared, and the white stallion flew past. Karali turned him and charged again.

"Draw your sword! Defend yourself!" whispered the voices, but Mana sat paralyzed.

A pale gold mare raced past her. Calomil seized the spear and ripped it from Karali's hands, then hurled it into the woods. He motioned Mana to go, and she urged Ting forward.

Then the horrible woods were past, and they raced along the track in the late afternoon sun. Minors lined the rail in front of the grandstand. As Mana passed, one of them stepped forward onto the track. Looking back, she saw him hand a new spear to Karali. Her throat tightened.

The next obstacle was a great archway of stone. The trail led through it and split into five new trails all leading to new stone arches. Tricks of perspective made all trails look the same size, but when Mana started along one of them, it revealed itself to be a tiny trail leading to a miniature arch. She turned back toward the intersection.

Ahaha galloped past, her tail flying like a banner. She had no rider.

Mana screamed and peered back up the trail. Calomil rode up and grabbed her arm. "Ride, Mana!"

"But my mother!"

"She's all right. Karali just unhorsed her."

Mana nodded. An ordinary person like herself would go flat if unhorsed inside an obstacle, but Puflet's mindpowers would allow her to act. Mana followed Calomil along one of the trails. He seemed to have chosen correctly, for it led to an arch just broad enough for two horses to pass beneath it side-by-side.

Somewhere on the trail behind them a monstrous roaring erupted, followed by a thin shriek.

"Shell!" Mana gasped.

"She will be fine!" Calomil said. "Ride!"

The roaring grew like thunder around them. The sky darkened, and the arches on every side rocked and cracked, sending showers of stones bouncing across the large and small trails. Mana screamed as a burning skeleton horse with the skull of a horned dinosaur overtook them. Red-orange flames licked the blackened bones and seethed within the eye sockets of the spike-fringed skull. It was the personification of the cataclysm Morning Glory had foreseen. Puflet sat on its shoulders, the pendant with the green splinter ablaze on her chest.

"Mother!" Mana screamed.

"You have nothing I want," Puflet growled, and her monstrous steed shoved Calomil's mare aside with its nose horn.

Spacious plunged down a trail that had looked the same size and on the same level as the one they followed, but it was in fact far larger and on a level far below them. A tiny Calomil on a tiny gold mare skidded helplessly down the dangerous incline toward a vast but distant archway.

"You have something I want!" Puflet leaned toward Ting and snatched the red sword from its sheath, while Mana goggled helplessly.

"You don't recognize the thing I'm riding?" Puflet asked. "This is the black splinter. This is the form it's always taken for me. Deep-level artifacts can be tricky that way!"

With a joyous laugh, she rode on.

Mana stared down at Calomil. He motioned her to go on, then passed through the enormous distant arch. She rode.

The black splinter monster churned along the trail ahead of her, leaving a wake of foul smoke. Mana thought she could taste the bitterness of hatred and the evil of killers in every spidery wisp of it. As the monster bore down on the white stallion, Karali turned him and charged at Puflet with her moon-spear. The impact drove both steeds back onto their haunches. The moon-spear's crescent blade had caught between two spikes on the monster's skull. With a ponderous shake of its head, the monster ripped the weapon from her hands. Karali turned to flee, but the monster was upon her. The red sword flashed. Karali's head flew off and bounced along a small trail, becoming wedged in the arch at its end.

"Noooo! It can't end this way!" the head screamed.

Karali's body rode on, but Puflet leaped onto the white stallion's back and hurled it off. Laughing, riding Trat, she overtook Aspo on one side, while the monster overtook him on the other. "You have something I want." She whipped the violet sword from its sheath.

The trails and arches vanished, along with Puflet's monster. She led the way along the track on Eternal Trat, whirling a sword in either hand, yelling words that Mana couldn't make out. Mana looked back and saw Calomil and Katora emerge from the intersection. Virtuous closed the distance between them. "Imbecile!" Katora screamed. "You've let her get all the splinters! You've doomed us!"

The horses plunged into the next intersection.

They rode along a broad stone floor within a hall of enormous proportions, its ceiling and far wall too distant to see. On either side of them rose gargantuan stone statues depicting men, women, and beasts frozen in moments of heroic battle. The horses' hooves clattered across the stone.

"I will get one of the swords from her," Calomil said.

Katora sneered at him. "You're descended from Thermeon too, aren't you?"

"Through Maxuas," he admitted. Veering to one side, he leaned out and plucked the sword from the hand of one of the smaller figures around a statue's base.

"What will you do?" Mana stammered. Her emotions roiled. She didn't want something terrible to happen to Calomil, so she knew she had to act, do something to help him. But she felt too cowardly, too incompetent to be of any use.

He placed a finger across his lips to caution silence. Then Spacious surged away from Ting and Virtuous. Aspo raced a few lengths ahead of them on his white mare. Calomil drew even with him, then passed, and gained on Puflet and Trat.

The path through the great hall along which they galloped was straight for as far as the eye could see. With his long tail rippling behind him, the white stallion looked like a fluttering moth in the distance. Puflet laughed and sang, her voice filling the vast space of the hall.

"There will be a monument to me, me, me! Thermeon thinks he's the pinnacle of life, but I'll climb higher still, you'll see, see, see!"

Beside Mana, Katora muttered, "She's monstrous!"

"It-it's because of the black splinter!" Mana protested.

The blue-gray eyes regarded her with cold contempt.

Far ahead, Calomil had just caught up with the white stallion when the scene evaporated, and the home-level spatial expansion carried the two of them out of view.

The fourth intersection unfolded a refreshing and peaceful scene in blues and greens. The track had become a broad pathway of fine gravel that followed the edges of a series of polygonal ponds through an extensive and fragrant garden. Because the path turned back on itself as it went around the lakes, Mana could see the leading riders as she gazed across the still blue water. The white stallion began to pull away from Calomil's mare. Puflet's song reached across the lake.

"When I rule, I'll reach into every town! Pirates and slavers will go down, down, down!"

Beside Mana, Katora muttered, "Your Coder boyfriend didn't accomplish anything."

Virtuous was breathing hard, straining to keep up with Ting. Mana looked at Katora and saw something new in her face—a weariness, an aging, as if some vital power had been sucked away from her over the past year.

"It's too bad you don't have any children left to love," Mana said.

"I loved your father!" Tears streamed from the corners of Katora's eyes and flew back into her wind-whipped hair. "But Dino ruined him! All of Thermeon's offspring are so arrogant! I should have realized long before that he was no good as a father!"

Mana thought for a moment. Then she said, "Quintillion's children aren't arrogant. Shell and Aspo are beautiful people."

Katora gave her head a violent shake. "Quintillion was filled with evil."

"But, don't you see—it was because of the black splinter. But he didn't give the splinter to his children. He gave it to my mother."

"The black splinter?" Katora's eyes opened wide. "Do you mean to say, it required only the removal of that splinter, and Quintillion might have been redeemed?"

"I think so."

Katora didn't hear her. She was bawling at the top of her lungs.

Mana clucked to Ting, and the mare's ears pricked. She surged away from Virtuous and passed Aspo's Rational Shop. She closed the distance to Spacious as the white stallion continued to increase his lead and Puflet's triumphant song soared through the mild blue sky.

"I'll burn brighter than Katora's so-called Illuminated Age, and my fashion sense will be the rage, rage, rage!"

As Ting caught up with Spacious, Mana saw that Calomil held a sword. Its pommel burned with crimson fire. She gasped.

"A bit of sleight-of-hand," Calomil said. "But let's not let her get too far ahead."

As they urged their horses to accelerate, the lakes gave way to the curve of track before the final intersection. The screams of the crowds in the grandstand were distant and tinny. Mana didn't see any minors.

They were in the final obstacle. Every sound was magnified by the jagged walls and low-hanging rocky ceiling of the mine tunnel through which the horses galloped along a narrow, winding path. Lamps glimmered in nooks and alcoves, coaxing sparkles from the facets of gems that peeked from piles of rock everywhere. A melodious chanting came from deep shadows at the ends of branching tunnels, as if voiced by the gems themselves.

"The moment is mine, mine, mine!" Puflet sang out.

"Mine! Mine! Mine!" echoed the mine.

"My soul-gem I will design, design, design!"

"Sign! Sign! Sign!"

The narrow tunnel forced the horses to go in single file. Mana looked over her shoulder at Calomil, who was right behind her. He leaned over his mare's neck and extended the red sword toward her. She wondered how he had managed to keep hold of it while they were on home-level. But maybe Fuerida had been wrong to think an ordinary person would necessarily drop the swords. After all, just being mounted had been enough to let Mana hold the green splinter.

The mine's chant grew soaring and ethereal, and a heartbeat-like throbbing of drums resounded everywhere. Mana bit her lip. She needed to take the sword and win back the other splinters from her mother. Then she would need to secure the black splinter as well. Half measures would avail nothing.

"Form, you blasted, twistored thing!" Puflet screamed.

A deep and terrible roar answered her. The walls shook. Gems burst from their seams and tumbled down. The mine was voiding its bowels, horrified by the dark monster that had penetrated its secret places.

"Upward or downward?" thundered the voice of the black splinter.

"I want to soar, soar, soar!" Puflet sang. But her voice wavered.

"Ore! Ore! Ore!" echoed the mine.

The eyes of dinosaurs glinted from the shadows. Finned reptiles thrashed in the slimy black pools of side tunnels. Flying reptiles skimmed overhead, making Ting and Spacious snort. Manlike beings with great black eyes watched their passage and whispered,

"Remember!"

A strange, musty, odor filled the tunnel. It seemed to be trying to tell Mana something, and then she remembered how Quokisa had said that the black splinter left tracks of memory. All the creatures around them must be the expression of the black splinter.

"All of you!" Puflet screamed. "Respond to me! Melt and meld together!"

A trickle of luminous green ran back through the tunnel to meet Mana. From it sprang rows of sunflowers that twisted their heads to seek the hidden sun. Bees buzzed around them. Their wings seemed to murmur, "Home," and the breeze came warm and fragrant.

They were the expression of the green splinter.

Spires the color of evening sky rose in the shadows. Within their windows Mana saw the silhouettes of scholars and heard them exclaiming, "Ah! I understand now! Oh, the wonder! How marvelous is the universe!"

They were the expression of the violet splinter.

The red splinter that Calomil still held out to her flared and shot forth rays of fire that became warriors, comrades-in-arms marching forth together, slaying their enemies, some dying, others marching home to celebrate their victory with drink and song.

Mana knew she must seize the sword before the moment passed, use its fiery power to overwhelm her mother and collect all the splinters and forge her own brilliant future. But she heard the echo of her mother's voice.

"It's part of me."

She was certain then, that even though the skeleton monster appeared to rampage as a separate being, it remained rooted in her mother, and that severing their connection would kill Puflet. She met Calomil's eyes and shook her head.

Puflet's voice had continued to ring out in desperation. "Why won't you come together? Why won't you form the future I've chosen?"

All the splinters thundered, hummed, exclaimed, and sang in their separate voices, creating a cacophony that crashed against the jagged mine walls and rebounded in a vast drone of echoes. Everything was capped by Puflet's final uncomprehending howl, and then silence fell.

The horses were on the home stretch. Calomil and Mana called on Spacious and Ting to make the final effort. As they pounded up behind the white stallion and the still howling Puflet, Calomil waved the red sword.

Puflet's head swung around. She gaped at him, then looked down at the sword in her right hand. It was the sword from the great memorial hall. She let it fall. As it hit the track its fusion field blasted out a shower of dirt that struck them from behind, making the three horses spurt forward.

Showing her fangs, Puflet transferred the violet sword to her right hand and veered over to swing at Calomil's head.

Mana screamed.

Calomil blocked with the red sword, then executed a deft, circling movement that pried the weapon from Puflet's grasp. Next he grabbed her arm and unhorsed her. He looked at Mana and indicated the white stallion, who had slowed to look around for his rider.

As Calomil herded the stallion from the far side, Mana edged closer on Ting. She didn't want to desert her wonderful mare, but an emperor was expected to ride the white stallion. She gave Ting a fierce hug, and then leaned over to grab two fistfuls of the white mane. The white stallion slowed to a gentle canter, allowing Mana to scramble over onto his back. Once she was settled, she whispered, "Go," and he spurted ahead. He ran straight and smooth as a light beam.

When they passed under the finish line the screams of "Chosen One," engulfed Mana like a wave, and people spilled out onto the track. The white stallion stopped. She slid to the ground and stood on shaking legs. The newsers were clamoring, but she ignored them and waited for Morning Glory and Kusomba to worm their way to her and produce apples. Mana gave one to Trat. She called Ting, but the mare didn't come. Mana peered over the heads of the crowd to see her standing by the outer edge of the track, head down. A wave of regret hit Mana. She was about to embark upon a new life of power and importance, and she could never go back to the old life that she had loved.

As she stood there, sadly staring toward her mare, the crowd jostled and parted for an eerie series of cracklings and crystalline pops. Calomil stepped through the opening, holding the two naked swords and the pendant. Mana still wore a sword belt. She held out the sheath, and he slid the red sword into it. He set the pendant around her neck.

Moments later, Aspo and Shell galloped up side by side, and Morning Glory and Kusomba went to them to help them reward their horses. When the four of them rejoined Mana, she looked at the sword belt around Aspo's waist and the sword in Calomil's hand, and faced a decision. The newsers, a great crowd of them, had their eyes pinned on her every movement, and her actions would be exaggerated and endlessly interpreted to the galaxy. Should she indicate to Calomil to return the sword to Aspo, or should she indicate that Aspo should hand over the belt?

She took a deep breath, and tried to be a bit like her grandmother Katora, for once, and look into the future. But not by any feats of time travel, but simply by being open to possibilities the way Morning Glory had advised her, and the way Attequol had said she was. She couldn't let fears or pressures of current circumstances interfere with the big picture. And so she nodded to Aspo, who already had his hands on the belt, and he unbuckled it and passed it to Calomil, who buckled it on and sheathed the violet sword.

"The future I foresee for the empire," Mana told the newsers, "is a future free from the conflicts and the divisions of the past. Men and women of the Code and citizens of other faiths will see themselves as one people. Mindseas and those who have no mindpowers will respect one another for their different talents."

Then she sent Calomil a stern look and thought, *Why didn't you tell me you were a mindsea?*

He just smiled, but she knew that he had understood.

A faint patter of hoofs sounded. Katora had emerged from the final obstacle. The crowd swayed as some of the newsers turned their attention to her.

Mana stepped closer to Aspo and Shell and quietly said to them, "She is rethinking the last few thousand years of her life. If you ever hoped for a reconciliation with your mother, now would be the time to approach her."

"I-I wouldn't know what to say," Shell stammered.

"It's far too late," said Aspo.

Mana pushed past them and watched Katora's bedraggled approach. Woman and mare looked equally disconsolate.

"There is a woman who owes her children an abject apology," she declared, knowing the newsers would note her words.

She noticed her own mother crouched by the edge of the track, clutching her head. Mana's chest tightened. Their reconciliation would not be easy to accomplish, either.

Turning away from the defeated, she smiled at her friends and allies. "I think it's time to go," she said. According to the rules of the Challenge, the Wall would be sealed off until the winner of the Emperor Race arrived to take the imperial oath. This was to prevent anyone who might dislike the outcome—an imperial major who saw the end of their appointment coming, for instance—from trying to make themselves emperor. But it was still wise to move quickly, before plans to subvert the outcome by other means, such as assassination, could develop.

"I'll take you in my shuttle," Dino offered. "It's just over the horizon."

Orgmorgan shook his shaggy head. "I wouldn't trust myself to that death-trap!"

"The swiftest way would be to ride," Calomil said.

"Why don't you two go, then" Morning Glory said. "As long as you don't need any of us." She gave Mana a searching look. It was her gentle way of asking whether Mana planned to name Calomil as her major.

Mana nodded to Calomil, and they called their horses. Out of habit, Mana called Ting, but it was the white stallion who came to her. Ting had moved out onto the field. She was grazing, head down. She didn't look up as they passed.

Mana spent the first years of her reign concentrating on improving educational curricula, expanding horse racing programs, engineering further safeguards into glowworm systems, and cracking down on slavery, piracy, and hate crimes throughout the galaxy.

She also embarked upon a major remodeling of the imperial palace, with her Aunt Taana as head architect.

On the morning when Taana told her that the work had been completed and the palace was safe to move back into from temporary Palace headquarters in a replica of the old palace within the imperial museum, Mana had a full day planned, so she asked Taana to do the walk-through with her that evening.

The first thing on the day's agenda was the regular meeting of the Education Council. They gathered in a large circular nook in a quiet, softly-lit green-toned room. Rondo was there representing the ancient imperial tradition of face-to-face instruction. He sat across from experts from the various schools of bioid-to-crèche instruction. There was a representative of the Lalian peasant tradition, as well as those from other major indigenous populations. Calomil was there, of course, to speak for people of the Code, and Morning Glory's responsibility was to present the unexpected, deep-level perspective.

As usual, the meeting began with everyone—except for the

bioid instructor experts—looking for new ways to pull more young citizens away from bioid instructors, and ended with Mana and Calomil in their old argument about whether the Code teaching was science.

"Science means exploring possibilities," she said. "It doesn't mean deciding that one interpretation is comfortable and not ever looking beyond it."

"Code science is constantly looking beyond itself," he replied. "We know that the Goddess will always lie beyond our understanding."

"But some people choose not to call ultimate reality 'the Goddess,' and I think that they're entitled to do so! They may choose to call it 'the Tenets of Patternistics,' or 'the Great Nothingness,' or simply 'Existence.'"

"Certainly, they are free to choose. But how they choose affects their lives. So why would someone choose to believe that the universe is the accident of nothingness with all the depressing meaninglessness that implies, when it can be equally well interpreted as the creation of a wonderful goddess? Every child should be exposed to the message of the Code—as well as whatever their ancestors believed in."

"I think it is fine for some people to visualize the universe as the creation of a goddess. For for others, it can give them the notion that all they need do is lie back and let this mother-figure minister to them, as if they were infants forever. That's why I personally like to think that the Tenets of Patternistics lead the way to the truth—they're something one needs to work at. They keep the mind and spirit active."

"The Goddess also requires work," said Calomil.

"But, you must admit, some people can get the wrong impression. Like Thermeon."

Calomil scowled. "He has his own religion. It isn't ours. No son of the Code would dare imagine that he could possess the Goddess!"

"But nature loves variation!" Mana cried. "So don't you think it would be wrong if every citizen in the galaxy believed in one interpretation of reality?"

As Calomil knit his brows and searched for a reply, Rondo

cleared his throat. "I think that this has been a most useful discussion that could be reenacted for students with great benefit! However, our time is running out."

Quickly they went over the few points that had been decided, and then the meeting broke up.

Mana and Calomil traveled by air lifter to the new Code sanctuary that had been constructed in the Valley. Lal was not a geologically active planet, but the Fissure had created a hot springs that could feed the Pool of Revelation. They didn't go to the pool—such delights had to wait for the night—but lunched in a sandstone gazebo overlooking the craggy walls of the Fissure and the river that ran through it. The new palace could be seen on a distant cliff to the East. Mana couldn't take her eyes from it. She had based the concept on the expression of the violet splinter—letting Taana work out all the details, of course. The old palace had been a big gold fist giving the sky the finger, but the new palace was elegant and soaring. Its spires matched the color of the sky so that it seemed washed out and ethereal, like a morning moon.

"I will be glad to leave that museum for good," Calomil said. "Being in there is like being in Attequol's head."

Like most Coders, he still carried a grudge against Attequol for Ulona.

"Once we're settled," Mana said, "Let's see about getting riverboats running from the city to the sanctuary."

He nodded. "And someday, perhaps we could even find time to ride on one of them ourselves."

Returning to their air lifters, they flew to the far northern region of the Valley, where a new racetrack had been built near the place where Thermeon and Morning Glory had been born. Morning Glory had helped the track engineers to implement the natural deep-level intersections that she had sensed during her childhood wanderings.

Mana discussed horses and riders with Kusomba and her assistant stable manager, Fiesa, the granddaughter of the Peasant Champion, Miesa. Since the first crèche field trip had visited its border with the Plains of Possibility, thirty new horses had chosen riders.

"Have you heard from Aspo?" Kusomba asked.

Mana nodded. "There's no problem getting horses for the Bri racetrack, but there have been a number of incidents involving students from the pilot school—horses aboard ships or riding trays in the mess hall—that sort of thing. If Orgmorgan approves, Shell will become the pilot school's horse relations instructor. She has no problem communicating with other pilots, it seems."

Kusomba snickered.

"Katora's on Bri too," Mana said. "She's launched a movement to have the amusement park Quintillion built there declared a galactic historical site. I've seen newsclips of her and Aspo and Shell at the park together, but I don't know whether they've actually talked to each other."

They rode their horses out for a training race. The white stallion always seemed happy to romp, but Mana still missed Ting. A lot of her predecessors, like Katora and Pia, had kept their personal horses, riding Trat only on ceremonial occasions, but Ting had bonded with another rider.

As they reached the track, Dino rode up on Prog. "A rider at the Vuduna track saw Karali's head in an obstacle," he told them. "It was still shrieking."

Mana shivered. He was joking, she told herself.

Still, she felt a small pang of trepidation every time she entered an intersection. However, the worst obstacle they encountered that afternoon was a glacier that seemed to be composed of pure alcohol, one that Orgmorgan would no doubt have loved. The fumes had horses and humans reeling, but luckily, no one fell.

After the ride, Calomil flew to the sanctuary to meet with members of the Wamatuan Restoration Committee, while Mana returned to the interim palace to discuss the latest eruptions of space piracy in Sector Seven with her military advisers. Puflet was there. As she had at every meeting she attended, she berated Mana for thwarting her soul-gem.

"If you'd just let me complete the forging, we wouldn't have these endless communication problems with the fleet, and the pirates wouldn't be able to flee across the timelines. Did you think that I wouldn't forge it right? Did you think that I don't have any noble impulses? My monster has posed the question 'Upward or Downward?' innumerable times, and I wanted to choose upward! I wanted to lead our species onto the next level of awareness, into a future where there are no suffering slaves forgotten in the dark corners of society!"

"Maybe you can still forge it," Mana told her. "Meet me and Taana for the walk-through this evening."

Mana hurried from the meeting to a big, garden-themed playroom, where she joined Calomil, Nathimeon, and Fuerida in watching three little girls romp amid flowerbeds and ponds. Waving bubble wands, the children raced after Quokisa's fox. The two dark-haired girls, Sikori and Sayuta, were Nath and Fue's. The one with Luminary hair was Mana and Cal's. Genetic Algorithms had assigned her the name Quanuman, and they weren't quite sure yet what they would end up calling her. All three children seemed incredibly intelligent and talented.

Evening fell. Mana dined with Puflet and Taana in the museum, while Calomil met Raolin, Hube, and a couple other Members of the Circle at a restaurant on the Way.

Then it was time for the walk-through. Taana looked radiant as she showed off the new galleries, conference rooms, conservatories, water rooms, and wind towers. Puflet looked bored.

"What about having another go at the soul-gem?"

"I'm saving that for last," Mana said. "It might be dangerous."

She turned to Taana. "It's more beautiful than I could have imagined. I think that just looking at these new perspectives will help to lift citizens to an Age of Illumination."

Taana smiled. "Can you do the last bit without me? I have the feeling you'd like to see it alone with your mother."

"Of course," Mana said.

Taana bade them good night and walked off along a curving, luminous blue hallway.

Mana stood alone with her mother in an airy vaulted room beneath a small spire, the breeze playing melodies as it streamed through a wind-gate high overhead.

"You killed Eria," Mana stated. "You used your backdoors to the Palace and Bureau systems to override their safety algorithms so that the crusader could bring in her bomb."

Puflet shrugged. "I told them to kidnap the stupid woman. I figured it would distract my father and keep him out of the race.

Well, it worked anyhow, but what happened was a mistake."

"If a pirate gave that excuse, you'd have no mercy."

"So what are you going to do, execute me?"

"No. I'm going to give you a chance to redeem yourself by forging your soul-gem. If you want to. Because I think it will kill you."

Puflet laughed. "What makes you say that?"

"Your failure at the forging wasn't because of Calomil sneaking away the red splinter. I've thought over what I saw in that last intersection. He had it in his hand, but space and time are hardly real when you go that Deep. You still held it with your mind. I saw it respond to your call and send out its rays. All of the splinters responded to you."

Puflet frowned and tapped one foot against the marble floor. "So why didn't they meld?"

"Because you wouldn't release the black splinter. You told me it was part of you, that it gave you your mindpowers. To create the soul-gem, you would have to give up that part of yourself. But you couldn't do it."

Puflet snorted. "I wasn't going to give up the black splinter. I was going to join it with all of the others, within myself!" She flung up her head, her pale blue eyes alight. "Instead of just this one monstrous streak of power, I would possess a full and gleaming splendor, greater than my father, greater than old Besi, and far greater than Katora! I would be the true beacon of an Age of Illumination! Humanity would evolve in the glow of my rays!"

"Oh," said Mana. "Then maybe it didn't work because the intersection hadn't taken us quite deep enough. The splinters all were singing, so I think that we had reached their level, Deep Five. But we needed Deep Six."

Puflet tilted her head and regarded her with amusement. "So you think you know how to reach Deep Six now?"

"Yes," Mana said. "Come with me."

She led the way to the restored Chamber of Planets, the room where Palace officials gathered before Wall Speakings. An armored minor awaited them there, wearing Mana's brown horsehead insignia on his green surcoat, green plumes rising from his helmet. He wore Hush and Rush on either hip, and the pendant on his chest.

Puflet gave a hop when she saw the splinters, and Mana saw a hand unconsciously reach out as if to grab at the green gem before her mother pulled it back. "You're not planning to humiliate me with a surprise Speaking, are you?"

"Of course not," Mana said. "I'm going to do just what I said I'd do."

She nodded to the minor, and he unlocked a door that would not be used for Speakings.

"I had your backdoor removed from the Palace system," Mana told Puflet as she led the way down a twisting tunnel. "So don't try to sneak in here alone."

The tunnel debouched into a very high, long, but narrow room that ran along the back of the Wall, providing the view of the edifice that Mana and Karali had seen on that day they had walked around it after the emergency Wall Speaking.

"This is strange," Puflet said.

"Yes," Mana agreed. "You see all those holes? Sort of like very tall, narrow honeycomb chambers? I recognized them in one of the patterns that Attequol laid out on my table at the stable, and he told me that was all I needed to know. He didn't lay out the whole Wall, just a piece of it, and various holes were paired with solids that I recognized—much later, of course—as symbolizing the splinters. So now I just need to count the holes and insert the splinters in their proper places."

Mana counted, then indicated to the minor where to place the swords and the pendant. He handled them easily, but respectfully. She had needed someone with mindsize for the task, and she wondered whether he was the same man who had survived Thermeon's Bolt, but he remained anonymous behind his golden mask.

When the splinters had been inserted into the Wall, Mana counted some more, and then pointed out an alcove-like opening to her mother. "That is where the fourth splinter needs to go, if you want to forge the soul-gem. Those four points have some connection in Deep Six that can't be seen from home-level. But Attequol assured me that this patternistic method would allow you to work on Deep Six."

Puflet looked the Wall up and down. "It's not going to drop a block on me?"

Mana shook her head. "I've come to the conclusion that the Wall didn't drop a block on Rathax. Probably the thing that fell and killed him was a splinter from the soul-gem that he was destroying."

"That makes a kind of sense," Puflet agreed.

"Soul-gems are dangerous, so if you don't want to try this, let's leave."

"Wait! You're saying that if I walk into that hole, the four splinters will intersect on Deep Six?"

"Yes. They'll meld. But I think it might kill you."

Puflet tossed her head. A triumphant smile bloomed on her face. "No! It will make me a goddess!"

She walked into the hole.

Blinking her eyes, Mana tried to focus on the vague blue shapes around her. After a moment, she identified the new imperial bed chamber. She was stretched out in the bed, Calomil hovering beside her. Her head swirled when she tried to sit. He hugged her, then let her lie back.

She frowned. "I don't recall anything after she completed the pattern. What happened?"

"The minor says there was a mind-blast. You weren't hurt physically." He paused. "You've been out for a while."

She pushed the question of how long aside. There were more important matters. "Was the soul-gem forged?"

"It will take a while before statistics from galaxy-wide communications and travel come in. No one can actually see it, since it's on Deep Six."

"I saw it!" cried a voice.

Thermeon strode into the room, grinning and resplendent in a Deep-woven white and pale indigo costume. "I saw it from the mountain that rises from the Plains of Possibility. It was brilliant and amazing! More beautiful by far than Horl's soul-gem, or mine. Puflet is a little unhappy, though, since she's now trapped inside the Wall. She says that Attequol tricked her into eating him so that certain trace elements that had been in his body would signal the Wall to confine her."

"That's ... that's...." Mana couldn't find words.

"I like your new setting." Thermeon turned slowly to take in the airy room with its skylights and fishpond and hanging blue ferns. "But now for the important news." His grin broadened. "I have realized the true identity of my goddess-star!"

Mana clutched her head. Calomil rose and stared at her grandfather with a concerned expression.

"She is Quokisa!" Thermeon gushed. "How could I have not realized that the moment she appeared, wearing those two splinters and a fox, and riding that wild black mare! Unfortunately, I was distracted by Eria. I feel very regretful now that I caused her so much needless agitation, and perhaps even contributed to the circumstances that led to her death. Why didn't someone point out Quokisa to me?"

Mana blinked at him. Calomil sighed.

"Well, without a doubt, Quokisa is my goddess! Her eyes are pure, piercing, golden starlight! I imagine that she is amused by my stupidity, and awaits my coming to my senses and declaring my love. Do either of you know where she is?"

ACKNOWLEDGMENTS

Mana would never have completed her long journey to the finish line without the support and encouragement of my fellow writers from the Science Fiction Association of Bergen County, the Piscataway Library Writers Group, and the Taos Toolbox class of '07, especially Oz Drummond and Rebecca Stefoff. And, of course, my daughter, Ezra, and my son, Ben, were always on hand to offer advice.

Most of all, I would like to thank the horses of my teenage years: Gypsy, Kiko, and Filly. They were always eager for a ride, and they patiently put up with the fantasies my sister, brother, and I enacted with them, whether we wanted to be cowpokes, racing jockeys, trick riders, or knights.

ABOUT THE EMPIRE

Information about the Mindsea Empire, including glossary, historical outline, and planetary list, may be found at www.bonniebrunish.com.

The white stallion and the black mare, along with other Torsa horses from pre-imperial times, appear in a number of free apps. Check www.puflet.com for details.

www.ingramcontent.com/pod-product-compliance
Lightning Source LLC
Chambersburg PA
CBHW071452170626
46811CB00007B/2556